ON THE EDGE OF

DAYLIGHT

A NOVEL
OF THE TITANIC

GISELLE

BEAUMONT

TREK PRESS
SAN FRANCISCO | TILLAMOOK | SANTA CRUZ

Copyright © 2018 Giselle Beaumont

ISBN: 978-0-692-09406-8

Design by Giselle Beaumont.
Artwork and Cover © Giselle Beaumont.
Lyrics: "Eternal Father, Strong to Save" © William Whiting.

10 9 8 7 6 5 4 3 2 1

First Edition.

To those who were here
from the beginning.

CONTENTS

I find the great thing in this world is not so much where we stand as in what direction we are moving: To reach the port of heaven, we must sail sometimes with the wind, and sometimes against it—

But we must sail, and not drift, nor lie at anchor.

—OLIVER WENDELL HOLMES

PREFACE

The story you are about to read is fictitious. Its plot and narrative are merely inspired by true events, while its cast of characters are loosely based on their real-life counterparts.

This novel does not intend to mock, slander, adulterate, disrespect, or exploit any historical figures involved in the disaster, while the protagonist, Esther Bailey, is not meant to represent the courageous officers who risked their lives that tragic night. She is an imaginary character designed to explore the world of maritime tradition and move the romantic narrative along. However, despite the romance, adult themes, and fictional characters woven into this storyline, every effort has been made to stay as close to history as possible. This is especially true for the chapters leading up to, during, and after the sinking. Details have been carefully researched from survivor accounts and inquiry testimonials to blend fiction with fact, and create a story that will tug the heartstrings.

Although *On the Edge of Daylight* is not a one hundred percent accurate representation of the RMS *Titanic* and her officers, it still seeks to highlight the honorable traditions of White Star Line officership, to correct common misconceptions raised or reiterated within the 1997 film, such as Officer Murdoch's bribe, and to show the duty, bravery, and sacrifice of the crew who are so easily forgotten—or even unknown—by society today.

CHARACTERS

Edward John Smith. Captain of *Titanic*; was previously in command of the RMS *Olympic*.

Henry Tingle Wilde. Chief Officer; previously held the same role aboard the RMS *Olympic*.

William McMaster Murdoch. First Officer of *Titanic*; formerly chief officer before the reshuffle.

Charles Herbert Lightoller. Second Officer; formerly first.

Herbert "Bert" John Pitman. Third Officer.

Joseph Groves Boxhall. Fourth Officer.

Harold Godfrey Lowe. Fifth Officer.

James "Jim" Paul Moody. Sixth Officer.

Esther Anna Bailey. Seventh Officer in training.

Thomas Andrews Jr. Shipwright of the RMS *Titanic*; employed by Harland and Wolff.

J. Bruce Ismay. Chairman and managing director of White Star Line.

John "Jack" Phillips. Senior Wireless Operator.

Harold Sydney Bride. Junior Wireless Operator.

Booker Hamilton Bailey. Apprentice to Thomas Andrews; Esther's older brother.

Callum Lockerbie. Son of railroad tycoon Niles Lockerbie; fiancé to Fay Harlow.

Gideon Slate. Former Pinkerton; Callum's personal valet.

ONE

ARRIVAL

April 6, 1912 | 06:20

IT RAINED THE day she arrived in Southampton, watching the cold, sodden port drawing nearer and knowing her life would never be the same.

Esther Bailey sat in silence, mirroring the sleepy quiet of her driver as their motorcar bumped along a road long-gutted by tire tracks, the deeper ruts already swollen with rainwater. Beyond the fogged window, she could see the swirl of waves foaming against the docks, dark and vaguely blue beneath the daybreak sky.

Esther shivered underneath her woolen coat. Not merely from the cold, but from the sheer excitement of what awaited her at port: the RMS *Titanic*. The luxury steamship all the papers, newsboys and bustling folks across London were calling "*The Ship of Dreams.*" A true marvel of steel and manmade opulence bound for New York in five days' time.

And she would soon become one of its newest junior officers.

A *woman* officer, at that.

Esther tried to keep such a trivial detail from plaguing her thoughts. But she could still feel it swirl through her mind like floodwaters, tearing away the wonder and anticipation she had thrived on these last few weeks. She wasn't simple-minded; she knew female officers were unheard of. She had braced herself to expect the worst from her crewmates, whether it be indifference, disapproval—or outright prejudice.

This wouldn't be easy, Esther knew. But she was perfectly qualified for the role. Her magnate uncle, being the practical businessman that he was, hadn't wanted to waste her talents. Rather than turn his nose up at her aspirations, he had used his influence with White Star Line to secure two positions, one each for her and her brother, aboard the glittering new steamer.

Esther sighed, slipping the chain of her silver locket through shaky fingertips. Booker would be just fine aboard *Titanic*. Her brother had studied shipbuilding and design at the Institute of Marine Engineering and Science in London. He would work underneath Thomas Andrews, *Titanic*'s shipwright, in a formal apprenticeship these next few weeks.

But Booker was an accomplished *male* student of twenty-nine. Esther was a lady of twenty-six, and although she'd studied with a small pool of female scholars at the very same institute, and knew her maritime laws like she knew the back of her hand, she was still a woman entering a world traditionally reserved for men. It was a first for the maritime business—a first for White Star Line, undoubtedly enough—and she wasn't sure how her new shipmates would react to such a peculiarity.

They'll be ecstatic, I'm sure, Esther told herself, unable to keep the sarcasm from her nervous thoughts as she watched the raindrops glitter past the window.

The motorcar came to a shuddering halt before the rain-slick platform of the nearest loading dock, headlights blooming out across the dark shapes of berthed ships and cargo cranes. The driver swung around in his seat to look at her, cocking his head to one side.

"Y'sure yer in the right place, ma'am?"

"If I wasn't," Esther said lightly, "I would have told you by now, don't you think?" She smiled at him before stepping out into the frigid air.

A short walk brought her past a handful of sailors and seafarers tending to their ships in the early morn, many watching her pass with puzzled looks. In the distance, a sliver of light strained its way through layers of fog and rainclouds; weak though it was, Esther hoped it meant that the dreary weather might clear at last.

Hands buried deep in her pockets, she continued onward through the maze of docks, winding her way to Berth 44. But it wasn't until she rounded a row of Cunard ships that she finally saw it, and her breath caught in her throat.

The RMS *Titanic* loomed out of the downpour, a giantess of gleaming steel and metalwork that put the berthed ships around her to shame.

Never had Esther seen a steamer so impossibly grand. Yellow light poured from portholes and promenades, seeping into the watery blue darkness. She gaped at the ship's colossal size as it towered above her, nearly reminiscent of the skyscrapers she'd seen in New York, and she had to tilt her head back to take it all in: the buff-colored funnels soaring high above her, illuminated by lights at each base; the white paintwork sweeping across decks, davits and roaming promenades, as smooth and pristine as if the coats had dried only yesterday; and finally, the enormous mast that speared the sky, linked by a sprawl of crisscrossed cables and wirework. *Titanic* was every bit as stunning as the papers and newsboys in London claimed her to be—if not more.

"Good Heavens," Esther murmured, standing rigid with her eyes flooded with awe. "She's unbelievable."

Suddenly, everything she had fretted over during the journey to port—every concern regarding her gender, her purpose, her place—vanished from her mind. Her eagerness returned, and Esther found herself thinking only of the days ahead, when she would cross the North Atlantic on the grandest ship she had ever laid eyes on.

06:50

Sixth Officer James Moody had never liked the rain.

He fought to ignore its sting of icy droplets as he crossed the sprawling docks, cursing himself for forgetting an umbrella this morning.

Although he had donned leather gloves and a thick, blue-black greatcoat made of heavy wool, his attire could do little to bar the freezing chill. He quickened his stride, vigorously rubbing his hands together for warmth and dreading how much colder the nights at sea would be.

He had originally been assigned to the RMS *Oceanic* for a summer voyage this year, until White Star Line—for reasons unbeknownst to anyone—had transferred him to *Titanic* instead. Less than thrilled by his new assignment and not wanting to brave the harsh April weather, Moody had put in a request for leave…only to have it denied a *day* later.

He tried to swallow down his bitterness as he imagined his fellow *Oceanic* officers preparing for a much warmer, much more jovial transatlantic crossing. On the one hand, *Titanic* was a gem of a ship—a steamer that outclassed any other vessel Moody had worked in his career. Aside from boasting luxury and lavishness, she had performed incredibly well during her sea trials in Belfast, steaming her way through all manner of turns with a speed that had impressed him.

But despite *Titanic*'s excellence, Moody was still disappointed this trip would consist of chilled nights, cold watches and frozen seas, rather than the calm summer voyage *Oceanic* had promised him.

Well, he thought idly, *doesn't get much better than this.*

The downpour began to lighten, falling in a drizzle that was more mist than rain. Moody listened to the tides hissing and foaming against the slipway as he strolled toward Berth 44, heading straight for the port shell door where a gangway and a handful of seamen awaited him.

He was about to give the crew a cursory nod when he stopped in his tracks, taken aback by the odd sight before him.

A short, slender woman donned in a heavy coat two sizes too big for her stood alone at the far end of the dock. She was gazing up at *Titanic*'s behemoth mass, the glow from the portholes glittering like starlight in her eyes. She seemed frozen, almost—though whether she was in a daze or simply ridden by the cold, Moody couldn't say. But there was no reason for a girl like her to be on the docks, anyway, least of all at such an early hour. He made his way toward her at once, brow knitted into a frown.

"Miss?" Moody said, hoping the crisp formality of his voice was enough to conceal his bewilderment.

But the woman didn't even look at him; she remained hopelessly transfixed on *Titanic*, studying her sleek hull and speckling of rivets with soft-eyed wonder.

Trying not to feel miffed, Moody pressed on, "Forgive my intrusion, miss, but may I ask what…you're…doing?"

"*Oh!*"

Her gasp vaulted across the berth, catching the air in a cloud of fog. She swung around to look at Moody, her cheeks rosy pink with cold and embarrassment, her gaze widening as she took in the officer beside her.

The woman was young—perhaps his age—with dark, shoulder-length hair still wet with rain and tucked behind both ears. She had golden skin that reminded him of a Greek woman he'd met last week in Belfast. Her eyes were long and almond-shaped, their color like shallow green seawater, and there was a speckling of wild freckles across the bridge of her admittedly pointed nose that he found endearing.

"I apologize," the woman said, speaking quickly in an already-speedy American drawl. "It's just—I've never seen such a ship. I couldn't help but stop and stare, you know?"

For a moment, Moody felt an unexpected twinge of pride and kinship toward *Titanic*. It was the first *real* optimism he'd felt toward the liner since White Star Line had snatched him away from *Oceanic*, and it caught him by surprise. He smiled, lifting his chin in a dignified manner and hoping to impress the pretty girl in her too-long coat.

"Ah, yes. She is rather impressive, isn't she? Triple-screws, forty-six thousand tons, more than eight-hundred feet in length—and so well-constructed, God *himself* couldn't sink her if he tried. I daresay she's the finest steamer you'll ever set foot on."

"Jesus, I believe it." The woman tipped her head back, eyes tracing the tips of the funnels all the way down to the plated black hull. She gave a low whistle. "Never dreamed I'd be working on a ship like this."

"Oh?" Moody asked curiously. "You're a stewardess?"

She laughed. "What, do I strike you as a stewardess type?"

He studied her glossy black hair and cashmere coat, noting she was more well-dressed than he'd realized. There were pearls at her ears and a thin silver locket around her neck, while her shoes were a glittering, midnight-blue.

Heels, Moody observed, and he almost scoffed. *On the docks. In the rain. Good Lord.*

But the woman looked completely at ease in them, standing patiently on the dock as Moody struggled to comprehend what purpose she had here, and *why* she was standing by her lonesome at port. Then he cleared his throat, deciding he'd rather not know. It was too early and too bloody cold to dwell on the odd behavior of some stranger—especially when he already expected a visitor of his own this morning.

"Beg pardon, miss," Moody said. "I actually must be off—I'm afraid I have other matters to attend to elsewhere. A colleague of mine is coming aboard today, see, and I'm due to meet him any moment now."

"Very well," the woman said, and to his surprise, she was smirking. "I suppose it would be best not to keep *him* waiting." A sly look crossed her face as she added, "Oh, and I didn't catch your name, Officer …?"

She must have recognized the gold trim on his uniform. He stood straighter and said a little tersely, "Moody. Now if you'll excuse me…"

"Right." She was still regarding him with amusement. "Goodbye, Mr. Moody."

"Goodbye."

He started for *Titanic's* port side without another word, smoothing out his greatcoat and refusing to glance over his shoulder.

Pretty woman. But puzzling, very puzzling. And why on earth had she been smiling at him like *that?* Moody didn't have the faintest clue, but he refused to let himself care. Nodding at the sailors lining the shell door, he pulled a heavy pocket watch from his coat to inspect the time. The new junior officer in training should have been here by now, but there was no sign of him along the rainy sprawl of Berth 44. Some chap by the name of Bailey, according to the report—and already he was late. Moody's lip curled with disapproval. How very promising.

Lightoller won't be happy, he thought. *He'll skin that poor fellow alive.*

Dipping his watch back into its pocket, Moody stood taller and folded his hands behind his back. As he surveyed the docks, cold and annoyed and still waiting for some tardy seventh officer to arrive, he realized the woman with the long coat was strolling toward him.

Now what? Moody raised an eyebrow as she neared, all the while considering whether to ask some dockhand or another to escort her from the premises.

"You forgot to ask my name, Mr. Moody," she said. Her tone was bright. Facetious, almost. "Junior Officer Esther Bailey. Requesting permission to come aboard, sir."

Moody froze, all decorum lost to the winds as he goggled at this girl and her mischievous green eyes.

It felt like an eternity before he managed to compose himself, smoothing away his astonishment and slipping back into his mannerly poise. Still somewhat perplexed, he rummaged around his pocket for the small notebook carrying the seventh officer's details. His eyes raced across the paper slip, and he almost had to bite the inside of his cheek to keep from cursing his shock.

Esther, it read. *Esther Bailey.*

Moody hadn't even realized it was a *woman's* name—he had glossed over that little detail earlier this morning, when he'd been more interested in hot tea and a warm jacket above all else…

And now here he was, staring dumbfounded into the eyes of *Titanic's* newest recruit, who stood with her chin held high, a clever little grin spreading across her face.

"Right," Moody said, warmth rising in his cheeks.

He stood awkwardly beside the girl for a moment, not sure what to do or say next. But then he remembered his manners, and he offered a tentative hand. She wrung it hard, beaming, her grip tight and painfully enthusiastic in a way that almost made him wince.

When she finally released his hand, and Moody flexed his fingers to make sure none were crushed, he gestured toward the shell door with a hard swallow.

"Welcome aboard *Titanic*, Miss Bailey."

TWO

THE MEETING

April 6, 1912 | 07:10

THE BLEAK SKIES began to clear as First Officer Charles Lightoller left the bridge and made his way toward the smoking room.

A tall, wiry man with blue eyes and a prominent chin, he walked with an air of strict purpose as he crossed the freshly-waxed pinewood deck. He spared a passing glance at the waterfront, watching the daylight sift through the cloud cover, pale and shimmering across glass-smooth waves.

Good, he thought with satisfaction. *About time the weather broke.*

Then he straightened his cuffs and slipped inside the officers' smoking room, closing the door behind him with a snap.

The room was humbly furnished, its white-paneled walls affixed with coat hooks, brass light fixtures, and a pair of clocks displaying ship and destination time. A White Star Line sailing notice hung directly opposite of him, proclaiming *Titanic* and her twin, *Olympic,* to be "The Largest Steamers in the World."

A circular table of glossed teakwood sat at the center of the room, and it was here that Lightoller took his seat, laying the file on his newest officer flat before him. He scanned its contents with a weary sigh, lacing his fingers in quiet reserve as he struggled to process the unfortunate situation he now found himself in.

Esther Bailey, the file read, blue ink burning into his eyes like a dreadful poison. *Twenty-six. Born in San Francisco, California to Dr.*

Arthur Bailey. Graduated from the Institute of Marine Engineering, Science, and Technology in London with a specialty in maritime law and regulations (high marks, notable letters of recommendation). Attained Ordinary Master's Certification in 1909; fulfilled apprenticeship on the SS Maloja in 1911. Sister to Booker Bailey (apprentice under Thomas Andrews) and niece to J. DeWitt Bailey, co-founder of IMM Co. and White Star Line.

Lightoller snorted at the last line. *Of course,* he thought scathingly. *Nepotism at its finest.*

Had the girl not been related to this J.D. Bailey chap in some manner or another, no one in their right mind would *dare* commission her as an officer. Her brother wouldn't be an issue, none at all. As a graduate student and promising shipwright, he would work soundly under Thomas Andrews.

But to have a woman on the *bridge*, giving orders and working alongside his fellow officers…it was nearly unthinkable.

Lightoller was a man of order—of strict formality and conviction. He was a meticulous sailor who believed there was no gray when it came to following the rulebook, only black and white. *Never*, in all his years of seafaring, had he known a woman to become an officer. Women worked as stewardesses and *maids* and what have you. Not in a role that demanded physical and mental fortitude, respect for maritime tradition, and the ability to delegate in the face of danger—or perhaps even death.

He didn't have to meet the girl to know she lacked each of these traits in turn. Oh, there was no doubt about it. She would just be a damn nuisance, like a pebble trapped at the base of his boot.

Already the girl was causing a stir, and she hadn't even boarded the ship yet. Captain E.J. Smith was usually a collected man, blue eyes as calm as the ocean waves always stretching before him, but Lightoller had never seen him so agitated the day they'd received the news by wire. Smith had tried to reverse the decision, of course. But no amount of reasoning with White Star Line or IMM Co. executives could shift the tide. It seemed the girl's uncle had too much financial and political power at his fingertips, and Smith was neatly overruled. His only alternative would be to step down. And what sort of man would dare give up his captaincy aboard the crown jewel of White Star Line's fleet?

No one besides Smith and Lightoller knew their newest junior officer was a woman. The captain had wanted to keep it hushed for the time being, and Lightoller knew it was more out of shame than anything else.

But the men would know soon enough.

They would see her standing out on the bridge or inside the wheelhouse, donned in an officer's uniform and tie. A woman who belonged below decks arranging meals and bedding instead of working on the bridge of the most expensive ship in living history.

Sighing, Lightoller removed his cap and combed one hand through his sandy-brown hair.

Let's just get this over with, he thought, sweeping his hat back onto his head. *The girl's coming aboard, one way or another.*

A knock at the door saw him rise swiftly to his feet.

"Come in," Lightoller commanded, and he watched Officer Moody enter the room with a very freckled, very short girl who could only be Esther Bailey.

Lightoller went still, his eyes dark with undisguised scrutiny as he studied his new protégé. There was something unusual about her speckled complexion and wide green eyes. Where most Englishwomen tended to be fair-skinned, this girl had a warmness that suggested she spent a fair amount of time in the sun. Her attire was plain and unassuming, save for some pearl earrings and a pair of ridiculous blue heels that glittered lightly along the floor.

Well, at least she didn't come dressed to the nines, Lightoller thought scathingly.

Regardless, the heels and pearls were still inappropriate, and he hoped she would have enough sense in the future to leave the showy jewelry at home.

"Morning, Mr. Lightoller, sir," she said, her bright, bold American accent thundering through the quiet. "It's an honor to finally—"

Lightoller raised one hand to silence her, and her smile faltered.

"I take it you are Miss Esther Bailey, of San Francisco, California?" he asked indifferently.

The girl nodded. "Yessir. All my life."

Where she had once been beaming, there was now a discomfort about her, which she was clearly trying to hide. Her eyes struggled to meet his stern glare, and her fingers kept twisting together like baker's dough. She was nervous.

Lightoller turned to Moody. "Would you excuse us for a moment?"

"At once, sir."

Moody swiftly took his leave, and Lightoller sighed as he turned his attention to the scrawny girl before him.

"Have a seat, Miss Bailey."

The girl scrambled forward at once, though not before slamming her knee against the table in her earnestness. She uttered a filthy curse as she collided with the woodwork, wincing with pain, and Lightoller stared in disbelief, wondering how in Holy Christ some well-to-do *girl* could wield such a sailor's mouth.

"I said have a seat, Miss Bailey, not injure yourself," he snapped. "And watch your tongue."

"My apologies, sir." Her voice was small, her cheeks tinged pink as she pulled out the leather chair and promptly, but carefully, sat.

An awkward silence settled over the room as Lightoller considered what to say next. He hadn't prepared for this moment—especially since he was still struggling to come to terms with such a bewildering circumstance. It certainly didn't help that the girl's freckles were all too similar to his wife's.

But no wife or woman would have dared to step into an officer's uniform—save for the one sitting before him.

Why?

It was the only question Lightoller had. He brought his fingertips to his temples, frowning at the swirling wood grain etched in the teak table, then quickly collected himself, sitting straighter in his seat and fixing the girl with a piercing stare.

"First and foremost," he began, "I wish to make one thing clear. You are *only* here due to circumstances beyond the captain's control, and he would not have even considered taking you on otherwise."

Lightoller spoke the simple, blunt truth. He noticed her eyes narrow, but if she was offended, she gave no other indication.

"That being said," he pressed on, "we have still agreed to provide you with the same opportunities as each of our crewmen. We will treat you as we would treat any junior officer—just know that there will be no special treatment, no accommodations. You, as a *junior* officer, are to afford every assistance in the navigation of this vessel and attend strictly to all instructions of the officer in charge. You will be expected to perform your duties admirably, steadfastly, and without complaint. Anything less will be met with swift and decisive punishment. Do I make myself clear?"

She nodded. "Yes, sir."

"Good." Lightoller gave a brusque nod in return, while silently asking himself what the *blazes* was going on, and why White Star Line had allowed this nonsense to happen. His mood only seemed to worsen as he spent the next hour reviewing the girl's duties, summarizing their watch schedules and other such business matters. She hung on his every word, green eyes intent and respectful. But not even her attentiveness could ease the hostility smoldering inside him.

Lightoller was relieved when the clock struck nine, signaling the end of their meeting at last. He shot to his feet, struggling to cling to the last of his patience as he yanked open the door.

"I do believe we're done here," he said curtly. "Tomorrow, we will provide you with a detailed tour of the ship so you may familiarize yourself with every nook and cranny aboard. Come Tuesday, we will have you situated in your cabin. And on Wednesday, we set sail." He eyed her accessories disapprovingly. "Be sure to remove any and *all* jewelry before setting foot on the bridge. Understood?"

"Yes, sir."

"Oh," Lightoller added idly, "one more thing. Officers are required to collect their uniforms. I'll have Mr. Moody write down the address to our approved tailors in Southampton. Miller, Murphy, and Holm. They should be able to assist you."

His voice grew strained as he spoke those last words, for he simply could not fathom the difficulties of a woman being fitted in a naval tailor shop. Suppressing a wince, Lightoller continued, "While I don't expect your garb to be worn tomorrow—given that I *highly* doubt it will be ready by that time—I do expect you to wear it when we set sail. Do I make myself clear?"

"Perfectly clear, sir," the girl answered. This time, her words blazed with conviction.

"Right, then." His voice was short. "You are dismissed. Report to the ship tomorrow no later than nine o'clock."

Bailey nodded. "Very good, sir." She turned on her heel for the door, and the light caught the pearls at her ears. But then she paused, fingers gripping the brass doorknob tight, eyes boring into Lightoller's with resolution.

"I very much look forward to working with you, sir."

Lightoller hesitated. He knew he was being hard on her. Knew he ought to give her a chance. But he simply couldn't bring himself to do it. The girl was like a storm that appeared from nowhere, trapping him amidst an ocean of uncertainty. He felt as if he were sailing blindly into dark and unfamiliar waters—and he didn't like it one bit.

The first officer met her determined stare and merely nodded with dismissal.

"Good day, Miss Bailey."

09:40

By the time Esther left Southampton Port and made for her hotel, she was far less enthused about the journey ahead of her.

Where she had once felt an immeasurable excitement, she now felt small, lost and unwelcome, treading rough currents without a sense of belonging to keep her afloat.

Lightoller had been cold with her, and Moody hadn't even *realized* they were colleagues until she'd given him her name.

Esther could feel her cheeks burn with shame and humiliation as the motorcar bumped along the road, winding along cobbled avenues already thick with people. Southampton had come alive now that the rain had cleared and the sun had risen. And yet, all the seventh officer wanted to do was bury herself in her bed—deep into her blankets where she would never see the light of day again.

Esther had thought she'd dressed modestly in a plain skirt and simple wool overcoat, but Lightoller had scrutinized her attire anyway. The pearls and heels might have been a bit much, and she swore to dress more conservatively tomorrow. At least she would have a uniform by Monday, so blending in with the other officers wouldn't be much of an issue.

Other than the small, unavoidable detail of her being a *woman*, of course.

It wasn't until Esther entered the hotel suite and slammed the door shut that she truly let her emotions get the better of her. They billowed within the confines of her ribcage, a stormy wrath of shame and anger. She stalked across the elegant carpet in a temper, pacing back and forth in her heels and breathing through her nose like some kind of animal. She kicked at the leg of an end table in frustration, sending a bowl of pears tumbling to the floor in a heap. Cursing under her breath, she knelt down to collect them.

"I take it the meeting went rather well, then?"

Esther turned to see her brother strolling into the parlor, shutting the pocket watch at his waistcoat with a snap. He was freshly shaven this morning, suit pressed and ink-black hair slicked to perfection. While he and Esther shared the same freckled complexion and green-gray eyes, Booker was much taller than his sister, with a sharp jawline and thick eyebrows that matched the darkness of his tidy hair.

At his question, Esther straightened up with a snort.

"Oh no," she grumbled. "What gave you that idea?"

He laughed. "I doubt taking your anger out on bowls of fruit and furniture will do you any good, you know."

"It helps," she insisted stubbornly, returning the pears to their rightful place. "You ought to try it sometime."

"I would, but I happen to have a little thing we like to call *dignity*." He smiled teasingly at her scowl. Clearing his throat, he gestured toward a sitting chair. "Temper tantrums aside, come have a seat. Let's hear what happened."

Esther folded her arms across her chest, lips pressed together in defiance, eyes glowering at some spot on the patterned floor. And before she knew it, she was pacing across the parlor, spilling out the events of the morning in a heated rush. Her brother listened patiently to her outburst, one leg crossed over the other, eyes never leaving her troubled face.

"The *captain* doesn't even want me on board, for Christ's sake," Esther finished, chest heaving against the binds of her corset. "And that's *nothing* compared to Lightoller. I could practically *feel* the disgust coming off him when he was looking at me—like I was the sort of scum you find floating in a gutter or something."

"Scum, you say? That's somewhat of a compliment in your case, isn't it?"

"Hilarious, Booker," Esther said dryly. "I didn't realize you've become a goddamn comedian."

"Geez, keep your hair on. Lightoller will come around. They all will."

"Easy for you to say," she snapped back. "*You're* not the one who's a—"

But Esther stopped herself, suddenly flushed with guilt. She knew she had no right to turn her anger on her brother, so she fumbled for a hasty apology. "I'm sorry, Booker, I—"

"Don't bother," Booker said calmly, waving a dismissive hand. "Let it all out if you have to. I can stand to be a punching bag for a day, if that's what it takes. Just remember you've spent four *years* of your *womanly* life studying maritime law at one of the finest institutes in England. I wouldn't say that was for nothing, now, would you?" He waited until Esther numbly shook her head before continuing, "That Ordinary Master's Certification of yours was no picnic, either. You are *just* as qualified as the rest of those junior recruits; you being a woman shouldn't make the slightest difference. And if it does, then they're damn fools."

Esther smiled at her brother, all rage and humiliation momentarily forgotten. "You're right," she agreed, speaking with a fierce determination that surprised even herself. "I've spent too many years working toward this moment to let them ruin it. *I'm* a junior officer on the finest ship in the world—and by God, I'm going to give it my all, no matter what they say."

"That's the spirit," Booker said cheerfully. "See? It helps to talk these things out rather than keep them bottled up. You don't want to end up throwing a fit, kicking furniture and things..."

"Oh, shut up," Esther said over her brother's laughter.

He was still chuckling when the maid entered the room bearing a platter of hot coffee and iced oatmeal cakes.

"Thank you, Miss Josephine," Booker said, flourishing a dazzling smile. "As prompt and as lovely as ever."

Slightly pink, the maid gave a short curtsey and slipped from the room, her eyes lingering on Booker's sleek black hair. Esther wasn't surprised; her brother had always possessed a flirty charm that captivated both women and men alike—a trait that Esther almost certainly swore she lacked. She couldn't seem to turn a head these days, much less entice some gentleman to buy her a drink. But Booker …he never seemed to have any trouble catching attention.

"So, you never did tell me." Her brother hooked his mug with the crook of one finger and raised it to his lips. "What did you think of *Titanic*? Are you now a firm believer she's truly *the* Ship of Dreams—or whatever drivel they call her these days?"

Esther hesitated, her expression softening as she sought a heartfelt response. "She's indescribable," she breathed, eyes glowing as she recalled it *all*: the grace, the splendor, the sheer size of the impressive steamer. "I haven't seen much of her interior, though. Just the officers' smoking lounge on the boat deck so far."

Booker smiled. "Oh, just you wait. You haven't lived till you've seen the forward Grand Staircase. Mr. Andrews did a truly marvelous job; I'm honored to work beneath him."

Esther sat up straight, nearly spilling coffee down the front of her blouse. She'd been so preoccupied with her own matters that her brother's apprenticeship had slipped her mind.

"That's right!" she said excitedly. "How was your meeting with Mr. Andrews?"

"It went rather well, I think," Booker admitted. "He's an intelligent man. I hope to learn everything I can from him." He brought his cup to his lips, adding thoughtfully, "Hard to believe we're setting sail this coming week. I'm already scheduled to move into my quarters on Monday."

"Same as me," Esther mused. "But I'll have to visit a tailor shop beforehand to get fitted for my uniform. If I'm not in full dress on Tuesday, there's a slight chance Mr. Lightoller will murder me."

Booker did not respond immediately. The faintest look of uncertainty crossed his face, but it was fleeting, and she wondered if perhaps she'd imagined it.

"I see," her brother said in a smooth, careful voice. "Well, I have Monday morning free and can accompany you to the tailor, if you'd like."

Esther nodded, thinking tomorrow would be a new day. A brighter day, perhaps.

"It's a plan."

THREE

DEMOTION

April 6, 1912 | 13:10

CHARLES LIGHTOLLER WAS still reeling as he retraced his steps down the starboard boat deck, trying to soothe the erratic swirl of his thoughts.

Clouds had rolled into the port once again, paling the River Test to gray, while a rather nasty wind snarled in his ear. *Bizarre April weather,* he thought absentmindedly, tugging on his leather gloves and making a mental note to wear his greatcoat for the rest of the day. But he had much more to worry about than the cold. His mind was fixed on one single ruddy point amidst his universe, and that point was Esther Bailey.

Lightoller wanted nothing more than to slip inside his cabin unnoticed, where he could brood alone and accept the mortifying truth of the girl becoming his charge. But he had no sooner reached the officers' promenade when footsteps echoed ahead of him, and he found himself walking straight toward Chief Officer William Murdoch and Second Officer David Blair. His colleagues were chatting leisurely, greatcoats snapping in the saltwater breeze. But the sight of Lightoller's wan face drew them to a short stop.

"All right, Lights?" Murdoch asked, the rasp of his Scottish accent rolling off his tongue. His eyes—a deep, watery blue that so often reminded Lightoller of the sea itself—were filled with curiosity.

"You look as if you've seen a ghost," Blair added, amused.

I might as well have, Lightoller thought. He stood straighter and tipped his dimpled chin into the air, struggling to keep hold of his composure. But his efforts were useless; the words spilled out fast and irritable as he confided, "I had the pleasure of meeting our newest recruit this morning."

"Oh?" Blair said pleasantly. "The junior officer?"

"Yes." Lightoller spoke through gritted teeth. "And *she* is looking forward to working with us."

Murdoch had been idly rubbing his hands together to warm them. But now he was motionless, still as stone, eyes narrowed tight.

"Sorry?"

Lightoller inhaled sharply through his nose. "We are to welcome Miss Esther Bailey to the ship come tomorrow morning."

His words seemed to crack the air like a whip—harsh enough to split all sanity and reason apart.

"You must be *joking*," Blair gasped, looking thunderstruck, while Murdoch regarded Lightoller with frozen disbelief. "He's joking, Will."

"How I wish I was," Lightoller said. "Our seventh officer is a *girl*, relative to some lofty old executive of White Star Line and its parent company."

Murdoch frowned. "You're talking mince, Lights. I don't believe a word of it."

"You'll see her soon enough, Will. She'll be here tomorrow for a tour of the ship, and then she…" Lightoller pinched the bridge of his nose as if suffering from a headache. "She'll be moving into the officers' quarters come Monday."

Blair looked outraged. "*Our* quarters? But the captain—"

"—was overruled," Lightoller finished bluntly. He swallowed against the bile in his throat, his stomach churning with shame and dismay. "As I said before, the girl is a relative to the owner of our parent company. Nothing can be done. She is here to stay, as much as I loathe to say it."

"Do they have any idea what they're doing?" Murdoch asked in a quiet voice. "This is a proper working *ship*, this is. Not a parlor."

"Well, the girl does appear to have maritime experience," Lightoller pointed out. *Bloody hell,* he scolded himself. *Don't defend her.*

Murdoch arched a single eyebrow. "Does she, now?" he said flatly.

"So it seems. Her file says she's certified and spent four years studying maritime law in London. She even worked aboard a small liner in Nova Scotia earlier this spring—though I shudder to imagine how that played out."

"Bollocks," Blair muttered. "As if any of that makes a difference. She belongs with the other *stewardesses*. Not out on the bridge with the rest of our men." He shook his head, his cloudy eyes dark with disgust. "She'll hurt herself, she will. Or fall asleep on watch. Or chip a nail, aye? That sort of thing."

Lightoller regarded him with a pained expression. "I agree with you, Davy, I really do. But we've no say in the matter. We'll simply have to endure her for the time being, as unfortunate as it may be."

Though his colleagues wanted to discuss the matter further, Lightoller didn't think he could take much more of their conversation. Not now, for heaven's sake. Not when his composure was already threatening to splinter apart. Clearing his throat, he smoothly changed the subject.

"Never mind all this. What are you doing on the boat deck at this hour, anyway? I thought your shift didn't start until two, Will."

Blair exchanged a glance with Murdoch. "Actually, we were looking for you. The captain's called a meeting with all senior officers this afternoon."

"Good news?" Lightoller asked swiftly.

"He didn't say," Murdoch replied. "But Henry seems to think it may have something to do with our roles."

Lightoller frowned. "Henry Wilde?" he said in a gruff voice, thinking of the tall, commanding officer with his broad face and squinting gray eyes. "What does Wilde have to do with any of this? He isn't even assigned to our ship—he's *Olympic*'s chief officer, last I heard."

"Aye, that he is." Murdoch nodded, thoughtful, head tipped to one side. "Bit funny, isn't it?"

"Bothersome, more like," Blair said. "But I s'pose we'll find out soon enough."

Lightoller heaved a sigh, longing to be gone from his company—and from the unpleasant thoughts now prickling him, digging into his skin like a bad itch he couldn't quite scratch. "I'd best be getting on, then," he told his colleagues. "I must finish some last-minute paperwork regarding Miss Bailey. Or throw myself overboard," he added wryly, managing a grim smile. "One of the two." His fingertips met the brim of his cap in a gesture of farewell. "Good day, Will. Davy."

And with that, Lightoller started down the boat deck in a hurry, Oxfords thundering across the waxed wood beneath him.

His surroundings rushed past him in a blur: the tides swirling with seafoam and salt beneath him, the gulls chattering in the distance, the handymen still polishing and tending to the spotless ship.

But Lightoller was oblivious to it all. Between having the girl as his charge and hearing rumors of a shift in their chain of command, he was already beginning to feel the first cracks of stress.

His place as first officer was off to a bumpy start, that much was for certain, and Lightoller could only hope for smoother seas ahead.

16:40

A cold rain returned by late afternoon, swirling over the decks and bulwarks before tumbling in rivulets to the sea.

William McMaster Murdoch had a lot more than rain on his mind as he stood watch inside the wheelhouse, keeping his hands folded behind his back and his expression smoothed into a mask of practiced calm.

His eyes drifted from the teakwood helm attached to its telemotor, then to the row of engine-order telegraphs perched beyond it, their bold lettering shimmering across the rain-slick wetness of the bridge.

Stand by, some of them read. *Dead Slow, Slow, Half, Full, Astern.*

Murdoch straightened his spine and stretched the crick from his neck, quiet as he watched the downpour. Though he had his own misgivings about the female officer, he was more concerned with the journey ahead—specifically, what to expect as *Titanic*'s new chief officer.

Chief Officer Murdoch.

The title was still a peculiar thing, but it rolled off the tongue in a fine way, enough to make him swell with pride. There was no denying his excitement. Murdoch had waited for this moment for years now, working his way up through the ranks and manning the decks of White Star Line ships ranging from the *Arabic* to the *Germanic* to the *Olympic*. He was a steadfast man, more comfortable at sea than on land, who attended to his work with professionalism and level-headed ease. Now he was chief officer, donned in the proper garb depicting his senior rank: two golden stripes, with the third one looped—a reminder that he now had more authority, more *responsibility*, even, than he'd known in all his maritime career.

It was a humbling thought, and Murdoch was damn well determined to prove his worth not only to his captain, but to the entire lineage of his seafaring family. He would make his father proud. He would uphold the Murdoch name with propriety. And someday, hopefully…he would assume the rank of captain himself.

Wednesday could not come quickly enough; Murdoch was eager to set sail as soon as possible. He wanted to taste the saltwater air and see nothing but endless ocean stretching before him. He wanted to feel the rumble of *Titanic*'s steam engines and hear the roar of wind through her rigging; he longed for the pull of her speed as she cut across frozen waves and the deepest of waters, gracefully leading her crew to the American coast awaiting them.

And yet…despite the thrill of setting sail, something else lingered at the back of his mind. Something that needled him in the dead of night, and oftentimes stayed with him long until morning.

Murdoch touched the finger where his wedding band once rested, more out of habit than anything else. He swallowed hard against the lump in his throat, his chest twisting into a knot that nearly whisked the breath from his lungs.

He'd thought Ada had been happy. He'd thought their marriage was set in stone, sealed by a bond of mutual love and devotion.

Apparently not, he reminded himself, grazing his bare ring finger with one calloused thumb.

Murdoch knew he was partially to blame. He could have been there more. He could have taken shorter voyages rather than those long, extended trips across the Atlantic. But his love for the sea and the dedication to his career was stronger than forged steel—stronger than the bond of marriage, even—and Ada had taken notice.

He could still recall the day she'd left him, shortly after their row in which she'd pressed him and *pushed* him to give up his life at sea. She grew lonely in his absence, she'd said. She didn't want to be a seafarer's wife, spending weeks and oftentimes months waiting for her husband to come home. Instead, she wanted to settle down in the country. Start a family, perhaps. But Murdoch, being at the height of his career, hadn't been ready to father children.

And so, on the night he'd returned from his last assignment aboard *Olympic*, Ada had given him an ultimatum. Her words still lingered in his head, crackling at his temples like the splinter of a headache.

Make a choice, Will. It's me or the ocean. You can't have both.

Of course, Murdoch chose the ocean.

Standing before the vast stretch of sea now, with the gleaming woodwork and pristine white paint of the vessel before him, he was certain he had made the right decision. Absolutely, he had. It didn't quite snuff out the unbidden ache of losing his wife— of *missing* her, even—the remorse stinging him like an open wound meeting saltwater. But Murdoch found the loneliness was growing less and less each day, fading away into itself until one day, he'd wonder what became of it.

Heavy footfalls dragged him from his thoughts, and his expression became one of good-natured welcome as he spotted his old friend and colleague Henry Tingle Wilde on the bridge. While Murdoch stood at average height, Wilde was an absolute giant, towering over him with a strapping frame and eyes the color of cool slate.

"Daydreaming again, Will?" he asked, his voice rolling out in the deep, guttural drawl Murdoch had come to know since their camaraderie aboard *Olympic*.

"Caught me." Murdoch cracked a smile as they grasped hands. "Good to see you again, Henry."

Wilde smirked. "Oh, how I wish I could say the same." He studied Murdoch's uniform with approval, noting the distinctive gold trim and shoulder-boards. "Blimey, have a look at *that*. Chief officer now, eh?"

"Aye," Murdoch said, amused. "Not too intimidated, then?"

"Marginally, darling," Wilde answered with a careless grin. "Though I must say, I'm proud of you for getting this far. 'Specially with that ruddy accent of yours. No one can understand a lick of what you're saying half the time, you sad, Scottish bastard, and yet you've managed to climb the ranks—gibberish be damned."

Murdoch snorted. "That I have, ya dafty. And I'll be throwing your arse off the back of this *ship*, mind, if you don't shut your sorry mouth."

Wilde let out a bellow of good-natured laughter before slapping his palm against Murdoch's back. "Well, then. If you've finished being a salty git, that lad Mr. Moody sent me to fetch you. Seems we're wanted by

Smith in his sitting room."

"This ought to be interesting."

"Indeed. Any idea what this is all about?"

"Not a clue," Murdoch confessed, as they left the wheelhouse for the sitting room, leaving the rain long behind them. "Though there's rumor it might have something to do with officer positions."

Wilde looked bemused. "Can't imagine why I'm here, then. Unless old E.J. is offering me a job. You know I was scheduled for the *Olympic* last week? Then White Star Line asked me to stay behind in Southampton." He inhaled sharply through his nose. "Wankers. Should've told 'em to sod off, eh? Like I don't have anything better to do than sit around and wait for them to get their shit together."

Murdoch listened with a patient half-smile, completely unfazed by his colleague's gruff curses. Though Wilde was quite the professional mariner, and notorious throughout the industry for his intimidating stature and distinguished air, he had never learned—or bothered—to lose his sailor's mouth.

A handful of electric lamps greeted them in the captain's sitting room, dousing the mahogany walls with a lemony glow. Captain E.J. Smith sat upon an upholstered settee, his beard an unmistakable beacon of white, his eyes steadier than pools of untouched water. Lightoller and Blair were already present, seated before the end table, raindrops sparkling in the navy fabric of their coats. Murdoch shot Lightoller a quizzical look, but he said nothing as he turned his attention to the captain. They shook hands with Smith, exchanging the usual pleasantries.

"Mr. Murdoch. Mr. Wilde. Please, have a seat."

The officers obeyed at once, Murdoch settling across from Blair and struggling to ignore the icy foreboding slipping through his bones.

"Gentlemen," Smith began, surveying the faces gathered around him in turn. "As you know, we set sail for New York this coming Wednesday. I had hoped to avoid last-minute preparations or any such uncertainties before the maiden voyage, but I am afraid that simply cannot be the case."

The officers waited in silence, no one daring to move or breathe. It was so quiet, Murdoch could almost hear rain rattling on the roof above them. All eyes remained fixed upon the captain as he continued, "Due to certain events that have transpired, I have decided to reshuffle officer positions for the duration of our crossing. This was a personal choice on my part, and I believe it will ensure operations continue to run smoothly for all onboard."

Murdoch swallowed. He thought of the girl, the new *officer*, and wondered if this mishap was because of her. Anger rippled through his mind, threatening to break his composure like a hammer to glass. His hands tightened into fists beneath the table; blame and bitterness swelled in his chest.

"Mr. Wilde will be assigned to the position of chief officer," Smith said, and Murdoch felt as if he'd taken a blow to the stomach. "He will move into the chief officer's cabin as soon as possible. Mr. Murdoch, you will take up the role of first officer. The rank of second officer will go to you, Mr. Lightoller. And Mr. Blair." Smith hesitated, his voice weighing heavy with regret. "My apologies, Mr. Blair, but you will no longer be required on this voyage. If you will return to Southampton whenever you are able, White Star Line will see that you are transferred to a different ship."

He cleared his throat, lacing his fingers neatly before him. "I understand this may pose some difficulties, especially given that we've already established officer duties and lodging. But I will leave it to you fine gents to sort it out among yourselves. Are there any other questions?"

A long, uncomfortable silence followed his words as the officers processed the finality of their shifted ranks. Murdoch could not meet the eye of any man at the table. His gaze was downcast, his face drawn and stiff. He recalled the feeling of pride and elation he had felt only moments ago, standing amidst the splendor of the wheelhouse. He had been looking forward to his role as chief officer for months now. But now the opportunity was snatched away from him in seconds *flat*.

In hindsight, Murdoch knew he ought to have braced himself for something of this nature to happen.

He'd been a sailor long enough to know the unexpected could happen, just as sudden as storms rearing up from clear oceans and gulfs, turning waves into whitewater mountains, blue skies into walls of darkness and rain. The ocean was a volatile creature, unrestrained and often ruthless. Murdoch had long since expected this unpredictability to appear in his everyday life, so he had learned to adapt—to ride out the rougher currents and not think twice on it.

But *nothing* could have prepared him for this moment of relegated shame, and now Murdoch felt utterly caught off guard, trapped beneath shifting tides with no surface in sight.

When no one spoke, Smith seemed to sense the discomfort of his men and called an end to the meeting. One by one, the officers bade their farewells before shuffling outside in silence. The rain had become a violent downpour, blurring the forecastle from view. Even the mast and rigging were scarcely discernible, while the distant docks of Southampton were mere smudges of inky blue. Murdoch was lost in thought, his eyes on the sheeting rain. But he found himself suddenly jolted back to awareness when Wilde gripped his shoulder with a heavy hand.

"Will," he began, his voice gruff with remorse. "Will, listen. You know I would *never* agree to this if I could. I'm so sorry, mate. I'd no idea he would go and—"

"It's fine," Murdoch said shortly. "Believe me, Henry, it's all right. I don't blame you one bit—"

"That certainly makes one of us."

They all turned to see Lightoller standing stiffly, chin raised, eyes narrowed with flinty disdain.

Wilde turned slowly to him. "Oh, I'm sorry," he drawled. "Do you have something to say, *Mister* Lightoller? Go on then, spit it out."

As if giving Wilde his full attention was beneath him, Lightoller took care to adjust his gloves as he replied, "I have many things I'd like to say, Mr. Wilde, though none too polite."

"I'm a seaman, in case you've forgotten, darling," Wilde sneered. "So why don't you try me?"

"That's *enough!*" Murdoch bellowed, putting an end to their bickering with a hoarse shout that stunned them all—even himself. "The pair of you—pack it in, will you? What's done is done. The captain has his reasons, and Henry *certainly* isn't to blame. He's now the highest-ranking officer aboard this ship, in case you've forgotten, Lights."

The tension following his words was almost palpable, crackling the air like static electricity. Murdoch could understand Lightoller's attitude— they'd both been bumped down in rank, after all, and therefore also in pay. But there was no need for animosity. Least of all at a time like this.

It was Wilde who broke the silence, his mouth twisted into a crooked grimace as he surveyed the officers before him. "Listen, you lot. I know this ruddy reshuffle has us all hot under the collar, and that *some* have their knickers twisted more than others apparently—" He spared a meaningful glance at Lightoller, who scowled in return. "But regardless of what's happened, we've a job to do. And we can't let any sort of bad blood get in the way of that. So, let's move past this, shall we?"

"Easier said than done, I'm afraid," Lightoller retorted.

Wilde blinked innocently at him, his voice bright and patronizing, as if speaking to a sulking schoolchild. "Thank you, Charles, for your astonishingly constructive input—"

Patience withering, Murdoch turned away from the pair of them in disgust to address Blair instead. "Davy, I'm so sorry," he murmured, heart heavier than stone. "Truly, I am."

Blair heaved a low sigh. "S'no worries, Will. Be lying if I said I wasn't gutted, but...I suppose it wasn't meant to be." He shrugged, staring glumly at his feet, and Murdoch could think of nothing more to say, nothing that could convey his remorse. "Ah, well. Keep a sharp eye on this ship for me, hear? Best of luck to you, gents."

They shook hands. "And to you," Murdoch said quietly.

He stood between Lightoller and Wilde, and the three senior officers watched as Blair disappeared beyond the torrent of rain.

Wilde, in what Murdoch assumed was a desperate attempt to break the tension, said, "Well, then! Quite the unexpected turn of events, eh?"

Lightoller glared at him. "To say the least." He turned to Murdoch, his cold expression shifting to curiosity. "Since you're to assume my position, it seems Miss Bailey will now become your charge."

Murdoch was momentarily confused; in the turn of events this afternoon, he'd forgotten all about their newest recruit.
"My charge, you say?" he echoed distantly.

Lightoller nodded. "She's the responsibility of the first officer, so there you are. She'll be on the ship tomorrow morning, so you'll be the one to give her a tour, I imagine."

"Forgive me." Wilde glanced between his colleagues with a look of bafflement. "Perhaps my ears are deceiving me...but are you talking about a *woman?*"

"Yes." Lightoller gave a short sigh. "An officer."

"A *woman* officer?" Wilde boggled.

"*Yes*, a woman. Who is also an officer. Aboard this ship." Scowling, Lightoller checked his pocket watch. "If we're finished here, I'd best be off. I'd rather not keep this *company* any longer than need be." His frosty eyes passed over Wilde, regarding him with apparent distaste before he bade a friendlier goodbye to Murdoch. "Cheerio."

Wilde waited until the last of his footfalls disappeared before turning to Murdoch. "Think he fancies me?"

Murdoch snorted. "Clearly. Thought he was about to pop the question once or twice." He studied the downpour with a thoughtful expression, trying to keep a grasp on his flitting thoughts. "The reshuffle wasn't your fault, Henry, and Lights is just looking for someone to blame. He's fair scunnered now, but he'll come 'round. And who knows? Perhaps you'll become good mates by the time we reach New York."

"Good God," Wilde grunted. "I'd rather drink myself to death before that day comes, thanks. Speaking of which," he added carelessly, "why don't you join me in the smoking room? Have a touch of whisky. Take your mind off this whole reshuffle nonsense, perhaps."

Murdoch sighed. "I would, but I ought to get my quarters sorted. Still have to move my things from the chief officer's cabin to first."

Wilde frowned. "Surely it can wait until tomorrow?"

"Doubt it. Given I'm now a full-time nanny, it seems as though I'll be busy dealing with that girl officer from here on out." His voice was dull. "The *highlight* of my career, I daresay."

"Be as that may, it won't hurt to relax for an hour or two. We only have so little time left before we sail, mate. Might as well enjoy it while we can." Smoothing out his coat, Wilde crossed the room to open the wheelhouse door. A chill rushed in, and the room was awash with the drip and scatter of falling rain.

"Come on, Will," he teased, when Murdoch didn't move a muscle. "Before I have to order you."

Murdoch bit back a scoff. "That'll be the day, that will," he muttered. But he still shot his companion a grateful look as they stepped out into the downpour, hoping a drink might be enough to clear his head, and keep the shame of his demotion from crashing down on his shoulders again.

FOUR

THE GIRL

April 7, 1912 | 08:40

THE SOUND OF waves greeted Esther when she returned to the Port of Southampton, waters calm and swirling beneath a crisp blue sky.

Though the rain had disappeared overnight, the air was still as icy as the day before, if not worse. But Esther paid little mind to the cold as she wove around puddles and pools of rainwater. Her eyes were on the port, observing the vast huddle of ships' masts and prows cluttering the docks before her.

There was a diligent energy she had not seen yesterday morning, in the early hours before dawn. Stevedores and sailors called to each other as they worked, their voices boisterous, rising high above the jumble of equipment and electrical cranes. Motorcars glittered as they cut along the narrow streets dividing the storehouses, carrying the stench of exhaust and oil. There were sounds of hissing steam and shoveled coal, of box hooks snapping open cargo crates, and of engines whirring as they fired up along the shore. Esther could even catch the distant bellow of a whistle horn, its sound billowing across the port like thunder.

It was exciting, seeing all this commotion spread before her, and she could not look away as she watched the movement swell across every dock, every deck, every berthed ship.

She had remembered to dress more conservatively for today's meeting: a plain white blouse with a pleated skirt hugging her narrow waist, coupled with a long coat tumbling past her knees. Her boots were brown suede, simple and nondescript, and there were no pearls at her ears this time. But she'd left the silver locket hanging from her neck, with the photograph of her twin brothers—Booker and Brighton—nestled safely behind its clasp.

She couldn't see anything Lightoller might complain about today. Barring the obvious, of course. But she refused to let him put a damper on her thoughts as she continued onward, enjoying the salty sea breeze and curious sights all around her.

Titanic loomed at the end of the dock, breathtakingly perfect as she sat nested in swirling water, her hull swept by sunlit tints of azure, muddy turquoise, and foam-tipped blue. Esther hurried forward, her stride quickening in her eagerness to board, but the sight of a familiar face brought her skidding to a halt. There was certainly no mistaking his square jaw and round, dark eyes.

"Why, good morning, Mr. Moody!" Esther called pleasantly.

Officer Moody stopped short, the tails of his greatcoat whipping to one side. He made his way toward her after a moment's hesitation, wading through the throng of dockworkers and longshoremen with ease. Though his expression was carefully aloof, Esther didn't miss the rush of color blooming across his neck. Part of her wondered if he was thinking of yesterday, when she surprised him with her full name and rank. Even now, that gaping, gobsmacked look on his face still made her want to laugh.

"Miss Bailey," Moody said politely. "It's a pleasure to see you again."

"And you." She shook his gloved hand with a smile.

"I heard you were coming aboard today. For a tour of the ship, if I'm not mistaken?"

She nodded. "That's right. I'm scheduled to meet Mr. Lightoller on the boat deck in a quarter of an hour."

"Mr. Lightoller?" Moody echoed, puzzled. "Don't you mean—?"

But then he stopped himself, recovering from his momentary bemusement with a quick, nonchalant smile. "Never mind. I suppose they'll sort out all the details once you're on board."

While he seemed willing to drop the subject, Esther's curiosity only piqued tenfold. She opened her mouth to pry, but fell silent when Moody added, "Actually, I was wondering if I might have a word. Will you walk with me?"

He gestured toward the sweeping cement dock edging *Titanic*'s berth. Esther nodded, surprised, and the two junior officers were quiet as they fell into step together.

Moody kept his hands behind his back, his eyes staring determinedly ahead, and it wasn't until they'd passed through the teeming crowd that he spoke.

"I wanted to apologize for yesterday, Miss Bailey. It was sloppy of me to have overlooked you. I should have recognized you the moment you set foot in port, and I am terribly sorry if I inconvenienced you."

She laughed. "You're pulling my leg."

"Sorry?"

"You think you *inconvenienced* me?"

A light shade of pink colored his cheeks. "Quite."

He's embarrassed, Esther realized. She smiled at his sheepish expression, both touched and amused by his gesture.

"Oh, Mr. Moody," she said kindly, "not on your life. It was *funny*, if anything, not inconveniencing. To be fair, who in their right mind would think a lady at the dock was truly a ship's officer? If I'd been in your shoes, I probably wouldn't have believed that baloney either. So let's just forget about it, shall we?"

But then Esther paused for a moment, a mischievous grin playing across her face.

"On second thought," she added slyly, "Let's not."

Her words only seemed to embarrass Moody even further. His hands shot up to his throat, fumbling to straighten his already-perfect tie.

"Is there a *reason*?" he asked weakly.

"Well, to be perfectly honest with you, Mr. Moody, I don't think I can ever forget that goggle-eyed look of yours when you realized I was a 'miss' and not 'mister.'"

She offered him a quick imitation of the face in question, dropping her jaw wide open and bulging her eyes, and Moody couldn't stifle his laughter.

"*See?*" Esther said, laughing along with him. "I'm afraid it's *too* spectacular a face to be completely forgettable."

"I suppose you are right," Moody agreed with a grin. "Spectacular indeed."

She was pleased to see her humor brightened him up, albeit imperceptibly. His stiff posture seemed to relax, while his stoicism dripped away to reveal a dimpled smile.

He's quite the charming fellow, Esther decided. *When he's not all aloof and proper, that is.*

"Well, Mr. Moody," she said brightly, "I must be off. Mr. Lightoller's waiting for me topside, and I don't want him to have an aneurysm if I'm not on time."

Moody regarded her with amusement. "Probably for the best," he agreed, as he touched his forefinger to his cap in a salute of farewell. "Good day, Miss Bailey."

She saluted back. "Good day, Mr. Moody."

09:00

Murdoch spent most of the early morning in a state of agitation, lost in the tidewaters of his brooding thoughts.

He felt careworn and defeated, drowning in the worst of his misgivings as the day wore on. But although the newly-demoted officer was under stress, he certainly did not show it. He chatted with his colleagues over a short breakfast of tea and milled oats in the officers' mess. He roamed the decks with a sense of swift purpose, fulfilling his duties with ease. He met with the newly-arrived quartermasters, and greeted his captain with a salute and a smile. Murdoch was still every bit the professional seafarer, as cool and reserved and meticulous as could be.

But he could feel the hold on his composure weaken as the day dragged on, flooding him with the deepest waters of disappointment and shame.

He had been so close to the position of chief officer—so absurdly goddamn *close*—but one minor change sent the rank slipping from his grasp, trickling through his fingers like seawater.

Murdoch still couldn't believe it. He had been looking forward to his new title for *months* now. He'd spent these last few weeks rehearsing his duties and getting accustomed to his watch schedule. But it was all for naught, and he could not stop the slow burn of frustration simmering through him.

He would lose the wide, comfortable cabin only second in size to the captain's. He would lose the hefty raise promised to his pocketbook. His twice-daily watches would change, meaning he'd have to acclimate to a new sleep schedule all over again.

Worse even, he now had some lady officer tagging along after him—a reminder that White Star Line was becoming little more than a joke.

Murdoch didn't blame Wilde for his demotion. Not one bit. The choice had come from their captain, whom he assumed had been pressured by the higher-ups at White Star Line. Fleetingly, Murdoch wondered if the newest junior recruit might have had anything to do with it. She was a *girl*, after all, so perhaps they'd wanted to accommodate her by any means possible. The notion disgusted him, and Murdoch found himself dreading the thought of working alongside her day after day. Whoever organized the reshuffle clearly didn't know him very well; he was bloody terrible with women. His marriage was a well-enough testament to that fact.

The sky was a clear, cloudless blue as he made his way to the bridge wing on the starboard side of the ship. It was here where he was scheduled to meet Miss Esther Bailey and Mr. Harold Lowe, both of whom were newcomers to transoceanic crossings. Murdoch had been instructed to give the junior officers a tour of the ship this morning, while also briefing them on their respective watches and duties.

He tried not to let his misgivings get the better of him as he waited alone on deck, listening to the tides and longing for their murmur to steady him.

Quit your worrying, he told himself sharply. *It'll do no good.*

And yet, worrying was all he seemed able to do these days…

"Sir?"

A voice caught his attention, dragging him out of his brooding thoughts. Murdoch turned abruptly to see a young woman stepping toward him on the bridge wing, long overcoat rippling at her ankles and dark hair falling to her shoulders.

This must be the girl, he thought, swallowing his distaste as he swept a wary gaze over her. There was a glow to her freckled skin in the morning light, and her eyes—a pale green that oddly made him think of celery—studied him uncertainly.

"I'm sorry to trouble you," she said, "but I'm looking for Mr. Lightoller. I was supposed to meet him here at nine o'clock. Is he around?"

No one had informed her of the reshuffle, it seemed. Murdoch stared blankly at the girl for a moment, struggling to process the notion that this lass—who looked more like a first-class passenger rather than a sailor—was standing before him with that grating American accent, ready to step right into his world of maritime rules and tradition.

Or *kick* her way into it, more like.

Part of Murdoch was still convinced she was the reason for his demotion. The one broken, misplaced cog thrown into White Star Line's well-oiled machine.

If it weren't for her, he thought bitterly, *I might still be chief officer.*

If it weren't for her, damn it all, he wouldn't be standing on deck this very moment, wasting his time with some high-society *girl* who had no business being here in the first place.

Inhaling a deep breath, Murdoch willed his voice to remain curt but still carefully professional as he addressed her.

"'Fraid there's been a slight shifting of our ranks. I take it you are Junior Officer Esther Bailey?"

"That's correct, sir."

"Well, Miss Bailey. I regret to inform you that Mr. Lightoller has become *Titanic*'s second officer. Therefore, he will no longer be your superior."

Her eyes widened in astonishment. "He's second officer?"

"Did you not hear me the first time?" Murdoch demanded. His sharp rebuke surprised even himself. Nevertheless, he pressed on, "Mr. Lightoller has been moved to the rank of second officer. I have assumed his place as first." And then, more out of habit and formality than respect, he held out his hand. "William Murdoch."

They shook, and Murdoch was aware of the firmness of her grip, clenching with a strength not at all dissimilar to his own seafaring hands.

Lightoller said she had maritime experience, he reminded himself grudgingly.

"A pleasure to meet you, Mr. Murdoch," the girl said politely. "Mr. Moody mentioned yesterday that you were chief officer. Forgive me for asking, sir, but were you asked to step down as well?"

"Aye." Murdoch's lip curled. "I should think that would be obvious."

"If that's the case, sir, then permit me to ask…who is our new chief officer?"

"Mr. Henry Wilde," Murdoch answered shortly. "You'll meet him soon, I imagine, along with the rest of our crew. I understand you're moving into the officers' quarters tomorrow?"

"I am, sir."

"Good. We'll be holding a dinner with all officers Tuesday evening. As a way to break the ice, so to speak."

"I very much look forward to it, sir."

A brief, cool pause stretched between them as Murdoch studied the girl, brooding, wishing he could be rid of her already. Criticism darkened his gaze as he looked her up and down, scrutinizing everything from her skirt to her cashmere coat.

"Correct me if I'm wrong," he said in a bored voice, "but you seem to be missing something, Miss Bailey."

She flushed. "Forgive my lack of proper attire, sir. I have an appointment for my uniform fitting tomorrow, and—"

"I should certainly hope so," Murdoch interrupted stiffly, and he saw the momentary shock cross Bailey's face before it vanished behind a scowl. "Can't have you walking 'round in those clothes for much longer, can we? You're already unqualified enough as is; I don't need you setting a poor example with the crew any further."

Resentment flashed in her gaze as she looked up at him. "*Gee*, Mr. Murdoch," she remarked under her breath, "wouldn't that be a shame."

Murdoch narrowed his eyes. He hadn't missed her thinly-veiled sarcasm, and it irked him.

"About as shameful as having a woman on the bridge, I'm sure," he snapped back.

Her temper flared in response, its mild spark erupting into a firestorm of anger. Murdoch watched the girl rear up on her tiptoes, chest heaving, ready to blow off some cheeky retort. But he stopped her at once.

"Think carefully before you speak," Murdoch warned, his voice carrying an edge of quiet, menacing calm as he loomed over her, only marginally aware of their differences in height. "And do well to remember your *place*, Miss Bailey. You are a junior officer. I am your superior. Is that clear?"

She glowered up at him for a long moment, blazing eyes of green meeting steely blue.

"Yes, *sir*."

They spoke nothing more to each other, glaring at opposite ends of the ship and refusing to make eye contact. Bailey wore a scowl, red-faced and seething as she watched the tides. Murdoch could almost feel the tension sizzling the air between them, hot enough to scald his skin, and he was glad when Lowe came trotting across the boat deck with a wave.

"Morning, Will," the fifth officer called cheerfully.

A lean, broad-chested man nearing thirty, Lowe was an experienced mariner with a steadfast attitude and a keenness for the sea. Although Murdoch had only met him a few days earlier in Belfast, he'd been thoroughly impressed by the lad's tenacity for maritime work. *He* would have made a fine protégé during the maiden voyage. Murdoch was damn well sure of it. But a stroke of blinding misfortune put *the girl* in his charge, rather than the promising, able-bodied Welshman standing at his side.

Although Murdoch offered his colleague a short good morning, Lowe was too busy looking at Bailey to notice.

"Why, hello," he said politely, studying her with interest. "You must be Miss Bailey. Harold Lowe, Fifth Officer. Pleasure to meet you."

Bailey shook his hand. "Pleasure's all mine."

Although she offered Lowe a pretty smile, her voice was still quiet. Strained, almost. Murdoch turned away, spine stiffening, suddenly wondering if his harsh words were too much for her. But Good God, what did she expect would happen? She had spoken out of turn, so he had rebuked her, plain and simple. Murdoch wasn't about to tolerate such disrespect from any officer—least of all from the likes of *her*.

But even as he chatted with Lowe about the weather, he knew the girl was watching him, and he couldn't forget the burn of her angry green eyes.

───────────────── 06:50 ─────────────────

Esther was fuming.

It was a silent rage, but rage nonetheless. She could feel it swirl inside her, all darkness and smoldering heat, charring her insides until she might burst into flames.

And I thought Lightoller was the jackass, she thought angrily. *Boy, was I off the mark on that one.*

Only yesterday, Esther had sworn to never let her less-than-welcoming shipmates get under her skin. They might belittle her, or talk down to her, or shoot her sidelong glances—but what did it matter? She was better than the ornery men who let their pride and insecurities keep them from accepting a woman officer. She had a backbone of wit and a mind of maritime knowledge at her arsenal, didn't she? She could move past their animosity with tact, and compose herself with just as much dignity as the next man.

But still…there was something about this *Murdoch* fellow Esther didn't like.

Whereas Lightoller had been cold and standoffish, her new superior officer was downright insulting. His snide comment still echoed in her ears, lacing her nerves with blistering fire.

You're already unqualified enough as is; I don't need you setting a poor example with the crew any further.

In hindsight, Esther knew she should have held her tongue. Knew she should have acted tactfully, and let his slight go right over her head. But the look in his eyes and the belittling edge of his voice had been so *demeaning* that she couldn't stop herself. And now her sarcastic retort had created what felt like an ocean between them—deep, foaming and seemingly impossible to cross.

She was quiet as they began their tour of the boat deck, exploring the officers' promenade first, and examining the compass tower amidships not long after. But it wasn't until they reached the navigating bridge that Esther felt her surly mood turn to giddy, wide-eyed excitement. She had never set foot here until now, and it was nearly impossible to look away.

The bridge was a wide, bright space that commanded a magnificent view of the bow, and beyond that, the glimmering sea. Light poured through an array of square windows, catching specks of dust and illuminating floors of smooth, glossy pine. There were four enormous telegraphs and one binnacle as far as she could see, each one as polished and immaculate as the last. Behind her sat the wheelhouse, its far wall hidden behind a forest of instruments: two brass clocks, four telephones, an inclinometer used to show whether the ship was listing to starboard or port, watertight door switches, and a meticulous sprawl of junction boxes and circuity that she knew stretched to the furthest reaches of the ship.

For the briefest of moments, Esther felt her anger with Murdoch trickle from her mind. She couldn't remember ever feeling so weightlessly elated as she gazed around, marveling at the bridge and its gleaming instruments.

This was nothing like the rickety old steamer she'd worked off the Nova Scotian coast; while the SS *Maloja* was simple and bare-boned in design, *Titanic* was breathtaking with all her shiny equipment and attention to detail.

Lowe was grinning at the astounded look on her face. "What d'you think, then?"

"It's—" Esther began, eager to spill her heart out. But then she caught herself. Murdoch's eyes were on her, and she backtracked, tucking her short dark hair behind one ear. "It's more wonderful than I could have ever imagined," she said quietly, and she meant it. "Truly a sight."

Murdoch was looking curiously at her. But then his gaze hardened as he placed his hands behind his back, curiosity turning to criticism at once.

"So it's wonderful, then," he said shortly. "That's an astute observation, Miss Bailey, but there's a lot more to it than that. Do you even know what half the instruments in this room are meant for?"

Her eyes flashed at him in a challenge. *Cheeky Scot.*

"No, *sir*," Esther said innocently, her voice tinted with a faint sarcasm no one missed—not even Murdoch. "I almost certainly wouldn't be able to tell you that's a binnacle." She pointed at the enormous brass object with a facetious smile. "Which houses the compass and inclinometer, and is used for navigational purposes. And I absolutely can't tell you that the telemotor—" She pointed again. "—is powered by hydraulics and helps us steer the rudder of this ship. Or that those telegraphs over there send maneuver orders to the engine room, with instructions for speed and direction." She raised her chin at him, green eyes glittering with defiance. "My apologies, sir. I just don't rightly know."

Lowe, who looked on the verge of laughter, glanced down at the deck to hide his face beneath the brim of his cap. But Murdoch was not so amused. He stood straighter, brows raised as he looked down his nose at her.

"Well, Miss Bailey," he said indifferently. "Thank you for proving that you're not entirely *useless* after all."

Lowe's laughter disappeared at once; he let out a startled choking noise that he attempted to disguise as a cough. Esther stood still, the loathing on her face unmistakable. But Murdoch was unfazed. In fact, he looked rather pleased with himself.

"Shall we continue with the tour?" he offered, smirking.

"Yes, sir," Lowe agreed, but Esther merely glowered in reply as she followed them down the boat deck.

They spent the next few hours exploring the ship from bow to stern, with Murdoch leading the way and a very disgruntled Esther trailing behind. Once they had seen the entirety of the boat deck—including the officers' mess and smoking lounge, and the Marconi Room holding the wireless operating equipment—Murdoch led them down a long promenade and inside the extravagant interior of A Deck.

When they first came upon the Grand Staircase, and Esther saw the domed skylight of iron and opaque milk-glass vaulting its way high above them, she had to cover her mouth to stifle a gasp.

Christ Almighty, she thought with wonder.

This entire room had to be the sole culprit for *Titanic*'s staggering cost; Esther was damn near sure of it. Natural light fell like a glaze on tiled floors of black and cream; it shone on elegant balustrades of wrought-iron and gilt, and made polished wood gleam as if wet. The staircase was wide and sweeping, built of solid oak as smooth as marble. A chandelier of beaded crystals glittered at the apex of the dome, while an ornately-carved panel graced the topmost landing, overlooking the steps with a single clock ticking at its center.

Esther studied the room and all its extraordinary woodwork, committing every detail to memory: the dazzling airiness of the domed ceiling, the carved pineapple finials sweeping up from the posts, and finally, the bronze cherub perched at the base of the staircase, holding an illuminated torch to the sky. She could already imagine these steps spilling with hundreds of first-class passengers come Wednesday, the men in their fine suits and white-ties, the women in their silks and glittering jewels.

"Well?" Murdoch said suddenly, shaking Esther from her thoughts. "You haven't said much, Miss Bailey. I take it you're overwhelmed? Too *wonderful* of a sight, perhaps?"

He was mocking her again, but Esther was too distracted to care.

"Something of that nature, yes," she said absentmindedly, running a hand over the glossy back of the nearest banister. "This craftsmanship is…geez, I don't even have a word to describe it. I've never seen anything like this, in all my life…"

Her voice trailed away when she realized Murdoch was watching her, and she drew herself up with a scowl. "I mean. It's pretty." She tossed him a pointed look. "Shall we continue with the tour, Mr. Murdoch?"

Murdoch pursed his lips. "That would be wise," he said curtly. "We still have Decks B through G, all of Scotland Road, and the orlop deck, if we have the time." Clearing the last few steps of the Grand Staircase, he strolled purposefully toward the lift foyer. "Now step lively, Mr. Lowe, Miss Bailey. We don't have all day."

As they walked, Lowe hung back to speak with Esther, whispering in an undertone so Murdoch wouldn't overhear.

"Er…permit me to ask, Miss Bailey, but why does it seem as if you and Mr. Murdoch are at loggerheads?"

"Sorry?"

Lowe studied her with amusement, a faint smile pulling at a corner of his mouth. "Well, you're quarreling with each other…continually. And at *this* early in the morning? Really, now?"

Esther shook her head with a sigh. "Is he always this insufferable?"

"No, not that I know of. He's a decent chap. Good sense of humor. Dry humor, mind, but that's a Scot for you. Perhaps he's sour after losing out on the chief officer position."

Esther stole a glance at the first officer, who stood with his back to her as he faced the empty lifts, gloved hands straightening up his tie. She had half a mind to say Murdoch was at fault for all this quarreling—that he was a complete ass who had no respect for a junior officer lacking the proper gender for her role.

But then she stopped herself.

Esther wasn't exactly guiltless, either; she was the one who had spoke out of turn to her superior. The one who had foolishly let her short temper get the better of her. Murdoch was a jackass, sure, but his foul behavior did not excuse hers one bit.

Besides, she reasoned, *I'll bet he's not happy after Smith demoted him.*

And when all was said and done, who would be?

Her blazing eyes softened, and Esther blew out a resigned sigh.

Perhaps she and Murdoch ought to bury the hatchet. They had a long journey ahead of them, in any case, and crossing the North Atlantic on an enormous steamship was no simple task. Quarreling with her superior officer wouldn't make the voyage any easier—that much was for certain.

The wrought-iron grille clattered open as the lift to E Deck arrived. Murdoch nodded at the attendant before stepping inside, Lowe swift at his heels.

Esther, however, hung back. She was lost in thought, still pondering whether to swallow her pride and apologize to Murdoch. Not right this moment, of course. Not in front of Lowe. But later, perhaps, when she could speak with him in private and avoid being overheard...

Murdoch glanced at her over one shoulder.

"Are you going to get into the lift, Miss Bailey?" he called. "Or are you just going to stand there and continue to waste my time?"

Esther fought to suppress her anger as she met his hard blue eyes. But she could still feel it scorch the back of her throat, white-hot and ruthless, as if she'd swallowed a mouthful of liquid fire.

Apologize? she thought in disbelief. To *him?*

The idea had become laughable at this point. As she stood beside Officer Murdoch in the opulent little lift, Esther scowled at her feet and swore to never consider something so foolish again.

FIVE

THE TAILOR

April 8, 1912 | 10:50

A THICK, DENSE FOG spilled through the streets of Southampton early Monday morning, chilling Esther and her brother as they combed their way through midtown.

The roads were empty at the early hour, save for the occasional motorcar rumbling along past them, headlights beaming out through the gloom.

But Esther was feeling too weary to pay any notice to her surroundings. She'd spent nearly all last night packing her belongings for *Titanic*, cramming far more books than necessary into her suitcase, and when all was said and done, she'd only managed a few hours of good sleep.

Now she regarded the wispy fog and desolate streets with a bleary gaze, lost in her thoughts and trying not think of Officer Murdoch. But where Esther once might have ranted and raved about her frustrations, she now pulled herself inwards, quietly shuttering her emotions and not knowing what, exactly, to do with them.

Booker tried to break the silence as they walked, breath clouding the air to misty white.

"Christ, it's cold," he remarked with a grimace, rubbing his gloved hands together for warmth. "And we'll soon be getting on a ship bound for the goddamn North Atlantic. We're none too bright, are we?"

"No." Esther spoke softly, her eyes on her feet. "Perhaps we're not."

"Just think of all those *long* watches you'll have on the boat deck," Booker teased. "*I'll* be all nice and cozy inside the ship, sitting before a warm electric heater…and you? You'll become an icicle, I imagine."

He was trying to coax out a smile, but Esther was too lost in her thoughts to notice. "I don't doubt it," she murmured distantly.

Her reply didn't sit well with Booker, who stopped her on the street to scrutinize her, gripping her shoulder with one hand.

"All right, what's the matter with you?" he demanded. "You've been moping about ever since you returned to the hotel yesterday, and you won't even tell me what's wrong."

"I'm a far cry from *moping*," Esther said defensively, the fire returning to her voice. "I just have a lot on my mind."

"Like what? You can talk to me. Is it that Lightoller fellow again?"

She shook her head. "No, not at all. He's not even my mentor anymore."

Booker regarded her with surprise. "He's not? Who's the first officer, then?"

Esther gritted her teeth, wishing she could drift away with the fog and be long gone from this conversation. "William Murdoch."

"Murdoch?" Booker echoed, eyebrows knotting together in puzzlement. "The Scotsman, right? Kind of a stocky fellow, with dark hair that has a bit of gray?" When she nodded, he frowned and said, "Odd. I met him the other day with Mr. Andrews, and he was quite the charming gentleman."

Esther snorted. "*I* certainly didn't see any of that charm," she said dully. "Must've missed it."

Her brother raised an eyebrow. "I don't understand. What on earth happened between you two?"

"Nothing," Esther lied. "We just…got off on the wrong foot, is all."

"And?"

Esther rounded on him, the exasperation thick in her blood.

"And what else do you want me to say?" she demanded. "He doesn't like me much, Booker. And trust me when I say the feeling is *very* mutual. I'd rather chew glass than deal with his piss-poor attitude again."

A long silence stretched between them as Esther glared down at the cobbled path beneath their feet. Booker studied his sister with a sigh, his voice soft with reason, his levelheadedness putting her short temper to shame.

"You realize this is your superior officer we're talking about, right?"

he reminded her. "You're partnered with him for *all* of *Titanic's* maiden voyage, dummy. You'll be working beside him day and night, won't you? So how can you think this sort of animosity is even remotely acceptable?"

Her eyes snapped up at him, blazing with cold fire.

"I don't think that," she insisted. "In fact, I was *this* close to apologizing to him yesterday. I spoke out of turn—I'll admit it, all right? I wanted to make things right with him. But it's hard to do so when you're dealing with a man who has a stick so far up his ass, he can't even see straight—"

"Oh, boy." Booker shook his head with stern disapproval. "Listen, I don't know what happened between the two of you, but you *need* to stop being so stubborn and make amends with him."

She opened her mouth to protest, but he swiftly raised his voice to silence her.

"Doesn't matter who said what, Es, you still have to do it. You're his subordinate. He's your superior. Just be polite and *civil*, for Christ's sake. And if he insults you, well, you'll simply have to learn to take it in stride. Like a *professional*."

"A professional?" Esther echoed hollowly, shutting her eyes tight as the freezing wind snarled past. "Booker, he thanked me," she mumbled, "for proving that I wasn't *useless*. Right in front of another junior officer and quartermaster. Do you have any idea how humiliating that was?"

Her brother said nothing, and Esther sucked in a deep breath, fighting to keep the tremble from her voice. But she could feel herself breaking, like a pane of glass waiting to buckle, the cracks trickling out further and further until she thought her angry tears might fall. The fire in her chest that fueled her temper was close to guttering out. It withered fast, crisping away her resolve and leaving embers of hurt and humiliation as she rambled on, "That was just *one* of the many nasty remarks he said to me. He's impossible. He won't even give me a chance!"

Her shout echoed off the desolate streets, spiraling toward the frozen gray sky, and she shrank a little as passers-by stared.

A flicker of sympathy crossed her brother's face. "I said it before about Lightoller, and I'll say it again about Murdoch: he'll come around. Give it time. You don't have to like the man, but you do need to make sure your working relationship is—at the very least—*functional*."

"Try telling that to Murdoch," Esther gritted out, unable to keep the bitterness from her voice.

At length, their destination came into view, looming before them through the fog bank. It was a nondescript little shop nestled on the ground floor of some housing complex, windows glazed with a thin layer of morning frost. Peeling gold letters above the entryway read *Miller, Murphy, Holm Ltd: Naval, Military & Shipping Outfitters.* Esther reached into her pocket and withdrew the order form Murdoch gave her.

> *On behalf of White Star Line, we request your fine tailoring to assist our officer with the purchase and fitting of the following:*
>
> *Three full uniforms of service dress, consisting of:*
> *(3) Melton reefer jackets adorned with eight*
> *   brass buttons apiece*
> *(3) white cotton dress shirts*
> *(3) pleated skirts (imported o.k.)*
> *(3) waistcoats*
>
> *We further request:*
> *(1) greatcoat and frockcoat each*
> *(2) pairs of black leather gloves*
> *(2) black silk ties*
> *(1) White Star Line cap*
> *(1) pair of leather Oxfords*

She read the order aloud to her brother, and when she glanced up, she was surprised to see his face as hard as stone.

"What?" Esther asked. "What's wrong?"

But Booker waved her concern away. "Nothing," he said idly, starting toward the shop without pause. "Let's go inside."

A bell trickled above their heads as they stepped over the threshold, leaving the fog and biting chill behind. Esther rubbed her nose, which was raw and red with cold, and looked around the shop. Rows of officer uniforms stood on display, their woven wool a deep, dark blue almost black in color, their brass buttons glittering beneath a pool of amber lamplight. A woman's soft singing voice poured from the phonograph in one corner, crackling with static and filling the dingy room with charm.

While Esther roamed around the shop, studying the smart uniforms with utmost longing, her brother made straight for the counter. But his finger barely touched the silver bell before a thin, reedy man with a salt-and-pepper mustache came hurrying from the back room.

"You must be the Baileys," the man said with welcome, smoothing out his waistcoat with spindly fingers. "We've been expecting you. John Miller, founder of our humble little shop."

The three of them shook hands before Miller went straight to business.

"Now then," he said, "I'll be assisting you this morning. We need only take a few measurements, and my tailors and I will get to work straight away. White Star Line officers are our foremost priority, naturally, so we should have the uniforms delivered to *Titanic*'s berth no later than tomorrow."

"That's wonderful," Esther said, impressed. "Thank you."

"Oh, it's no trouble at all," the tailor replied. But he wasn't even looking at her; he approached Booker instead, eyeing him up and down as if sizing a racehorse.

Booker raised his eyebrows at Esther, who shrugged back in bewilderment. Miller must have been satisfied with what he saw, however, because he clapped his hands and said, "Right this way, Mr. Bailey. We'll get you fitted as quickly as possible. I trust you have the order form provided by White Star Line?"

But Booker didn't move a muscle. "You are mistaken, sir," he said, sparing a glance at Esther's crestfallen face. "I'm no officer. These uniforms are meant for my sister."

Miller gaped at him before dissolving into a fit of scratchy laughter, the sound more menacing than it was humorous.

"You jest, Mr. Bailey," he said, still chuckling under his breath. "How very funny. Now right this way, if you please. We'll start with your height first—"

"Sir." Booker flashed a thin smile, eyes boring into the tailor's face.

Although his voice was measured, there was a steeliness about it that made Esther stare, and she now understood why her brother had wanted to accompany her this morning. "I wasn't being funny. Look at her license. And the order form. Both say Esther Bailey, Seventh Officer of the RMS *Titanic*."

"Preposterous," Miller huffed. He didn't even glance at the order form when Esther lamely held it out to him. "There are no women officers aboard *Titanic*."

"Funny," Booker retorted, "because I'm pretty sure you're looking at one, pal."

The tailor's eyes bulged, a deep red the color of wine spreading across his blotchy face. "My dear boy, do you expect me to stand here and believe that you're in my shop to buy uniforms for her?" He thrust one rude finger at Esther, who wanted nothing more than to ball up her first and sock him square in the nose.

"I have the order form here, sir," she said indignantly. "If you take a look, it'll show you my name and my rank and—"

But the tailor set his jaw against her. "Not damn likely. Not a chance."

Too flustered and too angry to speak, Esther watched her brother smoothly step forward to intervene. He towered over the tailor with his lanky figure, a lethal calm settling over his handsome face.

"Look, mister, we ain't looking for a fight. See to my sister and we'll be on our way."

"What don't you understand? We only fit men here. *Not* women. Take your nonsense elsewhere, you ruddy yanks. I've no time for games today."

But his refusal only angered Esther even further. "Just *look*, would you, it's right *here*—"

"Are you deaf, or just plain stupid, woman?" Miller snarled, spit spraying from his mouth. "I said no!"

Esther flinched, her boiling blood crystallizing to ice in her veins.

"Booker." She couldn't say her brother's name without hearing her voice crack, and she swallowed against the dryness in her throat, completely at a loss for what to do. Her fingers tightened, threatening to crumple the order form in one fist. She couldn't imagine returning to the ship without her officer's garb. Already she could see Lightoller's cold, disapproving eyes, and Murdoch's sneer when he realized she was truly useless after all.

Can't even buy a proper uniform, he'd say. He would never come to take her seriously as an officer. None of them would.

But Booker refused to back down. "Do you realize who you're talking to?" he demanded. "We are the niece and nephew of J.D. Bailey, who *owns* White Star Line as a subsidiary, which is responsible for more than *half* your business—"

"Yeah?" Miller shot back. "Well, sonny, I don't give a damn who you are. She's not getting fitted, and that's that. Now, you can either turn 'round and walk out of my shop, or I'll see to it that you're *thrown* out." He stormed toward the back room, swinging the curtained partition closed behind him. "Good day!"

Esther was the first to step outside. Her brother followed after a moment's hesitation, muttering a string of curses that would have made their mother roll over in her grave.

"Miserable *sonofabitch*," Booker hissed. He was seething, smoothing back his hair with one agitated hand, but Esther was feeling too glum to match his anger. She started down the street in a daze, needing to get herself far away from the tailor shop and no longer caring where her feet might take her.

It wasn't until she reached a thin, crooked alleyway that she stopped, pressed her back against the brick wall, and closed her eyes.

"I never should have done this." Her voice trembled as she spoke.

"Done what?" her brother demanded. "Become an officer?" When she nodded meekly in reply, Booker stared at her in outrage. "Oh, for heaven's *sake*. Don't be ridiculous, of course you should have!"

He was glaring at her now, as if he couldn't believe the timid girl standing before him was truly his strong-willed sister. "And don't you dare give me that defeatist attitude, either," he scolded. "I want you to wait here. I'll be right back. And *don't* you move, you hear me? We're going to get this sorted out."

Esther wanted to believe him.

But she couldn't help but feel doubtful as she stood in the crooked little alleyway, wishing she could sink into the sooty bricks at her back, and leave her shame and humiliation behind her.

11:30

Murdoch was finishing up his breakfast when the message came, sipping down the last of his tea with the morning paper sprawled upon his lap.

He was feeling somewhat listless, eyes glazed with exhaustion as he stirred milk and sugar into the steaming mug before him. He'd spent most of the night making final preparations for the voyage ahead: checking all the navigational instruments, winding the chronometers, scribbling out lifeboat assignments for the officers, and so on.

It had been tedious but necessary work, with most of his duties stretching well into the early hours of dawn, and he'd been relieved to finally retire to the mess for a moment's peace. There was no one to bother him here, no one to ask *why* he was relegated from chief officer to first, no one to pepper him with questions or crude obscenities about the Bailey girl. It was just Murdoch and his cup of tea, the slats of sunlight warming his back, the distant tang of saltwater brine filling his nose.

He hadn't expected company this morning, so he was surprised to see the senior Marconi Wireless Operator—a slim, wiry man donned in a sleek black waistcoat—entering the mess hall.

"Mr. Phillips," Murdoch said, nodding in acknowledgment.

"Mr. Murdoch," Jack Phillips greeted. "Mr. Wilde said I might find you here. There's a message for you from shore, sir."

"Come again?" Murdoch was too weary to process his words.

"Er, someone telephoned the Southampton Port Office and left a message for you, since they can't contact *Titanic* directly. The shore operator then relayed the message to me." Although Phillips looked curious, he kept to business as he went on, "I wrote down a transcript of what was said, sir, if you'd like to have a look."

"Sure." Murdoch rubbed his eyes, stifling a groan of disinterest. "Cheers."

He waited until Phillips left the room before laying the marconigram on the table before him. His eyes scanned scribbled words only once— and suddenly he was on his feet, throwing down the dregs of his tea and shoving the transcript in his pocket.

He hurried to his cabin, where he splashed cold water on his face and ran a comb through his short dark hair. God only knew why he did it, but he figured it wouldn't hurt anyway.

He was just swinging on his greatcoat and staggering out the door when Wilde caught him.

"Where you off to, Will? Thought you were on lunch."

"Change of plans," Murdoch explained, hurrying for the staircase with Wilde trailing curiously along after him. "I'm headed to town."

Wilde seemed surprised. "Really? Whatever for?"

Murdoch kept his voice cool and his steps brisk, not wanting to explain himself just yet. "I need to sort a few things out," he replied, Scottish burr ringing out across the empty deck. "Be back in a mo'."

"Never known you to skip a meal," Wilde remarked, amused. "Must be pretty important, then."

"Aye." Murdoch nodded, striding quickly as he tugged on leather gloves. "I believe it is."

He wasn't sure what to expect by the time he reached Oxford Street, weaving his way through the crowds with his greatcoat swirling along behind him. He had half a mind to turn around and head right back to the ship—back to a cuppa and the quiet brood of his thoughts. But the wireless message kept ringing through his head, leading him onward, deeper into the fog and hurrying concourses of people.

> *The tailor in Southampton has refused to offer his services to my sister. As you are her superior, I am afraid you may be the only one who can help.*
>
> *We are waiting on the corner of Oxford and Oak. Please assist if you can.*
>
> *Booker H. Bailey.*

Well, of course Murdoch was going to help; he damn near didn't have a choice. Maddening though she was, the girl was still his charge, and therefore his responsibility. He couldn't very well have her boarding the ship without a uniform—especially when it would only reflect poorly on him. What else would she even wear in the meantime? Some lacy blouse, with a string of *pearls* to go along with it?

Christ in Heaven, Murdoch was wincing at the thought.

No, it would be better to sort this mess out now, and ensure the girl would have a full uniform come sailing day. This would keep Smith happy, no doubt, while also keeping Murdoch from losing his mind.

Sure enough, he found the Bailey siblings standing at the end of the cobblestone street, murmuring to each other as people streamed past. Murdoch recognized Booker Bailey at once—Thomas Andrews' tall, handsome apprentice whom he had met only a few days ago. They had been introduced during a time when Murdoch had no knowledge of Booker and Esther's kinship whatsoever. But walking toward them now, he was momentarily stunned by their likeness: same dark hair and freckled complexions, same pointed noses and pale green eyes. They only seemed to differ in height and, well—*gender*, obviously, with Miss Bailey hovering timidly at her brother's side.

She was the first to spot him on the street, and Murdoch saw her worrisome expression turn to undisguised incredulity as she recognized him in the crowd. He was almost certain he heard her mutter an oath as he neared, and it only deepened his dislike for her even further.

Part of him almost wanted to turn on his heel and walk *straight* back to port. She was clearly less than thrilled to see him, so why should he even lend her a hand? He should go, and let the damn girl fend for herself.

That'll teach her a lesson, that will, Murdoch thought scathingly. But he kept walking, and it wasn't until he stopped short in front of her that he offered a patronizing smile.

"Having a pleasant morning?"

Bailey ignored him. "What are you doing here?" she blurted. But then she paused, as if realizing her question was rude, and added grudgingly, "Sir?"

Murdoch raised his brows. "Well, Miss Bailey. I, like you, have business in Southampton today. My gloves," he lied smoothly, lifting one hand, "don't fit like they used to. I'm here for a more comfortable pair."

"I see," Bailey said, although she still looked suspicious. "How…nice."

Murdoch cleared his throat, nodding at the tailor shop behind her. "I believe you said you were being fitted for your uniforms today, weren't you? So why don't you come along with me, then? We can head back to *Titanic* once we're finished. Do you have your order form?"

Her eyes widened in astonishment. "I do, sir…but the man inside the shop won't…he won't…"

"Won't what? You're going to have to speak clearly, Miss Bailey, my ears aren't accustomed to gibberish."

She glowered at him, but her voice came out clear as crystal as she grumbled, "He won't sell me my uniforms."

"That so?" Murdoch carelessly straightened up his tie. "Well, we'll see about that, won't we?"

He wasn't at *all* surprised when Bailey opened her mouth to argue, but her brother quickly pulled her aside.

"Just do as he says," Booker insisted, a note of impatience in his voice. "I'll head back to the hotel and get our belongings readied for the ship in the meantime, all right? See you on board." His eyes lingered on Murdoch, and he added, "You're in good hands. Trust me. And remember what I told you earlier. *Professional.*"

Bailey still looked as if she wanted to protest. But she seemed to think better of it, muttering a pitiful farewell instead. Booker stepped forward to offer Murdoch his thanks, wringing his hand with a kindly smile. And then he was off, striding into the veil of icy fog and leaving the two officers standing awkwardly side by side.

Murdoch waited until he disappeared before turning his attention to his subordinate. Studying her now, he was suddenly aware of how miserable she looked. Her eyes were downcast, and there was a weariness about her he didn't like. Christ, he was almost feeling *sorry* for her. He cleared his throat.

"Let's get this over with," he said idly, opening the shop door to admit her inside. "Keep next to me. And pass me the order form. Now."

Bailey wordlessly slid the document into his hands, and the glum look in her eyes became a baleful glower when Miller stepped into view. Murdoch strode forward to greet him, nodding at her to follow.

"Morning, Mr. Miller."

"Good morning, Officer Murdoch," the tailor crowed back. "I confess I wasn't expecting you t—" But he stopped cold at the sight of Bailey standing alongside Murdoch, his eyes crinkling tight with disgust. "You know this girl, then?"

Murdoch raised a brow. "Certainly do. Else I wouldn't be standing right here with her, would I?"

Despite the measured calm of his voice, he still felt a peculiar ire stir within him. It was quiet and dark, like the subtle shift in weather before the onset of violent storms, but Murdoch welcomed it nonetheless, wanting nothing more than to defend the girl at his side. Although he didn't particularly care for Bailey—*or* her cheeky mouth, for that matter— he was still furious that any tailor would *dare* refuse service to a maritime officer. Woman or not, she was White Star Line crew. And therefore, she was entitled to a uniform. It was as simple as that.

Hooking his hands behind his back, Murdoch spoke with a cool, crisp civility that belied the anger storming inside him.

"Allow me to introduce Esther Bailey." He gestured toward his subordinate, who stood a little taller at his words. "Seventh Officer of the RMS *Titanic* and my newest protégé. I believe she's in need of new uniforms this morning, courtesy of White Star Line." His eyes narrowed, and a slight edge came to his voice as he added curtly, "But I'm sure you were already aware of that when you turned her out the door."

Miller fumbled for words. "This—this must be a joke, sir," he spluttered, looking aghast. "*Surely.*"

Murdoch felt his calm waver as he stepped forward. Anger leaked into his eyes, darkening them like oil to ocean water.

"Does it look as if I am joking?" he demanded.

Miller flinched, paling beneath his handlebar mustache, and Murdoch felt a rush of satisfaction as he watched the tailor get his well-deserved comeuppance. No one was going to mistreat any White Star Line officer with such disrespect—not if Murdoch had anything to say about it. With a nod at his subordinate, he added, "Miss Bailey and I have a *very* busy schedule ahead of us. So why don't you stop wasting our time and let us finish our business so we can be well on our way? Sound pleasant?"

"Absolutely, sir," Miller said at once. "I apologize, sir. It was my mistake."

"Clearly." Murdoch handed him the order form with a level stare. "These are for Miss Bailey. You will take her measurements and ensure her garments are delivered to the ship as quickly as possible. I trust that won't be an issue?"

"No, sir."

"Good. As for myself, I'll need a new pair of gloves. Black leather, if you please."

Miller bowed his head, clearly recognizing defeat. "Very well, Mr. Murdoch. I'll see to it at once." He turned to Bailey, forcing a smile that didn't meet his resentful eyes. "Right this way, miss."

Bailey looked stunned. She timidly stepped forward, glancing over her shoulder at Murdoch with a glowing expression of deep gratitude. He watched her go, eyes lingering on her short dark hair, and it wasn't until she disappeared behind the fitting room curtains that Murdoch wondered whether he'd done the right thing after all.

12:15

By the time Esther was properly measured, and every item in her new wardrobe was paid for, she was in a much cheerier mood.

Where she had once been fretful and nervous, agonizing over what might happen if she boarded the ship without her garb, she was now bubbling with a peppiness that brightened her spirits and coaxed out her usual lively grin.

She was well on her way to becoming an officer now. That jackass of a tailor was long behind her, the uniforms would be delivered to *Titanic* without issue—and *Murdoch*, of all people, had stood up for her.

Esther couldn't resist smiling at him as they stepped out onto the street, and was about to thank him for his unexpected kindness when he looked her in the eye and said, "I didn't realize that my duties as first officer would include being your nanny."

The words *thank you* caught in her throat, clotting her windpipe as if she had swallowed a mouthful sand. She bristled at him, all warmth and cheeriness gone.

"Are you always this charming, Mr. Murdoch?" she demanded.

"Funny. I was about to ask the same of you, *lass*."

He spoke the last word almost mockingly. Scowling, Esther grumbled, "No one asked you to come here."

"Your brother did," Murdoch replied, and for a moment, Esther was frozen with shock. She made a mental note to throttle Booker as her superior continued, "He telephoned the Southampton shore operator at port, who relayed his message to our Marconi telegraphist, who then delivered it to me. And it's damn well good that I did show up. Otherwise, how else would you have gotten your uniform?"

"I would've found a way," Esther insisted.

"*Really*, now?" Murdoch raised an eyebrow. "That's rich, because something tells me you would've returned to the ship empty-handed."

"Better that than having to stand here and listen to you antagonize me," Esther said shortly.

She turned on her heel and stormed straight toward port, praying Murdoch wouldn't follow. But he did, much to her annoyance, his pace smooth and swift as he matched her angry stride.

"Shouldn't you be thanking me right about now?" he demanded.

"Sure thing." Esther stopped in her tracks, swinging around until she stood face-to-face with her superior officer, their coats nearly brushing in the cool mid-morning.

"Thank *you*, Mr. Murdoch," she said pointedly, not sounding very thankful at all, "for helping me purchase my uniforms today so I won't be walking the deck in my skivvies tomorrow."

Murdoch paled, and she wondered if he was searching for some snarky retort or another. Or thinking of her in her skivvies, perhaps. But he composed himself within a matter of seconds, lifting his chin and offering her a thin, humorless smile.

"You're *very* welcome, Miss Bailey," he said dryly. "It was all I could do to keep from subjecting my men to such a ghastly sight."

Esther stood remarkably still, nose scrunched up in a scowl, mind cranking like a caught gear as she scoured for a retort.

And then, without thinking—without even considering that she was an officer meant to keep a dignified composure—her self-control dissolved, and she snorted with laughter.

Murdoch stared at her in utter disbelief, as if he had never seen anyone so simple. But Esther couldn't help it; their repartee was becoming all too ridiculous at this point. Comical, even. She never thought she'd end up having this sort of conversation with a superior *officer*, and yet here she was, going toe-to-toe with him and refusing to accept that his quick wit might actually put her own to shame.

But while she found their banter funny, Murdoch did not seem to share in her humor.

"Have you finished?" he asked flatly, shaking his head.

Esther straightened up, stifling the last of her laughter.

"Just about," she assured him breathlessly. But she was still fighting back a smile as she cocked her head at him, her eyes sweeping him up and down with amusement. "*Ghastly*? Really? You flatter me, Mr. Murdoch."

She braced herself for another snide quip, but Murdoch remained oddly quiet. He was watching her closely, but there was neither a smile nor a sneer on his face—only a vague unease. It was as if seeing her laugh had flustered him somehow, and he wasn't sure what to make of it.

"We'd best get back to the ship, then," he said quietly.

She studied him for a moment, looking curiously into those insufferable blue eyes and wondering what was ailing him.

"*Today*, if you don't mind," he snapped, pointing one impatient finger toward port.

Esther did not need to be told twice. She marched down the street without pause, all interest in Murdoch and his lousy blue eyes fading like a grain of sand lost to a stormy sea.

SIX

MOVING IN

April 8, 1912 | 16:20

THE TRANSITION FROM shore to ship was an easy one, much to Esther's surprise.

No mishaps, no messy complications—and most fortunately of all, no Murdoch to stand around and criticize her.

The first officer had made himself scarce since their dispute with the Southampton tailor, and it was only after boarding the ship that Esther came to learn why: Murdoch was spending most of his time conferring with Captain Smith and Chief Officer Henry Wilde, both of whom she had yet to meet. It seemed the three of them were making last-minute preparations for tomorrow, everything from lifeboat drills to provisioning arrangements, health inspections to lengthy cargo manifests.

It was busy work, by the sound of things—especially given all the hullabaloo surrounding *Titanic*'s maiden voyage. Despite being cut from the same steel as her sister, *Olympic*, it was *Titanic* who had been coined "The Ship of Dreams." Which meant all the crewmen were working twice as hard to live up to her title, ensuring she had a smooth, flawless crossing ahead.

With Murdoch busy, it was Moody who showed her to her cabin late Monday afternoon, and the sixth officer was surprisingly chipper as he escorted her to their quarters.

Esther was impressed by the whirlwind of activity around them, as crew and handymen alike hurried to put the last finishing touches on the ship. Painters applied fresh coats to the white walls, electricians tested bulbs encased in crystal fixtures, florists tended to potted plants and palms.

A group of hired workers scrambled to finish the provisioning, bringing aboard crate after crate of foodstuffs ranging from perishable eggs to ice cream, mineral water to beer.

The officers made their way topside, picking their way through the last-minute chaos before coming to a cool white passage. It was quiet here, tucked away from all the hectic preparations and the turmoil of a busy ship, and Esther gazed around with interest as Moody led her down the corridor.

"Right this way, miss," he said cheerfully. "Your cabin's beside mine. Our quarters are arranged in order of rank. Chief officer is closest to the captain, first officer is closest to the chief, and so forth. Except for Boxhall, of course," he chuckled, "who's in the middle of nowhere. We're down at the end, see, closest to the lavatory."

Esther clutched her suitcase in one hand, peering curiously down the long passage still gleaming beneath its fresh coat of paint.

"Not too shabby," she said when they arrived at her cabin.

No, not too shabby at all. It was a cozy little room filled with a collection of mahogany furniture: a writing desk and simple bedstead with drawer storage underneath, a wardrobe waiting to be filled with clothing, and one squat cabinet boasting a mirror and washbasin cut entirely from marble. A slat of light streamed through the only window, catching motes of dust before tumbling on a coverlet of pure white.

"What do you think?" Moody asked, hovering in the doorway as she stepped inside.

Esther crossed the brilliantly-lit room to inspect the window above her bed. She was pleased to find it swung out on a hinge, opening to a magnificent view of the officers' promenade. Beyond the boat deck, she spotted the jumbled rooftops of Southampton, and the glimmer of a distant sea. She turned to face Moody, beaming.

"It's lovely! And you simply can't beat that view. Goddamn."

Moody seemed somewhat taken aback by the casualness of her curse, but he made no mention of it as he went on. "I'm glad to hear it. The captain wasn't sure it would be to your liking."

She flinched. "Why's that?"

"He…thought you might prefer a larger stateroom."

Esther looked away, trying to hide her hurt. "I'm not some uppity snob, you know," she insisted. "This cabin is more than suitable. It's perfect. And just *look* at that sink." She pointed excitedly at the glistening washbasin. "Is it really solid marble?"

"It is indeed," he said, amused. "Quite nice, isn't it?"

"Very."

Esther made to close the window, but the brass latch seemed to have stuck. She struggled with it for a moment, sweating and puffing, and when it refused to budge, she turned to Moody for help. "Hey, you mind giving me a hand, here?"

But he remained in the doorway, fidgeting with his cuff and shifting from one foot to the other.

"I'm afraid I can't do that, Miss Bailey."

She laughed. "And just why not? I won't bite, you know."

"It's …well, I can't enter your cabin, miss. I must remain out in the hall."

Esther stared at him uncomprehendingly, her laughter fading, one hand frozen on the window latch. "Why?" she asked quickly.

Moody stole a glance down the corridor, a discomfort in his eyes as he explained, "All officers have been prohibited from entering your cabin under any circumstances, miss. And if we are in any other room alone with you, the door must be kept open at all times." He regarded her look of astonishment with sympathy. "I'm sorry, Miss Bailey, but it's captain's orders. I'm sure you understand."

Esther stared at the floor, her fingertips turning frozen and numb as she weighed the implication of his words. She knew Smith's order was only a measure of precaution, but still…It was enough to make her feel even more estranged from the crew. The realization her own colleague couldn't enter her room to help with some shoddy window hatch only made it worse. It was another reminder that Esther would never be their equal, no matter her experience, or her work ethic, or her maritime knowledge. She was an unwelcome addition to their world. A mild inconvenience who would be better off scrubbing floors and washing bedding than joining their ranks.

The thought sickened her. Esther yanked and tugged on the window latch once more, snarling under her breath. But it refused to yield to her hand, and she surrendered out of frustration.

Sighing, Esther turned to Moody. "Would you mind leaving me for a moment, please? I need to unpack my belongings."

"Certainly," he said. "I'll see you in the mess for dinner, perhaps?"

She managed a distracted smile. "Sure thing."

Moody tipped his cap in farewell, and Esther waited until the last murmurs of his footfalls disappeared before closing the door.

She roved around the tiny cabin, cramming nightgowns into her wardrobe and stowing away all her miscellaneous items: maritime books as thick as *Titanic*'s hull, a jar of her favorite peppermint candies, and one large, sturdy medical kit she'd kept from her old nursing days. She'd even brought along her most cherished photographs, which she arranged on the mahogany desk. Her eyes roamed across the monochrome array of landscapes and loved ones, studying everything from the Bailey family portrait to the countless photos of beachside vacations. She even had a picture of a younger Lockerbie with her brothers, captured in an old snapshot from some childhood summer long ago, though Christ only knew why she'd kept the damn thing when she hadn't spoken to the man in years...

Not wanting to dwell on some moron from her past, Esther turned her attention to her brothers instead. She thought of a time long ago, when they had vacationed in Santa Cruz and she'd chased them through sand dunes and sparkling cold surf. They'd eaten blue cotton candy, swam in the seaside natatorium, and teased Booker when he'd lost carnival games along the boardwalk.

Even to this day, Esther could still remember the waves lapping at her toes, the rare laughter of their father, and the tide pools Brighton had encouraged her to explore, kneeling to show Esther some spindly sea creature or another.

It won't hurt you, he'd laughed, when she was too nervous to run a finger across a spongy anemone. *See, Es?*

Esther sank onto her bed, unable to shut her mind against the flood of recollections. Her head felt muzzy and waterlogged, as if she were sinking to the bottom of a deep pool, and she closed her eyes.

She could feel it again—the visceral, bone-deep ache of loss that would often overwhelm her, tearing through the barriers of her resolve and reminding her of the brother she had lost.

It seemed like only yesterday she had seen him alive. Brighton—Booker's tall, quiet twin with a heart of gold and dreams of sailing the world.

He had been the one to find Esther after her engagement party all those years ago. Even now, as she tugged back her sleeve and chased her fingertips across the lingering scars, she could still recall the events of that night. The deadly look in Brighton's eyes when he'd found her curled up on the bathroom floor. The way her brother had tended to her wounds, clearing broken glass from her cuts and applying ice to the worst of her bruises.

Brighton had been there for her that terrible night—just as he'd been there for her years later, when she'd summoned up her wits and gone to her father with a revelation. Rather than continue nursing at the family hospital, she would leave for London to study maritime law. And nothing, or no one, was going to stop her.

Her brothers had been understanding. Her father, not in the slightest. They had fought and argued and spat words to the brink of him disowning her and stripping her of her inheritance entirely.

But Esther hadn't cared.

She would work at sea with or without her father's blessing, and so Brighton stepped in to help with the travel and schooling costs. He had supported her until the day he'd died.

Were it not for his encouragement—and Booker's, too, when all was said and done—Esther wouldn't be sitting in this cozy little cabin on the grandest damn ship in the world. She wouldn't be carrying the title of seventh officer on her shoulders, nor would she be paving the way for those women still hoping to enter the maritime industry.

Christ, if only Brighton were here to *see* it—

A ship horn bellowed in the distance, wrenching Esther from the dark waters of her wistful thoughts.

Come on, girl, she scolded, struggling to get a grip on herself as she smoothed her hair and dried her eyes. *Don't disappoint Brighton by crying like a ninny when you've finally made it. There's still an awful lot to do.*

And if you don't do it, who will?

April 9, 1912 | 16:40

Lightoller resisted the urge to straighten his tie as he stood in the passageway of the officers' quarters, waiting for the Bailey girl to answer her door.

Although she had moved into her cabin late yesterday, bringing with her a single suitcase and an armful of books, the realization that a woman would be living among his fellow officers was still a peculiar thing.

A *worrying* thing.

The fact that he would now have to tiptoe around the lavatory— willing with all his might not to run into the girl—was enough to make him stew in his unease.

But despite his misgivings, Lightoller knew it was time to swallow his doubts and accept the hard truth: the girl was a member of the crew. She was an officer, and therefore, she was deserving of an agreeable work relationship. He could at least offer her that much, unbearable as it was.

Lightoller rapped his knuckles on the door again, impatient this time, and Bailey emerged from her cabin at last. Her eyes were puffy from sleep, her hair slightly mussed, but she greeted him with a smile nonetheless.

"Mr. Lightoller, sir."

"Miss Bailey," Lightoller acknowledged. He peered over her shoulder to study her cabin, noting the books dumped over the bed, and the open drawers haphazardly stuffed with unfolded clothes. *Not exactly tidy, is she?* he thought. "I trust you're all settled in?"

"I am, sir, thank you."

"Good," he said swiftly, swallowing back his discomfort to make pleasant conversation. "And the cabin? What do you make of it so far?"

She tucked a strand of hair behind one ear. "It's nice, sir. Very comfortable. I'm looking forward to staying here."

Lightoller raised his brows in mild surprise. Like the captain, he'd assumed she would find the cabin less than accommodating. It was rather small, in any case—nothing compared to the elegant staterooms she was no doubt used to, what with her being the daughter of a wealthy San Francisco surgeon, and the niece of some well-to-do magnate. But here she was, standing at attention and politely answering his questions. No complaints, no criticisms, and none of that backtalk Murdoch had warned him about. The girl didn't seem to be too much of an inconvenience.

So far, at least, he reminded himself.

Sweeping a level gaze over Bailey, Lightoller added, "I come bearing good news. Your uniforms were delivered this morning and are available for pickup at the purser's office."

"That's wonderful, sir. I'll head there straight away."

But Lightoller shook his head. "Later, perhaps," he drawled. "For now, we're needed on the bridge." He started down the corridor, tossing an expectant glance over one shoulder.

"Well? What are you dawdling for? Come along, Miss Bailey. The captain is waiting to meet you."

The girl quickly shut her cabin door and scrambled after him, struggling to keep pace with his swift, long-legged strides. He led her through the wheelhouse and out into the open airiness of the bridge, where an assortment of quartermasters and deckhands milled about in the icy sunlight. Captain Smith stood in the port bridge wing, impressively venerable as usual, medals of war glinting across his coat. Lightoller heard Bailey draw a sharp intake of breath at his side, and he wondered if she was nervous.

"No need to fret," he told her idly. "The captain is a kind man, and he wants to make your acquaintance."

Lightoller wasn't sure why he was trying to console her, though he figured it was more out of pity than anything else. As he ushered the girl forward, Smith turned at the sound of their footsteps. He swept a calculating gaze over Bailey, regarding her short hair and simple plainclothes. But then he removed his cap and stepped toward her with his hand outstretched.

"Esther Bailey, is it?" Smith greeted, offering a stilted smile Lightoller knew masked his true disdain for the girl. "A pleasure to finally meet you."

They shook, with Bailey standing at attention, eyes never wavering from his face.

"And you, sir," she said, inclining her head. "It's an honor, sir."

Her bold American accent was surprisingly controlled, Lightoller noted, almost soft with respect as she stood before her captain. Perhaps she hoped to make a decent impression.

She's wasting her time, that girl, he thought. *Smith doesn't want her here. He only has to tolerate her.*

The captain continued to study Bailey, scrutinizing her up and down. But there was no warmth or welcome in his eyes—only a stiff, calculated formality, as if they were discussing stringent business matters.

"I hope you're settling in well on the ship, then?" he finally asked. "And I trust you have met the rest of your colleagues as well?"

"I've been introduced to Misters Murdoch, Moody, and Lowe, sir, but I have yet to meet the others."

Lightoller stepped forward to interject. "We've arranged a dinner in the officers' mess this evening, sir," he explained. "She will have the opportunity to better make their acquaintance then."

"Very good," Smith said, though he could not have looked any less enthused by the prospect. He peered over Lightoller's shoulder, eyes lingering on some spot in the distance, and he mused, "Though it seems she will be meeting our chief officer sooner than expected."

Swallowing down his distaste, Lightoller turned to see Henry Wilde emerging from the A Deck Stairwell with Murdoch sauntering along at his side. The pair were chatting animatedly, but their voices fell into dutiful silence as they approached their captain. Murdoch was the first to offer the usual salute of the cap, exchanging words of pleasant greeting and minute details of the day. Wilde, on the other hand, only had eyes for Bailey, staring as if he had never seen anything quite like her.

It was only after Smith bade farewell and moved on to greet Boxhall that Wilde finally spoke.

"So this is the girl I've heard so much about," he said curiously. "Chief Officer Henry Wilde, at your service, my dear."

The girl barely came up to his chest, but it didn't deter her in the slightest. "Esther Bailey," she answered brightly, standing on tiptoe to wring his enormous hand. "Pleased to meet you, sir."

They shook, her slender fingers disappearing into his thick, weathered ones. A faint smirk played on the corner of Wilde's mouth as he towered over her, his expression halfway between skepticism and amusement. "You know," he remarked, "you're much shorter than I thought you'd be."

Lightoller squared his jaw with disapproval at the untoward comment, nostrils flaring wide. But Bailey didn't seem to mind. Something wily flickered in her eyes as she stood before her chief officer—some crafty gleam hinting at a challenge.

"And you're more observant than I thought you'd be, Mr. Wilde," she replied. "How positively uncanny."

Her wit was startlingly cool and quick, narrowed down to a point, and while Murdoch's lips thinned, Wilde released a hearty bellow of laughter.

"Cheeky one, aren't you?" he said, amused. "You'll fit right in around here. Though I hear you'll be working under this bloke." Wilde gestured toward Murdoch, whose face was expressionless, still as stone. "Bully for you. He hasn't been making your life *too* miserable, I hope? Uttered any unintelligible Scottish words as of late, perhaps?"

The girl shook her head, her boldness faltering. "Neither, sir," she said a little too quickly, sparing a cursory glance in Murdoch's direction.

The lie could not have been more obvious, and Wilde did not hesitate to call her out on the spot. "Cheeky *and* a liar. You're just like my eldest daughter. Only she's not so American." Glancing again at Murdoch, he chuckled, "You'll have to keep an eye on this one, Will."

Murdoch's stoic expression didn't waver; he seemed to be looking everywhere but the Bailey girl.

"Duly noted," he said wryly.

"Jolly good, then." Straightening up, Wilde rolled back his shoulders with a kindly smile. "Well, Miss Bailey. I do believe I've yet to have your signature for our Crew Particulars of Engagement form. It's just a ruddy formality, but I'll need you to fill out your name and details all the same." He started across the bridge, motioning for her to follow. "Join me in the chart room, if you please. And try not to look Mr. Lightoller in the eyes, will you? That grouchy old face of his isn't a pretty sight. Give you nightmares for weeks, it will."

Lightoller waited until a smirking Wilde disappeared beyond the wheelhouse door before sneering, "Git."

Murdoch shot him a chiding look. "Easy, Lights," he warned. But he was still staring at the wheelhouse, too, watching the hem of Bailey's coat vanish inside the chart room. "He seems to get along well with her, at least. Wasn't expecting that from Henry."

"It was all *flattery* on his part. He simply likes the attention."

"Let him have it, then. They'd be much better off putting the girl in his charge, if you ask me."

Lightoller shrugged. "Possibly. But at least you'll have an extra pair of hands during the voyage, eh? Should make your shifts that much simpler, I suspect."

"This isn't a matter of her being able to simplify my *job*," Murdoch said tersely. "I don't give a damn about that, Lights. It's the fact that she's even here in the first place."

"Will," Lightoller reasoned, looking surprised as he met his colleague's hardened stare. "I'm not at all thrilled she's here, either. But I'm willing to give her a chance. We set sail on the morrow, and I'll wait to reserve my judgment until then. If she's useless, she's useless. But if she proves her worth, then I will have no further qualms on the matter."

"Give her a chance?" Murdoch echoed in disbelief.

He stormed toward the officers' promenade with a look of disgust, Lightoller trailing quietly behind him. They stopped before one of the lifeboats, and Murdoch leaned close to mutter, "You do realize this reshuffle was because of her, aye?"

"You can't know that. Especially when you're missing the most obvious reason of them all."

"Oh?" Murdoch's voice was dull. "Enlighten me."

"Well, Wilde was *Olympic's* former chief officer, was he not? So perhaps they wanted to mirror that oaf's experience to her sister ship. Makes sense, doesn't it?"

When Murdoch was dead silent, staring unblinkingly into the waves of foamy blue, Lightoller sighed. He wasn't sure *why* he was trying to defend the girl, but damn it all, he couldn't seem to hold his tongue.

"Listen, Will," he said, dropping one hand on his colleague's shoulder. "I wasn't thrilled with the reshuffle either. In fact, I was pretty damn gutted, same as you. But I'm not going to dwell on it—*or* let myself think an innocent woman is to blame. We have a job to do, for God's sake. Get your head together."

Their gazes locked until Murdoch managed a grudging nod, blue eyes flinty and bitter, and the two officers set off once again, a heavy silence hanging in their wake.

SEVEN

THE OFFICERS

April 9, 1912 | 18:10

ESTHER WAS NERVOUS as she stood in the dim light of her cabin, hurrying to stow away her new uniforms.

Her mind was elsewhere, her fitful thoughts washing in and out like the tide.

Although she was already acquainted with half her colleagues, the thought of dining with the entire group filled her stomach with butterflies. Lowe, Moody, and Wilde were perfectly agreeable. She would sit with them, most likely. Lightoller seemed to be coming around, though his standoffish attitude had only seen marginal improvement.

But it was the others Esther worried about.

Boxhall, Pitman—and naturally, Murdoch.

She had welcomed the distance between her and her superior officer today, as he hurried around the ship making preparations. And in all honesty, she wasn't cherishing the thought of seeing him again.

By the time six o'clock came around, and Esther was donned head to toe in her new uniform, she swallowed down her nerves with grace and started down the corridor.

Her jacket was neatly buttoned and her long work skirt swirled at her feet. No heels, no earrings, and nothing shimmery that might warrant disapproval. In fact, her wardrobe was nearly identical to her colleagues', save for the skirt, the slimmer fit, and the silver locket glistening around her neck.

The greatcoat had surprised her; it was a heavy thing, but the dense, woolen fabric blocked out the cold with ease. She gratefully drew its lapels around her neck as she crossed the freezing boat deck, only distantly aware of the eyes lingering and heads turning as she passed.

When she finally entered the cozy warmth of the mess, she found most of the seats already full. Moody and Lowe chatted over tea at the far end of the table. Lightoller was there as well, back straight and fingers laced together as he spoke with two gentlemen Esther didn't know. The officers had all removed their caps and greatcoats, revealing black waistcoats and long-sleeved shirts of white underneath. But others were still missing, she noted. Wilde, and—*blessedly*—Murdoch.

Good, she thought with relief. *Here's hoping he doesn't show at all.*

With a deep breath, Esther crossed the room and made her way toward her colleagues.

There was a brief lull in conversation as she approached, trickling away into silence before picking up again. It was clear they weren't comfortable with her yet. Not all of them, at least. Esther could see it plainly in their eyes. The wariness, the hesitation—the unease at having a woman among their ranks. But she paid it little mind, seating herself between Moody and Lowe with confidence and shrugging her greatcoat from her shoulders.

"Blimey." Lowe nodded with approval as he looked her up and down. "You clean up well, miss."

"You sound so surprised," Esther laughed.

He studied her for a moment before proclaiming, "It's the skirt, I think. It's real tidy, like. Very nice."

She teased, "Well, if you ever want to borrow it, you need only ask."

Lowe dissolved into good-natured laughter, while Moody hid a snicker behind his teacup. Esther started to laugh herself when a throat cleared across the table, and she turned to see Lightoller looking at her expectantly.

"Miss Bailey," he said, gesturing toward the two officers sitting beside him, "allow me to introduce your colleagues. Mr. Herbert Pitman of Somerset." He indicated the friendlier-looking of the two men, a stocky gentleman with brilliant hazel eyes who nodded warmly in her direction. "And Mr. Joseph Boxhall of Dorset."

While Pitman was more than welcoming, his dark-haired companion remained quiet and taciturn, regarding her like some vile insect beneath his shoe. Esther swallowed against the tightness in her throat, her nerves fizzing wild once more, but she refused to falter before Boxhall's wary eyes.

Kill 'em with kindness, she reminded herself, making a point of beaming at him despite the lightning storm of defiance trembling through her.

Lowe spared Boxhall a cautionary glance before turning to Esther.

"Miss Bailey," he said quickly, "I've a story to share with you, and I reckon it's something you'll enjoy."

Esther smiled at him, grateful he was distracting her from Boxhall's foul stare. "Oh? What happened? Let's hear it."

Grinning, Lowe launched right into his tale. "Well, we were walking along A Deck Promenade, see, when we spotted someone who looked *awfully* familiar. Real familiar, almost uncanny like. So Jim here, bless him—" He waved one hand toward Moody, who sank a bit lower in his seat. "—called, 'Miss Bailey!' at the top of his lungs, all chipper and such. And I don't need to tell you who turned around in surprise."

Esther nearly spat her sip of water across the table. She glanced between Lowe and Moody, torn between amusement and indignation as the realization set in.

"It was my brother, wasn't it? Jesus, we don't look *that* alike!"

Moody fumbled for words, his face redder than wine. "You do indeed," he mumbled sheepishly. "And if you must know, Miss Bailey, I hadn't met him until then. In fact, I'd no idea you had a brother in the first place."

"Well, *now* you know," Lowe snorted. "And you'll damn near never forget it, will you?" With a carefree laugh, he leaned back in his chair and folded his muscled arms across his chest. "Christ, that was proper funny. You should have seen the look on Jim's face. Made my sodding *week*, to be honest. Your brother thought it was funny as well. He's a friendly bloke."

"He is," Esther agreed. She opened her mouth to say something more, but heavy footfalls made her turn in her seat.

Wilde and Murdoch had arrived at last, removing their caps and tugging off their greatcoats as they joined the crowded table. Esther studied her superior in the yellowing lamplight, surprised by how *different* he looked without his cap. His hair was dark and glossy, threaded with a bit of gray that indicated his near-forties age. But he didn't look half bad, she thought grudgingly, with his sleeved shirt freshly-pressed and his eyes deeper and bluer than ever.

Doesn't excuse his lousy attitude, though, Esther reminded herself.

She was staring at Murdoch longer than she should have—long enough for him to notice. He swept a neutral gaze over her, eyes meeting hers, and she quickly looked away, busying herself with her water glass at once.

"What's all this laughing about?" Wilde demanded, dropping himself into a chair beside Esther and stuffing a cigarette into the corner of his crooked mouth. Murdoch settled at the head of the table, closest to Lightoller and across from Esther, his face impassive as usual.

Lowe smirked at Wilde's question, ready to recount his tale, but Moody was quick to speak over him.

"What are we having for dinner?" he asked loudly, shooting Lowe a silencing glare.

"That's what I'm wondering," Pitman said, rubbing his stomach with a groan. "S'pose we'll find out soon enough. Better enjoy dinner tonight, gents, it'll be the last decent meal we'll have for a while." His eyes slid briefly to Esther, and he added, "Oh, right. Gents *and* lady."

But Esther waved away the oversight. "Last dinner?"

Pitman raised his brows. "Ah. Yes, well, I hate to be the bearer of bad tidings, love, but we don't have dinner relief after our watches often. Breakfast and lunch relief, sure—but that's because the food's already prepared for the passengers. We eat what they eat, see." He smiled at the incredulous look on her face. "Don't you worry, miss," he assured her. "By the time you've finished with your second watch, you'll *want* to crawl straight into bed. Dinner will be the furthest thing from your mind, you mark my words."

"I don't know about that, sir," Esther said dubiously.

He chuckled. "You'll get used to it. Just takes time. What's your watch schedule, anyway?"

"Er…" Esther combed her thoughts, struggling to remember, until Murdoch's soft, scratchy voice answered for her.

"Ten in the morning till two in the afternoon," he answered. "Then again at ten at night till two in the morning. But we'll be up earlier than usual tomorrow to prepare for launch." His blue eyes raked over his subordinate, and he added curtly, "Isn't that *right*, Miss Bailey?"

Esther suppressed a scowl as she met his condescending stare. "That's right, sir," she said firmly, smoothing out the lines in her skirt and refusing to let him belittle her again.

Stewardesses soon fluttered inside the mess hall, bringing with them an assortment of delicious food: crystalline bowls filled with creamed barley soups, silver platters laden with steamed oysters and filet mignon, saffron rice and roasted lamb swimming in mint sauce, and an assortment of other exquisite dishes that made Esther's mouth water. There were crisp celery stalks and Waldorf pudding for dessert, and a fresh stack of cigars to go along with them.

The aromas were enticing, delicious—and Esther inhaled deeply, all too aware of how hungry she was. She felt the stewardesses' eyes linger on her uniform as they roamed around the table, setting out bowls and plates of steaming hot food. But Esther dutifully ignored them, more interested in the entrees laid before her than in their scrutinizing stares.

"Tuck in, everyone," Pitman said cheerfully.

Esther did not need to be told twice. She started with rice and roasted duck first, passing over the heavier meats, which she never favored. Conversation stuttered as they ate, stumbling between topics before settling into an awkward quiet. It was as if the officers were testing the waters, not entirely sure how to act or what to say in the company of their newest recruit. But talk soon turned to the simpler matters—their pasts, their previous ships, the places they called home—and Esther found herself learning bits and pieces about the men gathered around her.

Wilde had worked at sea for more than twenty years. Hailing from Liverpool, he had two strapping sons and two beautiful daughters waiting for him back home. Lightoller was a Lancashire man married to a woman from Australia; he had worked aboard many steamships and windjammers since the age of thirteen, and had spent some time braving the gold rush in Yukon Territory before calling it quits and returning to the sea.

At some point during the conversation, Murdoch—whether deliberate or accidental—let slip about Lightoller's tattoo, and it was only after the rest of the group hounded him to show it that he drew up his sleeve, revealing the initials of his mother's name etched into his left arm.

But Lightoller wasn't the only tattooed officer, much to Esther's surprise. Even Lowe had his initials enclosed in the typical sailor's heart, inked on his forearm by some shipmate during his time along the West African coast. *Titanic* would be his first transoceanic crossing, he told them, despite having worked the *Belgic* and the *Tropic* in his career.

"And I'm damn well looking forward to it," he said stoutly, grinning at Esther.

Pitman had joined the maritime industry later in life after leaving his farming roots behind, while Boxhall had become a mariner at an early age, upholding his family's tradition of working at sea. Moody was the youngest of the group; he had formerly worked aboard *Oceanic*, and while he told his colleagues that he enjoyed seafaring, he merely saw it as another career and little else.

As for Murdoch, he kept the details about himself relatively short. Like Wilde, he had worked at sea for over twenty years. He came from Dalbeattie, Scotland. And he had sailed to almost every corner of the world.

Esther listened intently to his words, fascinated, her own curiosity taking her by surprise. She couldn't help but envy him, wishing she, too, could travel across every open ocean and sea.

One day, perhaps, Esther promised herself.

Eventually, all attention turned to her—as she had dreaded.

"And what of you, Miss Bailey?" Lowe asked.

"Whu—?" she mumbled, mouth chock-full of food.

He smiled, his eyes dancing curiously across her face. "Come on, let's hear it, then. I'd be lying if I said we weren't all the least bit curious how you ended up in the maritime business."

Suddenly nervous, Esther lowered her fork and wiped her mouth, her pulse hammering in the depths of her chest. She wasn't sure where to start, but she tucked away her rattling nerves and decided to give it a try.

"Er, I'm from San Francisco originally," she said. "Born and raised there, along with my older brothers. But we moved to Santa Cruz for a short while after the Great Earthquake, then back to San Francisco once they'd rebuilt the city. That was the year my father opened a new hospital."

She breathed deeply for a moment, weighing what to disclose, and what to quietly omit. Her past was a dark, winding river she preferred to steer clear from, never wanting to dip her toes in lest she be dragged away by the strongest currents. But her colleagues were watching her, so she bravely threw down another sip of water before pressing on.

"It was a well-known hospital among the upper-class. Or New Money. Whatever you call 'em. My father was the chief surgeon, my late brother the foremost physician. I worked there as a nurse for a year when I was eighteen or so. I'd just finished medical school and was assigned to the children's wing."

Moody stared at her in astonishment, one hand hovering over the brim of his tea, sugar spoon frozen between his fingertips.

"You were a nurse?"

Esther tried not to flush. She seemed to have caught everyone's attention now; even Murdoch was looking at her.

Lowe cocked his head to one side. "That's a very…*interesting* change of professions there, miss."

"It is," Esther admitted with a nod. "But I was involved in an accident when I was twenty, and nursing, well…" She shrugged, silently praying they wouldn't see through her lie. "Let's just say it didn't end up working out after that."

"But why settle on the maritime industry?" Wilde asked around his cigar. "That's what I've been trying to figure out! No offense, miss, but I'll just come out and say it: you being here is a *bit* of a shock. I mean, we're all still happy you're here, aren't we lads?"

He glared around the table as if daring someone to say otherwise. There was a general murmur of assent among the officers—with the exception of Lightoller, Boxhall, and Murdoch, of course. Wilde snorted at them before turning back to Esther.

"But we want to know *why*," he implored. "Why join the pride of the merchant marine?"

Esther met his inquisitive stare with a smile. "I didn't always like ships, Mr. Wilde. My uncle had a schooner when we lived in San Francisco, and I remember one day he sailed us out into the bay. I must've been eight or nine, perhaps. I don't really know what happened, but my brothers and I were roughhousing—stupid as we were—and I fell overboard."

Her eyes grew distant as she recalled the freezing water that stung her mouth with salt and sucked the breath from her lungs.

"They fished me right out, of course. But it still had a lasting impression on me, and not a very positive one, at that. I was terrified of the ocean for the longest time after that day. It took some coaxing, but eventually my uncle convinced me to face my fears. I'd sail with him out in the bay every weekend, learning all I could about ships and the tides. It grew on me, and I ended up harboring a soft spot for marine work. So when my nursing career went south, and my brother told me the Marine Institute in London was accepting women as part of an inclusion initiative, I jumped right on it at once."

The table was quiet now, with every eye fixed upon her. Self-conscious and flushed with pink, Esther looked down at her plate.

"I wanted to do something different," she said, shrugging. "Be someone different. So I spent four years working toward my degree in maritime law, then another year fulfilling my apprenticeship on the SS *Maloja*. My uncle had connections with White Star Line, and arranged something for me upon my graduation, so…here I am, I guess."

Murdoch suddenly spoke up from across the table. "And here you are," he echoed, eyes narrowed with cool derision. "Nepotism and all."

Silence followed his words.

It was the first time Murdoch had put Esther down in front of the entire group, and the officers all seemed to react differently to his slight. Some nodded with approval, as if they didn't believe a person ought to be handed a role that others worked their entire life to achieve. But a few officers—Moody and Pitman included—stared in shock.

"Honestly, Will." Wilde's voice was gruff, carrying the faint note of a warning. "There's no need for that."

He turned to Esther, who clenched her jaw tight, hiding her fury behind a pearly-white smile. "Don't pay the grumpy old Scot any mind," Wilde said, jerking his chin in Murdoch's direction. "We're glad to have you here, Miss Bailey."

"Hear, hear," Moody agreed, while Lowe raised his glass in a toast.

"Thank you," Esther murmured.

But it was Murdoch she was looking at, and she found herself thinking how much easier life would be if her superior officer shared Wilde's sentiments.

Esther made her way to the lavatory after dinner, all qualms with Murdoch momentarily forgotten.

Sailing day was tomorrow, much to her excitement, so she would report to the bridge in less than twenty-four hours' time. Determined to make a decent impression, she decided to have a quick bath and retire early this evening. It would give her enough time to tidy up, wind her alarm, and have a good night's rest before the real work began.

Lowe had tried to convince her otherwise, asking her to join him and the officers for a round of poker and a pint. They wanted to celebrate the maiden voyage, he said, and there were a fair few bottles of ale and boxed cigars waiting for them in the smoking room.

It was tempting, Esther had to admit. Though she wasn't necessarily fond of alcohol, she'd always enjoyed a competitive game of blackjack every now and then. And besides, it would be interesting to see how rowdy her colleagues could become.

But deep down, Esther knew better.

There was little time for fun and games given the monumental journey ahead of them—especially in her case. She was the lesser officer in their eyes. The one dumped upon their ranks in a flourish of nepotism and nothing more. She had to work twice as hard to prove her worth. She had to remain disciplined, ensuring she was prepared for every task, rule and requirement demanded of her.

So she declined Lowe's invitation, collecting her dressing robe from her cabin and trying not to feel disappointed as she watched her colleagues amble toward the smoking room.

The officers' quarters had two lavatories—one on the port side, the other positioned starboard—and Esther slipped inside the one facing port, where she cranked on the crystal faucets and let the clawfoot tub fill with glistening hot water. The taps gushed as she started to undress, kicking off her Oxfords and peeling off her greatcoat in a heap.

She was just stripping out of her hosiery when the door she could have *sworn* she'd locked snapped open with a click, and someone strode inside.

Esther froze, rooted in place as she found herself face-to-face with the last damn person she wanted to see.

First Officer Murdoch was looking at her as if he had stumbled upon some grisly automobile wreck, one hand gripping the doorknob, the other clutching a cotton towel.

There was a moment of silence as the officers stared at each other.

Then, in a frantic scramble of movement, Murdoch dropped his towel to shield his eyes, his face a brilliant, beet-red as he grappled for the doorway behind him.

"*Jings, crivvens n' God in heaven!*"

He bellowed out some Scottish oaths Esther couldn't understand, though it was clear he was shouting more out of shock than actual anger.

"Did *no one* teach you how to lock a bleedin' door, lass!"

Incredulous, Esther watched him stagger backward, fumbling at the doorframe as if trying to flee from death itself. She snorted, and the words came tumbling out before she could stop them.

"And did no one teach you how to knock before entering a room?" she demanded. "*Sir?*"

Her cheek seemed to momentarily anger Murdoch, blazing right through his panicked haste; he stopped dead in his tracks, lowering his hand from his eyes until their gazes locked tight. Upon seeing her fully dressed—save for her discarded coat and stockings—his sense of urgency withered away at once. He merely stood in the doorway instead of fleeing through it, glaring at her, ready to reprimand.

"Good grief," he gritted out, his thick Scottish burr fading and becoming far less pronounced as he regained a level calm. But his chest still heaved, swelling up and down as he struggled for breath. "The hell's the matter with you? Lavatory doors are meant to be locked if they're occupied, you dafty. I could've—could've—"

He seemed to struggle for words, but Esther was quick to cut in.

"Could've seen me stark naked in the tub?" she suggested carelessly.

Murdoch blanched, the color draining from his face. She nearly smirked; it was nice, really, seeing him flustered when he was usually so goddamn caustic.

"I'm still decent, sir," she reasoned, shrugging. "Still clothed. So I'd say we dodged a bullet, wouldn't you?"

Murdoch snorted. "That's debatable." Shaking his head, he rushed one agitated hand through his dark hair. "Damn near gave me a heart attack. Lightoller was right. We ought to establish a designated lavatory for you and you *alone*. You'd do well to take the one closer to the starboard side, you know. Away from the cabins."

"This one's closer," Esther said simply. "And it has saltwater taps."

"So?"

"So I've never seen them before, and I wouldn't mind giving them a try."

Murdoch made a disparaging noise in his throat, as if tired of dealing with someone so simple-minded, and Esther retorted, "Forgive me, sir, but it's hardly fair to shunt me away to another washroom simply because you don't understand common courtesy."

Murdoch opened his mouth to argue, but a trickling noise made them turn.

The clawfoot tub was overflowing.

Water spilled over the sides in cascading sheets, slithering across the tiles of blue-veined marble and soaking into the hosiery she left on the floor.

"*Shit*," Esther groaned.

She'd been so preoccupied with Murdoch's unsolicited visit that she left the bathwater running, taps gushing at full blast.

Cursing, Esther scrambled toward the tub and scrabbled at the handle, frantically trying to crank the faucet off. The torrent stopped, and she didn't bother pushing up her sleeve before plunging her hand into the bathwater and uncorking the brass stopper at its bottom.

A low whistle of relief escaped her lips as the tub began to drain itself, water swirling its way out of sight. Esther slumped to the floor, the hem of her skirt drenched, and peered around for Murdoch. But her superior officer was nowhere in sight. He must've taken off the moment she'd hurried to stop the running faucets, and it irked her.

Of course, Esther thought crossly. *Typical jackass.*

She rolled her eyes, about to curse the man to high heaven—but the words caught in her throat when Murdoch came hurrying into the room seconds later.

"Here," he said gruffly.

He carried extra towels in his hands, and she watched in stunned silence as he wrenched up his sleeves, knelt on the floor, and began to clear away the excess water. Wordlessly Esther grabbed another towel and joined him, trying her hardest to avoid meeting his eyes.

They were quiet as they cleaned the wet tiles, soaking up the puddles here and there, and it wasn't until the last drop of water was cleared away that Esther finally broke the silence.

"Thanks," she murmured.

Murdoch rose to his feet. His sleeves were wet despite having rolled them up, and she saw lean muscle through the sheer, damp fabric.

"Don't thank me," he said tersely. "It was my fault for intruding on you. I only came for a quick rinse—I didn't think anyone would be in here at this hour." Shrugging, he added, "Everyone went to the smoking room for a pint. I thought you'd done the same."

She shook her head. "I decided to pass. Never liked that sort of thing, anyway."

"Poker?"

"Drinking."

Esther threw the damp towels into the hamper before turning to Murdoch in surprise. Was he actually *admitting* his fault? It was baffling, especially since her superior officer seemed too snarky and too high-minded to consider such a thing. She bit her lip as she stood before him, suddenly wanting to match his courtesy with her own.

"I forgot to lock the door," she said politely, trying to be friendly for once. "I'm at fault, too, sir. I'll be more careful next time."

But Murdoch wasn't paying attention. With the sleeves of her blouse shoved up to her elbows, his eyes lingered on the ugly scars mapping her right forearm—an everyday reminder of the brandy bottle that once splintered her skin apart. He was quiet long enough to make her self-conscious.

"It's rude to stare, Mr. Murdoch," she told him, sliding her sleeves back down.

"Sorry," he muttered, looking away from the scars and up at her scowling face instead. His brows knotted into a frown, and he asked, "That's what you were talking about earlier, wasn't it?"

"Pardon?"

"At dinner. You said you left your nursing career at twenty. Because you were involved in an accident of some sort."

Esther was surprised he even remembered. "You were listening," she said thoughtfully, kneeling to gather up her soaked stockings.

"Yes." Murdoch's voice was wry. "I've been known to do that from time to time." When Esther said nothing, he crossed his arms and studied her with a questioning look. "So, what happened, then? If you don't mind my asking, that is."

"I don't think you want to know," Esther admitted. *Or even care*, she added silently to herself.

Murdoch raised a single brow. "Try me."

Esther went pale. She had no intention of discussing the muddy waters of her past with anyone, and certainly not with Murdoch.

But he had asked her outright, so what could she say now?

Her eyes darted across his face, tracing the faint smatter of freckles along his nose, and she felt the pulse of her heartbeat turn erratic as she wondered how to work her way out of the corner she'd found herself in.

Murdoch waited, surprisingly patient, a look of respectful curiosity spread over his face. This was rare for him, Esther noted. Rare enough that she almost didn't like it. Flustered, she tucked a strand of hair behind one ear, trying to think of some clever ruse. But she had always been a poor liar, so she found herself blurting out the first thing to come to mind.

"It was a grizzly bear," she said, nearly wincing at how ridiculous it sounded aloud. "Happened when I was on holiday in, er… the northwest. Oregon, to be precise. Never saw the damn thing coming. Clawed me up quite a bit, but it could've been mighty worse."

Esther shrugged, hating the heat rising in her cheeks and hoping she wasn't pink in the face. "So, there you have it. That's how those scars came about, sir."

Murdoch stared at her for a long moment before declaring, "That's the stupidest thing I've ever heard. If you're going to lie, you might as well make an effort, lass."

She smiled innocently. "With all due respect sir, you don't know what the American West is like. You haven't a clue what goes on out there."

"I have a *vague* idea, Miss Bailey, and I doubt it includes you grappling with the likes of some wild animal." He was shaking his head at her, although there was a faint smile on his lips that he seemed to be trying his damnedest to hold back. "But I'm willing to suspend disbelief for your sake," he added dryly. "So let's just leave it at that."

A short silence followed his words as Esther looked up at him, grateful he hadn't pried—and amazed he was actually behaving himself. She'd expected him to utter a snide quip by now, similar to the backhanded comment he'd made at dinner. Hurt and humiliation tightened in her stomach at the memory, and the words came spilling out before Esther could stop them.

"It wasn't only nepotism, by the way."

His eyes met hers, deep blue and impossible to read, but she did not look away as she continued, "I mean, I'm not stupid, Mr. Murdoch. I know I wouldn't have gotten this job without the help of my uncle. But I still worked very, *very* hard to get here, sir. Don't make the mistake of thinking I didn't."

Murdoch studied her for a long moment, his expression unreadable.

But instead of offering an apology, he simply spun on his heel and stalked for the door, pulling down his sleeves and reverting to his usual indifferent demeanor.

"If you've finished prattling," he scolded, "you'd best wash up and head to bed. We've a long day ahead of us tomorrow."

Fuming, Esther merely nodded in response.

"Remember, six o'clock sharp on the bridge, and not a minute after." Narrowing his eyes, he added curtly, "Do try to avoid sleeping through your alarm, will you? I'd rather not deal with that sort of embarrassment so early in the morning."

Esther gritted her teeth against the curse she longed to hurl at him. She merely glowered at her superior officer until he left the room, and it took every last bit of restraint she had to keep from slamming the door behind him as he went.

EIGHT

THE BRIDGE

April 10, 1912 | 05:00

I T WAS THE key-wound alarm clock that woke Murdoch early Wednesday morning, ringing shrilly in his ears and dragging him from the comfort of deep sleep. He sat up at once, tapping the top of his Westclox to silence it.

5 o'clock, the numbers read through the gloom.

Murdoch rubbed his eyes and gave his head a quick shake, as if trying to scatter away the last remnants of drowsiness. His blankets were still ridiculously warm against his skin—all fleece and soft flannel—and although he wanted nothing more than to crawl back underneath them, he knew better. Almost two decades of seafaring hadn't taught him to snooze the morning away, tempting though it was. Murdoch was a senior officer with the highest of expectations. Timeliness at odd hours of the day wasn't only a requirement after all these years; it was second nature.

So he sighed, blinking in the dim lamplight seeping through the frosted glass window.

Go on, get up, you lump, he chided himself.

Within moments, Murdoch was on his feet, meticulously smoothing out the bed covers and rewinding the alarm for his later shift. He moved to the wardrobe next, pulling out the components of the traditional officer's uniform. First the thick greatcoat for the cold awaiting him outside, then a pair of fine Merino wool socks, and finally, the rest of the ensemble: reefer jacket, waistcoat, sleeved cotton shirt, tie, cap, slacks. All neatly pressed, without so much as a wrinkle in sight.

Thoughts of what the day would bring coursed through his mind as he dressed, buttoning up his shirt and tightening the dark silk tie at his neck. Sailing day had come at last, and although Murdoch was a reserved man who had seen more than his fair share of ships off to sea, even *he* couldn't ignore the exhilaration swelling in the depths of his chest.

Over a thousand people would board at noon—everyone from millionaires to aristocrats, stewardesses to stokers—and cargo holds would fill with enormous stockpiles of food, textiles, and mailbags bound for the American coast. *Titanic* would make a short journey from Southampton to Cherbourg later in the evening, with only one more stop in Queenstown the following day. And then they'd be off, sailing across the North Atlantic with only a blue ocean and brilliant constellations to guide them.

But that was all very distant, Murdoch knew, and there was still a great deal of work to attend to first. Ticket processing, lifeboat safety drills, sea and anchor duties come departure...The list of preparations stretched on and on. He was eager to start the day, of course. There was certainly no denying that. And yet, he couldn't stop his irritations from needling him, reminding him once again that he was stuck with the *girl*.

Misgivings tore into him as he shaved, splashed his face with cold water, and rubbed aftershave along his jaw. Murdoch was certain that the girl would find some way to embarrass him in front of his captain and crew. Christ, how he dreaded seeing her this morning.

It didn't help that he was still reeling from their encounter in the lavatory last night, unable to scrub away the sickening shame of walking in on the girl and almost finding her in a state of undress.

All you had to do was knock, he thought sullenly. *Daft bastard.*

In all honesty, Murdoch knew he ought to give her a chance. She was a sharp girl with a decent sense of humor. And she wasn't hard on the eyes, he had to admit.

But she had too much cheek. Too much fire.

Wilde might have found it *adorable*, but Murdoch wasn't about to let a junior officer get away with such disrespect. He would sooner jump into the icy sea than deal with that sort of nonsense.

By half-past five, Murdoch stood before the mirror to make sure he was decent. A pair of steady blue eyes gazed back at him, as calm and professional as could be. He drew in a deep breath. Straightened his tie and cuffs one last time. And then he was off, slinging on his greatcoat and closing the door quietly behind him.

As he made his way toward the mess for breakfast, Murdoch spared an idle glance at the seventh officer's cabin. Gleaming white wood looked back at him, and for the briefest of moments, he almost considered knocking to see if the girl was awake.

But then he stopped himself. As an officer of the ship, it was *her* responsibility to set her alarm and wake up on time—*not* his. If she slept in like some do-nothing shirker, well, it was her own damn fault.

At least, that was what Murdoch kept trying to tell himself.

She'll have to learn the hard way, he thought firmly. *I'm not her nanny. It's not my job to hold her hand.*

Murdoch pushed the girl from his mind as he headed aft, crossing the length of the boat deck to the officers' mess. The room was drenched in weary quiet as his colleagues filled up on tea, coffee and steaming hot food. But a buzz of anticipation still hummed in the air, and Murdoch knew they—like him—were eager to set sail.

He found Wilde sitting at the far end of the mess, smoking a cigarette with the usual breakfast sprawled before him: bowls of porridge and fried bread, fresh tomatoes and baked beans, black pudding sausages with bacon and over-easy eggs. But not even a hearty breakfast seemed to brighten up Wilde, who looked exhausted as he slid Murdoch a mug of hot tea.

"Mornin'," he greeted, voice gruff and eyes still glazed with sleep.

Murdoch settled beside his colleague, wordlessly mixing a bit of milk and sugar into his drink. Only after a long sip did he turn his attention to Wilde. "You look like hell," he remarked honestly.

"Do I?" Wilde lifted one hand to his mouth, stifling a deep, enormous yawn. "Been up since two. Still getting used to my watch schedule—and what a *shit* schedule it is. Absolute rubbish. You're bloody lucky you'll be on the ten-to-two circuit once we're underway. I'd gladly give my left bollock to trade places with you."

Murdoch smiled wistfully. "Aye, but if we were to trade, then you wouldn't be chief officer, remember?"

Wilde stole a quick glance around the room before leaning closer to Murdoch. "I'll be honest with you, mate, chief officer ain't as fancy as it looks. You know one of my foremost duties is to ensure 'cleanliness and discipline throughout the ship,' yeah? Meaning it's my responsibility to make sure the ruddy decks are washed down, and all the brass is spick and span by eight."

He took a short drag from his cigarette, scowling, gray eyes crinkling into slits. "Every *damn day* I have to stand around and supervise the crew as they clean. I'm going to shoot myself in the brains before we're in New York, Will. I wasn't made for this kind of tedium. Not even the *Olympic* was this bloody particular."

"Come off it," Murdoch scoffed.

He tried to ignore the jealousy bubbling in his stomach as he chewed a spoonful of oats, but it was useless; the recollection of his demotion still cut into him like a blazing, white-hot knife. It was *Wilde* wearing the chief officer's uniform, not him, and Murdoch would forever be reminded of this fact. But he forced himself to swallow down his grudge, keeping his voice carefully neutral as he reasoned, "You're making it sound plenty worse than it is. You're in charge of standard inspections and watch duties, aye? It's not simply endless *cleaning*."

Wilde waved this away with one hand. "Sure, but it's not enough. I'd be lying if I said I didn't envy you, Will. Your place is on the bridge for a good chunk of the day. You get to be in the thick of things. I know you were none too thrilled about being bumped down a rank, but I daresay you got the fairer deal, if you ask me."

"Hardly," Murdoch retorted, and this time, he was unable to keep the bitterness from his voice.

"You can sit there and be sour as a lemon, but you know it's damn well true." Wilde leaned back in his chair with an ungentlemanly slouch, cigarette nestled between his thick fingers, wisps of blue-tinted tobacco smoke pooling from the corner of his mouth. "And if I'd had a choice, I honestly would've turned down working on *Titanic* altogether. There's something about this ship I don't *like*."

"How do you mean?"

"I dunno. I just have a queer feeling about it, Will. Can't rightly explain why, but I feel it in the pit of my stomach. In my bones, even."

Murdoch's voice was wry. "Did you ever consider it's simply indigestion?"

Wilde drummed his fingers on the table, looking close to rolling his eyes. "Blimey," he snorted. "You're just as cheeky as that Bailey. Two of a kind, I'd wager." Chuckling at the incredulous look on Murdoch's face, Wilde took a moment to glance around the mess hall. "Where's your girl, anyway?"

"Sleeping through her alarm, no doubt."

"Oh, come now," Wilde chided. "You ought to give her a bit more credit than that! She's a sensible girl. Reminds me of Jennie a bit, to be honest," he added thoughtfully, referring to his eldest daughter, and Murdoch shook his head in disbelief. "I'm sure she'll be on the bridge before six."

"We'll see," Murdoch said thinly. "How I wish I could share your optimism, Henry."

He glowered down at his tea, silent and brooding, until his companion tentatively spoke.

"Why do I get the feeling there's something you're not telling me?" Wilde asked. "Is everything well between the two of you, Will?"

Murdoch breathed out an irritable sigh. "I'm surprised you even have to *ask*. Nothing but pure cheek, that girl. Stubborn little lass, too." He coursed one hand through his dark, gray-threaded hair, wishing he could wind back time so Lightoller would be the one dealing with this mess, *not* him. "I've never met someone so damn infuriating," he went on. "She'll be the death of me, I'm sure of it."

"Oh, nonsense." Wilde looked on the verge of laughter. "You're being *far* too dramatic for a Wednesday morning, you realize that?"

"I am not. You've seen her, Henry. You know what she's like. And let's not forget her most *exemplary* qualities…reckless, impudent, temperamental…behaves *nothing* at all like an officer should—"

"She treats me fine all the same," Wilde said cheerfully. When Murdoch scoffed, he shrugged and said, "Listen, you've not been warm to her, either, you grump. It's no wonder she's biting back. Give it a few days, will you? I'm sure the pair of you will warm up to each other in time."

"Aye, we will," Murdoch said dully. "When hell freezes over."

His temper crackled as the girl's defiant green gaze flooded his mind, only worsening his mood. "The lass is a complete pain in my arse who has *no* place being an officer. None at all. And yet, they still decided to punt her to me, so *I'm* the one dealing with her day in and day out. Dafties."

"And it's a fine thing they did," Wilde reasoned calmly. "You might be a sarcastic little git at times, and you lay on the Scottish a *bit* too thick—but you're a damn good sailor, and you'll make an even better mentor. I'm sure of it. She's lucky to have you, mate, and you're lucky to have her. I daresay she'll keep you on your toes, she will." Smirking, he added as an afterthought, "Can you bloody *imagine* if she was stuck working with Mr. Lightoller? I do believe I'd run for the hills, wouldn't you?"

Murdoch was saved from answering when the door cracked open, and two officers stepped inside. He swallowed hard, expecting to see Bailey, perhaps—but it was only Moody and Lowe. They settled at the table, pulling dishes and cups of tea toward them.

"Good morning, gents," Moody said brightly.

Unlike the rest of the officers at the table, there was no grogginess about the sixth officer this morning; he looked refreshed and ready for the day, cuffs neat and tie impeccably knotted at his throat. Murdoch wasn't surprised; Moody seemed to be the most meticulous of the bunch, striving for decorum in even the most trivial of manners: the way he brushed his teeth, combed his hair—prepared his morning *tea*, even.

But while Moody seemed content to sip gingerly from his teacup, Lowe was the exact opposite, snagging every dish in sight. Poached eggs, currant buns, griddle cakes, kippered herrings—he devoured it all, silverware clattering almost furiously across his plate. He damn near came close to splattering egg yolk on his white cuffs, earning a look of outrage from the ever perfectly-dressed Moody sitting at his side.

Murdoch watched the fifth officer with amusement. "Bit hungry, are you?"

"Starved," Lowe mumbled, mouth bursting with kippers.

Moody laughed, and Wilde passed his cigarette to the other side of his mouth with a snort.

"That's an understatement if I've ever heard one," the chief officer remarked. "Try not to choke, yeah? I don't think the captain will be all too pleased to find his fifth officer dead before we've even left *port*."

"Yes, at least wait till we're at sea to choke," Murdoch deadpanned. "Be courteous, lad."

Lowe chuckled, but his laugh was more nervous than anything.

"Sorry," he apologized. "I tend to eat when I'm nervous. Old habit, I s'pose."

Murdoch glanced up from his tea; he had forgotten this voyage was Lowe's first transatlantic crossing. The poor bloke was looking a bit peaky, as if suffering from a dreadful case of *mal-de-mer*—which was surprising considering his typical air of haughty confidence.

"Nothing to be nervous about," Murdoch assured him. "You'll do fine, lad. We're all professionals here; we'll make sure the crossing's as smooth as possible." His thoughts turned to Bailey, and he glanced at Moody to ask, "You haven't seen Miss Bailey around, have you?"

Moody looked thoughtful. "I haven't," he admitted. "Perhaps she's still getting herself ready."

"Perhaps," Murdoch echoed distantly. But he couldn't stop the worry threading its way through his veins, colder than crackling ice. His concern only turned to irritation as the minutes ticked past. He spotted Boxhall entering the mess for breakfast, looking drowsy but lucid all the same. A shivering, red-nosed Pitman appeared not long after, nearly bowling Lowe over in his desperation to reach the hot food and drink.

But still…no Bailey.

At twenty minutes to six, the officers filed out of the mess hall and made their way toward the bridge. As they crossed the boat deck and stepped down the long corridor of their sleeping quarters, Murdoch stole one last glance at Bailey's cabin door.

Her own damn fault, he reminded himself.

A glacial wind swept across his skin as he stepped out onto the bridge, soaking right through his greatcoat. The space was brilliantly lit, its electric lamps and glowing telegraphs a welcome contrast to the cold darkness shrouding the port. Thin, milky fog lingered around the harbor, hovering above the glassy waves, while the distant horizon glowed with the gray light of dawn. Murdoch peered around, eyes roaming from each bridge wing to the wheelhouse and back again. But no Bailey in sight.

Wilde let out a low whistle at his side. "Whew! Bloody cold, eh? I don't fancy this April weather. Not one bit."

Murdoch nodded vaguely, eyes still scouring the bridge for his charge. "Mind you, it'll be colder once we're at sea."

"Good Lord, *don't* remind me. This is dreadful enough as is." A deep sigh rumbled in the depths of Wilde's chest as he chafed his hands together for warmth, studying the slow-moving activity on the bridge. But his eyes narrowed when Lightoller rounded the corner of the officers' promenade in a swirl of his long greatcoat, and he muttered, "Oh, how *wonderful*. Just the miserable old codger I wanted to see."

When Murdoch sighed, Wilde asked innocently, "What?"

"Now's not the time nor the place, Henry."

"He's a prat, though. Keeps blaming me for bumping him down to second officer, and you ruddy well know that wasn't my fault—"

Murdoch shot him a warning look, and Wilde grudgingly fell silent as Lightoller stopped before them, tugging on a pair of leather gloves.

"There you are," he drawled, nodding in a friendly manner at Murdoch. But his eyes were not so merry as they swept over Wilde. "The captain's waiting for us in the navigating room. Says he wishes to speak with all senior officers immediately."

Wilde and Murdoch exchanged bewildered glances, but they said nothing as they ambled toward the navigating room.

They found Smith standing before a heavy teakwood desk, studying a sprawl of maps depicting North and South Atlantic shipping routes. But upon hearing their footsteps, he turned to greet them.

"Good morning. I do hope you're well rested and ready for the day?"

The officers murmured their assent, and Smith nodded approvingly before pressing on. "Excellent. Now, I've gathered you here to review our itinerary for the day, but also to discuss a rather...trivial issue at hand. But it's an issue I'd like to address all the same." He cleared his throat, standing straighter with a hint of calm authority in his gaze. "From what I understand, Mr. Murdoch, you and Miss Bailey are assigned to lifeboat drills and ticket processing for first-class passengers prior to launch."

Wordlessly Murdoch nodded, though he didn't have the faintest idea what Smith was getting at. But he held his tongue, keeping attentive as the captain continued, "I've given it some thought, and I am somewhat hesitant to have Miss Bailey present during the boarding process. Mostly due to my concerns of how the passengers might treat her...and of how she might behave in return. What are your thoughts?"

Wilde was the first to speak, his deep voice full of confidence. "I believe it is a non-issue, sir. She'll be fine."

"I disagree," Lightoller added stiffly, and Wilde's lips thinned. "I do believe she would be better suited working on the bridge until noon. A woman officer is unusual enough as is; I think it would be prudent to avoid any unwanted attention."

"And what say you, Mr. Murdoch?" Smith asked. "You've come to know her better than anyone aboard insofar."

Murdoch hesitated, clasping his hands tightly behind his back. On the one hand, he wouldn't mind being rid of Bailey for a few hours out of the day. She would be far from him, stationed on the bridge while he attended to the port gangways before setting sail. There would be no risk of her embarrassing him. No witticisms or backtalk or piercing green eyes. It was in his best interests to agree with Lightoller, was it not? Simply shunt her away to the bridge and avoid having the passengers see her altogether.

And yet…Murdoch could not bring himself to do such a thing.

Something held him back—something foreign and beyond understanding—and it made him uneasy.

"Well?" Smith pressed, expectant.

Murdoch stepped forward. "Sir," he began with measured calm, lifting his chin and standing as tall as his five-foot-ten stature would allow. "I agree with Mr. Wilde. Even if Miss Bailey were to face maltreatment from the passengers, I do believe she would be able to work past it and continue to perform her duties tactfully and professionally."

God in Heaven, a voice in his head groaned. *You know she bloody well won't. So why are you telling the captain otherwise?*

Smith studied Murdoch for a long moment, as if quietly weighing his input. Eventually, he nodded.

"Very well," he said. "I trust your judgment, Mr. Murdoch, and I will allow her to be present during the boarding process."

"Very good, sir," Murdoch said. But his throat felt dry, and he spent the next ten minutes or so immersed in a flood of his own thoughts, scarcely listening to Smith as he reviewed their itinerary for the day.

By the time they were dismissed, Murdoch was grateful to breathe in the cold, salty air of daybreak once more. Lightoller and Wilde were bickering yet again, but Murdoch paid them little mind. He stood in the starboard bridge wing, listening to the lazy swirl of the tides and struggling to calm himself. But his thoughts were like a gale that refused to quit, howling in his ears and spreading an icy numbness to his fingertips. What in God's name was the *matter* with him? Why had he defended the Bailey girl? Worse even, why had he *willingly* agreed to let her spend the entire morning with him? Either he was growing soft, or he was just plain daft.

Likely the latter, Murdoch reckoned, pinching the bridge of his nose and inhaling a sharp breath of frustration.

But it didn't matter now. He'd made his choice, however senseless it was. Now he had to deal with the consequences.

Murdoch stole a cursory glance at the clock. One minute to six, and Bailey still wasn't on the bridge. He knew he should have knocked on her door. But he'd held back, not wanting to coddle her. Now she was likely fast asleep in her cabin, tucked beneath the cozy blankets while the rest of her counterparts stood on deck, ready and willing to greet the day.

Another minute passed. Irritable, Murdoch tapped his foot on the pine decking. *Six o'clock,* the little brass clock in the wheelhouse seemed to blare at him. Smith was due out on the bridge any moment now, where he would address the assembled crew as per custom. And yet, Bailey still wasn't here. Damn it all, she was nowhere in *sight—*

There was a crescendo of frantic stumbling as the girl came barreling past the officers' corridors, through the door of the wheelhouse, and out onto the open bridge.

Everyone stared as she made her grand entrance. Some regarded her with confusion, others with varying degrees of disgust or astonishment. Lowe was clearly holding back a grin, and both Moody and Lightoller looked absolutely scandalized. But Murdoch was one of the few who stared at her in sheer, raging disbelief.

She looked downright haggard, as if she'd climbed out of bed only seconds ago. Her eyes were heavy with sleep, her hair uncombed and messy beneath a lopsided cap. She hadn't even bothered to lace up her Oxfords properly—*or* cuff her sleeves, for that matter. Her collar was askew, and worst of all, she was completely missing her tie.

Murdoch had *never* seen such a shameful sight, in all his seafaring years. He didn't know if he was more embarrassed by her lack of timeliness or bedraggled appearance. Both, probably. But he didn't have a moment to consider it. Within seconds he was storming toward her, his anger burning hot enough to warm him from the morning chill. He snagged her by the arm and ushered her away from the crew, tugging her over to the starboard bridge wing where they wouldn't be overheard.

"I thought I told you to be *timely*," he snapped, the words a quiet snarl against her ear.

Her run to the bridge must have winded her, because she was still breathing heavily through her nose. "It's six o'clock, isn't it?" Bailey gasped, one hand clutching her side. "I *am* on time, sir."

Fuming, Murdoch yanked his pocket watch from the folds of his coat and thrust it under her nose. Bailey squinted down at its face with a frown, and her jaw plummeted when she realized the time.

"Shit—I mean, shoot. Two minutes past six, then."

"Firstly, you watch your mouth when you're on the bridge. Secondly, I don't care if it's two minutes or twenty. You're still late." Murdoch regarded her with a look of deep disgust. "Though I can't say I'm surprised," he added scathingly, snapping his watch shut and plunging it back into his coat pocket. "I expected nothing less from you. You're a pure disgrace. Why you even *bothered* to become an officer if you don't even know how to be punctual or presentable is beyond me."

Murdoch waited for her to snap back. In fact, he was nearly bracing himself for it. But the girl actually kept *quiet* for once, bowing her head and refusing to meet his eyes. There was no fire. No sharp tongue. Just a young woman standing ashamed in her disheveled uniform.

"I'm sorry, sir," Bailey whispered. Her eyes were glassy, though whether it was from sleepiness or from the first beginnings of tears, Murdoch couldn't say. "There's no excuse for my tardiness. I swear to you, sir, it won't happen again."

Sincerity flooded her voice, true and apologetic, and for a moment, Murdoch's anger seemed to dissipate altogether. He studied the girl uncertainly, not sure what to say—and not wanting to admit that he was more disappointed in her than he was angry.

But then he collected himself, his authority returning in a blaze of disapproval. "It'd better not," he warned, "or I will throw you overboard myself. Make no mistake of it, lass."

And with that, Murdoch turned sharply on his heel and stalked toward the bridge, greatcoat swishing along his calves. Bailey followed him in silence, shuffling forward to stand beside Moody, and he heard the sixth officer hiss under his breath, "Where on *earth* is your tie?"

Bailey rubbed a hand over her tired eyes. "Don't ask," she groaned.

Shaking his head, Murdoch bit back an exasperated sigh. He was relieved when Smith appeared, distracting him from the squall of his agitated thoughts. Like the rest of the officers, Murdoch swept his fingers to his temple in salute, and he thanked the stars that Bailey remembered to do the same.

A hush descended on the crew as they faced their captain, who looked impressively venerable in his full uniform. There was no sound, no noise to trouble the deck—save for the distant sounds of a waking Southampton, and the lull of waves flowing far beneath them.

Chin raised high, Smith called out into the quiet, "We have a long and promising journey ahead of us, gentlemen."

Murdoch resisted the urge to glance at Bailey, though he could almost picture her nose wrinkling at the captain's oversight.

"Do well to remember I have faith in every one of you. You are among the finest seafarers of the merchant marine, and I am proud to stand here as your captain. With the eyes of God upon us, we shall uphold the name of White Star Line with honor and propriety. We shall ensure the safety and comfort of all on board. And we shall make it our foremost duty to see our Ship of Dreams complete her maiden voyage with ease."

His eyes roved across the crowd, looking from one face to the next, and he smiled. "Best of luck to you all on this splendid day."

And with that, they were all dismissed. There was a rush of movement as every officer, quartermaster, lookout, and able seaman shuffled off to their stations. Wilde was among the first to leave the bridge, regarding Murdoch and Bailey with mild amusement as he went. Murdoch shot him a sullen look before rounding on his subordinate. She blinked in the electric lamplight with a pair of bleary eyes, her clothing all mussed and hair frizzing beneath her cap. It was an embarrassing sight.

"We must check the gear on the docking bridge," Murdoch said shortly. "After that, we'll see to lifeboat safety drills 'round seven. Then we're wanted on the gangways to take passenger tickets at eight. Come departure, we'll be positioned at the stern. Any questions?"

"None, sir."

Incredulous, Murdoch watched her stifle a yawn with the back of her palm, and it took every scrap of restraint he had left in his bones to keep from shouting at her.

"Miss Bailey," he sighed. "Am I right to assume you didn't have any sort of pick-me-up this morning before stumbling your way onto the bridge?"

When she merely shrugged in response, almost determinedly avoiding eye contact, Murdoch sighed again and started for the officers' mess.

Christ. Perhaps he *was* becoming her nanny after all.

"Come on, then," he called over his shoulder. "I'm not about to work alongside you for the entire day if you haven't at least had a cup of tea. You'll only slow me down." He impatiently drew his pocket watch from his coat and clicked it open to inspect the time. "We can spare no more than five minutes, so it'll have to be quick. I hope you like your tea cold, Miss Bailey, because that's probably all that's left."

"But Mr. Murdoch!" she spluttered, as she hurried alongside him. "I don't need anything. I'm ready and wide awake, sir. I'm good to go."

"Yes," Murdoch said wryly, scrutinizing her unkempt hair and clothes. "And your sloppy appearance this morning is testament enough to that fact."

"Sir—" she protested again.

But he refused to hear a word of it. "Mess hall, Miss Bailey. Now. That is an order, in case you couldn't tell."

Once again, Murdoch waited for his subordinate to lash out with some defiant remark or another. But she was oddly silent, staring down at her cuffs and refusing to meet his stern gaze.

He frowned at the girl, and although his expression was reserved and careful, his eyes were sharp with wariness. What the hell was going on with her? Her attitude this morning—or lack thereof—was almost beginning to bother him. He had grown accustomed to hearing her witty retorts throughout the day, as ridiculous and inappropriate as they were.

But now she was quiet. Subdued. Dull as dishwater.

Murdoch tried to keep himself from dwelling on his subordinate as he led her down the boat deck, the pair of them lost in an awkward silence. There was still much to do today, after all. And he wasn't about to let the peculiar behavior of some irrelevant girl distract him.

NINE

SETTING SAIL

April 10, 1912 | 06:20

ESTHER WAS QUIET as she followed Murdoch down the starboard boat deck, breathing in the cold, stinging air of an early dawn.

The morning was still dark as pitch by the time they left the mess hall, its daybreak light struggling to wake along the horizon. Waves of deep black swirled against the plated hull far below, while the illuminated funnels glowed like gold pillars high above them. The seventh officer could feel her grogginess fade at last, tapering to bright-eyed clarity thanks to the cup of lukewarm tea Murdoch ordered her to chug. But as they headed aft down the promenade, and Esther gradually became more alert in the morning darkness, she could not stop the anger from swelling mercilessly within her.

She wasn't angry at the Scotsman at her side. No, not at all.

She was angry at *herself*.

Esther couldn't believe she'd been late to the bridge. Two minutes late, but it had been enough to earn Murdoch's criticism, and scathing stares from the rest of the crewmen. Everything had gone to shit this morning, to put it plainly, and Esther knew she had no one to blame but herself. She'd slept through her alarm like a fool, not waking until ten minutes before her shift. Then she'd stumbled around her cabin in a flurry of panic, struggling to put on a uniform still bulky and foreign to her.

And the tie—the stupid, miserable, goddamn *tie*—she'd spent nearly five minutes trying to figure the damn thing out, after having worn only neckerchiefs throughout her maritime career.

But once Esther had realized she was running out of time, she'd thrown the tie on the bed and flown out the door.

She thought she'd made it to the bridge on time.

She had been so *close*. But not close enough.

And now, as she walked solemnly alongside Murdoch with a heart full of humiliation, she couldn't stop worrying that she had disappointed him. Embarrassed him, even. Despite his foul attitude, Murdoch was still her superior and one of the highest-ranking officers aboard the ship. Of *course* she had wanted to impress him. And not only Murdoch, but the rest of her crewmates who doubted her. She'd wanted to prove she wasn't some worthless, harebrained girl who had no place working on a luxury liner— and she had failed spectacularly. The very realization was enough to shock her into shameful silence.

Quiet and subdued, Esther trudged after her superior as he climbed the steps to the stern deck. They spent nearly an hour fulfilling their duties on the aft docking bridge—checking the life rings for punctures, ensuring all equipment was in working order, and finally, deploying the Blue Ensign flag from the white railing along the stern. Murdoch ignored her the entire time, as if trying to pretend he didn't have a lady officer padding around after him. And when the time came for lifeboat inspections, Esther almost had to sprint down the boat deck as he marched away without her.

The sun rose as they assembled before Lifeboat No. 13, shedding a pale, silvery light across the rippling water. It was chilly, Esther noted, but not freezing—nothing compared to what awaited them in the North Atlantic. Board of Trade surveyors stood with their clipboards in hand, and beyond them lingered a small concourse of officers and seamen awaiting orders.

Murdoch broke away from Esther without so much as a word or a passing glance, so she stood between Moody and Lowe to watch the inspection unfold. After a while, Lowe seemed to grow bored with the proceedings. He leaned over to whisper to her, his thick Welsh accent scarcely audible over the creaking winches and booming shouts of Chief Officer Wilde.

"How's everything with ol' Murdoch?" he asked. "Not still sour about earlier, is he?"

Esther studied her superior officer, observing the way he roamed the deck and prepped the Welin davits with deft hands.

"I've been mulling it over, Mr. Lowe," she said. "And I've come to the conclusion that he hates me."

Lowe laughed. "Rubbish. Bit of an overstatement, don't you think?"

"What else would you call it, then? If not hatred?"

He pondered this. "Hmm. I'd say it's more of a pronounced dislike."

Esther gave him a flat, dull look. "Well, that's certainly a relief," she remarked sarcastically.

"Only joking, miss," Lowe teased. "Mr. Murdoch is a decent chap, but he's quite the professional if I've ever seen one. You being late set him off good and proper, all right, but he's not cruel. Bit strict, more like. Just make sure to keep your head down and do as he says. And when you're on watch with him this evening, remember two things: one, bridge operations are taken very seriously by White Star Line, so don't be surprised to find it quiet as a morgue. Especially under the command of someone like Murdoch." He nodded at the first officer before continuing, "Two, you'll likely be conducting celestial observations along with compass readings n' such, so try to brush up on your stars beforehand."

Esther bit her lip, suddenly uncertain. "Celestial observations?" she echoed. The skill had never been her strong point; even now, her thoughts raced as she struggled to remember all fifty-eight navigational stars and their constellations.

Polaris, she thought wildly, nose wrinkled up in concentration. *Vega, Regulus, Spica, Aludra—oh no, wait, that's Atria. Shit.*

Lowe smiled at her expression. "They can be proper tricky," he said, leaning even closer so that his voice was discernible over the noise of the davits. "But I could help you review 'em, if you'd like."

Esther glanced up in surprise. "Really?"

"Absolutely, miss. And judging by that befuddled look on your face, I'd wager you need all the help you can get."

"Oh, shush."

He grinned. "I've a spare nautical almanac and a few star charts that might be of some help. What d'you say? Lunch relief would be a perfect time to get to work."

Esther beamed at him, eyes shining with gratitude. "That would be wonderful, Mr. Lowe. I can't thank you enough."

Lowe opened his mouth to reply, but Wilde barked at him to man the frapping lines; Esther, too, was given the same task. She didn't hesitate to answer her chief.

"*Yes, sir!*"

The rope felt thick and heavy in her hands, but Esther was familiar with this sort of work. She tugged with all her might, the line sliding through her gloved grip as she helped Lowe and a handful of crew hoist the lifeboat to freedom. The men huddled around the deck watched her every move, a few sneering or shaking their heads in disbelief. But Esther kept at it, refusing to let their skepticism deter her. Even Murdoch had a narrowed gaze on his subordinate, and their eyes met for a half second before he glanced away again, busying himself with some supply list or another.

By the time the boat was swung out and ready on its falls, and she was red in the face from exertion, all junior officers except Esther were given oars and ordered to step aboard. She rounded on Murdoch, indignant, wiping the gleam of sweat from her brow.

"Why am I not going with them?" she demanded.

Murdoch arched one eyebrow.

"You want to be out there rowing, is that it?"

"*Yes,*" she said firmly. "I've done these drills before, sir. I know how to pull an oar; I can help."

But Murdoch did not seem convinced—and neither did he seem to care, for that matter.

"While I admire your enthusiasm, Miss Bailey," he said dryly, "we're unfortunately needed elsewhere." He started for the nearest stairwell, signaling with one gloved hand for Esther to follow. She did, albeit reluctantly, sparing a longing glance at the lifeboats as she went.

"First-class passengers are due to board in fifteen minutes' time," Murdoch explained as they walked. "We'll be taking their tickets on D Deck. You are to check the manifest for their name and provide them with the corresponding cabin number."

"Doesn't sound too difficult," Esther said confidently.

Murdoch shot her a stern glare. "Aye, and it won't be, so long as you avoid giving the passengers any sort of attitude, Miss Bailey. Do try and remain professional, won't you? I think you've already caused enough trouble for today."

Esther resisted the urge to slap him round the face as they filed down the stairs to D Deck Reception, crossing through the calm, empty quiet of a ship still awaiting her passengers. The reception room was enormous, and she gazed around in awe as they wove their way around wickerwork furniture and potted palms, their footsteps silenced by a sweeping carpet of pale emerald and persimmon. A massive piano sat in the far corner, its keys glossy and untouched, while elegant signage near the lifts read *D Deck* in gilt letters. Beyond the open shell door and its sloped gangway, Esther could see the dense, bustling crowds swelling along the waterfront. The rumble of a busy port reached her ears—honking horns, clattering horseshoes, jubilant yelps and chatter—and she stepped closer, captivated, staring out in surprise.

Good *God*, she had never seen so many people.

Thousands of them milled about in the bright sunlight, all from different walks of life: she glimpsed the elegant women dressed in jewels and day gowns that likely cost a fortune, and others who wore humble clothes of worn wool and tweed. An assortment of vehicles crawled their way through the throng, with polished motorcars weaving past horse-drawn carriages and lorries. Even a sleek locomotive whistled from its station beyond the quay, pistons hissing and steam billowing in the distance.

Electrical cranes hoisted machinery and a shiny new Renault into the air. Porters rushed to and fro, sorting through luggage and enormous mailbags bound for America, Ireland and France. Esther spotted families embracing in farewell, crewmen calling out for health inspections, and photographers cranking the handles of their cameras as they captured the magnificent steamer before them.

The anticipation was palpable, hovering in the crisp morning air like a dazzling mist. It was a marvelous sight, and Esther felt almost giddy as she watched all the commotion unfold before her.

"Have you finished ogling?" Murdoch demanded, impatiently thrusting a copy of the manifest into her hands.

"No," she answered honestly. "I've never seen anything like this before. There're so many people…It's incredible, sir."

"You'll get used to it," Murdoch said, his voice dismissive in a way that made her scowl. "Now, hurry along. There's work to be done, in case you've forgotten."

The boarding process was nothing short of tedious. It was the same "Name, sir?" or "Name, madam?" as a parade of first-class passengers streamed inside. Esther would take their ticket, mark their name on the manifest, and list off the cabin in which they were roomed. After about an hour of the same dull routine, she tried to entertain herself by silently guessing the cost of each woman's extravagant dress, or every gentleman's tailored suit. While most passengers didn't even look twice at her, a few stopped short, gawking as if she were a menagerie animal on display.

Esther paid them little mind; she was used to it by now. No use in letting their foul stares bother her, *especially* when they couldn't hold a candle to the scathing looks Murdoch so often threw her way.

"Next!" she called out into the din. "Right this way, please!"

A svelte woman wearing periwinkle-blue silks drifted forward next. Her hair gleamed like dark lacquer beneath the brim of a wide, ostrich-feathered hat, while her dress seemed to flow behind her in rippling waves. She was so beautiful that even Murdoch glanced twice at her; he was subtle about it, all right, but Esther didn't miss the way his eyes lingered on the woman's silky hair and elegant features. The seventh officer felt a peculiar emotion tighten within her stomach—something bitter like anger, but not quite. She ignored it, however, turning to ask, "May I have your name, madam?"

"Elisabeth Allen," the woman said politely, peering at Esther with mild interest. She was quiet for a moment before she mused aloud, "My goodness, I thought my eyes were deceiving me at first! But you truly are a lady—and a ship's officer, no less. How very peculiar. Are there more of you aboard, my dear?"

"It's just me, madam," Esther replied, distracted as she flipped through the manifest for the name Allen.

"Such a shame," the woman said. She sounded disappointed, and Esther glanced up from the manifest in surprise. "You never see women working aboard these ships, unless they're stewardesses of some sort. I daresay it's a pleasant change."

Esther beamed at her, both taken aback and elated. "Thank you, ma'am. Oh, yes, and—" She stole a quick glance down at the clipboard in her hands. "—you'll be in cabin B-5. Welcome aboard *Titanic*."

And with that, the woman passed her a smile and a warm nod before disappearing down the corridor.

Brighton had a saying when she was younger, that for every positive event that occurs, there will always come a negative. Life operated on a fragile balance, he said, always seeking a counterweight to avoid tipping the scales. And his words could not have been truer to Esther as the morning went on. For every kindly passenger she encountered, she had the misfortune of meeting a spiteful one in turn. But she kept a straight face, not yielding, and *never* letting any nasty remarks get under her skin.

Murdoch kept an eye on her throughout their shift, watching her, no doubt waiting for her to slip. But Esther was determined. She'd already disappointed her superior once today. She wasn't about to do it again.

A slim, middle-aged American in a dark traveling suit was next in line. Esther studied the enormous rings on his fingers and the solid-gold fountain pen tucked neatly into his breast pocket before offering a smile.

"Good morning, sir. May I have your name and ticket?"

Her question earned her a patronizing stare. "That won't be necessary, kid."

Esther hesitated. She glanced uncertainly at Murdoch, unsure whether to ask for his assistance. But he was busy dealing with some other fussy passenger, so she decided to take matters into her own hands.

Squaring her shoulders, Esther addressed the man with a calm, business-like bearing. "I beg your pardon, sir, but it *is* necessary. I'll need your name and your ticket for you to proceed beyond this point."

The passenger merely laughed. There was a dark amusement in his coal-black eyes, as if he found her words comical.

"And why would I hand my ticket to the likes you?"

"Because I'm an officer?" Esther suggested brazenly, before she could stop herself.

So much for professionalism, then.

He sneered as he looked her over. "Bullshit. You're a *woman*."

"Really?" Esther raised an eyebrow. "I hadn't noticed, sir. You have a keen eye."

"Keen enough to tell you're no officer," the man retorted. "Just a foolish little girl playing dress-up in her daddy's uniform. I won't have you handling my ticket, understand? So why don't you run along, back to the parlors and the kitchens and the shitters where you rightfully belong."

Esther bristled at him in a fury, her patience finally lost.

"Then I hope you enjoy your stay in Southampton," she snapped, "because you're not getting on this ship unless I get that ticket."

The man took a sharp step forward, his expression twisted with outrage as he loomed over her, but she held her ground.

"Is there a problem?"

Esther whirled around to see Murdoch making his way toward them, hands folded behind his back. Though he maintained an air of professionalism, his blue eyes were cutting as he looked between the angry passenger and his fuming subordinate.

Livid and snarling, the man rounded on Murdoch next. "What does it look like? This little *tramp* is not only disrespectful, she's stark raving mad. Seems to think she's an officer of some kind. I won't humor this sort of lunacy, my good man, so I'll have *you* see to my ticket instead."

He thrust the slip of paper forward, but Murdoch didn't even acknowledge it. His expression hardened to stone, and it was clear he didn't like hearing his subordinate referred to as tramp. Not one bit.

"I apologize, sir," he said dispassionately, not sounding very apologetic at all, "but you will need to go through Miss Bailey here for ticket processing. She is a qualified officer of this ship. And she will be the one to assist you this morning."

"Like hell she will," the man retaliated, storming forward to point one threatening finger in Murdoch's face. "She's not getting my ticket, and that's that."

Murdoch's jaw tightened. "Well," he said with a shrug, "I s'pose this means you won't be boarding the ship, then."

"I won't be—I *beg* your pardon?"

"I do believe I made myself quite clear, sir. You won't be boarding unless you hand her your ticket."

Esther grasped her hands behind her back, clenching them so tightly that if she hadn't been wearing gloves, her nails might've punctured skin. She was dumbfounded. Murdoch could have simply scorned her, checked the ticket for himself, and waved the quarrelsome passenger through. It would have been quick and effortless, and the man would have been placated within a matter of seconds. But Murdoch…he was actually *defending* her. By refusing to accept the ticket himself, he was essentially forcing the man to turn and acknowledge Esther as a standing officer.

"This is ludicrous!" the passenger seethed. "Give me your names at *once*. I shall inform White Star Line of your behavior, make no mistake of it!"

"As you like," Murdoch said idly. "First Officer William Murdoch—that's Murdoch with a 'ch' at the end, just so you're aware—and Seventh Officer Esther Anna Bailey. Please feel free to address your concerns to our headquarters at 30 James Street, Liverpool, England. I'm certain someone will set aside their most pressing of business matters to prioritize your…*issues*."

Though his face was flawlessly composed, Esther didn't miss the faint sarcastic sneer in his voice. She watched in astonishment as Murdoch returned his gaze to the manifest, flipping through its pages as if he couldn't be bothered by their conversation any longer.

"Now, if you're not going to present your ticket to my colleague," he said, "then I must ask you to kindly step aside. You're holding up the line."

The man hesitated, his ire faltering as he took in the impatient passengers twittering and tapping their feet behind him. With a withering glower of defeat, he wordlessly shoved his ticket into Esther's hands, and she scoured through the manifest for his name and cabin number, wanting him out of her sight as quickly as possible.

"Your cabin is C-110, Mister—" she started to say, but the passenger was already stalking down the corridor, muttering a string of heated curses under his breath. Esther didn't even register the slurs; she was too busy staring at Murdoch, her eyes almost glowing with gratitude. She wanted to speak with him, but the crowd of passengers had grown thick after the brief hiccup in the queue, so she was forced to turn her attention to them instead.

Nearly twenty minutes passed before there was a lull in the flow of people, and Esther finally managed to tell Murdoch, "Thank you."

He wasn't even looking at her; his blue eyes were fixed on the manifest in his hands. "For what?" he asked indifferently.

Esther stared at him in surprise. "For standing up for me," she said, her voice soft.

Murdoch glanced down at her, his face unreadable. "I wasn't doing it for you," he said curtly. "I was doing it to set an example. No passenger is allowed to talk to an officer in that manner, first-class or not. You let it happen once, Miss Bailey, and they'll end up disregarding your authority altogether."

She bit her lip. "Well, even so…thanks."

Their eyes met for a long moment. Too long, perhaps.

Then Murdoch sharply turned away, calling out to the passengers ambling up the gangway's brine-weathered wood.

"Next! Step forward, miss. Quickly, if you please."

Esther suddenly felt too hot beneath her greatcoat, the warmth rising from her neck all the way up to her freckled cheeks. Though she kept her expression nonchalant, she could still feel a peculiar curiosity work its way through her, as cool and bracing as the seawater billowing along the shore. It trickled into the cracks of her resolve and seeped its way into her bones—and before she knew it, she was staring at Murdoch again. Studying him, wondering what was going on behind those impassive blue eyes of his.

He was insufferable and patronizing more often than not—and yet he had come to her defense not once, but twice. First with the haughty tailor back in Southampton, and now with some unruly prick of a first-class passenger. Esther was bewildered. She'd thought she had Murdoch all figured out. She'd thought he was just some cold, ill-tempered officer who resented having her on the ship.

But standing beside him now, well…she wasn't so sure that was the case.

Murdoch did not seem to notice her inquisitive gaze, as he was busy waving forward the next retinue of first-class passengers. Esther dragged her attention away from him to study the new arrivals, noting their exquisite clothes and sophisticated poise. The woman at the head of the group looked to be the oldest, dressed in a plum-colored gown with a necklace of pearls and a high-necked lace collar of midnight-blue. Behind her trailed a younger woman who appeared to be her sister, given their identical cornflower-blue eyes and silvery blonde hair. The younger girl wore a walking dress of sweeping ivory and fitted lavender chiffon, her rosy lips astonishingly vivid beneath the brim of an enormous peacock-feathered hat. She walked with an air of refinement as she crossed the gangway, clinging to the arm of a tall gentleman at her side—a gentleman who looked oddly familiar to Esther, though she could not place where she might have seen him before.

Then he turned his head in her direction, and the breath whooshed right from her lungs.

Sonofabitch.

Esther glanced around the vestibule, frantic, wondering if she should shove Murdoch out of her way and make a break for it.

Of all the people to come aboard *Titanic* this morning, she would have never expected Callum Lockerbie—heir to the multimillion-dollar Lockerbie Oil empire—to be one of them.

And yet here he was, stepping across the gangway in a tailored suit of charcoal gray, his sharp hazel eyes marveling up at the steamer towering before him. His hair was sleek and dark beneath a bowler hat, while his gloved hand carried a glossy walking stick at his side. He still looked as ridiculously handsome as Esther remembered, if only a bit older. Even his old manservant, Slate, trailed along in his wake.

But there was something different about him. And it didn't have anything to do with the pretty blonde hanging on his arm.

Esther narrowed her eyes at Lockerbie, regarding his showy suit and sleek hair, wishing she'd ripped up the photograph sitting in her cabin— the one of him lounging along some oceanfront with her twin brothers. He was no longer the sickly boy she'd met at her father's hospital, weak and recovering from a bout of pneumonia. Nor was he the young man who caused all manner of mischief with her brothers, the three of them sneaking into town to flirt with the local girls on weekends, or nicking aged bourbon from her father's private stores. Lockerbie certainly wasn't the dashing teen who'd once laughed and pulled her into the store cupboard at his family's manor—and she wasn't the foolish girl who'd let his hands shift up her blouse in the darkness, roaming and straying where they shouldn't have.

They had shared a long, secretive kiss in that cramped little cupboard. Her first kiss. How odd it was to think they had once been so recklessly intimate. She remembered wanting to marry him afterward, for she was a naïve girl who thought she understood the complexities of love. But when she'd brought up marriage, Lockerbie had promptly dismissed it.

Your family's wealthy, Es, he'd told her, on the day he'd left California for Harvard. *But not wealthy enough.*

Looking at him now, however, Esther realized she felt nothing. No anger, no bitterness, no lingering heartache. She was stronger and wiser than the lovesick young girl who had once cried for days on end because she wasn't good enough for Callum Lockerbie. She had struggled and persevered to end up here, aboard the RMS *Titanic*, fulfilling her dream of working at sea.

So she remained where she stood, watching calmly as Lockerbie and his entourage entered the gleaming foyer.

"Names, please?" Murdoch asked the group.

"Lockerbie, Callum," came the smooth, drawling reply. "Florence and Fay Harlow ought to be listed under my name. Gideon Slate as well."

As Murdoch rifled through the manifest, Lockerbie swept his lidded eyes over Esther, regarding her with cool appraisal. But then he frowned.

"Booker?"

Esther offered him a thin half-smile. "Close, Mr. Lockerbie," she said. "But not quite."

Lockerbie stepped closer, peering underneath the brim of her cap to better see her face. Recognition flickered in his eyes as he registered her feminine voice, her long eyelashes, her full lips. She saw his shock, but it disappeared within seconds as he smoothly composed himself. He was always good at that.

"Esther Bailey," Lockerbie said at last, raising his brows as he looked her up and down. "Goodness, I didn't even recognize you. What in *God's* name are you wearing?"

"My uniform," Esther said shortly, trying to ignore the way Murdoch was watching her. "I'm employed as an officer aboard this ship." She stretched out her hand. "Tickets?"

Lockerbie blinked, as if trying to scatter away his incredulity. As he passed her the small stack of tickets, the older blonde at his side turned to Esther with disgust.

"And you *willingly* chose such a profession?" she demanded.

While her beady eyes were dark and reproachful, her younger sister was in every way her contrast, studying the seventh officer with unabashed curiosity.

Esther shrugged. "Why, yes madam," she said casually, enjoying the look of outrage spreading across the woman's face. "That's about the size of it."

"A female officer working the Unsinkable Ship." Lockerbie released a false laugh that bordered on derisive. "How...*astonishing*, Esther. I didn't even realize ladies were allowed to *do* such a thing."

They're also allowed to deck you in the face, Esther thought irritably. *Pompous bastard.*

Though she longed to speak her mind aloud, she forced herself to keep quiet, shuttering her raw anger behind a pearly smile. After nearly two hours of dealing with impolite passengers, her temper was damn near close to breaking, and she knew it was wise to keep her mouth shut altogether. *Especially* since Murdoch would only admonish her for speaking out of turn.

Or worse, she added silently to herself, remembering his earlier threat to chuck her overboard and into the sea.

Glancing down at the manifest, Esther found the names and listed off, "Your cabins are B-52, 54, and 56. Enjoy your stay aboard *Titanic*."

She waited for Lockerbie to leave with his boarding party. But he hesitated, smirking, his hard, calculating eyes lingering on her greatcoat and officer's cap.

"Don't take this the wrong way, my dear," he said lazily. "But I *don't* believe you're suited for this kind of sorry work."

Esther felt Murdoch stiffen at her side, and only then did she feel the first blaze of blinding anger. There was nothing "sorry" about this line of work. Seafaring was a proud, time-honored profession that took years of dedication and discipline to master. Something Lockerbie—with his sacks of cash and oil-backed inheritance—could *never* understand.

Rage thundered and crackled through Esther like a bolt of lightning as she met his callous gaze. Her leather gloves stretched and flexed as she balled her hands into fists. She could hear the blood roaring in her ears— could feel her heart slamming furiously against her ribcage.

"With all due respect, Mr. Lockerbie," she said with steely calm, "I disagree. Good day."

Lockerbie's lips thinned. But then he merely shrugged, as if the conversation was beneath him, and disappeared with the stunning blonde still hanging on his arm.

11:30

Another hour slipped past.

The sun was bright, the crisp air smelling of seawater and buzzing with excitement. Esther remained dutifully at her post the entire morning, watching the queue of passengers slow to a thin trickle. When there was no one left to board, the crewmen detached the gangways while Murdoch and another quartermaster closed the shell door with a final, resounding *slam*. Esther watched her superior officer hike himself up on the tips of his Oxfords, sealing the latch handles and sliding the wrought-iron gate shut. Only then did he turn to face his subordinate.

"Just sea and anchor detail left now, Miss Bailey," he said, and she was surprised to hear the keenness in his voice. "Follow me."

He led her up a narrow flight of stairs and out into the bright, blinding sun of high noon. Now that they were topside, Esther had a clear view of the quay, which was scarcely visible beneath an enormous sea of well-wishers and onlookers. Steam plumed from the funnels in great, deafening bursts of smoky white, blotting out the roar of the crowds. The atmosphere was joyous, lively—with passengers crammed all along the port side railings and promenades, cheering and waving in farewell. Esther scrambled after Murdoch as he moved aft, weaving his way through the jostling tide of people.

"Quickly, lass," he called over one shoulder, and she hurried faster, suddenly sweltering beneath her thick woolen greatcoat.

When they climbed the stairs to the stern at last, Murdoch left Esther to oversee the mooring lines and tugboat hawsers. There was no task for her here; she was simply meant to observe. And so she hung back by the cargo crane to watch Murdoch work, impressed by how swiftly he moved and how effortlessly he barked orders into the din.

"*Ready the stern lines!*" he commanded, Scottish burr bellowing hoarse above the clamor. "*Steady, lads!*"

Though Murdoch was much shorter than the tall, burly seamen assembled at the stern, there was still a masterful strength and confidence about him, and Esther could see exactly why he was an accomplished senior officer. Even with all the animosity and bad blood between them, she was *glad* to work under such a distinguished mariner. Murdoch had over twenty years of seafaring experience under his belt, after all. There was much he could teach her—and even more she could learn in return. All he had to do was stop being so *surly*, for Christ's sake, and actually give her a chance…

Pitman sidled up next to her, shielding his eyes from the sun. "Enjoying the view?" he asked cheerfully.

For one wild moment, Esther thought he was talking about Murdoch, since she had been staring at her superior officer for the better part of twenty minutes. But then she realized Pitman was merely referring to the wonderful sights before them—all the crowds and the crew and the glittering, blue-green water—and she almost laughed aloud at her ridiculousness.

"Well, Mr. Pitman," she said with a pleasant smile, "I could say it's incredible, but that would be the understatement of a lifetime, I think."

"Couldn't agree more, miss."

A faint, vibrating shudder followed his words, and Esther gasped aloud as she felt the engines rumble to life.

Pitman shot her a grin. "I do believe it's time."

She raced to the railing and gripped it tight, beaming as she gazed across the port. Her breath hitched as the steam whistle bellowed once more, signaling their departure. Murdoch called for the lines to be cast off, while Pitman rushed up the stairs to the docking bridge—and before she knew it, they were *moving*.

Esther grinned as she felt *Titanic* lurch forward, easing away from her berth with six—yes, *six*—goddamn tugboats to guide her. A collective cheer rose up from the crowds as they witnessed the Ship of Dreams set sail at last, the wind snapping at her Blue Ensign flag, the howl of her baritone whistle-horn rumbling through the air. She was unlike anything Esther had seen, so colossal and queenly as she parted the glass-smooth waves, dwarfing the ships along the quay with her propellers churning and foaming the water behind her.

Esther could scarcely contain her excitement. She was bouncing on the balls of her feet as she waved at everyone and everything in sight, completely disregarding the professional stoicism an officer on duty was meant to have.

"Goodbye!" she cried at the top of her lungs. "Farewell! *Au revoir! Auf Wiedersehen!*"

Despite the tremendous noise flooding the port, Esther caught a series of heavy footfalls along the deck. She turned to see Murdoch stepping toward her, his hands clasped behind his back and eyes a brilliant blue in the crisp sunlight. Her smile vanished at his approach, and she quickly stood at attention, knowing fully well that her lack of a dignified composure would only warrant his criticism.

But he didn't reprimand her, much to her surprise. Instead, he merely nodded.

"At ease, Miss Bailey."

Esther stared at him, stunned he was actually speaking to her in a civil tone for once. She relaxed slightly, rolling back her shoulders and managing a small smile as he joined her at the rail.

They were quiet for a long while, staring out across the foaming backwash as the distance between the ship and Southampton grew, and the waters turned deeper, bluer. Esther didn't know how much time passed before she decided to break the silence.

"What are you thinking, sir?"

Her question seemed to catch Murdoch by surprise. He studied her for a long moment before answering thoughtfully, "That days like today make me glad I chose this job." There was no animosity in his voice. No acerbic wit. Just a soft, meaningful honesty that made her stare. "You?"

Esther closed her eyes. Strands of hair had escaped her cap and were now whisking about in the wind, but she paid it little mind. She stood very still, drinking in the saltwater air and savoring the roar of parting waves, the cries of joyful crowds, the hiss of escaping steam.

She thought today was one of the happiest moments of her life.

Truly, she did.

And that was exactly what she told him, only moments before she heard an ear-splitting *crack* like a gunshot, and *Titanic* gave a shuddering, unexpected jolt beneath her feet.

TEN

INVITATION

April 10, 1912 | 12:10

NOTHING COULD HAVE prepared Esther for the screams that followed, cleaving through the cool sea air and shattering the joyous calm.

Her eyes snapped open, and there was a split moment where she and Murdoch simply stared at one other, equal parts wary and mystified. But Esther watched her superior officer collect himself within seconds, the bemused look on his face darkening to urgency at once. He sped off without a word, greatcoat whirling behind him, blue eyes sharpened with a seriousness she'd never seen before.

"Mr. Murdoch!"

She shouted his name as she hurried after him, desperate to keep pace with his brisk, fleet-footed strides.

Murdoch didn't go very far, much to her relief. He clambered up the ladder to the aft docking bridge, pausing only to offer Esther his gloved hand. She didn't give the gesture any thought; she merely clasped his fingers tight and without hesitation, letting him hoist her up on the platform with him. They stood together, Pitman at their side, looking out across the frothed inlet waters—and Esther had to clench her teeth to keep from cursing at the sight before her.

An enormous ocean liner had broken from its moorings along the quayside, steel hawsers snapped and frayed, hemp cables dangling limply down its hull. Esther watched, breathless with shock, as the damn ship came jutting *straight* for them, careening its way across *Titanic*'s foaming backwash as though dragged by an invisible undercurrent.

"The propellers," Murdoch said slowly at her side. "Her engines will have to be run full astern."

His voice was astonishingly calm, as if speaking over a cup of morning tea. He didn't even bat an eye despite the massive steamer closing in on them, dragged along by the churn of silt and seawater. Esther was surprised by his cool professionalism. But then again, she supposed officers didn't have time to bow to their emotions during times of crisis. Even Pitman kept relatively controlled, save for a flicker of unease in his watchful eyes.

"I'll call to the tugs nearby," the third officer said, snagging a megaphone tucked away near the equipment. "See if they can help."

"Aye." Murdoch started for the telephone with a nod. "I'll send word to the bridge, then." His eyes lingered on Esther as he passed, and he added, "Head to the port rail and keep an eye on that liner, lass. Call out to me the *moment* it comes too close. Understood?"

"Yes, sir," Esther answered at once.

She scurried down the ladder, picking her way through the swell of crewmen crammed along the port-side rails. Esther was too short to see above their towering shoulders, so she kept pushing to the front, determined and willful, Murdoch's order still ringing in her mind. But when she tried to squeeze her way past one of the heavier seamen, he took one look at her and shoved her away like some bothersome child. She lost her balance, toppling down to the deck and landing on her hands and knees, *hard*.

"Sod off, kitten," he growled. "This ain't a place for the likes of you."

Hunched over the damp, freezing deck with the tangle of limbs surrounding her from all sides, Esther was almost too shocked to breathe. Her palms were sore from where she'd caught her fall; had it not been for her gloves, she might have chafed the skin away. She felt a gut-wrenching nausea billow up her throat as the cold shock gave way to hurt, her breaths catching, threatening to turn to uncontrollable heaves—

Until she realized Murdoch was watching her.

Even though he stood high up on the docking bridge with the telephone at his ear, he only had eyes for his subordinate.

And as their gazes met, Esther felt something shift inside her. It was enough to drag her away from her own emotions and back to the crisis at hand, her resolve fortified to steel as she scrambled to her feet. She couldn't allow any shipmate to treat her in such a demeaning manner. She was an *officer*, for God's sake. Like Pitman and Murdoch, she was entitled to respect, wasn't she? And if she had to fight for it, well…so be it, then.

Esther stormed forward, defiant, glowering at the brutish seaman and the dark, oily pits of his eyes.

"Do you not see my uniform?" she demanded. "Disrespect me like that again, sailor, and I'll damn well make sure you're unemployed by the time we reach Cherbourg." Hair frizzed and eyes wild, she shoved her way past him. "Now get out of my way!"

Esther didn't care if the man was angry at her, and neither did she care if Murdoch was still watching. She kept pushing forward until she finally reached the rail, clenching it with her sore hands and squinting her eyes against the salty spray. Far below, the massive liner drew closer by the second, whisked along by turbid wash of sea. SS *New York* read the chipped white lettering along its hull. Pitman's voice bled through the megaphone further aft, beckoning to the boats in the distance, and before long, one of the larger tugs mercifully set out to help.

Everything seemed to happen so quickly afterwards. *Titanic* reversed her engines, running them full astern just as Murdoch had predicted. The nearest tugboat threw a line to the *New York* and steered it away, chugging along at full steam. And an hour later, after all was said and done, a collective sigh of relief rose from the crew as *Titanic* steamed onward, unscathed and ready to begin her journey once more.

Pitman was laughing at the ordeal by the time the officers were relieved for lunch, the three of them strolling down the boat deck with Esther and a quiet Murdoch trailing behind.

"Can you believe this bloody ship?" he chuckled. "Hardly even left *port* and already she's making trouble." He shook his head. "Blimey. What'll she try to hit next, I wonder?"

"Five bucks says it's a Cunard ship," Esther chipped in, and Pitman snorted aloud with laughter. Murdoch, however, didn't even crack a smile. He was unusually quiet, watching the tides with a small, thoughtful crease upon his brow. But Esther paid it little mind. Better silence than having to deal with his usual antagonism, anyway.

When they came upon the officers' mess, Esther tipped her cap in polite farewell and continued walking. Pitman raised his brows after her. "You're not hungry?" he asked, sounding almost outraged.

"Oh, trust me, I am," Esther assured him. "I need to have a short word with my brother first." She hadn't spoken to Booker since yesterday, what with their respective duties and busywork they'd seen to before setting sail. But with *Titanic* now comfortably adrift, turbines and steam engines running smooth as silk, Esther figured she ought to seek him out. Starting down the promenade, she called over her shoulder, "I'll join you in a moment!"

But she had barely taken another step before a quiet, authoritative voice stopped her in her tracks.

"Not so fast."

Esther turned to see Murdoch looking expectantly at her, hands hooked behind his back.

"Sir?" she asked hesitantly, bracing herself for the worst.

"I saw you fall." His voice was indifferent, but something else lingered in his eyes as he stepped closer. "Are you hurt?"

Her cheeks burned, but she still met his gaze. "No, sir. I'm fine."

"You're sure?"

"*Yes*, sir," she insisted, more firmly this time.

Murdoch straightened his cuffs in an aloof manner, the peculiar look in his eyes vanishing at once. "Good," he said, his voice short. "Because God forbid we have an injured officer on board—least of all an officer who's not even qualified to be here in the first place."

And there it is, Esther grumbled to herself, unable to suppress a scowl. *Typical snark.*

She glowered at Murdoch as he turned toward the mess again, clasping the handle with one hand. But then he paused, keeping his eyes fixed on the doorknob as he quietly spoke.

"I can find the name of that sailor, if you'd like," he told her. "The one who knocked you down."

What, so you can congratulate him? Esther thought sourly, unable to keep the cynicism from her thoughts. She'd rather throw herself into the sea than accept his help, so she lifted her chin in cold defiance. "That won't be necessary, sir."

He shrugged. "If you insist," he said idly, disappearing into the mess hall without a parting glance.

As the door swung shut behind him, and Esther started down the boat deck in a huff, she found herself thinking of that peculiar look in his eyes. Found herself wondering if, perhaps, there *might* have been a sliver of concern hidden beyond the emotionless fortress of his gaze.

But then she dismissed it—scrubbed it from her mind, even—too jaded and too cynical to think her superior officer might have cared for her well-being after all.

17:30

Murdoch awoke to his alarm clock once again, its shrill noise splitting in his ears and rousing him from a short-lived nap.

Although the first officer was quick to silence it, he did not bother to rise to his feet, as he usually would have done. He merely lay in the comfort of his bed for a long while instead, staring up at the ceiling as the fading sunset washed his cabin in rusty, reddish-gold light.

Images from this morning kept flitting across his mind, cascading through his thoughts in a flourish of color and noise: the joyous cries of passengers waving along the rails in farewell; the roar of blue-green water parting before *Titanic*'s hull, sweeping aside to admit her graceful mass; and of course, the collision they had so narrowly avoided, thanks to quick-thinking and the timely help of the tugboats surrounding them.

But there was something *else* Murdoch couldn't stop thinking about. One single, ruddy image that refused to leave his thoughts as he lay in bed, blinking up at the ceiling.

It was the sight of Bailey standing at the stern, gazing across the foaming backwash with the wind stirring her hair across her freckled face.

Simple though it was, there had been a spirited glow of excitement and wonder in her eyes that Murdoch couldn't seem to forget. He didn't think he'd ever seen the girl so happy, in all the days he since he came to know her. And in some way, that look on her face had been reminiscent of his youthful self. Murdoch could still recall his first transatlantic voyage more than twenty years ago, when he was a mere fifteen-year-old apprentice working on a barque bound for San Francisco. He could close his eyes and almost *feel* those past emotions of awe and joy and nervous anticipation sweeping through him. Bailey had reminded him of those sentiments today, as she gazed earnestly out at the sea awaiting them.

Even now, he couldn't stop dwelling on what she'd told him at the stern, her words so soft-spoken, he had to lean closer just to hear them.

"Honestly? This is one of the happiest moments of my life, sir. I don't think I'll ever forget it."

Her response had been so heartfelt and so damn *familiar* that he could still feel it resonate within him now, making him wonder if they were truly alike after all. Seafaring was not only in his blood, but in his heart; perhaps it lingered in hers as well.

Murdoch pondered this as he clambered out of bed, rewound his Westclox, and lumbered to the washbasin. He spent a good five minutes splashing icy water on his face, hoping the cold shock might bring him a semblance of normalcy—or, at the very least, drag him back to his senses.

But the image of Bailey kept cropping up again and again, until he was gripping the sides of the washbasin with white knuckles. It was like a wave that refused to quit, quick and constant as it swept along the shores of his troubled mind. There was some foreign, mystifying sensation stirring within him now. He could feel it crackling along his nerves as he dried his face, ran a comb through his short hair, and pulled on the components of his uniform once more. Even the memory of a defiant, red-faced Bailey scrambling to her feet after being shoved to the ground was mercilessly etched into his mind.

These thoughts were unavoidable, no matter how hard he tried to cast them away.

And that worried him.

It means nothing, he tried to reassure himself, standing before his mirror and staring hard at the orderly man looking back at him. *And she means nothing. Remember that.*

Once he was fully dressed—tie impeccably straight and brass buttons fastened along the front of his greatcoat—Murdoch left his cabin and made his way down the long corridor. A quick glance at his pocket watch told him they would reach the deepwater port of Cherbourg in less than an hour's time. There they would drop anchor, and he and Bailey would help more than two hundred passengers aboard.

He found himself glancing at her cabin as he passed, wondering whether he ought to check and see if she was awake. Murdoch was *very* nearly tempted to make his way to the bridge without her. But the memory of her tardiness from earlier this morning was fresh in his mind, and he sighed, stepping forward to knock on her door.

"Miss Bailey?"

Murdoch kept his voice at a low murmur, lest someone see him standing before her cabin, rousing her like some sort of dutiful nanny. He didn't think he could stomach the shame. "Miss Bailey," he called softly once more. "Are you decent?"

Still, no response. No indication she might have heard him. Murdoch sighed again, and although all instincts shouted at him not to do so, he tried the handle. Locked.

Probably still snoozing, he thought scathingly. *Damn near has to be.*

"Esther *Bailey?*" Murdoch repeated, his voice now irritable. He rapped his knuckles on the door once again, louder this time, no longer caring who might see.

"I see you've finally learned how to knock, sir."

The words almost made him jump out of his skin. Staggering slightly, Murdoch spun around to see Bailey standing right behind him in the corridor, looking innocent and nonchalant as if she'd been there the entire time. She wore an amused look as she regarded his startled expression and wide eyes, a cup of coffee nestled in her gloved hands.

He blinked at her for a moment, surprised to see how *different* she looked in comparison to her disheveled appearance earlier. It was almost like night and day. Her uniform was impressively tidy, collar straight and jacket carefully buttoned at the waist, and Murdoch was taken aback by how well the ensemble fit her wiry frame. Her eyes were sharp and attentive, no drowsiness in sight, and it looked as if she'd run a comb through her hair this time. She was the image of a proper officer, everything from her cap down to her polished shoes. The only thing out of place seemed to be her tie, which looked as though it were knotted by a three-year-old. Murdoch tried not to snort at the lumpy mess of a knot as he straightened up.

"Aye," he said with indifference. "And you've finally learned how to wake up on time. I must say, I'm impressed."

She brushed off his sarcasm with little effort. "Not nearly as impressed as I am," she quipped coolly. There was a playful smirk on her face, and for one terrifying moment, Murdoch wondered if perhaps she was flirting with him. "Actually *knocking* before entering a room? I didn't think you had it in you, sir."

Murdoch swallowed, trying not to think of the night he'd barged inside the lavatory and found her in a state of undress. But he could still feel his cheeks warm, and he prayed he wasn't red in the face.

"How else was I going to make certain you wouldn't be late to your shift a second time?" he demanded, suddenly on the defensive.

"You could trust me." She toyed with the edge of her glove, no longer witty, her voice quiet but earnest. "I meant what I said earlier, sir. I won't be tardy again, so long as I'm on this ship and in your charge."

"That so?" Murdoch arched one disbelieving eyebrow. "Well, we have a *long* voyage ahead of us, Miss Bailey. There's still seven more days left at sea for you to disappoint me."

"Or seven more days to prove you wrong," she snapped back.

The fire had returned to her eyes, blazing green and defiant, but Murdoch didn't mind. He was actually *relieved* to see her attitude again. It was just another reminder that she was his irritatingly brazen subordinate and nothing more—no matter what his unbidden thoughts were trying to convince him.

"We'll see," Murdoch said shrewdly. "I'll be holding you to your word till we arrive in New York. Do well to keep that in mind, lass."

A short silence fell over the officers as Bailey seethed, looking as if she was barely holding back her rage. Murdoch felt the tension sizzling between them yet again, but he kept to business as he said, "We're due to reach Cherbourg soon. But we still have some time before we're needed at the starboard gangways. About half an hour, I imagine." His eyes traveled to the coffee cup in her hands. "I take it you've already been to the mess hall?"

She was still glaring at him. "I have," she said through gritted teeth.

"So what are you still doing in the officers' quarters?"

Bailey scowled at his accusatory tone. "If you must know, I was hoping to find Mr. Lowe, sir."

"Lowe?" Murdoch echoed, surprised. "What do you need him for?"

Her anger with him seemed to dissipate, replaced by mild puzzlement as she explained, "Well, I thought he said he was on duty this evening, but I didn't see him on the bridge." She lifted the mug brimming with dark liquid. "I made some coffee in the mess and figured I might as well bring him some. He was kind enough to help me review some celestial charts earlier, so I thought this would be a good way of saying thanks."

Murdoch stiffened, an unexpected twinge of displeasure prickling at his skin. He didn't know what to make of it, so he quickly cleared his throat.

"How very thoughtful," he said sardonically. "But I do believe Mr. Lowe had the afternoon watch. So he's either finishing his rounds or else asleep in his cabin at the moment."

"Dammit." Her face fell, but then she gave a good-natured shrug. "Well, I'd be lying like a dog if I said I didn't need more of this stuff." Lifting the mug to her lips, Bailey downed a quick drink of coffee before starting down the corridor. "I'll be out on the boat deck until our shift," she called blithely over her shoulder. "Wouldn't mind a bit of fresh air. See ya 'round six-thirty, sir."

Murdoch watched her go, studying her short hair and the sight of her lean frame in an officer's uniform. He knew he ought to let her leave. Ought to start for the mess hall on his own accord and let the two of them go their separate ways. So he couldn't understand why he called her back.

"Wait, Miss Bailey. A moment, please."

She stopped short at once.

"Sir?" Her eyes were wary, almost, as if she expected him to reprimand her right then and there.

With a deep breath, Murdoch clasped his hands behind his back and chose his next words carefully. "I was thinking coffee doesn't sound half bad this evening," he said, willing his voice to remain pleasant. "And if there's any left in the mess hall, I wouldn't mind a cup of my own."

He almost couldn't believe what he was saying. But he was only being *friendly*, was he not? There was no harm in with sharing a drink with a fellow officer. He would do the same with Wilde or Lightoller—or any other crewmate, for that matter. The woman standing before him was certainly no different.

He'd expected Bailey to react to his offer with surprise—or skepticism, perhaps—so he didn't understand why she smiled at him, her expression shifting to curiosity.

"I thought you only liked tea," she remarked.

Murdoch frowned. "No? What could have possibly given you that idea?"

"Well," Bailey said with a crafty grin, tucking one stray strand of hair behind an ear, "it's *all* I've ever seen you drink, sir. Tea with milk and one lump of sugar, if I recall correctly."

"I didn't realize you were so observant, Miss Bailey, well done."

She shrugged at his deadpan tone. "It's just something I noticed. And it's not only you, sir. It's the entire crew. I didn't even think there *was* anything but Earl Gray and English Breakfast in the mess till I rummaged around and finally found a can of grounds. Still sealed and untouched, of course." Bailey smirked, her eyes glittering mischievously at him. "But I suppose I shouldn't be surprised. You British sure love your tea, don't you?"

Murdoch raised his brows, wondering if she was taking the piss. "And you Americans sure love your stupid preconceptions," he said dully.

Bailey dissolved into hearty laughter, which only made Murdoch even more uncomfortable. "I know you drink more than just tea, sir," she said, amused. "You do know I'm merely teasing, right? I'm not *that* simple-minded!"

"Could've fooled me, all right."

She snorted. "Gee, thanks. Charming as ever, aren't you?"

Murdoch said nothing at this. He regarded her with wary eyes as she stepped toward him—a little too close for his liking, to be honest—but he held his ground. Her sharp, seawater-green eyes were fixed on his, but there was no anger or frustration in their depths. Just a gleam of amusement that appeared the moment he'd asked her for coffee.

"Look," she said simply, "if you're done being an ol' curmudgeon, I'm willing to brew you a cup. I don't think there's any coffee left in the mess, but I can make you another batch, if you'd like."

Murdoch hesitated. Now that she was no longer irritated with him, her breezy, good-natured humor was starting to throw him off, and he wondered if perhaps he should keep his distance after all.

But then he swallowed his misgivings in a stroke of boldness and gestured down the corridor.

"Very well. After you, Miss Bailey."

They were quiet as they left the officers' quarters and crossed the boat deck, which was awash in the brilliant light of a setting sun. *Titanic* was still on course, gliding south to Cherbourg. It was much colder now, the day's warmth all but disappearing beneath chilly winds blowing in from the sea, and Murdoch was glad he'd thought to pull on his greatcoat for this evening. He watched Bailey stare out across the deck, clearly transfixed by the ocean rippling beneath a glaze of golden light, and the same look he'd seen on her face earlier this morning suddenly returned. It was an expression of awe and sheer adoration, something he was certain only those whose hearts belonged to the sea could truly understand.

"I could get used to this view," she murmured, seemingly more to herself than to Murdoch at her side.

Sunset light surrounded her like liquid fire, glowing across her freckled skin, but Murdoch tried not to notice as he led her aft, crossing through the gated partition dividing the officers' promenade from that of first-class. They had no sooner stepped beyond it when a familiar voice called out to them, rising above the rush of sea spray and salt-ridden wind.

"Hey, Esther! Mr. Murdoch, sir!"

Murdoch turned to see Bailey's tall, handsome brother strolling toward them, arms laden with a stack of rolled blueprints. He was not alone, either; a second, shorter man walked alongside him, donned in a fine herringbone cloak with his salt-and-pepper hair combed into sleek waves. Murdoch recognized Mr. Thomas Andrews, and he tipped the brim of his cap in polite greeting.

"Why, good evening Mr. Murdoch!" Andrews called merrily. He gave Murdoch a firm handshake before turning to Bailey with a curious smile. "And *this* must be Esther. Your brother has told me a great deal about you these last few days. How delightful it is to finally make your acquaintance."

Bailey rushed forward, nearly shoving a disgruntled Murdoch aside in her eagerness to wring the shipwright's hand.

"And you as well, Mr. Andrews," she said breathlessly, unable to contain her excitement. "This ship of yours is truly a masterpiece, sir. I've never seen anything quite like it."

"You're too kind, Esther." Andrews gave a humble dip of his head. "My men and I have built a good, sound ship; I like to think she has many years at sea ahead of her."

Booker stole a proud glance at his mentor. "Undoubtedly, sir," he said with confidence, and Andrews smiled fondly at him. "*Titanic* is quite the engineering feat. I daresay she's your finest work yet." Turning to Murdoch, he added, "I'm glad I caught you, Mr. Murdoch. I never had a chance to formally thank you for helping my sister with her fittings back in Southampton. That was very gracious of you, and we are both grateful for your assistance. Aren't we, Esther?"

Bailey didn't seem to want to look at her superior officer. It was as if the memory that day had doused her in an embarrassed silence, and she kept her eyes downcast, the color rising high in her cheeks.

"Exceptionally grateful," she mumbled.

Booker nodded. "Which is why we would be honored if you would dine with us tomorrow evening—"

The words barely left his lips before his sister inhaled a sharp intake of breath. Everyone looked at her, and she quickly turned away, covering her gasp behind a hasty cough. Booker shot her a scornful look, but Andrews didn't seem to mind.

"It would be marvelous to have you attend, Mr. Murdoch," the shipwright said brightly. "Officer Wilde and Captain Smith will be present as well, and I am certain the guests would love to hear of your experiences working with our first and finest woman officer." He nodded at Bailey with a warm smile.

Murdoch was at a loss for words, his thoughts winding and creaking like unoiled clockwork. He simply couldn't fathom the grueling thought of dining with the glittering decadence of high society—and with *Bailey* at his side, no less. While the captain and chief officer were expected to dine in the First-Class Saloon from time to time, it was a formality Murdoch still had yet to experience, and he certainly was in no hurry to change that.

His eyes slid to Bailey, noting the slouch in her shoulders and the small, disappointed crease of her brow. While her brother stood before him with bright eyes and a benevolent smile, his sister was his stark contrast; any witty humor she'd displayed earlier was now eclipsed by unabashed chagrin, and it was clear she did not want him to attend. Murdoch didn't blame her. He had been nothing but cold and dismissive since the day they were first introduced. Perhaps if he'd been kinder to her, in ways Lowe and Wilde and Moody already were, *she* would be the one asking him to dinner. Not her brother.

The thought made him weary, and he was quick to clear his throat. "That's very kind of you, Mr. Bailey," he said quietly. "But I must respectfully decline."

He didn't miss Bailey's soft sigh of relief. Andrews looked surprised, but Booker wasn't willing to take no for an answer.

"Please," he said earnestly. "I *must* insist. You've been a great help to my kin, Mr. Murdoch; it would be a pleasure to have you dine with us. Even the captain is looking forward to having you there," he added, and Murdoch bit back a curse. "So what do you say? Six o'clock tomorrow? That way you and Esther will have time to return to your watches later in the evening."

Murdoch could see no way out of the corner he now found himself in; he couldn't even muster up a good enough excuse, for God's sake. Teeth gritted and fists clenched, he merely said, "Of course. My thanks, Mr. Bailey. I look forward to being there."

He turned to his subordinate, who wore a look of outrage and disbelief likely mirroring his own. "Well," he said stiffly, "we're needed at the gangways in a half hour, so I do believe Miss Bailey and I must be on our way."

Andrews nodded in farewell before addressing Bailey. "It was a pleasure meeting you, young Esther."

"And you, Mr. Andrews," she said, smiling as she looked into the shipwright's kindly eyes. But her expression turned cold when she rounded on her brother. Murdoch sensed there were some colorful words she wanted to say, but she merely grumbled out a goodbye.

"See you."

"Have a *wonderful* shift," Booker called cheerfully. His eyes lingered on her wardrobe as she turned away, and he teased after her retreating back, "But be sure to sort out that necktie of yours first, ya mangy hooligan. Looks like you tied it with both eyes shut."

Bailey said nothing at the jest, and Murdoch could almost feel the heat of her ire scorch him as she stormed away, sloppy tie, short temper and all.

ELEVEN

CHERBOURG

April 10, 1912 | 08:10

THE SKIES DEEPENED to shades of rose and indigo as Esther marched aft, trying to ignore the first officer strolling quietly beside her.

She drew in slow, deep breaths to steady herself, but the anger within her was far too strong, tearing through her like the icy darkness of a savage maelstrom. Esther was angry at her brother. Angry she was now forced to keep company with first-class patrons who cared only for their luxuries and lofty incomes. And *angry* Booker had extended the invitation to her superior officer without even discussing it with her beforehand.

Esther still didn't know what to make of Murdoch. She was grateful for the ways he had helped her so far, sticking up for her in front of unkindly people and passengers. She'd even had a bit of fun exchanging witty banter with him only moments ago. But the very notion of *dining* with the man—when already she despised that first-class realm of glamour and gentry and lousy social graces—was frustrating enough to darken her mood entirely.

Would Murdoch find some way to ridicule her in front of the guests? He had certainly spent a great deal of time scolding and belittling her, so why would tomorrow evening be any different?

At least Chief Officer Wilde would be there, with all his charm and paternal kindliness. As would her brother, whom she knew wouldn't stand for any sort of cruelty. The dinner wouldn't be *too* much of a chore, Esther reasoned. But still, she couldn't help but scour her thoughts for a last-minute excuse.

She could feign seasickness. Or a stomach virus, perhaps. *Anything* to keep from dining with the foul-tempered officer at her side.

She couldn't bear to look at him as they slipped inside the mess hall, leaving the velvety hiss of parting seawater behind them. The room was empty and dark, save for one or two lit bulbs that sent yellow light pooling above the countertops. Esther was about to make for the kettle when a hand caught her shoulder and pulled her back.

"Wait."

She turned and found herself facing Murdoch in the darkness. He was so close she could almost count the faint freckles scattered along his nose and broad jaw.

"Your brother's right, you know," he murmured, almost to himself. And then he held out his hand expectantly. "Tie."

"Sorry?"

"Hand me your *tie*, Miss Bailey."

Her anger with him still burned strong, threatening to boil over as she snapped, "I don't need your help, sir. I can fix it on my own."

"Nonsense." Murdoch's soft, Scottish tone was remarkably calm. "Judging by that right awful mess hanging about your neck, you've probably never tied one in your life, have you?"

Esther glowered at him, but Murdoch didn't seem to notice as he peeled off his leather gloves and stuffed them into his coat pocket. She studied him inquiringly, and he explained, "Easier with bare hands."

Wordlessly, grudgingly, she unloosed her tie and offered the ends to him, the bulk remaining in place around her neck. He was quiet as he worked, his eyes fixed on the dark silk fabric in his hands, his face unreadable. Esther kept very still, trying to ignore how close they stood to each other, and how she could distinctly catch his smell of aftershave. It was subtle, she thought. Something like sandalwood or spices. She couldn't quite place her finger on it. But it was surprisingly *nice*, and she didn't mind it all the same.

His hands made another loop, then another tug. And all the while, Esther wondered if he could hear her heartbeat pounding in her chest. She gripped her hands tightly behind her back, fidgeting with the corner of one glove and praying she didn't look too nervous. She had never been this close to him before, and the narrow distance between them was nothing short of awkward and uncomfortable. Her eyes raced around the room, almost desperately avoiding his face before settling on his hands instead. Esther studied them, inspecting the callouses along his palms, and the faint scar cut along one weathered knuckle. Signs of a man who made his living through hard work, not through the softness of sorting bills and pushing papers.

But then she couldn't help it. She snuck a look at Murdoch's ring finger and was surprised to find it bare.

He isn't married? Esther thought wonderingly. And then she chided herself. *Oh, for Christ's sake. Why do I even care...?*

As Murdoch slid the wider end of the tie through its second loop, taking care not to bump the heat of her neck, he said quietly, "You should know I don't want to attend the dinner any more than you do, lass."

She finally looked up at him, but their eyes did not meet; his still lingered on the tie.

"Why did you agree to it, then?" she asked.

"I'm not so sure." His hands continued to work around her neck, swift and surprisingly gentle. "Your brother is a kind man. I s'pose I didn't want to disappoint him." He paused his tie-tying, one hand resting softly on her collarbone, head tilted to one side. "But it seems I've disappointed someone else in turn, haven't I?"

Her cheeks bloomed pink at the implication of his words.

"I've no idea what you're talking about, sir."

"Aye, right." His thin smile was disbelieving. Weary, almost. "I'm afraid you lie just as poorly as you knot ties, Miss Bailey."

Esther met his steady gaze, her stomach twisting with unease. Murdoch knew she didn't want him at the dinner; it could not have been plainer on his face. But could he blame her, honestly, after all the quarreling and animosity and utter bullshit existing between them? She wanted nothing to do with William Murdoch. There was no one else on God's green earth who seemed to get on her nerves more than him— which was a goddamn astounding *feat* considering they'd only known each other for less than a week now.

But even so, Esther couldn't stop her heart from flooding with guilt as she looked into his hooded eyes. It was wrong of her to take her frustrations out on him, and even more foolish to jump to conclusions over what might happen tomorrow night. For all she knew, he might very well behave himself. Shouldn't she be willing to give him a chance?

Esther was about to muster up an apology when the door behind them banged open, and the words caught like sand in her throat.

Lamps flared to life, erasing the shadows in the mess and washing Murdoch and Esther in golden light.

They turned to see Wilde strolling into the room, whistling with a plate of black pudding in hand. But upon seeing the two officers standing so close together, he stopped dead in his tracks.

"Am I interrupting something?"

Murdoch was quick. "Not at all," he said mildly. "I was merely helping Miss Bailey here with her tie." His deft hands tightened the knot, sliding it upward until it rested against her slender throat. She felt his fingers brush her skin there before he pulled away, and she swallowed, a sudden, inexplicable heat pooling across her face.

"Not too tight, is it?" Murdoch asked.

Christ, she couldn't even look at him. "No, sir," she mumbled, cheeks still burning like a wildfire. "It's fine."

Wilde stalked toward her, cigarette hanging from his crooked mouth, platter of sausages in hand. "Let's have a look, then," he said gruffly, leaning forward to inspect the tidy knot now looped around her neck. Esther kept still, not sure whether to laugh, and when her eyes slid to Murdoch, she saw him shaking his head.

"Hmm…" Wilde scrunched up his gray eyes tight. "An admirable effort, mate," he said. "But I can definitely do better."

Murdoch laughed aloud at this, and Esther stared at him in astonishment. Smiles were rare enough for the first officer—but hearing him laugh was even rarer.

"Shove it up your arse, won't you?" Murdoch snorted, knocking one fist against Wilde's broad shoulder. "Don't think I asked for your opinion anyhow, eh? Ya dafty." He tugged on his leather gloves before reaching into the folds of his coat for his pocket watch. Only after checking the time did he turn to Esther, his smile fading.

"Well, Miss Bailey. Much as it pains me to say, I don't think we'll have enough time to brew your coffee this evening."

"I thought not. You seem pretty darn cut-up about it, though, sir."

"Devastated."

Esther glowered at his dry retort; it was as if those last quiet minutes in the darkness of the mess hall had never happened, and they were back to their usual tongue-in-cheek banter. She watched Murdoch cross the room, calling over his shoulder, "There's tea ready on the kettle here—allow me to pour a quick cup, and we can be on our way."

With a wordless nod, Esther settled at the table beside Wilde and listened to him share an amusing story about his youngest daughter. Something about the time she'd caught newts in the mossy little pond beyond their home and tried to keep them as pets. Wilde was smiling as he recalled his wife's horror when she came home.

"And there they were, swimming in the tub, nearly a *dozen* of the little buggars." He laughed in between his words, lazy wisps of tobacco smoke whisking around him. "My wife—she was bloody terrified, poor thing. So naturally, I did what any respectable husband would. I scooped two of 'em up and chased her 'round the house for a good fifteen minutes."

Esther couldn't help but smile and laugh along with him. She liked hearing Wilde share these personal stories; it softened him up, almost. Separated the tall man in the uniform from the affectionate, hardworking father and husband he truly was.

But while he seemed content to share stories of his family, Esther couldn't help but notice the way his eyes grew clouded at the mention of his wife. She didn't have time to ponder it any further, however, because Murdoch had already flung down his tea and made for the door.

"Are you coming?" he demanded, impatient.

Esther rose to her feet with a scowl, and the two officers set off for D Deck to fulfill the boarding process once again.

It was the same tedious routine as earlier, only without the excited crowds and teeming quay. The SS *Nomadic* sidled up alongside *Titanic*, porthole lights sparkling across the black ocean water. Crewmen assembled the gangplanks, shell doors were thrown open wide, and before long, wealthy passengers dressed in their finery came streaming inside the ship. Once the *Nomadic* emptied, a second tender, the SS *Traffic*, arrived with even more people, including a handful of posh women who glittered with so many diamonds that Esther couldn't stop staring.

The entire process was fairly uneventful, much to her relief—save for one peculiar circumstance involving her superior officer.

Esther had been assisting a confused passenger at the time, so she didn't get the gist of what was happening until it was already over. But it seemed Murdoch had denied passage to some French naval commander following a short disagreement. As for what they had disagreed on, Esther couldn't fathom. But she'd noticed the tall, mustachioed commander pointing in her direction with one angry finger, spitting rapidly in French to the assistant at his side. Though her grasp of the language was rusty, having not studied it since her days in secondary school, she'd caught a few familiar words. *Outragé* was discernible, along with *fille* and *officier*. Esther put two and two together and glowered at the commander with intense dislike.

It was only after Captain Smith was called down from the bridge that the naval commander was permitted to board, and Murdoch—who looked none too happy about this—was cold for the rest of the evening. He refused to look at Esther, and when Pitman asked what happened, he merely snapped, "Nothing worth discussing."

Though Esther was still prickling with curiosity, she forced herself to turn and greet the next passenger in line. Her expression became one of mild astonishment as she watched a heavyset American woman march through the shell door as if she owned the place, gloved hands laden with an assortment of luggage. Her lips were a luminous red, and she wore an exquisite mauve evening suit with a mink scarf draped over her shoulders. Something about her immediately caught Esther's eye. Though whether it was because of her boisterous voice or the confident manner in which she held herself, the seventh officer couldn't say. All she knew was that she was intrigued, and her interest only grew when the woman passed over Murdoch's line and charged straight toward her.

"Good evening—" Esther started to say.

But her words were drowned out by the thundering boom of the woman's roughened American twang.

"Well, I'll be *darned*." She ogled at Esther, a wide grin spreading across her crimson lips. "Since when did White Star Line grow some backbone and start hiring up gals like you, huh?"

Esther opened her mouth to respond, but the woman was already chattering up a storm again.

"Took 'em long enough, the chump bastards," she said stoutly. "Can't tell you how doggone happy I am to see a lady in uniform. I tell ya, it's a nice change from all these stuffed shirts we usually get 'round here."

Esther knew she ought to keep her mouth shut, but the words came spilling out before she could stop them. "Couldn't agree more, ma'am."

The woman let out a bellow of breathy laughter. "Oh, I like you," she said, her eyes sparkling at Esther with interest. "What's your name, darlin'?"

"Esther Bailey," the seventh officer replied. Her eyes found Murdoch, and she nearly laughed at the look of incredulity on his face. "And yours, ma'am?"

"Margaret Brown. But you can call me Molly, honey."

They shook, and Esther found her hand squashed underneath a strong, crushing grip. She flexed her fingers to make sure none were broken before glancing down at the manifest with a merry smile. "Your cabin is B-4, Molly."

"Sounds good to me." With a wink, the woman stooped to collect her massive trunks. "See ya 'round, Esther," she called, before parading down the hall and barking at the porters to pick up the pace.

Esther, still dazed by the rowdy whirlwind of Margaret Brown, suddenly realized Murdoch stood before her, his lips pressed into a hard line.

"If you've finished making friends," he said waspishly, "we're all done here. You're free to rest until the start of our watch. Ten o'clock sharp." His blue eyes were cutting, and it was clear he was still in a foul mood after his ordeal with the French commander. "*Don't* be late, Miss Bailey."

"I wasn't planning on it, *Mr. Murdoch*," she snapped back.

They glared at each other, the silence between them deafening, heavy with mutual dislike. Then Murdoch spun on his heel and started for the Grand Staircase, and Esther, who was still seething, couldn't even force a smile when Pitman chuckled at her side. "Do you two *ever* stop bickering?"

No, Esther thought savagely, her frustrations charring their way through her flesh like oil to flame.

No, they most certainly did not.

Esther was terribly cold.

A drafty chill crawled into her bones when she awoke at half-past nine, still slouched in her swivel chair with the alarm clock clanging unpleasantly in her ears.

She'd fallen asleep at her desk some hours ago, cheek smashed against the celestial almanac Lowe had lent her, drool dribbled into its pages.

The exhaustion of the day had finally caught up with her, and so she'd nodded off within minutes of propping open her book. Christ, she hadn't even undressed; she was still donned head to toe in her uniform, greatcoat, Oxfords and all.

Esther sighed, shivering, wanting nothing more than to crawl into her bed, bury herself underneath the blankets, and call it a night. But the mere thought of Murdoch's stony disappointment sent her scrambling to her feet, slamming her hand on her alarm and silencing it at once.

It took only a handful of moments to splash her face with cold water and comb the snags out of her hair. Esther straightened the tie Murdoch had knotted for her earlier before slipping out into the hall, quick and quiet, bracing herself for her first watch as a White Star Line officer.

The bridge was dark when Esther reported for duty, but she wasn't surprised; it was customary to dim the lamps to improve visibility of the open waters ahead. A few sources of light were still left: the glowing lettering of the telegraphs, the red and green running lights hanging from the bulwarks of each bridge wing, and the luminous oil lamps shining within the bellies of each binnacle. But other than those instruments, the bridge remained cloaked in the blue shadows of night, with thin sheets of moonlight streaming through the windows.

The quiet here…it's oddly comforting, Esther thought. There was something serene about it that calmed her nerves and soothed her pulse altogether. Quartermaster Rowe stood before the helm, silent as he steered, eyes fixed unblinkingly ahead. Moody stood in the far corner of the bridge, his back to her as he scribbled in the logbook; he hadn't noticed her arrival. Esther could hear the engines humming deep within the ship, a reminder that they were well on their way to Queenstown. And when she looked east, she could see the glittering lights of Cherbourg fading well into the distance, winking into the watery darkness.

Esther glanced around for Murdoch and found him standing in the starboard bridge wing with a weary Lightoller. She started toward them, smoothing out her greatcoat and praying she looked presentable.

"Nothing of note to report," Lightoller said. "We're expected to maintain speed and heading from now until morning—fifteen knots through the Channel to Queenstown, due northwest."

"And the weather?" Murdoch asked.

"Bit chilly. Clear visibility, though, with light wind and little sea. Not too bad at all." Lightoller paused his briefing, turning at Esther's footsteps. "Ah, Miss Bailey," he greeted, recognizing her in the dim light. "There you are." His tired eyes swept over her orderly clothes and combed hair, and he nodded with approval. "You're looking significantly less...disheveled, I see."

Esther almost stared daggers at him—until she realized that his tone was one of mild jest, and she offered a smile instead. "How kind of you to notice, Mr. Lightoller."

"I daresay it's impossible not to. You've gone from a complete eyesore to a bloody proper officer. And you've even done up your tie, well done."

Esther spared a cursory glance at Murdoch, who didn't seem interested in their banter. He merely adjusted the lapels of his greatcoat to shield his neck from the biting chill, his expression almost bored. With a shy smile, she admitted, "I have Mr. Murdoch to thank for that. It was his handiwork, really."

"Indeed?" Lightoller glanced at his colleague, eyes full of surprise and amusement. "Ever the gentleman, Will."

Murdoch's voice was dull. "I try."

Laughing tiredly, Lightoller turned his attention back to Esther. "Well, miss. Given your improved wardrobe and impeccable tie, I trust this means you're all ready for the watch?"

"I am, sir."

"Very good. I'll leave you to it, then." Lightoller stepped down from the bridge platform and started for the wheelhouse, long legs clearing the deck with ease. He paused before the door, adding over his shoulder, "Oh, yes. One more thing, Will. You might want to ask around and see if anyone's spotted the binoculars. They've been missing since yesterday, and it's rather a nuisance to watch the horizon without them."

Murdoch nodded. "I'll see to it at once. Cheers, Lights."

They exchanged pleasant farewells before Lightoller strolled away, heading aft to begin his rounds. Murdoch watched him leave before reluctantly turning to Esther. She was glad to see *some* improvement in his nasty attitude, any former irritability smoothed away by his usual cool indifference. Which wasn't saying much, really.

"Miss Bailey," he said in a crisp voice, "please observe the compass and log the heading. Once finished, you are to supervise Quartermaster Rowe at the helm until instructed otherwise. Is that understood?"

"Yes, sir."

"You *do* remember where to find the compass, then?" he demanded.

Other than up your ass? Esther thought, green eyes swelling with anger at his patronizing tone. She was halfway close to snapping at him. But she held back, squaring her shoulders and swallowing her temper with grace as she answered dully, "The binnacle." *Obviously.*

Murdoch merely gave a stern nod. "Good. Off you go, then."

Esther marched past him without another word, trying not to scowl as she made for the binnacle. Light glittered on plated brass and washed her gloves in gold as she peeled open its hood to inspect the enormous compass nestled inside. The task was fairly short, and once she'd finished scribbling the heading in the logbook, she left the wheelhouse to fulfill her place on the bridge. It was here where Esther stood for the next four hours, dutifully silent, her hands behind her back and gaze watchful as she monitored the helmsman. Murdoch hadn't moved from the starboard bridge wing, save for a quick visit to the wheelhouse to telephone the crow's nest and hear a brief weather report from Pitman. He was motionless otherwise, blue eyes never wavering from the stillness of the deep, black, endless sea.

The temperature dipped with each passing hour, but if any of the crew were cold, they certainly did not show it. They were professionals, shaped by discipline and a shared love for the sea, and Esther glowed with pride knowing she stood among them.

She was called away from her post only twice in the hours she was expected to stand at attention. The first time was around one in the morning, when Murdoch instructed her to lower a bucket to the sea and hoist it back up to check the water's temperature. The second was much later, when he required her assistance for celestial sights. Esther stood at his side with the logbook in hand, ready to record time and measurement. She watched, fascinated, as Murdoch held the sextant up to his eye and swung it back and forth. Her eyes followed the slow movement of his hands, and she couldn't help but think of how gently they had brushed the skin of her neck earlier. The memory sent a rush of heat billowing across her cheeks, and she was immensely relieved when Murdoch completed his observations and sent her along to the bridge.

Around two in the morning, when Esther was beginning to feel cold and weary, Wilde came marching smartly out of the wheelhouse. He looked refreshed and well-rested despite the early hour, greatcoat draped over his tall, towering frame.

"Morning, all," he announced to the gathered crew, his rumbling voice an almost improper contrast to the deep, wordless silence filling the bridge. He spared a glance at Murdoch, smirking as he tutted, "Dear me. Your tie's looking a wee bit crooked there, William."

Murdoch's retort was swift but good-natured. "Aye, and your nose'll be a wee bit crooked if you don't watch yourself."

The two senior officers chatted for a few moments, discussing the navigational minutiae with a few tongue-in-cheek remarks thrown in between. Esther kept by the helm throughout their briefing, listening to the conversation with only halfhearted interest as she struggled to fight off the fuzz of drowsiness. Eventually, she looked up at the sound of footfalls to see Murdoch strolling past.

"Rounds next," he said briskly, not even looking at her as he went. "Come along."

She hesitated, suddenly uncertain. "The two of us?"

"No, you and the quartermaster." He looked on the verge of rolling his eyes. "*Yes*, the two of us. I'll be escorting you for now, Miss Bailey, since you still need to familiarize yourself with the ship well enough to know where to go, and what to look for. But until that *shining* day comes, I'm afraid we must conduct our rounds together."

Esther wasn't at all pleased by this, and judging by Murdoch's flinty attitude, he was none too thrilled, either. But she nodded wordlessly, falling into step alongside her superior officer as he led her aft.

They were quiet as they walked, passing a handful of seamen scrubbing the decks with wide, bristled brushes and watered-down soap. Murdoch's stride was much slower than his usual purposeful gait, and Esther wondered if he was tired. They'd had a long night, after all, stretching well into the early hours of the dark morning. Already she longed for her bed, wanting nothing more than to crawl under an ocean of warm blankets and call it a night. But they still had another hour of rounds ahead of them, and she sighed, her breath clouding the air in a billow of mist.

Shivering, Esther drew the lapels of her coat closer to her neck, and that was when Murdoch finally looked at her.

"Cold?" he asked idly.

"No," she said stubbornly, and when he looked skeptical, she decided to tell the truth. "Okay, a little," she admitted. "It's chilly, yes, but not freezing. Reminds me of home a bit."

"San Francisco?"

She nodded, surprised he even remembered. "That's right. Ever been?"

He studied the tides, his voice wistful. "Aye, ages ago."

"No kidding!" Esther gaped at him, suddenly bright with interest. "So you were in my neck of the woods, eh? What on earth brought you all the way out there?"

Murdoch shrugged. "It was my first apprenticeship. I was just a lad then. Fifteen—maybe sixteen, perhaps. Can't quite remember after all these years."

"Did you sail from Southampton?"

He shook his head. "Liverpool. It was a long journey. Mostly because we had to steer 'round Cape Horn before making our way northward through the Pacific."

"And what did you think?" she pressed eagerly. "Of San Francisco, I mean."

Murdoch's reply was thoughtful. "That it was *bloody* cold for July. Foggy, too. We'd been expecting sun and warm weather, but it was dead *dreich*, it was."

Esther tilted her head to one side, momentarily bemused. Though she was still growing accustomed to Murdoch's thick Scottish accent, there were times when he'd toss phrases into casual conversation that were unfamiliar to her. He must have noticed the wrinkle in her nose and the puzzled crease between her brow, because he turned to her and said impatiently, "*Dreich*. Cold and wet, aye? Miserable, even. Was like being in Scotland all over again."

Esther laughed. "Well, we get the most fog between June and August. I've no idea why, we just do." She grinned at him, tucking her hair behind one ear as the cold ocean wind shivered past. "You ought to visit again, sir. In the spring, perhaps. It's very lovely."

"Doubt I'll be making my way out west anytime soon," Murdoch snorted. "What with working aboard one of the busiest transatlantic luxury liners, and all that."

"True," she agreed. "I suppose that *might* be more of a priority."

"Just a wee bit," he said wryly. "Besides, I'm looking at another eight or nine years at sea before I command ship of my own. So San Francisco will have to wait, unfortunately."

"You'd like to become a captain, then?"

He nodded. "Like my father, and his father before him."

Esther smiled at the thought, and Murdoch turned to her with a frown.

"Something funny?" he demanded.

"I'm simply imagining your future title, sir. *Captain* William Murdoch. Huh. Doesn't sound too shabby, if you ask me."

"'Doesn't sound too shabby,'" he quoted, eyebrow raised. "*Quality* praise, lass. Means a lot coming from you, it does."

She laughed heartily, once again struck by his dry humor. He could be perfectly comical when he wanted to be—when he wasn't driving her up the damn wall, of course.

"What of you, Miss Bailey?" Murdoch asked, as they continued along the desolate promenade. "When the maiden voyage is over, and we've docked in New York, where are you headed? San Francisco, perhaps?"

Esther shook her head. "Not a chance. I plan on sticking with *Titanic* for a long while, though I wouldn't mind transferring to another ship sometime within the year. Preferably one that's not so…*restricted* to the North Atlantic."

"And what, pray, is your reasoning behind that?"

"Simple. There's so much out there, Mr. Murdoch. So many new oceans and continents I could explore instead. I mean, *look* at you, for example." She gestured at the first officer with one gloved hand, hoping the envy didn't show on her face. "You've been at sea for what, twenty years now? I bet you've been all over the world."

"Nearly," he admitted. His voice was weary, but Esther kept prying, longing to hear more.

"Where?" she asked. "If you don't mind my asking."

Murdoch pondered her question, blue eyes clouded and distant, as if scouring his thoughts to remember them all. "Chile, Mauritius, the Netherlands," he answered softly. "South Africa, Peru…Germany, Belgium, Sweden. Australia, briefly, aboard the *Medic* with Mr. Lightoller. And China as well."

"*China?*" she gasped. "Get outta town. What was *that* like?"

"Shanghai was…different, to say the least." He smirked a little, as if enjoying a private joke. "Unusual people and food, aye, but it quickly became one of my favorite cities. With the exception of Valparaíso, I'll admit. There's nothing quite like the Chilean coast. Damn near unforgettable."

"Jesus." Esther let out a low whistle. "You really have traveled the world, sir."

"There's loads to see out there," he admitted. "But it does grow tiring after a while, Miss Bailey."

"Well," she said with a confident grin, "I suppose I'll simply have to find that out for myself."

"As you like. But don't say I didn't warn you." Shaking his head, Murdoch raised his eyebrows in disbelief. "Have you given any thought as to *where* you'd be going? This might come as a bit of a shock, but you should probably establish that first."

"Anywhere," Esther said simply.

Her eyes glimmered with excitement as she imagined the far-off regions she had yet to see: windy fjords cut by ribbons of deep saltwater, crystal-blue seas broken by reefs and white shoals, basalt beaches dotted with stones and buffeted by choppy surf. Those places were distant, nameless—and yet, she knew she'd reach them someday. Of course she would. She *had* to. Her way through life had been winding until now, like an unruly stream stumbling its way over hurdles and bumps, oftentimes trickling into those dark, unexpected cracks.

But she was like water. Persistent, versatile, never willing to wait.

Everything that had once hurt or hindered Esther was long behind her. She'd carved a different path than most, determined to fight not only for herself, but for those women still seeking to dip their toes in the maritime industry. It was a heavy burden to bear, knowing she was responsible for setting a good example. And although she was scared she might fail, Esther knew she had to keep going. Life had led her to this career, to the *Titanic*, to the sea—and one day, it would lead her to all the wild, wonderful places she dreamed of visiting as well.

"I've never been to New Zealand," she told Murdoch. "Or South America. And I've never sailed through the Java Sea, or along the coast of Greece. I'd like to do all those things someday, sir. While I'm still young and able. And childless," she added with a snort.

Murdoch was watching her intently now. Only there was no criticism in his gaze, just curiosity—and a wary curiosity, at that.

"What?" she asked, feeling self-conscious but shamelessly pleased by the way he was looking at her.

He merely said, "You surprise me, Miss Bailey."

"Oh." She hadn't been expecting that. "In a good or bad way, sir?"

Murdoch wrenched his eyes away and fixed them on the sea, his expression guarded once more. "Both, I'm afraid."

A silence fell between them again. Esther could think of nothing more to say, so she simply listened to the dark, foamy water storming like thunder beneath them. Neither officer spoke a word as they crossed around the stern and headed afore this time, stepping down the sprawling length of B Deck Promenade, then C Deck, D Deck, and so on.

By the time they finished their rounds, and Murdoch's pocket watch announced that it was three in the morning, Esther was dead tired. She stumbled into the officers' quarters with Murdoch trailing behind her, more than ready to throw herself into bed and not wake until sunrise. But she paused when she reached her door, suddenly remembering a question she wanted to ask—a question that had burned on the tip of her tongue for hours now.

"Mr. Murdoch," she said, and he stopped short, rubbing his tired eyes.

"May I ask you something?" When he nodded cautiously, she inhaled a deep breath and asked, "What happened between you and the French commander earlier?"

Murdoch shook his head at the question, blue eyes weary as he met her beseeching gaze. "It *doesn't* matter, Miss Bailey," he sighed, voice soft with exhaustion.

"Forgive me, sir, but I believe it does." Studying her feet, Esther tucked a stray piece of hair behind her ear. "I've a vague idea of what happened, because I overheard the man talking with his assistant in French. But still..." She looked meaningfully at him again, holding his gaze with hers. "I would like to hear it from you, if it's not too much trouble. Please."

Perhaps it was out of pity, or perhaps he simply wanted to hurry the conversation along and go to bed—but whatever the reason, her superior decided to oblige her.

"Commander Leloup was not at all happy to see a woman in uniform," Murdoch explained quietly. "He wanted you removed from his sight whilst boarding. I told him that wouldn't be possible, obviously, since you were assisting other passengers at that time. So he got a bit shirty with me after that. Started saying some...right awful things about you as well, and..." His voice trailed away, hoarse and simmering with disgust. But he cleared his throat, mastering himself and his emotions as he continued on. "I wasn't about to let some brute like that onboard, naval commander be damned. The captain overruled me, of course. As he should. But it doesn't matter. I did what I thought was right."

Esther gaped at him. "But you went against maritime law!" she protested fiercely, her voice ringing out with indignation. "You shouldn't have done that, sir. You could have lost your job!"

His eyes flashed at her for a moment, dark with anger and a trace of bitterness. "Would you rather I permitted him to board and shunted you out of the room?" he demanded.

She bit her lip, suddenly uncomfortable. "No. No, of course not."

"That's what I thought."

Esther stared at her superior officer, frustrated and completely at a loss for what to say. Maritime law and regulation had been her line of study at university, after all; she knew the consequences better than anyone, and she couldn't fathom why a distinguished senior officer like Murdoch would dare cross such a line.

When Esther spoke, her voice was quiet. "I don't understand. That's the third time you've stood up for me."

"And I would do the same for any officer," Murdoch said dismissively. "Don't take it personally, lass."

"I *know* that," Esther insisted. She looked down again, feeling nervous as she toyed with her glove. "But even so, Mr. Murdoch, I…"

Her words drifted away into silence. Their eyes met for a long moment, but neither officer seemed to want to look away. Esther braved a step closer, once again struck by the unusual color of his eyes.

Such a deep, dark blue, she thought. Like the sea, almost.

She expected Murdoch to back away. Reprimand her for getting too close, perhaps. And yet he remained right where he stood, watching her, a question in his gaze. Her hand reached out unthinkingly, brushing his forearm in what was intended to be a gesture of gratitude, nothing more. But the touch of her fingertips against his greatcoat only seemed to fluster him, and he snapped his eyes away from hers, taking a hasty step back.

"That's *enough*."

Murdoch's snarl was like a sharp slap to the face, and Esther flinched, quickly drawing her arm back to her side. "What on earth is the matter with you?" he demanded, blue eyes no longer calm as ocean waves, but frozen and opaque, cold as sheeted ice. "I told you I'd do the same for any officer, you numpty, and I meant it. Quit trying to make yourself feel special. We're due in Queenstown later today, in case you've forgotten. So why don't you do us both a favor and get some bleedin' sleep?"

He stormed down the hall, shaking his head in exasperation.

"Good*night*, Miss Bailey."

Esther did not move. Shock coated her thoughts like oil, darkened and slippery. She stared after her superior in silence, turning away only when he'd disappeared inside his cabin and slammed the door shut behind him.

Her heart felt heavier than stone, and she couldn't keep the bitterness from cutting into her voice as she spoke quietly in the deserted corridor.

"Goodnight, Mr. Murdoch."

TWELVE

OPEN OCEAN

April 11, 1912 | 07:45

A COLD, CALM SEA stretched before Lightoller as he stood watch, gloved hands folded dutifully behind his back.

He was quiet as he gazed across the glimmering ocean, breathing in the smell of saltwater, blue eyes fixed on even bluer waves. The morning fog had burned away at long last, and now there was only sunlight—crisp and dazzling and white—washing everything from the telegraphs to the pine decking beneath his feet.

The bridge was bright and airy as usual, dead silent but still brimming with tireless energy as crew and officers alike ambled through. And although Lightoller had spent the greater part of his morning barking out orders and reviewing the ship's course, there was a good deal of work to attend to before their arrival in Queenstown. His watch would end early, for one thing, and then he'd report to the gangways for boarding duty while Officer Wilde would man the bridge in his place.

But as Lightoller faced the motionless stretch of glassy sea, with the roar of water in his ears and the murmur of *Titanic*'s engines far beneath him, he found himself thinking not only of his work, but of his wife.

He had scribbled out a hasty letter to Sylvia in the early hours of the morning, sending it away to the mail hold for delivery upon their arrival in Queenstown. But the words he'd pressed into the paper could not convey how much he missed her.

Though Lightoller took pride in his work—and maintained just as much quiet dignity as the next sailor—he had never been able to stomach his woeful heartache whenever he was forced to part with his wife.

Even now, his thoughts were fixed on Sylvia: on her smooth porcelain skin always smelling of lavender and lilac; her sleek tresses of honey-colored hair he loved to comb his fingers through after long, tiring journeys at sea; and of course, the sound of her laughter whenever he made some stupid, self-deprecating joke or another.

Sylvia Lightoller was the light of his life, and every day he spent away from her only deepened his yearning to see her again.

As Lightoller was the only married man among his colleagues, there was no one he could truly confide in—no one who could understand the extent of his feelings. The exception was Wilde, perhaps, who lost his wife a little more than a year ago. But that was a different situation, Lightoller knew. More of a raw grief than his own simple pining. Besides, he and Henry Wilde were hardly the *merriest* of chums. Lightoller wasn't about to go spewing off his emotions to him—especially when he could hardly stand to look at the man.

He wished he could confide in Will more than anyone. But the first officer had left Ada nearly a year ago, and had shown no interest in another woman since. As for Boxhall, Pitman, Moody, and Lowe—all four officers were unmarried bachelors, as far as Lightoller knew, but he wouldn't be surprised if they had ladies waiting in the wings back home. Perhaps they were as lonely as he was.

A cool breeze ruffled the short, sandy brown hair sticking out beneath his cap, and Lightoller heaved a quiet sigh.

There were still many more days left at sea. Still weeks before he would see Sylvia again. He could swallow down the loneliness for now, as simple as throwing back a sizzling shot of whisky. But he was only human, after all. Though he was daydreaming of his wife's stunning eyes and sweet laughter, he was having *other* thoughts regarding her as well. Namely, all the things he would do to her when he was home—and none of which were very proper. Even now, as he finished up the last few minutes of his watch, he could close his eyes and almost imagine his hands trailing their way up her smooth thighs, pushing up her skirt before spinning her round so he could have his way with her from behind—

"Morning, handsome!"

A deep, sonorous voice split the air behind him, and Lightoller pressed his lips together to keep from bellowing his surprise.

He spun around, heart racing in his chest—and found himself face-to-face with none other than Henry Wilde. The chief officer stood tall as usual, one hand held in a stately manner behind his back, and—like Lightoller—he had discarded his greatcoat for a reefer jacket in response to the warming weather. He wore a crooked smirk on the corner of his mouth as he approached his colleague, slate-gray eyes squinting against the harsh sunlight.

"Lovely day for it, eh, Mr. Lightoller?"

Lightoller ignored him. "Can you think of no other way to announce your presence, Mr. Wilde?" he demanded with a scowl. "Or do you simply *relish* being as loud as humanly possible?"

"Loud as possible, naturally. I should think you'd be used to it by now, old chap."

"Decidedly not."

Smirking, Wilde stepped closer. He looked mildly amused as he observed Lightoller's obvious annoyance—the curled lip, the flared nostrils, the ramrod-straight spine—and he remarked, "Blimey. If I'd known you'd be so crabby this morning, I'd have taken my sweet time in the mess instead of hurrying along to relieve you from duty."

"Yet here you are. So if you're finished here, Mr. Wilde, I'd like to get on with my rounds."

"Rounds can wait. I'd like a quick word with you first."

"Regarding *what*, exactly?"

"Your attitude, Mr. Lightoller. Much as I enjoy all this bad blood between us, it's getting a bit *stale* for my tastes. Perhaps it's time we put aside our differences. Forgive and forget, and all that. What d'you say?"

Lightoller lifted his chin. "Give me one good reason, Mr. Wilde."

Wilde's answering taunt was almost lazy. "You mean, other than the fact that I'm your superior and you'd damn well better listen to me?"

When Lightoller merely glowered at him in reply, the chief officer took a slow, lumbering step forward. His smile was mirthless, but there was still a sharp glint of authority to his cool gray eyes. "Listen, I know you were none too chuffed about being bumped down a rank. Hell, I'd feel the same. But like Will, you need to put it behind you. I didn't ask to become chief officer. It was per captain's orders. I had no choice but to follow through."

"I am aware of that, Mr. Wilde," Lightoller snapped, yanking the edge of his glove a little too harshly.

"Wonderful! So how about you stop being such a smarmy git and let bygones be bygones, eh?"

And with that, Wilde offered his hand. Lightoller hesitated, jaw clenched and eyes glittering darkly with disbelief. The thought of shaking Wilde's hand was about as desirable as licking dirt off the decking beneath them. But he didn't have much of a choice, he knew, so he gritted his teeth before grasping the chief officer's thick fingers. As they shook, he couldn't help but speak the blunt truth.

"I'm willing to be agreeable for the sake of our jobs," he said. "But I still don't like you, Mr. Wilde."

"Oh, *dear*. I'll try not to lose sleep over it."

They released hands, and Lightoller flinched as Wilde slammed a heavy palm against his back, hard enough to knock the breath from his lungs. Perhaps the gesture was meant to be encouraging, but it was mostly painful, and his eyes stung as he registered the throbbing in his spine. Wilde, however, looked thoroughly satisfied as he said, "Jolly good. Now that we've got *that* business out of the way, you are officially relieved of your watch duties, Mr. Lightoller. You're free to make your rounds and retire to lunch before we drop anchor in Queenstown."

Lightoller nodded, his face still as stone. He turned to leave, but Wilde's grating voice stopped him in his tracks once more.

"One more thing: if you happen to see Will this morning, can you do me a favor and figure out what the blazes is going on with him?"

"What do you mean?" Lightoller asked, all irritation immediately swept away by concern for Murdoch. "Is he unwell?"

Wilde hesitated. He stole a cautious glance around the bridge wing before leaning close to Lightoller to murmur, "That's the thing—I'm not so sure. I dunno all the details, but it seems our charming Scottish friend has been acting rather *odd* as of late. The captain called a meeting with me today to discuss it. Said Will denied boarding to a French commander last night in Cherbourg, and—"

Lightoller stared in stunned disbelief. "He *didn't*."

"He most certainly did. And that's only the half of it. A first-class passenger filed a complaint with the purser's office yesterday, stating Will tried to prohibit *him* from boarding as well." Wilde shook his head. "He's lost his marbles, he has."

Lightoller fell silent, eyes narrowed as he studied the distant sea.

"Rubbish," he finally said. "That doesn't sound like Will at all."

If there was one thing he'd come to learn about Murdoch over the years, it was that his colleague was nothing short of professional—cool, capable, and always on his toes. His loyalty stretched not only to his fellow officers and crew, but to maritime code as a whole. He was the kind of man who did everything by the book and didn't think twice on it—which was why Lightoller simply refused to believe what he was hearing.

Wilde heaved a deep, weary sigh. "Listen," he said gruffly. "I know neither of us sees eye to eye, but the one thing we have in common is that we both care about Will. I doubt I'll be able to see him until this evening, so just...make sure he's all right, will you? Give him a good hard slap 'round the face for me, perhaps."

Lightoller laughed despite himself. "Just the one?"

"Or five. Might be the thing to snap him out of it, eh? You never know."

"I suppose that's not a bad idea, Mr. Wilde," Lightoller agreed, the faintest smile cracking at the corner of his lips. "I'll see what I can do."

Without another word, he bade farewell to his superior and started aft down the officers' promenade, his thoughts suddenly muddied, heavy with worry for his friend. His rounds were uneventful, save for a brief argument he'd had to break up between two quarreling seamen. But other than that minor hiccup, the decks were peaceful at the early hour, with very few passengers in sight.

It wasn't until Lightoller circled to the port side of the ship that he noticed a familiar officer standing alone by the deck rails, sipping from a mug as he studied the tides. There was no mistaking his dark hair and sturdy build, and Lightoller made to join him.

"So," he said nonchalantly, as he came up beside the first officer. "Are you going to tell me what's the matter, or must I pry?"

Murdoch stiffened but didn't turn, blue eyes lingering on the waves.

"I've no idea what you're talking about," he said flatly.

"Oh? Because I spoke with Mr. Wilde only moments ago, and he informed me that you denied boarding not only to a first-class passenger, but to a French commander as well. *While* we were docked in French waters, no less. Is this true?"

Shrugging, Murdoch brought his cup of tea to his lips. "Aye."

"Sodding hell." Lightoller's voice was a soft hiss of disbelief. "I've *never* known you to behave like this, in all the years we've worked together— and neither has Wilde, for that matter. What on earth is going on with you, Will?"

Murdoch glared at the sea, ears reddening with anger. "Doesn't matter," he said dismissively. "What's done is done, and I'd rather not discuss the matter any further—"

"Don't be such a prat," Lightoller snorted. "If you won't come right out and say what happened, I'll keep harassing you till we dock in New York. I mean it, Will. And that's not even the worst of it," he added warningly. "I daresay Mr. Wilde will slap you to oblivion if you don't cut this nonsense out, you stubborn Scot."

Murdoch rounded on him with an exasperated sigh. "*Jings*, Lights! Is there no one else on this damn ship you can bother this morning?"

"Only you, I'm afraid," Lightoller replied, clapping one hand on his colleague's shoulder. "So start talking."

A long silence stretched between the two officers, broken only by the rushing wind and sea. It was a while before Murdoch spoke.

"If you must know, I was acting in defense of one of the junior officers," he explained, his voice carrying an edge of annoyance. "Those two men were nothing short of offensive. Complete and utter dobbers, the pair of 'em. And you know me, Lights. I'm loyal to the crew. I wasn't about to stand there and let them disrespect any White Star Line employee, let alone an *officer*, for Christ's sake." He looked away, studying the dregs in his teacup. "I'm not saying what I did was the most sensible thing. But it damn well made me feel better."

Lightoller was about to ask the name of the officer when the obvious realization dawned upon him. "It was Miss Bailey, wasn't it?"

"Naturally."

"I *see*. So you've finally warmed up to her, have you?"

"I wouldn't go that far," Murdoch scoffed. "I simply didn't want to see *any* colleague of mine treated in that manner. The commander was disgusting. The things he was saying about her...calling her whore and such...She's a proper bleedin' officer, not a doormat. She doesn't deserve that. No one does."

Lightoller stared at the first officer, surprised to hear the anger sizzling in his voice. Murdoch was usually reserved, shuttering his emotions with practiced ease. But now his composure was beginning to crack, splintering like brittle glass. Lightoller could see all that emotion leaking through the fissures, and he wasn't sure what to make of it. He managed only a single question, as he stood beside Murdoch in the soft morning light.

"You care for the girl, don't you?"

Murdoch shrugged. "She's my charge, Lights. And my colleague. I've no choice but to care."

Lightoller raised his brows, unsure how to approach his next question. "I understand, Will," he said tentatively. "But I can't help but wonder if it's more than that. You seem quite…protective of her."

Murdoch stiffened at his side, eyes narrowing, but Lightoller pressed on, "You're not…*keen* on her, are you?"

There was a long moment of silence. Then Murdoch simply laughed.

"Don't be daft," he said. "She's my subordinate, Lights. To be keen on her would mean I'd have to forfeit my job, and you damn well know I'd never do that. I sacrificed my bloody *marriage* to work at sea, aye? I wouldn't risk my career for anything—least of all for the likes of someone as cheeky as Miss Bailey."

He pulled his watch from his pocket, silver casing glittering as it caught the light. "Now, if you've finished interrogating me," Murdoch added testily, "we ought to have a bite in the mess before Queenstown. C'mon."

And with that, he turned on his heel and stalked aft, greatcoat billowing at his heels. Still feeling dubious, Lightoller wordlessly followed. Although his colleague had dismissed the notion of being interested in Bailey, he couldn't shake the feeling that something was going on between the two officers. Something Murdoch was doing his damnedest to keep to himself.

Lightoller's suspicions only deepened during breakfast, when they joined Bailey, Boxhall, and Moody at their table. Bailey and Murdoch were cool and polite to one another—almost deliberately so. When Murdoch asked her to pass the marmalade, she did so without pause. But her pretty green eyes were oddly distant, and she seemed to be trying her hardest to avoid her superior's gaze.

It was all very *unusual*, Lightoller thought. Especially since the pair of them were usually exchanging some kind of snappy banter or another.

Before Lightoller could ponder their behavior any further, he looked up to see an energetic Officer Lowe ambling into the room.

"Mornin' all!" the fifth officer called brightly, settling beside Bailey and flashing her a handsome smile. His eyes fell upon the mountain of food obscuring the table, and he groaned. "Aah, what heaven, eh? You know it's gonna be a proper good day when you have this many pastries in front of you." Within seconds, he began piling his plate with an assortment of griddle cakes, currant buns, waffles, soda and sultana scones, and Scotch oatcakes. As he dribbled maple syrup onto his spoils—the intensity of his expression akin to that of a studious blacksmith welding his wares—Bailey started to laugh. It was the first sliver of cheeriness Lightoller had seen from her all morning, and her hearty laughter was surprisingly welcome as it filled the chilly room.

"Why do I get the feeling you're *only* working aboard *Titanic* for her food, and nothing else?" she demanded, regarding Lowe with amusement.

"'Cause that's the exact truth?" Lowe replied, lifting a sultana scone to his mouth and taking an enormous bite.

"So, let me get this straight. You're not here for the pay, or for the experience. Just for the meals."

"Spot on, Esther. Didn't think anyone would catch my true intentions, but there you are."

Moody, who was scribbling in a small notebook propped up on his knee, glanced at him from across the table. "You have syrup on your cuff," he said idly. "Did you know that?"

Lowe turned, crumbs littering his coat and cheeks bulging with food. "Mm," he said in a muffled voice, speaking with difficulty around a mouthful of scone. "Now I do. Thanks for looking out, mate."

Moody returned to his notebook with a lazy smile. "Any time."

Lowe swallowed down another enormous bite before turning to Bailey. Brown eyes sparkling, he pulled a pocket-sized almanac from his coat. "Oi, Esther. If you're up for it, we can spend a few minutes going over some more constellations. Maybe you'll *finally* be able to tell the difference between Ursa Major and Ursa Minor, eh? What d'you say?"

Although Bailey still looked distracted, she offered him a kindly smile. "That would be lovely, Harold. Thank you."

Lightoller raised his brows in surprise; it seemed the two junior officers were on friendly terms now, even going so far as to address each other by their given names. He kept a curious eye on them throughout breakfast, occasionally chiming in to offer a correct star or constellation Bailey couldn't place. Lowe kept leaning in to her as they worked, his pastries forgotten, more interested in her than in the food before him. In fact, he was looking at her in a *very* keen way that made Lightoller wonder whether *Lowe* was the one who fancied Bailey—not Murdoch.

But while the fifth officer was in high spirits, the seventh remained quiet and withdrawn, and Lightoller found himself wondering what was troubling her. He spotted her glancing at her superior officer a handful of times, but Murdoch was too busy stirring his tea and conversing with Boxhall to notice. So Bailey busied herself with the star charts instead, and it wasn't until she'd guessed incorrectly for a third time that she lapsed into frustration.

"Sonofa*bitch*," she grumbled, and almost every senior officer shot her a look of stern warning.

"Language," Lightoller reminded curtly.

"Sorry, sir," Bailey apologized. Sighing, she shoved the almanac toward Lowe with a wrinkle of frustration between her brows. "I give up, Harold. I'm no good at this."

"I can tell," Lowe teased, and when she glowered at him, he released a good-natured laugh. "You'll catch on," he encouraged. "Just takes a bit of practice, is all."

Nodding sagely, Lightoller chimed in, "Quite right. Stars may take a good while to master, Miss Bailey, but they're well worth the time. Say your vessel founders, and you're stuck on the open seas without any navigational instruments to guide you. What, then? Can't exactly pick one direction and pray it'll lead you to land, can you? That's why the stars are so important. Knowing them could very well mean the difference between life and death."

"At this rate, I'm pretty sure I'll end up dead at sea," Bailey muttered under her breath. "How can I memorize hundreds of maritime laws, but I can't remember fifty *stupid* stars?"

Her words coaxed Murdoch to look up from his tea. She flinched, as if expecting a rebuke, but his voice was surprisingly calm as he told her, "They're not stupid. They saved my life when I was twenty. Was sailing along the South American coast when my crew and I found ourselves in the middle of a nasty hurricane. We had nothing to guide us once our ship sank. Only the stars, *funnily* enough. And this."

He reached into his pocket and withdrew a tiny compass made entirely of brass, iron needle quivering until it held a steady point north. Bailey stared at it for a long while before Murdoch tucked it away into his greatcoat again. "Kept it on me ever since," he said. "Dead useful, this is. Just as useful as those 'stupid' stars, mind."

Bailey stared shamefacedly down at her coffee in reply, her cheeks a brilliant pink. Something about Murdoch's words must have humbled her, because she went straight back to her star charts without complaint. Around nine, she closed the almanac, downed the last of her coffee, and rose to her feet.

"Forgive me," she said politely, "but I promised my brother I'd meet him at the Grand Staircase this morning." Her eyes lingered on Murdoch, who stared hard at the water glass in his hand, and she quickly looked away again. "Erm…I'll be at the gangways by eleven. So…see you then, everyone."

Lowe waited until she had slipped out of the room before turning to his colleagues with a grin. "Right, gents," he said earnestly, "I want you to be honest with me. When we dock in New York, I was thinking of asking Miss Bailey out to dinner, and well…" His voice trailed away for a moment, one hand sheepishly ruffling up the back of his hair. "D'you suppose I have a chance?"

Boxhall looked disgusted. Moody opened his mouth to reply, a mischievous smile spreading across his face—but his superiors were far quicker.

"No," Murdoch answered bluntly, while Lightoller said in concurrence, "Absolutely not."

There was a long pause as the two senior officers stared at each other. Lightoller lowered his fork expectantly, waiting for his colleague to elaborate. But when Murdoch was dead silent, he took it upon himself to explain.

"Relationships between any and all crew members are expressly prohibited," he said sternly. "That goes for when we're docked *and* when we're at sea. You *know* this, Harold. You agreed to it the moment you signed your contract. Any violation is a form of gross misconduct that will warrant immediate dismissal. So don't even try it." He lowered his teacup with a look of unease. "Unless you truly think she's worth the loss of your job?"

Lowe did not reply. He leaned back in his seat until his shoulders struck the wood backing, the eager glint in his eyes fading like a drop of ink evaporating into water. Lightoller sighed as the guilt roiled through him, stronger than whitewater currents. But as a senior officer, it was *his* duty to lay down the law. He didn't want to see Lowe throw his entire maritime career down the gutter by pursuing a girl he couldn't have. *Especially* when that girl had a powerful relative perched at the executive level of the company.

"I'm sorry, Harold," Lightoller murmured sincerely. "But that's the honest truth of it."

"But she's *amazing*, Lights," Lowe protested, voice hollow with disappointment. "Pretty, funny, clever...and her *eyes*, mate. They're proper fetching, they are. I've never seen eyes that green—"

The noise of a scraping chair grated their ears as Murdoch suddenly rose to his feet. He was swift, quietly excusing himself before striding to the door, and although the look on his face was one of stoicism, Lightoller knew Lowe wasn't the only disappointed man in the room.

09:10

Esther had seen the Grand Staircase more than a few times since boarding the RMS *Titanic*. But even so, its opulence never failed to astound her.

She stood at the top balustrade overlooking the sweeping steps, marveling at everything from the enormous dome of milky glass high sweeping high above her head, to the Axminster carpets rippling with color beneath her feet.

First-class passengers spilled down the staircase at the early hour, no doubt making their way to D Deck Reception for breakfast. They were donned in their best as usual, and Esther nearly shook her head at the display of silks, lace, and glimmering jewels that must have cost more than her year's wages. It was a world of affluence and excessive luxury she'd never understood. Not even her parents—whose wealth and medical professions had easily ensured them a top spot amongst high society—had been so exorbitant. After the Great Earthquake and its raging fires tore through San Francisco, destroying their home, their hospital, and their livelihoods, they'd had no choice but to rebuild from the ashes. Start fresh, anew. In doing so, they had taught their children humility, encouraging Esther and her brothers to work hard and never take anything for granted. Their humble values had shaped Esther into the woman she was today, and as she watched the first-class passengers drift past, she was relieved to have dismissed such a soft life to work at sea instead.

At least I'll probably never have to wear a corset again, she reasoned, thinking of the fitted, simplistic brassier hugging her chest, and fighting to suppress a satisfied grin. *Thank you, Christ.*

Even tonight, Esther would be expected to wear her officer's uniform in the first-class dining saloon. No dress, no corset—no jewelry or other such frills. It was a relief, honestly, since she would be far more comfortable in her officer's garb than in anything else. But even so, she couldn't help but feel nervous. Not because she was worried about what first-class passengers would think of her—no, of course not.

She was nervous because Murdoch would be there.

The events last night—or early this morning, really—changed something between them, and not for the better.

Esther thought they'd had a great watch together. She had been interested to hear all about Murdoch's travels and the life he'd led before *Titanic.* She'd smiled imagining him as a captain, and she'd enjoyed the inquisitive way he was looking at her, staring as if she were some kind of puzzle he couldn't figure out.

But the thin sliver of amiability they'd built during their watch had crumbled between them, like waves washing castles of sand out to sea, and she kept wondering if it was her fault.

In hindsight, Esther shouldn't have reached out to touch his arm. But she hadn't *meant* anything by it. Nothing even remotely suggestive. She had simply been thankful for all the ways Murdoch had helped her—and appreciative of the stance he'd taken against that French commander. He'd stood up for her without thinking twice on it. But she'd crossed a boundary in her attempt to show gratitude, and here they were.

Esther knew she had no right to initiate physical contact with her superior officer. She had acted inappropriately, and she knew he was well within reason to rebuke her. But still…she'd be lying if she said her feelings weren't hurt, and she felt stupid because of it.

Even their working relationship felt mangled now. Their cool, awkward courtesy toward each other over breakfast had been a façade and nothing more, while her dismissal of the stars—stars that had once saved his *life*—hadn't helped the situation any.

Esther was suddenly lost. Murdoch was making her nervous now— not angry, but *nervous*—and it was clear that the more she came to know her superior officer, the less she understood of him. Actually *trying* to understand the man was comparable to tiptoeing across pools of quicksand or swimming against swells of rough, foamy seas with no lifebelt to keep her afloat. Esther couldn't do it anymore. She wouldn't even try. She would continue to do as Lowe suggested: keep her head down and follow Murdoch's every word. There would be no witty banter or curious questions. Just the strict, orderly professionalism of a respectable lady officer.

With a resigned sigh, Esther glanced around the room, seeking her brother's black hair and freckled face amidst the sea of passengers. Booker was supposed to be at the Grand Staircase by now, and yet he was nowhere in sight. Perhaps his meeting with Mr. Andrews was taking longer than planned. But Esther didn't mind; she was able to gawk at the Grand Staircase for a bit longer, at least, and that was perfectly all right with her.

Stepping around the balustrades with their wrought-iron scrollwork, Esther made her way toward the clock panel of *Honour and Glory*. She was studying the ornate carvings edging its crystal face when a smooth, drawling voice spoke behind her.

"Still wearing those unflattering clothes, I see."

Esther turned and found herself facing Callum Lockerbie, who stood before her in a fitted taupe suit with his glossy hair slicked back. A tie of blue silk hung around his neck, while the chain of a pocket watch glittered from his waistcoat. He carried a bowler hat in one gloved hand and a silver walking stick in the other, and she resisted the urge to sneer at his showy appearance as she looked him up and down.

"Yes," she said idly. "Because it's part of my job to wear these clothes. It's called a uniform, Mr. Lockerbie. Shocking, I know."

Smirking, he stepped closer. "Well, that's rather a pity. Because it certainly isn't doing you any favors, Esther."

She laughed aloud. "Yeah? As if you're any better in that overpriced suit of yours. You've even got a walking stick, for cryin' out loud. Is that even *necessary*, Mr. Lockerbie?"

"Enough with this 'Mister' Lockerbie business," he said with a grimace, hazel eyes narrowed to slits. "We've known each other for years now, have we not? I daresay we're far from being strangers."

Esther didn't like the implication behind his words. Nor did she like the stupid smirk crooking at the corner of his mouth. It was as if he was hinting at the times they'd flirted and kissed in the past—and it only tested her temper even further.

"I disagree," she said shrewdly. "Things change, people change. We haven't seen each other in years, *Mr. Lockerbie*. So I think it's fair to say we're both strangers in our own right."

Lockerbie's smirk faltered, but he recovered quickly, smoothing away his obvious irritation with her. "Well," he said in a stiff voice, "all the more reason to spend time catching up, then. I heard Booker is aboard as well. I'd like to see him."

"Lucky for you, I'm meeting him here this morning." Esther glanced around the room, which was bright beneath the glass dome, oaken woodwork and bronze embellishments glistening. "He should have been here by now. But I suppose he's simply running late."

Lockerbie seemed to brighten imperceptibly at this, but Esther wasn't surprised; between her twin brothers, Lockerbie always favored Booker the most—and she knew it was because Brighton had put up with less of Lockerbie's shit altogether.

"How is your brother?" Lockerbie asked. "Married yet?"

Esther shook her head. "No. He courted a woman in London a few years back, but that fell through, and I don't think he's been interested in anyone since."

"And you?" he asked casually, twirling his bowler hat in one hand.

"Last I heard, you were engaged to that doctor. Muir, or whatever his name was." His laugh was snide as he added, "Is he aware you're working aboard a ship, let alone wearing a man's uniform?"

Esther shrugged. "Well, he's dead, so probably not," she answered dully. "And our engagement fell through long before he died, so it's not as if he would've had a say in the matter, anyhow." Hatred glazed her heart as she spoke, and although Lockerbie studied her with an inquiring look, she was quick to change the subject. "How about that blonde you were with yesterday, huh? She's quite the stunner. Wife? Fiancée?"

She watched his mood shift to one of smugness. "Fiancée," he answered loftily. "Fay. We're to marry in Los Angeles come June, and—"

But Esther was no longer listening.

Her eyes were locked on the First Class Entrance, where she thought she caught the flash of an officer's uniform beyond the glittering concourse of well-dressed passengers and stewards. A navy-blue jacket so dark it was nearly black, sleeves trimmed in the gold stripes of a senior rank.

It was an officer, all right. But the breath hitched in her throat when she realized it wasn't Lowe, or Wilde, or any other shipmate she would have been pleased to see.

It was Murdoch.

Her superior officer crossed the foyer with his hands held behind his back, eyes roaming the staircase as if searching for someone. *Her*, probably. Why else would he have left the mess hall and made his way here, only minutes after she'd excused herself from breakfast?

Esther couldn't imagine what he wanted with her. But she sure as hell wasn't going to stick around and find out. She turned to Lockerbie, trying to contain the dread swelling like a cold water within her chest.

"Sorry, but—I've got to go," was all she managed to spit out.

Ignoring the affronted look on Lockerbie's face, Esther pushed past him and hurried down the Grand Staircase, moving as fast as her legs could carry her. She didn't know where she was going—she simply had to put as much distance between herself and Murdoch as possible. She kept moving, deeper into the belly of the ship, stepping quickly but carefully as she clambered from one extravagant deck to another.

It wasn't until Esther reached F Deck that she came to a halt. She braced herself against the nearest bulkhead, hunched over and wincing at the stitch in her side. Still breathing heavily through her nose, Esther started down the maze of narrow white passageways with aimless steps, passing along the sprawling mosaic tiles of the Turkish Baths before she came to the first-class swimming pool. Esther assumed it would be empty, since the men's hours ended at nine, and women weren't permitted to swim until ten. So she slipped inside, desperate for a quiet reserve—a solitary place where she could be alone and collect her frazzled self.

The Swimming Bath was deserted. Brightly-lit by slats of sun streaming through the portholes, a row of changing rooms stretched across the far wall, their cabinets piled high with crisp white towels and folded bathing suits. Esther paced around the pool, sidestepping turquoise waters as clear as cut crystal, before plopping herself down at its edge. She tugged off her Oxfords and high socks first, then carefully hitched up her work skirt. By the time she'd dipped her legs in the deep saltwater, she began to feel calmer and clearer, like a street washed clean by rain. She knew she shouldn't have run from Murdoch. It had been cowardly, and so *unlike* her. But she'd panicked.

And now she was all by her lonesome in the depths of the ship, wishing with all her heart that Lightoller was still her superior officer. *Not* Murdoch. Perhaps things would have been different. Perhaps she wouldn't be sitting with her feet drifting in pool water, wallowing in the tides of her confused, pathetic thoughts.

The door behind her clicked open, and a lazy voice said, "What on earth are you doing all the way down here?"

Esther started to scramble to her feet, heart hammering wildly in her chest—but stopped when she found herself face-to-face with her brother. Booker closed the door to the Swimming Bath and loped toward her, his expression one of amusement.

"How did you know where to find me?" Esther demanded.

Booker laughed at the question. "It wasn't difficult. I simply had to ask if anyone had seen the *bizarre* woman dressed in an officer's uniform." He settled along the poolside, grinning at the disgruntled look on her face. "What? You stand out like a sore thumb, you know. I must've spoken with no more than two stewards before they pointed me this way." His eyes narrowed questioningly, and he added, "I assume you're not here for a *swim*, so would you mind telling me what you're doing, and why you weren't up at the Grand Staircase?"

"You were late," Esther replied, trying not to feel defensive. "So I thought I'd wander off on my own for a bit."

"Yes, and I do apologize for that." He swept one hand through his sleek hair. "I'm afraid Mr. Andrews kept me a little longer than expected."

"Did your meeting go well, then?"

Her brother looked impatient. "Yes, as always. But don't change the subject. Why are you all the way down on F Deck?"

"I don't know." She shrugged, eyes boring into the pool, watching tendrils of light ripple across its tiled bottom. "I just ended up here."

Booker snorted. "Sometimes I don't even know why you bother to lie," he teased. "You're absolutely horrid at it."

Esther scowled, resisting the urge to splash water all over his slick hair and pristine suit. "Did you come all the way down here to insult me," she snapped, "or do you have some other purpose?"

"Geez, I'm only joking. You don't have to bite my head off."

"Sorry." Esther reached for her socks, temper fading, and tugged them on. "I'm just having a bad day, that's all."

Booker sniffed, shooting her a pointed glance. "I noticed." His expression shifted to one of curiosity as he added, "It wouldn't have anything to do with Murdoch, would it? He was up at the Grand Staircase, you know. Said he was looking for you. You're not in trouble, are you?"

Esther breathed a frustrated sigh. "No. Maybe. I don't know." She pressed one hand against her forehead, unable to look her brother in the eye. "I upset him, Booker," she mumbled. "I upset him, and I don't know how to fix it."

Esther was glad when Booker didn't pry. Instead, he kept his voice gentle as he said, "Apologizing isn't a bad place to start."

"I know." She dipped her hand in the crystalline water and stirred her fingers around, feeling weary as she watched the little waves spread and flow. "But I can't bring myself to do it."

"Oh, brother." Booker shook his head with a chiding smile. "Stubborn as always, aren't you?"

Esther fell silent. She didn't have the heart to tell him the truth—that it wasn't stubbornness keeping her from apologizing to Murdoch, but cowardice—and she turned away so her brother wouldn't see her shame.

11:00

By the time Esther parted with her brother and trudged up the steps of the Grand Staircase, *Titanic* had dropped anchor in Queenstown at last.

She'd barely reached E Deck when the ship came to a soft, shuddering halt. The rumble of engines faded to a distant murmur, while the familiar shipboard sounds—the creaking woodwork and rattling glass—lapsed into silence. A quick glance at her pocket watch told her she was due to report at the gangways in ten minutes' time, so Esther climbed the last steps to D Deck, arriving at the starboard shell doors to find Murdoch, Lightoller, and Moody already present.

While the rest of the officers nodded at her in polite greeting, Murdoch didn't even spare her a glance. In fact, her superior officer seemed almost determined to ignore her. Esther felt her throat tighten as she sidled up next to Moody, only distantly listening to his eager chatter as they waited for passengers to arrive.

Boarding was a smooth process, much to Esther's relief. Unlike the ports of Southampton and Cherbourg, there were no unruly passengers to cause any trouble, no commanders demanding that she be removed from sight. Most passengers simply regarded her with puzzlement or mild interest before moving on, but a few seemed fascinated by a woman in uniform. One tall, sharp-dressed man with a bushy mustache paused to compliment her, insisting she keep up the good work, and it was only after he departed for his cabin that she learned he was a Comstock Lode millionaire. Another bespectacled passenger held up his tiny pocket Kodak and kindly asked for her photograph before he disembarked; he looked to be clergy, judging by his high-necked collar and dark robes, and Esther tried not to feel awkward as she posed alongside Murdoch.

She'd expected her superior officer to excuse himself after the first photograph, but he merely leaned closer to her, a curiosity in his eyes.

"Enjoying the attention?" he asked mildly.

Esther shrugged, keeping motionless as the lens shutter snapped once more. "Not really," she admitted. "But I don't mind it. It's nice, sir. Not being treated like garbage for a change."

Murdoch hesitated, searching her face. A flicker of uneasiness appeared in his eyes, and Esther wondered if he was recalling his harsh words from last night. But it was a fleeting thought—a *useless* thought—and she gratefully wrenched her gaze from his when the cleric approached her, thanked her for the photographs, and departed the ship.

By noon, when the gangplanks were disassembled and the boarding passes all stacked together, Lightoller slipped away to fulfill his duties while Esther followed Moody and Murdoch topside to cast off. But they no sooner stepped emerged onto the boat deck when Murdoch spoke.

"You go on ahead, Mr. Moody. I must speak with Miss Bailey alone for a moment."

Shit.

Esther could feel her erratic heart thudding against her ribcage. She watched helplessly as Moody started down the promenade, leaving her standing alone on deck with her superior officer. Murdoch was looking very closely at her, and she dropped her gaze to her shoes, unwilling to meet the blue of his eyes. It was a while before he spoke.

"I don't need to tell you that you overstepped your bounds this morning," he said quietly. "But you weren't the only one. I overreacted, and for that, I apologize." Esther looked up at him, stunned, wondering if this was some kind of joke. But his eyes were steady, his voice sincere as he continued, "I think it would be in the best interests of our work relationship to forget all this and move on. What do you say?"

She hesitated, not even daring to believe it, a glint of skepticism in her eyes. "Are you being *serious*, sir?"

"Quite."

Esther broke into a smile, her expression full of a tentative hope that maybe they could be agreeable work partners after all. The knot of tension within her chest eased slightly, and she told him, "I would like that very much, Mr. Murdoch."

"That's settled, then." Murdoch didn't smile back, but his mood seemed considerably lighter, Esther thought. He straightened up, clearing his throat and getting back to business. "Well, lass. Now that we're on agreeable terms, I suppose this would be a good time to tell you that you're missing your tie."

Esther gasped, her smile vanishing as her hands flew up to find her throat utterly bare. She hadn't even realized she'd forgotten the damn thing. "Cripes! I'm so sorry! I can run to my cabin and get it, Mr.

Murdoch, it'll only take a moment."

"I'll go along with you, then." She glanced at Murdoch in bewilderment, and he added, "*Someone* has to tie it properly." He started down the boat deck, smirking a little as she wrinkled up her nose in a scowl. "Come along, lass, and be quick about it. Captain's waiting."

She scurried after him, heart sinking in dismay. "The captain? *He'll* be on the bridge during our shift?"

Though Murdoch wasn't looking at her, Esther still saw his eyebrows arch in disbelief. "I should think that would be obvious," he snorted. "We're heading out to open sea today, Miss Bailey. Where *else* would he be? The boiler room?"

Esther fell silent at this. Smith intimidated her, and she had never been able to shake the feeling that her captain was none too pleased to have her aboard. He'd been forced into it, after all, and she wouldn't be surprised if there was a hint of resentment buried underneath his venerable façade. Her thoughts spun with worry as she hurried down the corridor and inside her cabin, keeping her chin raised and posture straight in an effort to conceal her nerves. She was surprised when Murdoch followed her inside the room, pausing only to leave the door ajar. He swept his hands behind his back, sea-blue eyes studying her messy quarters with a curious expression, taking in everything from the peppermint candy wrappers littering the floor to the heavy maritime books dumped carelessly over her bed. A small smile crossed his face, as if something amused him, but she was too busy scouring the room for her tie to give it much thought.

Eventually, she found the damn thing bundled away in a pile of clothes, and she rose to her feet.

"Here," she said, trying not to look at him as she thrust the thin strip of silk into his waiting hands. "Since you think you can do better."

"Without question," Murdoch replied.

He stepped toward her, so close she could catch his heady smell of soap and aftershave. He swept the tie around her neck and worked quietly, twisting and looping in ways she still couldn't quite understand. She felt her heartbeat quicken as she faced him, and she wished he hadn't followed her inside her cabin. Her thoughts were straying where they shouldn't; she kept thinking of all the things his hands could do to her, rather than merely playing with her tie. She wondered if they would be gentle, trailing across her skin with quiet intimacy. Or strong and capable, yanking off her work skirt in a matter of seconds and pinning her down on her mattress with ease…

Stop that! Esther scolded herself, stamping out her filthy, unbidden imaginings at once. Already she could feel her cheeks flame with embarrassment. *He's your superior officer, you loony. Superior. Officer. You can't think about him like that.*

She was immensely relieved when Murdoch tightened the knot and withdrew his hands.

"There we are," he said in a wry voice. "I do believe you're suitable for the bridge now, Miss Bailey, though that's not saying m—"

"Great, that's great," Esther said distractedly, and before he could say another word, she barreled out the door at breakneck speed.

Murdoch followed, albeit at a slower pace. He was regarding her with amusement, and she knew it was likely because her cheeks were blazing pink. She tried not to notice as they crossed the hall and through the wheelhouse, emerging onto a bridge already bathed in warm afternoon light. Esther felt her flustered chagrin shift to awe as she noted the untroubled sea, the glimmering telegraphs, the air of anticipation hanging in the cool sea air. While Murdoch started for the starboard bridge wing, she assumed her place to the left of Moody. Her young colleague stood behind the helmsman, looking impressively dignified with his hands behind his back and chin raised into the air.

"Ready?" he asked her with a smile.

Esther nodded, her eyes fixed on the distant point where blue sky met brilliant sea. Excitement bubbled in the pit of her stomach as the whistle horn bellowed, signaling it was time to weigh anchor and set out at last.

Clouds of steam hissed and tumbled from the enormous funnels above their heads, while deckhands roamed across the bridge and the bow, ensuring all equipment was in working order. Murdoch gave the order for *Slow Ahead*, then *Half Ahead*, keeping a ready gaze fixed on the glistening sea. Foam trembled before the ship's prow like billows of frost, sheer and glittering. Esther felt the engines beat faster, deeper—echoing in time with the pounding of her heart—and before she knew it, *Titanic* was underway, gliding due west into the deep, chilly waters of the North Atlantic. The green swell of the Irish coast faded fast behind them, and soon there was nothing but open ocean, stretching as far as the eye could see.

Esther was so thoughtlessly captivated by the sight before her that she didn't realize Smith had emerged from the wheelhouse. He strolled to the starboard wing to join Murdoch, who studied the vast, blue water with pride. They spoke briefly, voices drowned out by the roar of wind and steam and seafoam. Esther didn't know what words passed between them, but Murdoch suddenly came strolling into the bridge with a relaxed grin, arms swinging confidently at his sides.

"All Ahead Full, Mr. Moody," he called, striding to the main engine-order telegraph and drawing back its lever in one fluid motion.

"Very good, sir."

Moody's reply was brisk, professional—but Esther could still hear the eagerness in his voice. She watched her colleague step promptly to the port engine-order telegraph, and bells within the heavy brass machine trilled as he yanked the lever to *Full Ahead*.

The change in speed was gradual, but once it picked up, it became nothing short of outstanding. Esther stood by the logometer, watching the needle rise before jotting the numbers down in the logbook.

Twenty-one knots.

She couldn't stop beaming as she returned to her post. Adrenaline coursed through her veins as she surveyed the sea, her eyes sparkling with wonder and awestruck delight. The sheer momentum of *Titanic* was an exhilarating thing, profound enough to make her shipmates stand tall and proud. It was a reminder that the giantess beneath them was a marvel of mechanical excellence, first and foremost, and not simply a floating palace of luxury. It was a truly impressive sight to behold—breathtaking, even— and Esther knew she would never forget it.

Eventually her attention wandered elsewhere, and she peered toward the bridge wing where Murdoch stood, curious to see his reaction to all this excitement. Esther thought he would be gazing out at the ocean. Or conversing with the captain, perhaps. So when she casually looked his way, she didn't expect to find the first officer looking straight at her.

Their eyes met for a half second before he quickly glanced away, staring almost determinedly at the horizon—and Esther felt a wild flutter in her chest that had nothing to do with the thrilling speed of *Titanic* beneath her.

THIRTEEN

THE DINNER

April 11, 1912 | 17:45

M URDOCH WAS FEELING restless as he paced back and forth along the officers' promenade, waiting for his subordinate to join him.

It was chilly out, the waves rumbling as usual, the ocean winds bitter and smelling strongly of brine. But Murdoch paid little mind to the cold or salty air as he roamed the deck, passing the bulky lifeboats and listening to their tarpaulins flit about in the wind.

While his expression was remarkably composed—a simple feat thanks to years of practice and formality—it was his eyes that betrayed him.

Murdoch was usually able to keep his emotions under control, tucked away where no one might see them. But now his apprehension was all too visible, slipping through his gaze like light shining through the edges of a doorframe.

The professionalism he prided himself on was slowly but surely dissolving, and the more he dwelled on what the evening would bring, the more agitated he became. Though he admittedly wouldn't mind keeping company with Bailey tonight, Murdoch found himself wishing he'd never agreed to attend in the first place. His pacing grew even more feverish as he imagined sitting amongst the first-class passengers, surrounded by crystal and champagne and delicacies he couldn't pronounce, and he ran a hand through his dark hair to steady himself.

But despite his nerves, Murdoch was still every bit the distinguished senior officer. He'd donned the traditional full company dress for the occasion—something he had only worn a handful of times since joining the ranks of White Star Line. It was similar to his everyday uniform, the only differences being a long, double-breasted frock coat tumbling to his knees, and a pair of white gloves that were quite the contrast to his standard ones of black leather. He knew Bailey would be wearing similar attire, and his thoughts turned to her as he circled back and forth beneath the stars.

While Murdoch was glad he and the girl were on agreeable terms, smoothing out the rougher edges of their relationship at last, she still made him nervous in some ways.

Many ways, actually.

And he wasn't sure what to do about it.

Murdoch had never been an uncertain man. He had always known he would work at sea, from the time he was just a lad running around in Dalbeattie, eager to follow in his father's footsteps. He'd led his life with a sense of purpose and propriety, always working toward that singular goal of becoming a sea captain. He'd never once wandered from the path he'd built for himself. Never once let any hesitancy or second thoughts stand in his way.

But meeting Bailey had changed that.

She had changed something in him. He felt as if his entire world shifted, like a breaking wave reversing the direction of its curl, suddenly foaming and swirling itself back into the sea.

Murdoch hated how he couldn't stop thinking of her. Of her freckles and wit and wild laughter. The way her nose wrinkled up whenever she was angry at him, or otherwise looking for a fight. How effortlessly she could counter his sarcasm, but could never tell a convincing lie. And how passionately she spoke of seeing new oceans and traveling the world.

But it didn't matter what he thought of her.

Murdoch was no fool. She was his subordinate, and he her superior officer. It was just as Lightoller had warned Lowe: White Star Line policy strictly forbade relationships or any other such intimacy between shipmates, whether that be stewardesses or stokers, electricians or cooks. Unless he wanted to lose his job—and everything he worked so hard for after all these years—he could do little more than swallow down his feelings before they destroyed his career entirely.

The door to the officer's quarters opened with a quiet click, and Murdoch drew in a slow breath as Bailey emerged onto the boat deck. Like him, she wore a frock coat that looked much too long for her and a pair of white gloves she hastily tugged on as she hurried toward him.

He studied her with surprise as she drew nearer, his brooding thoughts momentarily forgotten; the girl was still her normal self, short hair brushing her shoulders, freckled face clean and without cosmetics. Not that Murdoch minded, of course. He'd merely thought it was customary for women to beautify themselves for these sorts of fancy occasions. That was how Ada had been, at least, always applying creams to her skin, and painting her lips in pale pink, and styling her beautiful, billowing hair. She'd been stunning enough to make heads turn and eyes linger no matter where they went, her shapely figure filling out her dresses and day gowns with ease. The scrawny, green-eyed girl standing before him in her too-long coat and wild freckles was quite the contrast.

But still lovely in her own right, Murdoch thought, his throat turning dry as she stepped closer.

"I hope I'm not late," Bailey said, her bold accent echoing across the stillness of the deck. "I didn't have any white gloves, so I had to ask around for some."

"No matter," Murdoch said mildly. "We still have another five minutes or so." His eyes lingered on her necktie, which was expertly knotted against her throat, and he raised his brows. "Well, *this* is quite the miracle if I've ever seen one. Since when did you learn how to knot your tie?"

Bailey laughed, her expression good-natured. "I didn't. Harold was kind enough to fix mine up when he gave me his extra gloves. Said he couldn't stand to look at such an atrocity," she added with a snort.

Something peculiar swelled through Murdoch at her words—some cold, stinging jealousy that took him by surprise. He felt it in the pit of his stomach, twisting and vile, and clenched his teeth to keep his emotions at bay. The idea of Lowe being so close to Bailey—especially considering the fifth officer's blatant interest in her—was something Murdoch didn't like. His displeasure only deepened when he remembered that Lowe was a good ten or more years younger than him. Handsome, fit, charismatic—everything that would almost certainly catch Bailey's eye, and everything Murdoch was certain he himself lacked.

But he shoved away these unbidden thoughts and feelings, keeping his expression carefully neutral.

"Did he, now? Well, I can't rightly say I blame him. Knotting ties doesn't seem to be your forte, Miss Bailey. I suggest you take the time to learn."

"Couldn't you teach me?" she asked him with a smile.

Murdoch hesitated, feeling a thrill of pleasure mixed with unease when he heard the keenness in her voice. "Don't you have a brother who can assist you with this sort of thing?" he demanded.

"I do." Her eyes glittered at him. "Perhaps I could ask him, then, if you don't think you'd be up to the task…"

She was taunting him. But Murdoch didn't dissolve into anger or outright impatience, as he normally would have done. Something about her cheeky grin and clever banter seemed to intrigue him now, and he wanted more of it.

"Correct me if I'm wrong," he teased back, stepping closer to her with his hands folded behind him, "but I do believe you're challenging me, Miss Bailey."

"I do believe you're right, Mr. Murdoch."

Murdoch cracked a wry smile despite himself. "I'll consider it," he said evenly. "But for now, we'd best head downstairs. I'm certain your brother and the rest of the guests are waiting for us." He swept one hand toward the first-class entrance. "After you, lass."

The two officers fell silent as they entered the glossy interior of the ship. Warmth washed over them like bathwater, and Murdoch was glad to leave the North Atlantic chill behind them. He led his subordinate down the sweeping expanse of the Grand Staircase, the echo of their footsteps spiraling high to the domed ceiling of light and glass. Far below, he caught the chatter of conversation coupled with the murmur of ragtime music, and he sighed, wondering what he'd gotten himself into.

When they finally reached D Deck, the officers found themselves surrounded by a sea of first-class passengers, each one more exquisitely dressed than the last. The men wore handsome white ties and wing collars, while the beautiful women shone in their sparkling dresses and satin evening gloves. Murdoch, who had never known this world, felt somewhat out of place as he gazed around, noting the waiters with their trays of champagne and the melodic harmony of a string quartet playing in the far corner of the room. But although the first officer was ill at ease, he certainly did not show it. His face was smooth and professional as he weaved among the wealthy, chin raised and hands held in a stately manner behind his back.

At length, Murdoch spotted Wilde and Captain Smith chatting with a handful of first-class passengers near the saloon entrance. He started toward them, Bailey trailing reluctantly in his wake.

"Ah, Mr. Murdoch." Smith greeted him with a smile before turning to acknowledge his seventh officer. Although he regarded Bailey in a genial manner, the hesitancy in his voice was unmistakable as he added, "And Miss Bailey as well. A pleasure to see you both this fine evening."

The passengers around Smith studied the girl with various expressions of curiosity and puzzlement. Introductions were made, and Murdoch found himself face-to-face with magnates and aristocrats he had before known only by name: the Countess of Rothes, a tall, willowy woman with a beauty mark dotting one cheek, and an enormous collar of diamonds glittering around her neck; John Thayer, vice president of the Pennsylvania Railroad who stood linking arms with his wife, Marian; Margaret Brown, the boisterous American who'd charged her way on the ship back in Cherbourg; and finally, a lithe woman who smiled in his direction, donned in elegant pearls and a shimmering dress of indigo satin. She introduced herself as Elisabeth Allen, and Murdoch realized she was the same pretty passenger who'd caught his eye back in Southampton. Unlike the Countess or Mrs. Brown, she blushed wildly when Murdoch kissed her glove in perfunctory greeting, and he tried not to feel bemused.

More passengers trickled over to greet them, including a cluster of young women who seemed *very* interested in hanging around Wilde. But Murdoch, who was already growing weary of the chatter and pleasantries, nearly sighed with relief when Smith bade farewell at last.

"Forgive us, ladies and gentlemen, but I do believe our dinner party is already seated, and we oughtn't to keep them waiting any longer." Turning to Miss Allen, Smith offered his arm. "Shall I escort you to our table, my lady?"

He led the officers and their retinue of guests inside the saloon with its Jacobean furnishings and seamless white walls, meandering around dinner tables and waiters carrying trays of spirits and sparkling wine.

Murdoch glanced down at Bailey, who trudged along at his side. She was looking sullen for some reason, glowering down at her feet with a tiny crease between her brows. Murdoch couldn't imagine what was troubling her. But before he could ask, they spotted Booker waving them over.

The young architect was handsomely dressed in his white tie and tailcoat, ink-black hair smooth and slicked back.

"There you are!" he called brightly. "Come, have a seat."

Murdoch settled himself between Miss Allen and Bailey before glancing around the table, taking in the new faces before him.

He recognized Callum Lockerbie, the son of oil tycoon Niles Lockerbie. His narrowed hazel eyes were fixed on Bailey as he pressed a cigarette to his lips, his face unreadable. Bruce Ismay and Thomas Andrews were present as well, seated at the far end of the table beside the Thayers. But there were a handful of other passengers Murdoch couldn't quite name, including a portly man with a bushy silver mustache, and two women who were likely related given their likeness and blonde hair. Smith was quick to make introductions around the table, and Murdoch came to learn the mustached man was Archibald Gracie, while the two women were silver heiresses Fay and Florence Harlow. He nodded and introduced himself as well—though he admittedly wasn't paying much attention at this point. There were far too many names to remember in one night, and Murdoch was certain he'd forget half of them come morning.

Once all the guests had taken their seats, waiters clothed in white passed around bread rolls and filled glasses with bubbling champagne. As Andrews spread a napkin upon his lap, he cleared his throat.

"Pardon me, everyone," he said, "but I don't believe I've had the pleasure of introducing you to Booker Bailey, my apprentice and future shipwright for Harland and Wolff."

He gestured toward Booker, who sat straighter, eyes swelling with pride. Andrews studied him with a softness in his gaze before continuing, "And his sister, maritime graduate and White Star Line's newest junior officer, Esther Bailey."

A brief murmur of formalities and words of pleasant greeting flitted around the table. Murdoch stole a glance at his subordinate, who merely wore a passive half-smile, one hand resting on the stem of her water glass. Mrs. Brown winked at her, while Gracie lifted his glass toward the Bailey siblings in polite acknowledgment.

"A pleasure to finally meet the children of Dr. Bailey," he said kindly.

But others were not so courteous—namely Miss Florence, who scrutinized Bailey with a piercing stare, and Lockerbie, who was smirking at her in a peculiar manner.

Ismay chipped in, his lofty upper-class drawl sweeping across the table. "Esther and Booker are here on behalf of my good friend and business partner, J.D. Bailey. He spoke highly of his niece and nephew's talents and requested that we find suitable positions for them onboard."

"How splendid!" Miss Allen said, but Miss Florence Harlow was not so impressed.

"Forgive me, Mr. Ismay," she laughed sweetly. "But I fail to understand how the position of nautical officer is considered suitable for a woman. Surely the role of a stewardess would be more appropriate?"

Murdoch felt his hands tighten into fists beneath the table as a peculiar sensation seized him, hotter than molten steel. Mrs. Brown looked ready to breathe fire, but before Ismay could reply, Bailey cleared her throat.

"Yes," she said dully, "because I spent four years of my life studying maritime law to work as a stewardess."

A stunned silence followed her words, and while Andrews and Wilde looked amused, a few guests regarded her with varying degrees of disapproval—the captain included. Miss Florence went rigid in her seat, a look of outrage spreading across her pointed face. She opened her mouth to scold, but Mrs. Brown cut over her immediately.

"Four years!" she boomed, her voice so boisterous Murdoch wondered if those below decks could hear it. "Well, ain't that somethin'." She nodded at Bailey with approval, a warmth in her eyes. "Good on you, honey. You deserve to wear that uniform."

Bailey smiled. "Thank you, Molly."

Mr. Thayer laughed suddenly, as if their conversation was some kind of crude joke. "*I* don't believe women should be in uniform at all." Turning to Smith, he chuckled, "Aren't you worried what people might *say*, E.J.?"

Murdoch stiffened, knowing all too well of the captain's lukewarm acceptance of his seventh officer. But the bond between crew was a strong thing—a loyal thing—so Smith raised his chin as he replied, "What should anyone say? She has proven herself to be a capable officer, John. And she is welcome amongst our ranks."

Thayer fell silent, and Bailey leaned back in her seat, making little effort to hide her cheery grin behind her water cup.

There was a brief lull in conversation as waiters roved around once again, scooping caviar onto plates and refilling glasses with chilled water. For a moment, all was relatively calm. Miss Florence and Mrs. Thayer were engrossed in a conversation about wedding gowns. Booker leaned toward Lockerbie with a smirk, muttering something that made the pair of them dissolve into quiet laughter. Ismay seemed focused on the caviar and lemon wedges on his plate, while Andrews scribbled in a pocket-sized notebook, lost in his own world and utterly oblivious to the proceedings around him.

Murdoch somehow found himself chatting with the young woman on his left—Miss Allen, he recalled—who kept peppering him with questions about himself. Who he was, where he came from, what sort of business he attended to on the ship.

But even as Miss Allen smiled and batted her long lashes at him, and the guests drank their fill of champagne and fine wine, Murdoch could sense the interest in Bailey had not yet dwindled. It came as no surprise when they all turned their attention to her again.

"So, what prompted you to choose such a career, Miss Bailey?" Gracie asked over a spoonful of barley soup.

"An interest in travel and the sea, sir," Bailey replied.

Her tone of voice was polite but also terse, and Murdoch sensed she wanted to avoid talking about herself as much as possible. He certainly didn't blame her. He wouldn't have liked to be put on the spot, either. But then again, Bailey was quite the oddity. Sitting before them in her knotted tie and officer's coat, she was a zoo animal under their prying eyes.

A short pause lingered as everyone waited for Bailey to elaborate on her choice of profession. But when she remained wordlessly defiant, it was Lockerbie who spoke.

"Miss Bailey and I have been family friends for a long while," he said smoothly. "She used to talk about *nothing* but boats when we were young. I daresay Mr. Bailey and I couldn't go more than two feet without hearing her prattle on about them."

The table twittered with laughter, and even Booker cracked a smile.

"It's true," he chuckled. "She was mighty crazy about ships. Still is, to be honest."

Bailey didn't even glance at her brother. She was staring at Lockerbie with the flattest expression Murdoch had ever seen, eyes glazed over with boredom. She arched a single brow as Lockerbie went on, "Perhaps this, ah…charming little position aboard *Titanic* is her true calling after all."

He lowered his cigarette, his smile almost mocking.

"Since nursing didn't quite work out for her. Pity, really."

It was as if bait were dropped into a pool of sharks, and Miss Florence snapped it up at once.

"So you were a nurse once." She smiled at Bailey in a way that disgusted Murdoch. "I can't help but wonder what might have prompted you to abandon such an imperative field, Miss Bailey. Perhaps you can enlighten us?"

Bailey took a sip from her water glass, a challenge in her eyes. Murdoch wondered what she might say. He could remember all too well the night he and his colleagues dined in the officers' mess, and she'd told them snippets of her past. She'd said an accident prevented her from continuing her nursing career, but Murdoch damn well knew better. Those grisly scars all along her arms weren't from some bloody animal, either, no matter what lame excuse she'd tried to muster up. Motorcar accident seemed more likely to him, though he would never ask her outright. Not unless she was willing to share the truth with him. Murdoch would respect her privacy and keep his distance like a proper gentleman— unlike the nosy, narrow-minded people who seemed perfectly content to interrogate the poor girl throughout dinner.

"Well?" Miss Florence prompted, when Bailey remained silent. "We're waiting, officer."

Bailey lifted an eyebrow. "My sincerest apologies, ma'am," she said lightly, "but I'm afraid I won't be able to enlighten you this evening."

"Oh?" The woman's chilling smile faltered slightly. "And why not?"

"Because I don't think my personal affairs are any of your damn business, that's why."

Miss Fay Harlow had been staring distantly at her plate for most of the conversation, her beautiful face frozen as if carved from marble. But now she lifted her eyes to stare straight at Bailey, the corners of her crimson lips twitching up into a small smile. Wilde hid a smirk behind his champagne glass while Andrews glanced up from his notebook, shaking with silent laughter. But Smith was far less amused. His blue eyes snapped to Bailey, stern and sharp with authority.

"Miss Bailey," he warned. "Mind your attitude."

She bowed her head at his rebuke. "Yes, sir. I apologize."

Clearing his throat, Booker spoke quickly in an effort to control the damage. "My sister left our father's hospital on her own accord," he explained. "It was a conscious decision, and he obliged her."

"Did he *really*?" Mr. Thayer sneered. "Heavens, I'm not so sure that was wise."

"Quite the contrary." Booker's voice was cold. "It was the wisest choice of his life."

Murdoch stole a curious glance at his subordinate, but she was busy calling over another waiter for more water. Her face was utterly impassive, but he didn't miss the way her gloved hands clenched the armrests of her chair, gripping them as if they were her only tether to the world.

She's angry, Murdoch thought.

He could see it in the blaze of her green eyes. But despite her anger, the girl still remained straight-faced and dignified, refusing to let any question or criticism rattle her composure. And Murdoch—who knew all too well of her temper—was surprised.

She was in the captain's presence, after all. Perhaps she didn't want to say anything too nasty or uncouth that might reflect poorly on Smith...

Or on you, a small voice at the back of his head reminded him.

The fourth course soon arrived at the table, and the guests were momentarily distracted by the assortment of plates and bowls laid out before them: poached salmon and pan-seared filet mignon, creamed carrots and crisped Chateau potatoes. Steam coiled from a platter of roasted duckling and rice, while mint sauce dripped over platefuls of lamb.

While everyone tucked in, Bailey didn't touch any food or champagne, merely opting for water and a single dinner roll instead. She spent most of the evening ignoring the patrons at the table, preferring to converse with Mrs. Brown or Wilde instead. Murdoch found himself looking at her more often than he should, listening to her hearty laughter and trying to interpret the strange, light feeling in his chest.

By the time the sixth course rolled around, there were even more exotic dishes he could not name. He frowned at the questionable lump of paste slapped on his dinner plate, lathered in a dark sauce and sprinkled with some kind garnish.

Christ in Heaven, he thought. *The hell am I even looking at?*

Miss Allen spotted the bewildered look on his face and spared him a pearly smile.

"Something the matter, Mr. Murdoch?" she asked lightly.

"No, not at all," Murdoch replied. "I'm simply trying to figure out what this…is." He nodded at the slab of colorless meat on his plate.

"Why, pâté de foie gras, of course! Goose liver." Miss Allen laughed at the incredulous look on his face. "Goodness, Mr. Murdoch. Do you mean to say you've *never* eaten foie gras before?"

"'Fraid not." Murdoch's smile was wry. "I'm a simple man, miss. I fancy a good Scotch ale and a bit o' haggis above all else."

He was being facetious; such was his nature. But Miss Allen didn't seem to catch his tongue-in-cheek humor.

"Oh, I can imagine." She leaned closer to Murdoch, her large, pretty brown eyes sweeping him up and down with interest. "Tell me, Mr. Murdoch, is haggis any decent? I've not tried it before, but I suppose I wouldn't mind having a taste. Especially since it just so happens to be Scottish."

Murdoch raised a brow at her suggestive tone of voice. He was about to respond, but Bailey was quicker, speaking bluntly from his right. "Well, there's nothing more disgusting than foie gras. But haggis comes fairly close. *Too* close, I'd say."

"Thank you for sharing, Miss Bailey," Murdoch said flatly, and she smirked before turning her attention to Mrs. Brown.

Another hour passed before desserts were brought out for the tenth bloody course, everything from eclairs slathered in chocolate frosting to little crystal bowls piled with French ice cream and chartreuse jelly. But Murdoch had enough. If he'd have known that the damn dinner would have taken this long, he would have said no from the start. All the endless dining and trite conversation were beginning to wear on his nerves, to say nothing of the fancy dishes and their perplexing flavors.

He was just wondering whether to excuse himself when he caught the end of a conversation at the table.

"Oh, for Heaven's *sake*," Bailey huffed, while Miss Fay stared at her, eyes soft with astonishment and gratitude. "If she doesn't like roses, don't order roses. It's your sister's wedding, isn't it? Shouldn't she be the one deciding what kind of flowers to have?"

Miss Florence rounded on her with frosty eyes. "And what do you know of marriage and weddings?" she demanded crossly. "Do you even have a husband, Miss Bailey?"

Murdoch went very still. It was the same question he'd wondered for a while now, but never had had the gall to ask. Officers wore gloves while on duty, after all; he'd never once had a moment to inspect Bailey's bare fingers. But now he listened intently, his eyes burning into the water glass in his hands as Bailey answered, "No, ma'am. But that's neither here nor there—"

Lockerbie cut in, cold amusement in his eyes. "She was engaged," he said. "To Dr. Joseph Muir."

A murmur of surprise rippled across the table, and although Murdoch didn't have a clue who the doctor was, recognition seemed to flicker in the eyes of the American guests. Suddenly defensive, he glanced down at his subordinate on instinct and saw her hands clenching her armrests as if her life depended on it. She lifted her chin, her gaze full of fire, of defiance, as if daring someone to make a remark.

Mrs. Thayer was the first to speak, exchanging a glance with her husband before rounding on Bailey in disbelief. "*You* were engaged to New York's foremost surgeon? I don't believe it."

"She can't have been," Miss Florence scoffed. "The man killed himself. It was all over the papers several years ago."

"That's right." Gracie nodded. "I remember it well. Though I do believe the reports said he was engaged to the daughter of Dr. Arthur Bailey—and that he lost his medical license a year prior. Something to do with a crux of alcoholism, I believe, the poor fellow."

Miss Florence sighed, shaking her head in a theatrical display of false sympathy. "Terrible shame, terrible shame." Her thin, piercing blue eyes raked over Bailey, and she added loftily, "My, Miss Bailey, it's no wonder why your engagement fell through. Alcoholics are prone to violence, are they not? I do hope you weren't involved in any…altercations."

A shocked silence followed her words as the guests glanced uncomfortably at one another; Miss Florence had gone too far.

Murdoch could hear the blood roaring in his ears, his veins flooding with an anger so hot, it singed his skin.

"*Enough*, madam."

His voice was a quiet snarl; it was a miracle he'd managed to get out the words without bellowing them across the table. He was furious. But that was nothing compared to Booker, who looked ready to commit murder. Bailey, however, blinked at Miss Florence with steely calm.

"Your concern is overwhelming," she said, and this time, she did not bother to conceal her sarcasm. "But as I said before, the personal details of my life are none of your business. So perhaps you should let well enough alone, before you embarrass yourself any further."

She gracefully rose to her feet, smoothing out the front of her frock coat as she addressed the table. "Forgive me, everyone. As…delightful as this evening has been, I'm afraid I must retire early and prepare for my watch. Do excuse me."

Murdoch started to rise from his chair to go along with her. So did Booker. But Wilde was quicker than the pair of them.

Rage glittered in the chief officer's eyes as he assumed his full, towering height, and it was clear he was livid by the way Bailey had been treated. But he still addressed her with surprising gentleness—tender as though speaking to a daughter or a friend, not a fellow officer.

"May I escort you to the officers' quarters, miss?"

"No, thank you, Mr. Wilde."

"Please," Wilde implored, gray eyes soft with sympathy. "I insist."

But Bailey shook her head. "That's quite all right. I appreciate it, sir. But I'll be just fine on my own."

She offered him a polite smile before nodding at the table in farewell.

And then she was gone, striding out of the dining saloon and leaving only silence in her wake.

21:00

It wasn't until Esther stepped out onto the boat deck that the tears finally came to her eyes.

She had held it together for as long as she could. She had endured those passengers with their belittling stares and scrutiny throughout the evening. She had sat through a myriad of wretched criticisms and inquiries and insults, never once allowing herself to falter.

But now that she was long gone from the first-class dining saloon, she could feel herself start to unravel, falling apart at the seams.

Her tears of anger and humiliation pooled in her eyes until the decks and the dark ocean water were blurred from sight. Her throat burned as if scalded by fire, and she swallowed hard to keep from sobbing altogether.

Esther wasn't at all certain where she was going as she hurried afore, her vision glazed with tears and cheeks stinging with cold. She still had another hour left before her watch, and she didn't know what to do with herself in the meantime. Perhaps retreat to the darkness of her cabin, lock the door tight, and bury herself underneath an ocean of blankets. The thought sounded all too desirable, and she started for her quarters, still fighting back the sobs trapped in her throat.

But as her unwieldy footsteps brought her to the starboard side of the ship, she noticed a handful of deck crew smoking their cigarettes along the promenade, leering at her. Not wanting them to see an officer in tears, Esther quickly ducked inside the nearest room and swung the door shut behind her.

It took her teary eyes a moment to adjust to the gloom, and when she snapped on a light switch, she realized where she was.

The officers' smoking room.

She had been here only once before, during her introductory meeting with Lightoller so many days ago. It was a simple white-walled room with a circular table surrounded by leather chairs. There was a pantry in one corner, stuffed to the brim with packaged food and beer bottles, whistles, flashlights, shaving kits, and a heavy tin case of boxed cigars. A brass clock hung on the wall beside an array of coat hooks, while a slanted skylight stretched above her head, its glass rattling faintly with the engine vibrations as it displayed the heavens above.

Rubbing a palm over her eyes, Esther wiped the tears away and made for the pantry. She hadn't touched any food at the dinner out of righteous defiance, and now she realized how hungry she was. She snagged a box of crackers and a bottle of lager from the shelf before dropping herself into a chair, sniffing, eyes still blurred and watery.

Esther had always prided herself on being strong of will and mind. She'd never been one to cry if she could help it.

But now her strength was crumbling away, the fire in her heart withering to embers, charred and cold. She felt so goddamn vulnerable as she curled over in her seat, sobbing, salty tears spilling thick and fast down her cheeks.

And she *hated* it.

Perhaps if Muir hadn't been mentioned, she would have been fine. She would have been able to keep herself from crying. But dragging out those dark, personal details amidst a formal dinner—in front of her superiors and *Murdoch*, no less—was enough to make her crumple, bowing to the depths of her shame and sadness.

Even now, all the memories she once tucked away were flooding back: her fiancé's contorted face as he bellowed at her, the tang of brandy on his breath; the pain as she was dragged by her hair across their hotel room, scraping along the glass remains of a shattered table; the sound of a bottle whistling through the air before it exploded against her arm, slicing her skin and leaving the scars she still had to this day—but worst of all was the empty defeat of working beside Muir at the hospital, hiding her bruises behind cosmetics and pretending their engagement was the paradigm of perfection.

He was dead now, of course—and good riddance—but the scars remained, to say nothing of the deeper wounds that had never seemed to heal at all.

Esther wasn't sure how much time passed before the door clicked open, and someone stepped inside.

She could hear their footsteps, but she didn't bother to turn. Not even when a soft, Scottish voice filled the quiet space.

"You're a hard one to find."

Sniffling, Esther scrambled to dry her eyes on her cuff. She couldn't fathom what her superior officer was doing here, let alone why he'd sought her out in the first place.

Probably came to tell me off, I'll bet, she thought miserably, slouching lower in her seat and wishing he would go away.

But he didn't.

And Esther—desperate to pretend as if everything was right as rain—found herself reverting to her usual attitude.

"We're on a ship, Mr. Murdoch. It's not as if I can go very far."

His footfalls grew louder as he paced around the table, though his voice remained surprisingly calm.

"Your cheek is appreciated as always, lass."

Now that Murdoch was in her line of sight, Esther could see he had changed clothes, discarding his frock coat for his greatcoat and trading his white gloves for his traditional pair of black leather. He held a teacup in one hand and a cardboard container in the other, which he laid on the table before pulling out a chair.

"Mind if I join you?"

Esther turned her head away from him. "I'd prefer if you didn't," she mumbled. "I'd rather not subject myself to more ridicule, thanks."

"And who says I'm going to ridicule you?" he demanded. "I'm not entirely heartless, lass. Whatever you might think of me."

Wordlessly he settled at the table and slid the cardboard container toward her. "Here. Brought you some food from the mess. And tea, if you'd like."

Curious, Esther opened the container to find an assortment of cheeses and scones. She glanced up at Murdoch in astonishment, her wariness fading.

"Thank you, sir," she murmured gratefully.

She lowered the beer bottle and lifted the tea to her lips instead, glad for the soothing warmth it brought her. It was a welcome sensation, slipping through her veins like rich molten honey and chasing the cold hurt away. As she drank, Murdoch removed his cap and laced his fingers in quiet speculation, brow furrowed as if pondering what to say. After a long moment of silence, he spoke.

"Those people were despicable." His voice was a seething murmur, hoarse with anger and disgust. "Absolutely vile. I'm sorry you had to sit through that nonsense, Miss Bailey."

He's upset, Esther realized.

Somehow, hearing the emotion in his voice only tugged at her own.

She lowered her teacup, keeping her eyes downcast for fear of Murdoch seeing the tears billowing up once more.

"It's fine, Mr. Murdoch—"

"No, Miss Bailey," he insisted. "It bloody well isn't. You didn't deserve to be treated that way. It was nothing short of cruelty." He glanced down at his hands again, clenching them until his knuckles grew white. "I'm surprised you held it together so proper, to be honest. I had half a mind to think you'd throw a champagne bottle at Miss Florence's face."

"It was tempting," Esther admitted. "She's a wicked old bitch."

"To put it lightly." Murdoch's hooded eyes were dark; he looked so troubled by his own anger that he paid little mind to her sharp curse. "Nevertheless, you handled the situation with great tact, Miss Bailey. Even Smith and Wilde were impressed."

Esther trailed one finger around the edge of her teacup. "With people like that," she said, "you have to put on a mask and wear it well. You can never let them see that they get to you. Never give them that sort of satisfaction."

She looked up at Murdoch with a sniff. Her voice was stronger, bolder—and although her eyes were bloodshot, they were absent of tears. "I'm proud of who I am and what I've done, no matter what they say. I chose this life, sir. And I don't regret it one bit."

A silence fell between them as Esther sipped her tea, and Murdoch frowned at his interlocked hands. When he spoke again, his voice was gruff but still thoughtful.

"Well, as repulsive as that entire ordeal was, I s'pose I did learn a little more about you this evening. I'd no idea you were once engaged."

She shrugged. "You never asked."

Murdoch hesitated. He looked torn between wanting to know more of her, and wanting to keep a respectful distance. But it seemed his inquisitiveness got the better of him, because he softly asked, "Is it true, then? What they said at dinner?"

Esther nodded. She lowered the teacup on the table as she met her superior's careful stare, and the words came tumbling out before she could stop them.

"I met him when I was eighteen," she explained. "He was hired on as the chief surgeon at my father's hospital, and I was just a nurse in training at the time. We were engaged within the year."

It was odd, almost, opening up to Murdoch about her past when only days ago she'd desperately tried to shutter it from him. But she felt inexplicably...*closer* to her superior officer. He'd come to find her, after all, when he could have simply spurned her and continued on with his evening. He'd brought her tea and food. And he was still with her right this moment, keeping her company instead of letting her cry all by her lonesome.

So that meant *something*...right?

Esther continued without pause, eyes dry and voice steady, letting her secrets pour out like spilled ink and not caring where they might stain.

"I'd be lying if I said I wasn't madly in love with him. He was charming, and so very handsome. I was more than ready to be his wife. But things didn't work out as planned, as you learned at dinner."

"He was a drunkard." Murdoch's voice had grown quiet.

"Yes, Mr. Murdoch." She wrenched her eyes away from his, swallowing against the awful burn in her throat. "It's astounding how easily people can change once they've found the bottom of a whisky bottle."

Murdoch frowned at her, and his expression of puzzlement became one of sheer outrage as he studied her forearms. Although she kept them hidden beneath the sleeves of her long frock coat, Esther knew what he was envisioning. She watched him press his fingers to his temples and shut his eyes for a long moment, as if struggling to collect himself. And when he lowered his hand and made to look at her again, his gaze was cold with fury, storming with a dark, vicious hatred for a man he'd never known.

"*Christ* in Heaven," he gritted out, voice rough and slightly shaking, as if he could barely keep his rage contained. Esther didn't think she had ever seen him so angry. "I should've known. Your story about the animal was proper mince enough to make me think a bad motorcar crash was to blame." He swallowed hard, apple bobbing in his throat. "But it seems the truth is much worse."

Esther avoided his gaze and looked down at the table instead, studying the glossy wood grain swirling underneath her teacup.

"He beat me the night of our engagement party. Badly. That was the worst it had ever been, and I knew I had to get out before he ended up doing something worse. So I broke off the engagement, left my father's hospital for seafaring, and never looked back."

"Did he…did your father support you?"

She shook her head. "He didn't. My brothers did, though, and my uncle. I had them on my side, and that was all I needed." Drawing in another sip of tea, she added, "Regardless of what happened, sir, I don't let it trouble me. All in all, it brought me here. I was able to leave nursing behind to work as an officer. And I wouldn't trade that for anything." Her voice was sincere, her gaze meaningful and full of heart as it held his. "Truly, I wouldn't."

She smiled before sliding a scone toward him. Murdoch caught it effortlessly, and the anger in his eyes softened a little.

"Will you always work at sea?" he asked, seemingly wanting to change the subject. "You'll never marry or settle down?"

Esther snorted. "Settle down? God, no. Can you imagine how much of a bore that would be? Marriage just isn't in the cards for me, sir. I'm having far too much fun with this job to call it quits now." Her eyes traveled to his laced hands, and she couldn't help but ask, "And what of you? I assume you're not married, either? I haven't seen a ring."

"You were looking, then." He raised his eyebrows. "I'm flattered, lass."

The heat rushed right to her cheeks. "I wasn't *looking*," she lied, indignant. "I was simply…making an observation."

"Aye, right." Murdoch was smirking, and Esther sank lower in her chair, embarrassed, wishing she'd never said anything in the first place. "Well, Miss Bailey, if you must know, I was married once. But we divorced a year ago."

"May I ask what happened?"

Murdoch shrugged. "There's not much to say. She wanted to start a family. Settle down in the country. But I was always at sea, sometimes for months at a time."

Esther bit her lower lip, waiting for him to continue and trying to ignore the improper thrill of elation at knowing he was an unmarried man. *Jesus*, she thought, *Of all the things to think about.*

She silently scolded herself as Murdoch went on, "It was hard on her, you understand. I kept correspondence through letters as often as I could, but it was never enough. She wanted me to quit my job. Leave seafaring behind. I refused." He released a quiet sigh of resignation, one hand sifting through his dark, gray-threaded hair. "In the end, we simply couldn't move past our differences. We divorced last year, and I've not regretted the decision since."

Esther was quiet for a moment, staring down at the steam swirling from her tea. "Did you love her?" she asked, the words tumbling out before she could stop them.

Murdoch didn't seem offended by the inappropriateness of her question—only thoughtful.

"I used to think so," he admitted. "She was a right beauty, and I do miss her at times." He smiled wistfully. "But if I truly loved her, I'd have chosen her over my career. Without a doubt."

"But your career will always come first?"

"I don't know, Miss Bailey." His voice was weary; he seemed unwilling to meet her eyes. "I'm still trying to figure that out."

Esther tilted her head to one side, studying him curiously. "So, you've been a bachelor for some time, then. It's no wonder why Miss Allen was trying so hard to catch your eye at dinner."

Murdoch glanced up at once, his round ears suddenly reddening, and the chagrin on his face was enough to make her laugh aloud.

"Well, it's true," she chuckled. "She was quite flirty with you, sir."

"Was she, now?" he said flatly, arching a brow. "Can't say I noticed."

Esther was still laughing, too entertained by his awkward discomfort to let her own hidden jealousy of Miss Allen get the better of her. "You can play ignorant all you want, sir," she said breezily, "but it was damn obvious she was interested. Anyone with two eyes could see that."

Murdoch snorted, and she sipped her tea as she casually went on, "Perhaps she has a thing for men in uniforms."

"Perhaps," Murdoch said. And then he asked, "Do you?"

The question sent her heart fluttering against her chest.

"That depends on the gentleman wearing it," she said slyly.

"You don't say?" He laughed softly, but there was an inquisitive look in his eyes now. "And would you flirt with that gentleman, if you fancied him?"

"It's possible, sir," Esther confessed. "But unlike Miss Allen, I'd be more subtle about it."

Murdoch studied her with amusement, head tipped to one side, hands absentmindedly toying with his uneaten scone.

"Interesting," he remarked. "I didn't even know you were capable of subtlety, Miss Bailey. Let alone flirting."

"Then perhaps you're not paying much attention, Mr. Murdoch."

Heat flooded her cheeks as she regarded him—this stately senior officer who was leaning ever so slightly back in his chair, arms crossed over his chest, mouth twisted into a faint smirk as he weighed the implication of her words. Somehow, their conversation had crossed into a different kind of territory. There was an earnestness in his eyes as he held her gaze longer than he should have. Long enough to make her heartbeat turn erratic, sending electricity crackling across her skin.

And although Esther tried to fight it—tried to shove it out of her mind—she couldn't deny that she was attracted to him.

Christ, it was stupid, but she really was.

She didn't know if it was because of his dry wit that riled her up. Or because of his striking eyes that were bluer than ocean water. Or his raspy Scottish burr, perhaps.

All she knew was that they were alone together in this little smoking room, and that they had a good fifteen minutes to let off steam before their next shift. It was *more* than enough time for her to learn what his hands felt like. Enough time for him to take her right then and there— simply sweep her up on the table and be quick and filthy about it.

No one would know, in any case. The door had a deadbolt lock, and the smoking room was tucked well enough away that any moans of pleasure would have little risk of being overheard. He could splay her out on the table and have his way with her—and she with him.

Already she was aching for his touch—for strong hands snagging in her hair, or clutching her breasts, or gripping her hips as the table's woodwork rattled and swayed beneath them. Then they could make for the bridge shortly after, a bit breathless but still properly inconspicuous, going about business as usual with only the faint scent of sex lingering on their skin.

But Esther could feel the unfortunate truth pricking her like a shard of cut glass: he was her superior officer. She was his subordinate. Of course he wasn't interested in her like *that*.

There was no hope for any of the ridiculous obscenities she was fantasizing about, anyway—unless she wanted the two of them to lose their jobs.

So stop thinking about it, stupid, she snapped at herself.

Perhaps Murdoch had noticed the blush in her cheeks, or the yearning in her eyes, because his own earnestness vanished from his gaze within a matter of seconds. He shot to his feet, surprisingly cumbersome, nearly knocking aside his chair in his haste.

"As fascinating as this conversation has been, Miss Bailey," Murdoch said curtly, hands fumbling with his tie, "I think we've blathered long enough. We'd best prepare for our watch, so we don't keep Mr. Lightoller waiting." He looked her up and down with indifference before adding, "And change out of those clothes, will you? I'd better not see you on the bridge in that coat and those gloves."

She almost rolled her eyes. "Obviously not, Mr. Murdoch."

His expression was unreadable as he tugged on his gloves and swept his cap on his head. "Only making sure," he said idly. "See you in fifteen."

Murdoch turned to leave, but Esther's quiet voice had him stopping in his tracks.

"Sir?"

"Yes, Miss Bailey?"

She bit her lip, shy beneath his steady blue stare. "Thank you for keeping me company, sir. Especially after everything that happened this evening. I just...I..." Esther struggled for the meaningful words to convey what she truly felt. But when she came up short, she merely said once again, "Thank you."

His stern expression softened, and he sighed, "Don't mention it, lass."

Nodding farewell, Murdoch disappeared onto the boat deck in a rush of salt and cold, and Esther was left to wade through the improper thoughts she had no business having in the first place.

FOURTEEN

THE FIGHT

April 12, 1912 | 08:30

A DEEP CHILL PIERCED the air when Murdoch awoke early Friday morning, seeping into his skin and serving as yet another reminder of how forbidding the North Atlantic could be.

The first officer had never liked the cold much. While the freezing winters of Scotland were tolerable, this briny Atlantic chill was something else entirely. Murdoch could feel it burrow into his bones like needles, brushing his skin as if glazed in ice.

His thick woolen greatcoat certainly came in handy during the early mornings and late nights, but it was never enough. And it didn't help that his nose tended to redden like a sodding tomato whenever the temperatures plummeted—an unfortunate trait both Lightoller and Wilde never hesitated to taunt him about, the gits.

But this was a transoceanic crossing, not some merry holiday in the south of France. Glacial seas, stiff joints, and red, raw noses were all part of the job, as Murdoch knew too well.

He tried to convince himself the cold this morning wasn't entirely dreadful as he sat up and shoved the blankets away. But it was damn near impossible to think otherwise, and he quickly crossed the room to crank up the heater to full blast. Once he'd pulled on his dressing robe and snagged a towel from his cabinet, he headed off to the lavatory for a quick rinse, hoping the hot water might wash away the drafty chill and his own early-morning drowsiness.

The corridor was dead silent, which was typical at this hour. Lightoller was stationed on the bridge, Wilde was likely sound asleep in his cabin, and the remaining officers were either conducting their watches or snoozing as well. As for Bailey, well, Murdoch was certain she was preparing for their own shift at ten.

He couldn't help but steal a glance at her cabin door as he crossed the hall, and a peculiar, weightless sensation filled his chest as he recalled last night and the early hours of this morning.

Although their watch on the bridge had been silent and professional as per custom, something *unusual* had lingered between them the entire night. Some unspoken interest that had made their eyes meet more than once. When he and Bailey had left the bridge to make rounds, they'd ended up chatting about all manner of things, and not once had there been any animosity between them. Sure, they'd been witty and sarcastic at times, and they'd gotten into a bit of heated argument on whether or not haggis was edible—but other than that, everything had remained good-natured between them.

And the more they had walked and talked, the more Murdoch came to learn about his subordinate: how she loved the smell of redwoods in the rain, and the taste of clam chowder from her favorite pier in San Francisco; how she longed to sail to the islands of Polynesia, just to see if the water was truly as crystalline as people said; and how dearly she missed her late brother, Brighton.

She'd even prodded Murdoch with a few questions about himself, and he somehow ended up telling her all about Dalbeattie—everything from the little cottage where he grew up, to the sweeping Highlands where he used to hunt game with his father, to the hearty meals his mother used to prepare for Burns Night every winter.

All in all, it had been an enjoyable watch. Bailey had been good company, oddly enough, and it had been a relief to see her mood improve after the terrible fiasco at dinner. Murdoch had hated seeing her so out of sorts last night, hunched over with her eyes glossed with tears. But their talk had brightened her right up, it seemed. He was glad for that—and glad to have ended on a good note with her this morning, rather than shouting or storming away in frustration, as he once might have done.

But one thing kept circling his mind, and that was the sudden, precarious turn their conversation had taken in the officers' smoking room last night.

Their playful banter still echoed in his head like a ceaseless trickle of water, and he couldn't blot it out, no matter how hard he tried.

And would you flirt with that gentleman, if you fancied him?

It's possible, sir. But unlike Miss Allen, I'd be more subtle about it…

In hindsight, Murdoch should have never inquired about her flirting with a man in uniform. The question had not only been inappropriate, it had also been terribly foolish.

But he'd been curious.

And Bailey's crafty responses—coupled with the pink flush in her freckled cheeks—had intrigued him more than he'd anticipated. It was enough to make him ponder whether the feelings he'd begun to have for her were, in fact, mutual.

But while Murdoch wished he could be thrilled by the notion, he was feeling more uneasy.

It was one thing for him to be keen on his subordinate, but another thing entirely if that keenness was reciprocated.

Don't encourage her, Murdoch warned himself, as he stepped down the long corridor. *And if she flirts, don't you dare flirt back.*

These were dangerous waters he was treading—worse than those of stormy seas. And while he was attracted to Bailey, God help him, he wasn't willing to lose his job over her, let alone see her risk tarnishing her own seafaring career. No, he would simply have to reign in his emotions as strictly as possible, rather than tempt the fates and pursue her altogether.

He was brooding when he reached the lavatory tucked away on the port side of the ship. But Murdoch had barely grasped the doorknob when he heard a string of furious curses from inside.

"Stupid, goddamn, useless, piece of shoddy shit!"

Murdoch stopped dead as he recognized Bailey's snarling voice.

What in God's name…? he wondered in bewilderment.

He made to knock, but his knuckles barely brushed the white door when it flew open, and Bailey came storming out into the hall.

She nearly rammed right into him with her graceless, frantic pace—but Murdoch was swift, stepping to the side to avoid a collision.

"Jesus Christ!" she gasped, stumbling to an abrupt halt.

"Well." Murdoch arched a brow. "Good morning to you, too, lass."

He stood still for a moment, not sure what to make of her frazzled appearance.

She was dripping wet, her shoulder-length hair plastered to her neck and face, her freckled skin glistening beneath a sheen of water and suds. Her hands were furiously tightening up the sash of her dressing robe, but a sliver of skin was still visible, plunging deeply between her breasts.

Murdoch damn near wanted to turn on his heel when he saw this. Jump ship, even. But something kept him rooted in place, eyes narrowed in barely-disguised fascination as he studied his subordinate.

Bailey swept the sleeve of her robe across her forehead, wiping away the beads of water clinging there.

"You scared the bejeezus outta me, sir. What are you doing here?"

Murdoch frowned. "Is that even a question?" he demanded, incredulous. "I was headed for a rinse, obviously. Might I remind you that all officers share the lavatories, Miss Bailey. Since that seems to have slipped your mind."

"It hasn't." She breathed out a sigh of frustration. "Forgive me, sir. I'm not trying to be rude. I'm just…having issues this morning."

He snorted. "Really, now? I'd never have guessed." His eyes swept her up and down, taking in her soaked appearance but still desperately avoiding the slit of skin dipping between the folds of her robe. Funny how she hadn't made an effort to cover it up yet.

"So, what's going on, then?" he demanded. "Why all the racket?"

"It's nothing, really. The shower is just being awful stupid, that's all."

"And…?"

"And the confounded thing won't warm up, no matter what I do." Her words spilled out in an irritable hiss. "I don't know if it's because of faulty plumbing, or because Mr. Boxhall used up the hot water before me, but it went ice-cold within minutes. And I got a bit…frustrated."

"Yes, and I could hear those frustrations of yours loud and clear, Miss Bailey. Along with half the ship, I'm sure." Murdoch liked the way she tightened her nose up at him in a scowl; it was another thing he liked about her, silly though it was. "All melodramatics aside, you do realize we have a second lavatory with a second bath you may use, aye?"

"Of course, sir. I was on my way there when I ran into you."

"By all means, then," Murdoch said idly, gesturing down the hall with one hand. "Just be sure to let me know when you've finished, as I'm in need of a rinse myself."

"Sure thing." She smirked a little. "Though I can't promise there'll be any hot water left, sir."

Murdoch's voice was dull. "Lovely. And I suppose I'll simply have to freeze my arse off this morning, now, is that it?"

"Pretty much," Esther laughed. "Unless you'd want to share a tub, that is," she added, "and something tells me we both wouldn't fit."

"Oh? And you know that for certain, do you?"

The words tumbled out before he could stop them, and Murdoch couldn't help himself—he let his eyes trail down to her cleavage, noting the freckles dotted along the curves of her breasts, some of them dipping lower, trailing out of sight. Her nipples were hard against the chill, visible through the thin fabric of her robe, and he swallowed, suddenly beet-red, snapping his gaze up to her face again.

But Bailey must have noticed the enthralled curiosity in his straying eyes, because she answered it with a mischievous smile.

"Well," she replied in a nonchalant voice, "Not exactly...but I suppose we could always find out."

Christ in Heaven.

So much for trying not to flirt with the girl, then.

Murdoch sighed in exasperation, struggling not to think of how damn alluring she looked in that bleeding bathrobe of hers...and of what might lay underneath.

But he couldn't dwell on that. They had careers and futures to worry about, for heaven's sake—not some simple, fleeting, forbidden infatuation that appeared within the span of a week, and would likely die out by the time they docked in New York.

Keeping his voice sharp and expression stern, Murdoch snapped, "That is wholly inappropriate, Miss Bailey. You had damn well better be joking."

Her eyes glittered teasingly at him. "Obviously, sir. I wouldn't dare subject you to...what did you call it last week? A ghastly sight."

Murdoch clenched his jaw, not sure whether to laugh or start yelling. "How considerate," he said dryly. "Now stop wasting time and go bathe, Miss Bailey. We're still expected on the bridge by ten."

He started for his cabin, shaking his head and cursing whichever force on earth put the girl in his charge in the first place. But when she called after him, he came to an immediate halt.

"Will I see you in the mess for breakfast, sir?"

She was looking hopefully at him, and although Murdoch wished he was strong enough to deny her—and smart enough to keep his distance—he answered gruffly, "Aye. I'll save you a seat."

And with that, he started down the hall to his quarters in silence.

It wasn't until he'd closed the door behind him that he started pacing the room, his lips muttering curses while one hand rushed through his short hair.

You're a fool, Will, he told himself angrily.

A proper senior officer would put a stop to this nonsense, or else raise his concerns with the captain. But Murdoch was making little effort to end the peculiar relationship between him and his subordinate. And damn it all, he was certain this would be the end of him.

He decided to shave while he waited, and he wasn't sure how much time passed before there came a soft knock at the door.

"Mr. Murdoch?"

Bailey's voice drifted through the wood, and Murdoch, who was smoothing aftershave along his jaw above the washbasin, went still.

"I'm all finished," she said. "The lavatory is free for you to use, sir."

Reluctantly, Murdoch forced himself to call back, "Thank you, Miss Bailey."

He waited until her footsteps disappeared down the hall before making his way to the starboard lavatory. His shower was a quick affair. But even after he'd scrubbed and rinsed himself clean, he stood underneath the nozzle for a long while, watching the soapy water swirl and sluice its way down the drain. Christ's *sake*, how he wished his indecent thoughts of his subordinate could be washed away so easily. But they were etched into his head, seemingly permanent and unwilling to fade, like stained ink swept across the deep crevices of his mind.

As he stood in the shower and watched the water curtain down his limbs, he was still thinking of the split of skin showing between the folds of her dressing robe. Still wondering what might've happened if she'd peeled it open, and whether it would have ended with him pulling her into the shower along with him, clothing strewn upon the washroom floor, nothing but hot water and the heat of their bodies between them…

Blinded by sudden desire and blazing with want, Murdoch let his right hand inch downward, trailing beneath his waistline as the steam washed over him.

He breathed deeply, his mind consumed with thoughts of freckled skin, of soft whimpers and moans and the feel of hungry lips locked around his—

Stop.

The command was a sharp jolt in his mind, sending his fingers scrambling from his groin and toward the faucet like a madman.

Murdoch quickly yanked the water off, heart pounding deeply against his chest, lungs heaving as he fought to collect himself.

He couldn't do that. He *wouldn't* do that.

Even in the privacy of the shower, the notion of thinking of *her* like that felt so utterly, horribly wrong.

He clambered out of the tub at once, shoving his lewd thoughts out of his mind as he dried himself and flung on clothes in a hurry.

By the time he was fully dressed, gloves tugged on and greatcoat slung over his shoulders, Murdoch made his way across the boat deck, weaving among first-class passengers taking the morning air. He arrived at the officers' mess to find Wilde sitting with Bailey, the pair of them snorting with laughter at some joke or another. But when she saw Murdoch, she broke into a wonderful smile that brought a peculiar lump to his throat.

"Mr. Murdoch," she called brightly, freckled skin glowing and green eyes sparkling in the morning light, "I've made a pot of coffee, sir. Would you care for some?"

Murdoch seated himself beside Wilde, shrugging off his greatcoat and draping it over the chair's backing. "Think I'll pass."

"Well, too bad," Bailey said stubbornly. "You're getting a cup anyway, and you're going to like it."

She turned to Wilde, smirking a little as Murdoch looked incredulously at her. "May I fetch you a cup as well, sir?"

"That would be delightful," Wilde answered with a smile. "Cheers, miss." He waited until she crossed the room and busied herself with the coffeepot before leaning into Murdoch. "Well, well. She's looking a great deal more chipper than last night, isn't she?"

Murdoch shuffled his spoon around a bowl of oatmeal. "Aye," he said quietly. "That she is."

"Warms my heart, it does." Wilde reached into his pocket for a cigarette, stuffing it into the corner of his mouth. "And we owe it all to you, don't we?"

"Sorry?"

Wilde cracked a grin as he lit his cigarette; light flared from its tip, and suddenly he was wreathed in wisps of tobacco smoke.

"Bert said the pair of you were chattering away during your rounds this morning—even long after you were all finished. And he also said she was looking pretty damn chipper, too." He let out a rasp of deep laughter. "You must've cheered her right up, then. Well done, William darling."

Murdoch snorted. "Doubt I had anything to do with it," he said flatly, chewing on his oats and willing his face to remain impassive.

"And I'd be well inclined to say that is a load of bollocks," Wilde replied, looking amused. "Look, regardless of whether you think you helped her, I think we ought to be grateful she's well. I was worried, you know. Damn those first-class pricks for treating her like that. Wankers, the lot of 'em. Especially that one ruddy woman. Florence-whomever." His gray eyes crinkled into slits as he scowled. "Nasty little goblin-eyed witch. I despise that woman, I do. And if I ever see her wretched face again, I swear to you, I'm going to—"

"Here we are, Mr. Murdoch. Mr. Wilde."

Bailey had returned, bringing with her two White Star Line mugs brimming with black coffee. She placed them at their table before heading back to the counter to pour her own cup. As she stepped away, Murdoch lowered his spoon and braved a sip.

But then he froze, pressing his lips together to keep from spraying his mouthful across the table.

Bailey's coffee was horrendous, bitter and nasty as if made from liquefied tar. Murdoch stole a glance at Wilde, who swallowed down a gulp with a pained grunting noise. His colleague slowly lowered his mug then, his expression one of mingled shock and outrage.

"What the *devil* did I put in my mouth?" he hissed, keeping his voice low so Bailey wouldn't hear.

Murdoch sniffed the contents of his mug. "Coffee, I suspect. Or wet cement. I honestly can't tell the difference."

"God in Heaven." Wilde started to cough, eyes watering. "I do believe I'm going to die."

Bailey reappeared, dropping into a seat beside Murdoch with glowing eyes. "So! You like it?"

Murdoch might have supplied a sarcastic remark. In fact, he had a cutting quip on the tip of his tongue, ready to fire off. But something about the eager look on her face softened him, and so he kept quiet, sipping the foul coffee with a forced smile. Disgust bubbled at the back of his throat, but he was saved from answering when Wilde chimed in.

"Oh, yes. It's quite...*bold*." The chief officer paused, then added slyly, "Will here absolutely adores it. Says he wants you to make it for him every morning—"

Before Murdoch could aim a kick at him under the table, the door to the mess hall snapped open, and everyone turned to see Lowe poking his head inside.

"Oi, Esther!" he called cheerfully. "Your brother's looking for you out on the boat deck. Says he wants a word, real quick like."

"Oh." Bailey lowered her coffee mug in dismay. "Er...thank you, Harry. I'll head out straight away."

She didn't look all too enthused by this, and Murdoch wondered if she was still upset about the dinner. Perhaps she blamed her brother for the mishap entirely. Regardless, she rose to her feet and allowed Lowe to escort her to the door.

"Your tie's all funny again," the fifth officer laughed. "Let me fix it for you, once we're outside?"

"Sure," Bailey said with a pleasant smile. "Thanks."

Once the two junior officers left the room, Wilde rounded on Murdoch with a snort. "Well! Miss Bailey might know her way around a steamer, but she sure as shit can't make a pot of coffee to save her life."

"Aye." Murdoch was quiet now, his surly thoughts lingering on the keen way Lowe was looking at Bailey. He hated how seeing those two together only soured his mood. "Not one of her many talents, I'm afraid. Though that's not saying much," he added waspishly, "considering she never had much talent to begin with."

"Blimey, someone's a bit spiky this morning. We can hardly blame her, Will. Perhaps this is how Americans like their coffee."

"What a disturbing thought."

Wilde chuckled before reaching for another cigarette. "Dreadful coffee aside, what on earth is going on between our two junior officers, huh? Boxhall seems to think Lowe's soft on Bailey, or some nonsense."

Murdoch stiffened. "He is," he said dully. "And he was planning on asking her to dinner once we made port in New York."

"What?" Wilde lowered his cigarette in astonishment. "Did that policy Smith kept droning on about slip his mind? It's a wonder it did, we went over the damn thing for almost forty bleedin' minutes—"

"Perhaps he simply chose to forget it," Murdoch said, a faint edge to his voice. "But it's no matter. Lightoller was kind enough to remind him."

Wilde shook his head with a grimace. "Poor chap. She's a lovely girl, she is. I don't blame Lowe one bit for pining after her." He paused, gray eyes thoughtfully appraising Murdoch as he puffed on his cigarette. "But even if there *wasn't* a policy in place, I still reckon it wouldn't work out between them."

Murdoch raised an eyebrow. "What makes you say so?"

"Isn't it obvious?" Wilde laughed, smirking while Murdoch sat there looking bemused. "There's no use in Lowe chasing after that girl when she clearly has eyes for someone else."

"And who, pray tell, are you referring to?"

"Oh, I dunno," Wilde's said innocently. "Perhaps it's the stubborn Scotsman sitting before me."

"Me, stubborn?" Murdoch couldn't help but crack a small smile. "I'm hurt, Henry. Now you're just bordering on cruelty."

"Or honesty, more like," Wilde teased. "And by the by, I've seen the way that girl looks at you. She's sneaky about it, all right, but I've two daughters, mind. I catch these sorts of things rather easily."

Murdoch was quiet, the smile dripping from his face as he studied the ink-black coffee sitting before him. He snapped his eyes shut and pinched the bridge of his nose, a headache threatening at his temples. When he finally spoke, his voice was cautious.

"Even if I am keen on her—and I'm *not* saying I am—there's not a bloody thing I can do about it."

"'Course there is," Wilde insisted. "And I swear to you, Will, that I'll look the other way if it means you will find happiness. I mean it. You deserve that much, mate."

But Murdoch refused to hear a word of it.

"It's not that simple," he said quietly, rising to his feet and struggling to ignore the disappointment lying thick in his stomach. He felt nauseous, though whether it was from the sour coffee or his own unwieldy emotions, he couldn't say. "It's a question of morality. And that's not a line I dare to cross."

He fumbled with his greatcoat, hands imprecise as he slung it over his broad shoulders.

"Now forgive me, Henry. But I must be getting on."

And with that, he dropped the mug of vile coffee in the sink and hastened to the door, trying not to let Wilde's sound reasoning get the better of him.

09:45

Esther felt the bitter cold shock her skin as she thanked Lowe for his handiwork and headed aft, tie knotted perfectly against her throat.

It was freezing today, the temperature plummeting, the northern winds carrying the bite of salt and a nasty chill. The roar of water was thunderous as usual, storming the air as *Titanic's* steel prow rived the glassy ocean. But Esther was used to the sound by now, and it was a mere murmur in her ears as she meandered aft, passing along the line of squat lifeboats and first-class passengers out for a leisurely stroll.

Eventually she spotted her brother hovering near one of the Engelhardt collapsibles, one hand tucked into the pocket of his herringbone-gray overcoat, eyes fixed upon the calm sea. She stopped short before him, demanding, "Well? What do you want?"

Booker scowled. "That's a proper greeting if I've ever heard one."

"Yeah?" Esther growled back. "And that's all you deserve. You were the one who made me go to that stupid dinner."

Her brother sighed, one hand slipping through his hair. "I'm sorry," he apologized. "They were ghastly, Es, I had no idea they would behave like that—"

"Oh, you didn't, did you?" she demanded hotly. "Well, maybe you shouldn't have gone and invited Callum Lockerbie, then! Really, Booker? You might've told me. Then I wouldn't have even bothered to go at all!"

Though Booker looked uneasy, he tried to reason with her. "Come now, Esther. I know he jilted you in the past, but it's time you learned how to forgive and forget—"

"Excuse me?" Esther was livid. "That has nothing to do with it! The man's a conniving sack of shit, Booker. I see it, and so did Brighton, dammit. So why can't you?"

"Listen, I won't beat around the bush. I know his behavior at dinner was completely out of line—"

"You think?" Esther snorted, and Booker shot her a reproachful glare.

"Might I finish?" he snapped. "Jesus Christ. Look, I'll admit his goading was out of line, and he never should have brought up Muir. But he regrets it and wants to formally apologize to you, Esther. He said so after dinner."

Esther blinked as the outrage came crashing through her, stirring her temper until her gloved hands tightened into shaky fists.

"You kidding me? That's the last thing I want from that pompous bastard. As far as I'm concerned, he can take that apology, and shove it straight up his *a*—"

"Easy," Booker warned, glancing around the boat deck as first-class passengers stared. "I know you're upset. And you have every right to be. But just know that I am truly sorry for what happened, Es."

A long, uncomfortable silence stretched between them, broken only by the storming blue water far below. Esther's glare softened when she heard the sincerity in her brother's voice, and she heaved a sigh. "It's okay, Booker. It wasn't your fault, and I know that. Just don't expect me to attend another dinner, understand? I'd rather throw myself off the back of this goddamn ship than subject myself to their assholery a second time."

Booker cracked a smile. "Bit dramatic. But highly understandable." Shaking his head, he added, "Forgive me. I'd have apologized much sooner. But when I tried to find you after dinner, Officer Pitman said you weren't in your cabin."

"I was in our smoking room," she explained, trying her damnedest to hold back a smile. "With First Officer Murdoch."

Her brother's eyes flashed. "Murdoch?" he echoed, a note of wariness in his voice. "He wasn't reprimanding you again, was he?"

"No, not at all. He brought me some food and tea. And then we simply...talked. With some flirting in between, I might add."

"Flirting?" Booker stared at her, incredulous, brows wrenched together in a frown. "I thought you said he didn't like you?"

A blush of pink colored her cheeks. "I was mistaken. I think he likes me. And I like him very much. More than I should, really."

Booker hesitated, the disapproval on his face unmistakable. "It's fine to have a little infatuation," he said sternly. "But make sure you leave it at that. You don't want to do anything that might jeopardize your position— or even his, Esther. Besides," he added thoughtfully, "Murdoch strikes me as a man of convention. I doubt he'd ever consider acting outside of his ethics to pursue a subordinate, you know."

"No." Esther's voice was quiet. "I suppose not."

She tried to hide her disappointment by busying herself with her pocket watch, pulling it from her coat and holding it up to the light. But her blood ran cold when she realized the time, chilling her veins to ice.

"Cripes!" she gasped, all qualms with Murdoch forgotten. "I was supposed to be on the bridge five minutes ago!"

Esther stumbled down the deck and flat-out ran for it, tossing a hasty goodbye to Booker over one shoulder. Passengers gawked at her as she gracelessly flew past, stunned and scandalized by such an unladylike display. But Esther didn't care. She knew how strict Murdoch was about keeping timely; he'd damn near bit her head off the last time she'd been late to the bridge.

Christ, she could only imagine the earful she would get this morning. And so it came as no surprise when she staggered onto the bridge and found herself looking into Murdoch's narrowed, disdainful stare.

"Good of you to join us, Miss Bailey," he said curtly.

One hand was hooked behind his back, while the other held a small report on a wooden clipboard. Lightoller was at his side, looking curiously between the pair of them.

Breathless and winded, Esther tried to apologize. "I'm sorry I'm late, Mr. Murdoch, I was—"

"Riveting," Murdoch interrupted, indifferent to her excuses. "Now get to your station and be done with it."

She bit back a grumble. "At once, sir."

Shamefaced, Esther shuffled guiltily to her post. As she faced the brilliant swath of ocean, she listened to Murdoch and Lightoller converse in undertones, discussing some sort of issue in Boiler Room Six. Quartermaster Hichens steered the ship this morning, hands resting comfortably on the helm, while Lowe reviewed propeller revolutions in the logbook. The fifth officer glanced up at Esther from time to time, smiling in a shy way that bewildered her. But she tried not to notice, keeping her eyes fixed upon the glimmering sea instead.

The next few hours were fairly routine: Esther assisted with navigation, occasionally leaving the bridge to answer a telephone, post a chit in the chart room, or else retrieve messages from the wireless room. She always enjoyed running those errands, as Bride and Phillips were a chipper pair who always seemed happy to see her.

Murdoch, however, was standoffish all morning.

Although he wasn't angry at her outright, there was still a chilly disappointment about him that made the cold day that much colder. He wouldn't even look at her when she relayed a report from Phillips, and any words passed between them were stiff, layered with crisp formality.

Esther was frustrated. The man was almost ridiculously fickle. Friendly one moment, ill-tempered in the next.

But Esther knew it was her fault for being late this morning. Murdoch highly valued punctuality and professionalism on the bridge. She had no choice but to endure the consequences.

By noon, when the bridge was doused in pools of sheer, bright sunlight, Smith emerged from the wheelhouse. He looked calm and dignified as usual, chatting amiably with Murdoch before summoning Lowe over to join them. The fifth officer left the bridge not long after— to where, Esther hadn't a clue—but when he returned, he carried a teacup on its saucer. He presented the cup to Smith before returning to his position alongside Esther. His expression was a bit sullen, and she couldn't help but spare him a sympathetic glance.

"Is he sending you off to fetch his tea again?"

"Yes," Lowe muttered. "I'm a stinkin' officer, not some bloody tea courier."

Esther laughed. "I don't think Smith got the memorandum,

unfortunately."

"Clearly not." Lowe shook his head, brown eyes dark and indignant. "He's a fine man and all, and a proper decent captain, but I dunno why he thinks I should be the one fetching him a cuppa every waking minute. If anything, that should be *your* job—"

Esther suddenly went rigid, staring at him in shock. But then her anger and hurt came leaking through, spilling through her like stinging saltwater. "That's hitting a little below the belt, don't you think?"

Lowe gaped at her, horrified. "I'm sorry," he apologized. "It was just a joke, I didn't—"

"A joke?" Esther echoed flatly. "Boy, I'll be laughing at that one for days, Mr. Lowe. How positively comedic."

He tried to splutter out another apology, but Boxhall—who was passing along through the bridge on his way to Murdoch—ordered him to check the compass heading. Lowe shot her one last pained glance before stepping away, but Esther didn't care; she was glad to be rid of him. She was stunned, and admittedly angry. How could Lowe have said such a thing? Lowe, who was among the kindest of her colleagues, and who treated her with respect, and whose clever sense of humor always made her smile. He could be a bit cheeky at times, true, but this had been different. There had been neither jest nor cheek in his voice. Only a dull, blunt bitterness that made her wonder if they were truly amicable after all.

It wasn't until Wilde stepped onto the bridge to assume the watch that Murdoch made his way toward her.

"Rounds, then?" her superior officer asked idly, looking more even-tempered since their encounter this morning. He was rubbing his hands against the chill, but stopped abruptly at the dour look on her face. "What's the matter with you?"

"Nothing," Esther said through gritted teeth, marching toward the boat deck without pause. "Let's go."

"Esther, wait!"

They turned to see Lowe striding out of the wheelhouse, a thermos flask in hand, and Esther noticed Murdoch's eyes narrow slightly.

"Here," Lowe said sheepishly, offering the thermos to her. "I know you're off to take your rounds, so I was hoping this might keep you warm. Careful, though. It's real hot."

Esther felt her anger fade when he passed her the thermos flask, and she said quietly, "Thank you."

Lowe drew in a deep breath, and suddenly he was blurting out a flood of remorseful words.

"I want you to know that I regret what I said earlier. It was wrong and it was tactless, Esther. There was simply no excuse for it. And I hope you will accept my apology."

He was looking pleadingly at her, and as their eyes met, Esther couldn't help but forgive him. Lowe had always been kind to her, after all; a slip of the tongue was the last thing she'd let ruin their friendship.

"Don't worry about it," she said brightly. "I won't deny what you said was a bit boneheaded, but this tea certainly made up for it. It more than made up for it, in fact. You're very sweet, Harry, thank you."

Lowe grinned, a look of immense relief spreading across his handsome face. "'Course. I dunno how you like your tea, to be honest, so I didn't add any—"

But his words were cut short when Murdoch spoke behind them.

"I hate to break up such a profound conversation," he said stiffly, "but we have rounds to do, Miss Bailey, and they won't be fulfilled if you're having teatime with Mr. Lowe."

He started down the starboard promenade with his greatcoat snapping at his heels, hooded blue eyes colder than that of the sea. "Hurry up, won't you?" he added over his shoulder. "Else I'll be writing you both up for insubordination."

Lowe stared after him in surprise. "What's gotten into him?"

"I ask myself that same question almost every day," Esther sighed. She murmured a farewell to Lowe before hastening after her superior, unscrewing the thermos and blowing on the scalding hot tea as she walked. By the time she caught up with Murdoch, he was already stepping beyond the officers' promenade, Oxfords thrumming along with brisk purpose.

"Can't you slow down?" she demanded.

"No." Murdoch's voice was dull. "Walk faster."

Although she was still several paces behind him, she glared at the back of his cap. "Maybe you didn't notice, but I'm carrying tea. I don't want to spill it, sir."

"Aye, and that's your problem, lass. Not mine."

God, he was insufferable sometimes. Regardless, Esther shifted away from her indignation and decided to tease him instead.

"You're just cross because *I* have hot tea to keep me warm, courtesy of Harold Lowe—and you *don't*."

"Yes," Murdoch said sardonically, glancing at her over one shoulder with an eyebrow raised, "I can scarcely contain my envy."

She snorted. "Geez, Mr. Murdoch. Must you always be so sarcastic?"

Something about her taunt must have irked him, because he stopped abruptly, swinging around to face her in the icy afternoon light.

"And must you always be so impertinent?" he demanded, a flinty annoyance in his eyes. "I think you seem to be forgetting that I am your superior officer. You are my subordinate. If we are to remain agreeable, you will do well to put away your cheek, and address me with the proper respect a senior officer is entitled to receive. Is that understood?"

She glowered up at him. "No, *sir*."

"What a surprise." Murdoch usually had enough restraint to keep from rolling his eyes, but now he did so without pause. "So, why not, then? Do *tell*, Miss Bailey."

"Because you're frustrating me." Esther stormed closer, scowling up at his face, closing the distance between them until their coats were merely a hairsbreadth apart. "You're like night and day, you are. We were getting along fine this morning, and now you're all—all—grouchy again, and I just don't get it. I don't get you. *Sir*." She was speaking heatedly now, voice cracking with a mixture of ire and hurt. "It's maddening, sir. Especially since I enjoy your company, Mr. Murdoch. I just wish you actually enjoyed mine."

A deafening silence stretched between them, smothering the air like hot ash. Murdoch released a breathy sigh, eyes roving intently across her face. He seemed to be struggling for words, but when he finally spoke, his voice was soft in a way that made Esther stare.

"Miss Bailey, of course I—"

But his words were drowned out by loud, quarreling voices in the distance.

Murdoch's response was immediate; his gentle expression shifted to seriousness as he turned on his heel and set off to investigate, motioning for Esther to follow.

As they headed aft, twining their way through crowds of passengers and crew, Esther could see the source of the commotion: somehow, a scruffy steerage passenger in a heavy tweed coat and newsboy cap passed through the engineer's promenade to that of first-class. Moody stood before him, one arm flung out to prevent the unwelcome passenger from going any further.

"Sir," Moody was saying. "I'm terribly sorry, sir, but you're not allowed beyond this point. You'd best return whence you came."

But the man didn't seem to hear him; he was clearly drunk, his eyes half-closed, his movements odd and unsteady.

"Ain't goin' nowhere, lad," he rumbled. Even at a distance, Esther could catch the slur of his speech, and her pace quickened at once.

Moody's reply was terse. "Yes, well, I beg to differ."

"Pipe down, aye? Only wanna 'ave a quick look 'round first."

"Certainly *not*. You will return to steerage this moment, sir, otherwise the stewards and I will be forced to escort you ourselves."

"Like 'ell you will," the man grunted. "Bleedin' little prick."

And then he spat in Moody's face.

Esther didn't even look twice at Murdoch. She was already charging across the deck in her fury, tea sloshing from the uncapped thermos, fiery curses spilling from her lips.

Moody didn't bother wiping the phlegm from his cheek before he lunged forward, attempting to subdue the inebriated passenger. But the man was far bulkier and broad-chested compared to slim, slight Moody. He grasped the sixth officer by his necktie and swung him off his feet, slamming him into the white wall behind them.

Murdoch barreled past Esther in a blur, overtaking her with a stride as quick as lightning, his sharp, commanding bellow ripping hoarsely through the air.

"Lay off him!"

He hurried into the fray, wrenching the drunkard away from Moody with a strength that belied his shorter frame.

"*Lay off him, I say!*"

There was a brief tussle as Murdoch attempted to restrain the belligerent man; they staggered and stumbled about, while Moody struggled to climb to his feet, wiping the spit from his face.

A crowd had gathered now, watching the hullabaloo with varying expressions of shock and amazement. Whistles blared in the distance as first-class stewards came running toward the scene. But Esther wasn't about to wait for them. The man had twisted Murdoch's right wrist back, while his other hand reached up higher, grasping the first officer by the throat.

Murdoch winced, red-faced as he fought to wrestle the drunkard to the ground. But Esther could see his strength failing him as thick fingers crushed his windpipe, and that was enough to make her shout his name aloud.

"*Will!*"

Fire exploded through veins, ripping her composure to pieces and tearing her mind apart.

Esther could not think. She could not breathe.

She could only sprint forward, desperate to come to the aid of her superior officer.

Help him.

Those were the only words running through her mind. The only thought that mattered in her world. And while Esther was admittedly no brawler, small and wiry as she was, she did the one feasible thing she could think of.

She took her thermos of tea and flung it all over the drunken passenger.

Scorching liquid splattered across the man in an explosion of amber, and he released Murdoch's throat with a howl of rage and agony, hands scrabbling across his blistered skin.

By now, the stewards and seamen on duty arrived, moving swiftly to restrain him. Murdoch straightened up, breathing heavily and nursing his right wrist. His dark coat was mottled with flecks of tea, his cap and tie askew from the tussle. He stared at Esther, a bit flabbergasted and quite heedless of anything but her. But then he seemed to collect himself, slipping back into his cool, authoritative state.

"Take him to Dr. O'Loughlin first," he ordered of the stewards. "Then contact the Master-at-Arms as quick as you can, please. Inform him that this man is to be charged with disorderly conduct, public intoxication, and the aggravated assault of multiple officers, and see to it that the

Master-at-Arms contacts either myself or the captain whenever he is able."

The foremost steward nodded at once. "Aye, sir!"

As the steerage passenger was ushered away, and the crowds began to disperse, Murdoch turned to Moody.

"Are you all right, lad?" he asked, clapping one hand on his shoulder. "You may visit O'Loughlin if needed."

Moody massaged his neck, looking flustered but still unscathed. "No, no, that won't be necessary. He gripped my tie a bit hard, is all. But I'll be fine, sir."

"You're certain?"

"Quite."

Murdoch nodded. "Very well, then. Follow me, Jim. We'd best inform the captain of what happened forthwith. Then again," he added shortly, "I wouldn't be surprised if he's already been told. Word spreads quickly aboard this ship." His gaze slid to Esther, and he sighed, "You'd best come too, Miss Bailey. You'll have to tell the captain why you thought it prudent to assault a passenger, rather than wait for proper reinforcement to arrive."

Esther lowered her now-empty thermos, scowling at his accusatory tone. "No offense, sir, but you looked like you could use the help."

"Are you daft?" Murdoch demanded. "I'd hardly consider that display of yours to be *helping*."

"Well, I certainly do," she said indignantly. "That jackass was hurting you! And I saw the way he bent your wrist, sir. I couldn't very well stand there and do nothing!"

Murdoch hesitated. A softness filled his gaze as he studied her, head cocked to one side. But then it vanished as his expression hardened to steel.

"You disappoint me, lass," he said quietly, and Esther felt her heart sink in her chest. "While I'm grateful you sought to help me, that is simply not how officers behave. That man may have been aggressive and inebriated, aye, but that's no excuse. None at all. And now we have a passenger headed to the infirmary, suffering from burns thanks to your bloody negligence—"

"But Mr. Murdoch, I was only—"

"Quiet," Murdoch commanded, and Esther fell silent at once. "Please,

Miss Bailey, just hold your tongue. We will discuss this further with the captain."

He straightened his cap and started down the boat deck, eyes dark and narrowed. But Esther noticed the stiff manner that he held his right hand, and she frowned, her old nursing instincts kicking into high gear.

A sprain? she wondered fleetingly, biting down on her lower lip. *Please, be a sprain. Don't let it be a fracture.*

Esther wished he wasn't wearing gloves; she longed to look for swelling, or bruising, or any other such disfigurements that might confirm his injury. But if Murdoch was in pain, he certainly did not show it. His face was smoothed by stoicism, his voice curt as he spoke once again.

"Quickly now, Mr. Moody, Miss Bailey. We have a good deal of explaining to do." He shot his subordinate a withering glare. "Some more than others, I'm afraid."

Esther had no choice but to follow him, her heart swelling with icy trepidation as she realized the severity of her mistake.

FIFTEEN

IMPULSE

April 12, 1912 | 14:40

ESTHER FOUGHT TO calm her nerves as she filed inside the captain's sitting room, flanked by Moody and her stone-faced superior officer.

Her resolve was in ruins, her scattered thoughts racing like mad.

Christ. She had assaulted a passenger.

It didn't matter if she had acted in defense of Murdoch; she had still disregarded the propriety required of her rank. She had injured someone within the span of a few reckless seconds, and might very well have risked her career in turn.

But the sight of Murdoch being throttled had been enough to suspend all rational and reasonable thought. In that moment, the only thing Esther cared about was protecting him, and she had been willing to do whatever necessary to spare him from harm.

But why had she done it?

How could she have done something so unbearably stupid?

Murdoch was far from weak; he was a hardened, muscled sailor, wasn't he? If she'd waited only a second more, he likely would have gained the upper hand and thrown off his attacker.

But rash Esther—for God only knew what reason—hadn't been thinking logically. She'd thought Murdoch needed assistance right then and there, and so she had quickly leaped in to help him…by flinging a thermos of scalding tea all over his abuser.

Heavens to Betsy, she thought, her heart skittering with raw panic. *I'm done for. Fired. Finished.*

Esther stole a furtive glance at Murdoch, wondering what on earth he was thinking. But he avoided her gaze, his face unreadable.

"I'll do the talking," he said. "Is that understood?"

The junior officers nodded in silence, and Esther felt her pulse stutter as Murdoch left the room. She clasped her hands behind her back, gripping them tight to stay their trembling. Her frantic eyes traveled around the sitting room in a desperate attempt to distract herself, noting the smooth mahogany walls, the settee wreathed in Persian upholstery, and the glass bookcase displaying heavy tomes, maps, and a single spyglass.

But not even the opulent details of her surroundings could drag Esther from her fitful thoughts, and she sucked in a deep breath, trying to keep her nerves at bay before she lost it altogether.

At length, Captain Smith emerged from his quarters with Murdoch trailing behind him.

"Well?" the captain demanded, blue eyes crisp and calculating. "The Master-at-Arms telephoned me not long ago. He informed me that a second-class passenger has been detained for assaulting officers on deck, and that this man is now being treated for first-degree burns, of all things." His piercing stare roamed from one officer to the next. "What is the meaning of this? Explain yourselves, the lot of you."

Murdoch's reply was swift. "Allow me, sir. Miss Bailey and I were taking our afternoon rounds when we came upon Mr. Moody arguing with the passenger in question."

"And what was the nature of this argument, exactly?"

"From what I could gather, the passenger crossed the divider between the second-class and engineers' promenade. He was clearly intoxicated, I might add, smelling rather strongly of beer. I believe he was making his way toward first-class before Mr. Moody stopped him from going any further." His eyes slid to the sixth officer. "Isn't that right, lad?"

Moody nodded. "Indeed, sir."

Murdoch returned a cool gaze to the captain, hands respectfully held behind him. "It wasn't until he was asked to return to his designated area that he became belligerent. He then proceeded to assault Mr. Moody, spitting in his face and roughing him up by the necktie."

"Heavens," Smith murmured. "How vulgar." His expression became one of genuine concern as he turned to Moody. "Are you quite well, son?"

"Certainly, sir. Fighting fit." Moody gestured toward his colleagues. "Fortunately, Mr. Murdoch and Miss Bailey showed up in the nick of time. There was a bit of a scuffle, but we were able to restrain the man before he could cause more harm to himself and to others."

Smith nodded, but the approval in his gaze was marred by mild bewilderment. "That's all very well," he said tersely, "but it doesn't explain why he is now suffering from burns. Would anyone like to share how this came to be?"

At his question, Esther felt her heartbeat shudder to a halt, the blood seeping from her fingertips until they became little more than ice.

This was it, then.

The end of her maritime career as she knew it.

Everything she had worked so hard for these last few years was about to come crumbling down, whisked away by the tides of failure—and it was all thanks to one simple stroke of foolishness.

Her breathing grew shallow as she stood before her captain, her throat drier than desert sands.

And yet…a small sliver of hope still blossomed at the back of her mind, soothing her nerves with an oasis of calm. Perhaps Smith would be understanding if she told him the truth outright. Perhaps he would overlook her mistake, and see that she had acted with good intentions. It wouldn't be enough to guarantee a simple slap on the wrist, of course. But it might be the deciding factor of whether she could keep her job.

And that was worth a shot, wasn't it?

Esther drew a low breath as she stepped forward, armed with the words she would use to justify herself and her actions. But before she could speak, another voice filled the lingering quiet of the sitting room.

"I'm afraid that was my doing, sir."

Everyone turned to look at Murdoch. He stood with his back straight, blue eyes astonishingly calm as he explained, "Miss Bailey brought a thermos flask with her during our rounds. I knocked it from her hands as I hurried to assist Mr. Moody, and its contents splashed over the passenger. It was most unfortunate, sir, and I regret that my ungainliness caused injury."

His lie was smooth and effortless in a way that made Esther wonder if he'd been rehearsing it up until now. Or perhaps he was a practiced liar.

One of the two.

Smith regarded Murdoch thoughtfully for a moment. "Unfortunate indeed," he agreed. "But in moments of chaos, accidents are not entirely inescapable. So we must accept what has happened and move forward. I must thank you for bringing this to my attention, Mr. Murdoch. I know you have a long night ahead of you this evening, so why don't you and Miss Bailey retire early from your rounds? See to it you get some well-deserved rest before ten o'clock, and visit Dr. O'Loughlin if necessary." Glancing at his sixth officer, he added, "You as well, Mr. Moody."

Murdoch dipped his head. "Thank you, sir."

"Of course," Smith said with a kindly smile. "You are all dismissed."

The officers saluted and started for the door, footsteps whispering across the patterned emerald carpet. A crisp breeze greeted them as they emerged from the wheelhouse, still bracing but noticeably warmer than the bold chill from earlier. Heads turned and eyes lingered on them as they passed; clearly, their shipmates were curious to know what happened. But the officers said nothing, and only after entering their quarters did Moody break the silence.

"That was bloody brilliant, sir!" he proclaimed, grinning ear to ear as he looked between his colleagues.

But Murdoch did not share his warmth.

"I'd hardly classify lying to the captain as 'brilliant,' Jim," he said dully. "But I appreciate the commendation."

Moody looked taken aback, his smile fading. "Well, it kept Miss Bailey from being sacked, didn't it?"

"Aye, but you mustn't think my actions entirely permissible, lad. There's no brilliance in lying to your captain. Only a complete lack of honor and dignity, as it were." His voice was weary, and Esther bowed her head, wondering if he regretted his actions. "Nevertheless," he added, "sometimes it's better to sacrifice such principles for the sake of doing what is right. And in this case, it was saving Miss Bailey's arse from being almost certainly dismissed."

With a tired sigh, Murdoch removed his cap and glided one hand through his short hair.

"I trust you'll not speak a word of this to anyone, Jim?"

"Of course not!" Moody swore, beaming at Esther. "I am sworn to secrecy." But then he tilted his head to one side and said curiously, "Hold up, though. You don't suppose that man might go around saying Esther was responsible for burning his ugly old face off, do you? What if the truth gets out it wasn't accidental at all, and that she threw it on him intentionally? What then?"

"Who are people more inclined to believe?" Esther said quietly, her eyes on her cufflinks as she spoke. "The word of a first officer, or that of the drunkard?"

"Ah. Fair point."

Laughter echoed down the hall, and they turned to see Pitman and Lowe striding down the long corridor. It was Pitman who addressed them first, looking spent from his dog watch, but cheerful as always.

"*Hoi*! You lot!" he called. "What's all this gossip I'm hearing on the bridge, hey? Did some passenger really go mental and land himself in the infirmary?"

Moody spared a furtive glance at Esther. "It's a long story, I'm afraid."

"No matter," Pitman said merrily. "Harold and I are on lunch relief now; we've plenty of time to spare. Come join us in the mess, why don't you? We're dying to hear all the gritty details."

"Oh, yes." Lowe smirked. "Is it true Jim here got the stuffing kicked out of him? And that he cried his little heart out afterwards?"

Although Moody rolled his eyes in a dismissive manner, a touch of scarlet still colored his cheeks as he warned, "Only one who's going to be crying is you, Harry, if you don't shut your bleeding—"

"Play nicely, children," Pitman chided. He laughed at the miffed looks on their faces before clapping his hands together. "Well, no use standing 'round burning daylight, lady and gents. To the mess hall, then?"

Both Esther and Moody nodded their assent, but Murdoch shook his head. "I'll be in my cabin," he said distantly. "Could do with a nap, I think."

No, Esther thought sullenly, eyes lingering on the stiff, awkward hand at his side. *You could do with a medical opinion, you dunce.*

Pitman merely shrugged. "Suit yourself, then." He started down the corridor with Lowe and Moody good-naturedly bickering beside him, but when he realized Esther hadn't moved, he called, "Aren't you coming, Miss Bailey?"

She bit her lip. "You go on ahead. I'll meet you there in a moment."

Esther waited until her colleagues disappeared before turning to Murdoch, who still stood beside her in the corridor, blue eyes simmering with quiet reproach.

"You're welcome," he said gruffly, before she could even open her mouth.

She fumbled for something else to say. "Does this mean you're no longer cross with me?"

He laughed softly, mirthlessly. "Don't get ahead of yourself. You assaulted a passenger in an act of negligence, forced me to lie to our captain just to save your skin, and now you're standing between me and a good nap. So what do you think, Miss Bailey?"

"I'm not a mind-reader, sir," she scoffed. "You tell *me*."

Murdoch raised an eyebrow. "You're clever enough," he said shortly. "You'll figure it out."

Without another word, he turned on his heel and made for his cabin door. Esther scowled after him, chest heaving, but she wasn't about to let him go. She hurried along after her superior, nearly tripping over her Oxfords in her haste.

"Now wait just a darn minute!" she snapped. "Look, be angry with me all you want, Mr. Murdoch. I don't care. But I'm not about to let you retire to your cabin without seeing Dr. O'Loughlin first."

"And why on earth would I see O'Loughlin?"

She bristled at his feigned ignorance. "Oh, *please*. I saw what happened to your hand earlier, and I can see how stiff it looks now. You need medical attention, sir, and you need it right this moment!"

"The only thing I *need* is for you to stop shouting in my face, Miss Bailey." He brushed past her, reaching for the doorknob to his cabin. "Now, if you'll excuse me—"

But Esther stepped forward, squaring her shoulders as she stood between her superior and the glossy white door. A muscle twitched in Murdoch's cheek as looked down at her.

"Don't make this difficult, lass," he warned. "You are already treading on some *terribly* thin ice after what happened earlier. So I suggest you simply let well enough alone, rather than keep testing my patience any further."

But Esther refused to quit. "If you won't go to the doctor, then let me have a look instead. Please."

"While I don't doubt your nursing expertise, Miss Bailey, that really won't be necessary. Now kindly remove yourself from my cabin door."

She glared at him. "No."

He met the defiant blaze of her eyes with a weary sigh. "Why must everything be a bloody argument with you?"

"It wouldn't be, if only you'd stop being so *stubborn*, Mr. Murdoch."

"You're hardly any better," he retorted.

"Sure, but I'm not the one with the injured wrist," she said bluntly. "And if you're refusing because you're *embarrassed*, or trying to brush it off and be tough or something—"

"Nothing of the sort."

"Then there's no reason why you shouldn't let me help you!"

"I already told you no." His voice was relatively controlled throughout their quarrel, but now there was cold, ruthless authority cracking through. "Step *aside*, Miss Bailey," he said quietly, blue eyes boring into her. "That is an order. Follow it."

Esther finally shifted away from the door, recognizing defeat. But fire still danced along the rim of her heart, crisping her self-control to embers.

"Fine," she spat at him. "But don't come crying to me when you're in pain later on."

"I can assure you," Murdoch said curtly, "I won't."

He disappeared inside his cabin without another word, slamming the door shut behind him.

Fuming, Esther swung around and stormed down the hall, striding as fast as her feet could carry her. Christ, she was so angry with Murdoch she could scream. Start throwing things, even—preferably aimed at his lousy face.

Esther rushed out onto the boat deck in a temper, hoping the saltwater air and ocean waves might cool her boiling blood. She ended up pacing back and forth along the officers' promenade for a good fifteen minutes, biting back the curses she longed to mutter aloud.

Damn William Murdoch.

Damn him and his stubborn, fickle, frustrating nature.

So he'd lied to protect her position aboard *Titanic*. So what? He was still an insufferable ass, and he could sit in his stupid cabin with his stupid damaged wrist without so much as ice or painkillers, for all she cared.

Her pacing grew so fast and feverish that a wave of dizziness rolled over her, turning her thoughts muzzy and her knees unbearably weak. As she staggered, bracing herself against the nearest railing and gulping in the sea air, a voice spoke behind her.

"Miss Bailey? Are you quite well?"

Esther almost jumped out of her skin when she saw Officer Lightoller starting toward her. He was impeccably dressed as always, standing before her with his sophisticated air. Esther knew she must look a dreadful sight in comparison, hunched over with her hair frizzed and her temples drenched in cold sweat. She straightened up in a hurry, embarrassed, trying to drag herself out of her nausea.

"Yes, Mr. Lightoller, thank you. Just felt a little woozy. A case of *mal-de-mer*, I think."

"Shall I fetch you some seltzer water, perhaps?"

His genuine concern was enough to make her smile. "No, thank you," she said politely. "I'll be fine."

"Very well. But if you feel as if you are going to vomit, kindly check the wind and steer yourself away from me."

Although Esther felt lightheaded, she still choked out a laugh. Even Lightoller managed a thin smile. They were quiet for a moment, watching the sea glistening before them in endless shades of shifting blue. Eventually Lightoller spoke, his posh English lilt rising above the foaming whitewater. "Forgive my prying, Miss Bailey, but I can't help but wonder if something else is the matter."

"Erm…what makes you say so, Mr. Lightoller?"

"Well, don't take this the wrong way, but you're looking a bit hot under the collar. Has something upset you?"

Esther stifled a sigh. "Criminy. Is it that obvious, sir?"

"Not entirely," Lightoller laughed. "I'm able to pick up on these things rather easily. I've been married to my wife for nine years—and happily, I might add. But sometimes her emotions aren't hard to miss. And neither are yours, I'm afraid." His pale eyes studied her with curiosity. "So tell me. What's the matter, then?"

"I can't possibly bother you with something like this," Esther mumbled, looking away. "It's beneath your dignity, sir."

Lightoller seemed mildly taken aback by her choice of words. "The only thing beneath my dignity, Miss Bailey, is refusing to help another officer when they're so clearly out of sorts. Is this about the brawl on deck? I'd heard you were involved."

Esther shook her head, studying her feet. "No, it's not that."

"What is the problem, then?"

She sucked in a deep breath, hoping the briny air swelling inside her lungs would give her a peace of mind. Her hands twisted together, her teeth colliding hard with her bottom lip, and she couldn't look Lightoller in the eyes as she explained, "It's just…well, I can't help but wonder what things might've been like if you were still first officer. I think about it often, sir. I know we had a bit of a bumpy start at first, but you've been much kinder since we set out to sea, whereas Mr. Murdoch…"

Her voice trailed away, thinner than dust as it was lost to the sea winds. Esther felt her eyes burn, and she prayed the tears wouldn't come. Tears of anger, of frustration or hurt—it wouldn't make any difference. She didn't want them either way.

Lightoller regarded her with sympathy. "Miss Bailey…I know Will can be difficult at times. Trust me, we've been good mates for years now, and I've had to put up with his nonsense more times than I can count. But even so, he's quite loyal. Very strong of heart. And he means well, even if it might not seem like it."

Esther shook her head with a sigh. "Something tells me you and I know two very different William Murdochs, sir."

Lightoller gave her a small smile, but his voice carried a note of seriousness as he reminded her, "You are his charge, Miss Bailey. Don't think for a moment that he doesn't care for you and your well-being. He just…doesn't always know how to show it, I'm afraid."

Esther was quiet as she weighed his words, her eyes fixed upon the frigid cobalt water, and she found herself wishing more than anything that she could believe him.

17:05

Drowsiness caught up with Esther by late afternoon, sweeping over her like the tide and drawing her back into the soft comfort of her bed.

Lunch relief had taken her mind off things; Lightoller had chatted with her for a good hour or so, discussing her current workload and dropping helpful snippets of seafaring advice. He'd even lent her his ear when she'd rambled a little about Murdoch, surprisingly patient when her frustrations came spilling out. It was helpful, almost, and by the end of it, she'd felt as if some heavy weight had been lifted from her chest.

But while Esther had been grateful for the momentary reprieve their conversation brought her, she'd found even more enjoyment in prodding Lightoller about his wife. It had taken a great deal of encouragement, but eventually the second officer had opened up about her, describing her little quirks and eccentricities with shining eyes. And the more Lightoller spoke of his wife, the more Esther realized how much he adored her.

Though she was sorry to part with him when he'd left for the bridge, she'd found enjoyment in a few rounds of poker with Pitman, Moody, and Lowe in the smoking room not long after.

Esther had ended up winning two games out of five—once with four of a kind, and again with a straight flush. But while she'd wished her colleagues' rowdy laughter could distract her, she still found herself thinking of Murdoch. How he'd found her in the smoking room the night before, bringing her tea to brighten her up. How she'd shamelessly flirted with him, and he'd flirted right back. How he was likely tucked away in his cabin all by his lonesome, nursing either a sprained or fractured wrist— and she couldn't do a damn thing about it.

But now, hours later, as she burrowed into her blankets with the day long gone, she tried not to let her guilt get the better of her.

He didn't want my help, she reminded herself bitterly. *He brought it on himself.*

Sleep couldn't come quickly enough. Before long, Esther slipped from consciousness and plunged into her dreams, their iridescent colors and sounds and senses all jumbled, blurring together like watercolors soaking into parchment.

She could see her beautiful mother protecting her when the Great Earthquake struck, wrapping Esther in her arms as the walls of their hospital shuddered and crumbled, and falling medicine bottles shattered at their feet. She could see Brighton laughing with Booker as they skipped stones along the Presidio of San Francisco, barefoot and unfazed by the cold, the sight of them nearly lost to a wall of gusty fog. She could see herself sink deeply into bathwater as Muir raged beyond the door, dipping her head beneath the surface until the sounds of his drunken slurs were lost to watery quiet.

And Murdoch…she could see him, too, standing patiently at her side, tipping his cap at her. She could almost hear him, even. His Scottish burr was surprisingly clear as it slipped through her mind, but Christ, it was also loud as hell—

"Miss Bailey? Are you awake?"

Esther's eyes flew open when she realized this was no dream; Murdoch *was* speaking beyond her cabin door, his voice accompanied by a few brisk knocks.

Still dazed with sleep, Esther scrambled out of her bed and rushed to the door, opening it to find her superior officer standing alone in the hall.

His greatcoat was gone, revealing a creased waistcoat and white shirt underneath, while his tie hung loosely at his neck.

Esther gaped at him before she managed to find words.

"What is it, sir?"

"I suppose you were right, Miss Bailey." His voice was quiet. Bitter, almost. "The swelling on my wrist has gotten worse, to say nothing of the soreness. I was wondering if perhaps you might be able to help me?"

Esther hesitated, the memory of his stubborn dismissal all too sharp in his mind. Part of her wanted to tell him no—wanted to slam the door in his face, as he'd done to her earlier.

But then she nodded, her resentment for him yielding to the orderly, level-headed thinking of a nurse. "Of course, sir."

Murdoch peered over her shoulder, eyes lingering on her strewn clothes and scattered books, and he said, "There's more room in my cabin. Can you be there shortly?"

"Certainly. Let me get dressed and grab my medical kit."

Esther closed the door with a snap, and it wasn't until his footsteps faded down the hall that she started racing around the room, throwing on her clothes and yanking on her shoes.

She was stunned. Absolutely dumbfounded.

Even after all their quarreling, Murdoch had still come to her for help.

He'd come to her, when he could have simply walked below decks to fetch Dr. O'Loughlin or his assistant.

Some small, shameful part of her was pleased by this thought—even though she wished she could loathe the Scottish bastard instead.

Esther scrambled around the room, gathering her belongings with unwieldy haste. Her old medical kit was tucked away beneath her bed—a heavy green box with the first-aid cross slapped across the lid. She held it under her arm as she left her cabin and dashed to the mess, where she collected several chunks of ice and bundled them in a spare tea towel.

By the time Esther sprinted back to the officers' quarters and reached her superior's door, she was breathless. She knocked gracelessly, panting like mad and struggling to ignore the piercing stitch in her side.

Murdoch appeared at once, taking in her gasping, sweaty appearance with cool appraisal. He wordlessly opened the door to admit her inside, leaving it ajar behind her, as per captain's orders.

Esther clutched her medical kit tightly, feeling nervous as she stood in Murdoch's quarters. It was twice the size of her cabin, and meticulously tidy. The bedcovers were neatly made, smoothed to perfection. Every surface was spotless, devoid of any clutter, while clothing hung smart and orderly in the wardrobe across from her. His brass compass glistened on the bedside table, a relic of the brutal shipwreck he survived.

The only peculiar thing that caught her eye was a corkboard perched above the writing desk. It was dotted with a collection of postcards, letters, and one enormous world map speckled with blue push pins.

Esther was so mesmerized by the postcards—scouring for one of San Francisco, or Shanghai—that she didn't hear Murdoch step to her side.

"Should I sit, then?" he asked.

She could almost hear the wild stutter of her heart. "Please."

He dropped into a chair, wincing a little as he tugged off his gloves. While his left hand looked normal, the right one had become inflamed, the skin of his wrist raw and colored pink.

"May I?" Esther asked, and when he nodded, she gingerly took his hand. "I need to see if it's just a sprain or a possible distal radius fracture."

"English, please?"

Esther might have scowled at him, but she was too focused on examining his wrist to pay his snarkiness any mind.

"A broken wrist, if you will," she answered mildly.

There was no other chair in the room, so she knelt before him on the carpet, still scrutinizing his injury. She was aware of Murdoch watching her every move, but she refused to look up at him, for fear of her heart hammering wild once more. Twice she had him roll his wrist around, asking if he felt any mild to severe pain. The answer was always somewhere in the middle, which was a good enough sign, but it also made Esther wonder if her superior officer simply had a high pain tolerance. He was a mariner, after all, hardened by backbreaking work on the high seas; she wouldn't be surprised if he'd endured worse.

Regardless, his motor functions seemed relatively stable, and there were no odd angles or bruises indicative of a fracture. Esther finally looked up, beaming.

"I'm certain it's a sprain, sir! Nothing serious at all!"

Murdoch frowned, bewildered by her chipper response. "You make it sound so bloody terrific."

Esther laughed at the look on his face. "Well, it's better than a fracture, that's for certain," she told him brightly. "Your wrist has swelled quite a bit, but with some ice and elevation, it will be back to normal in no time, I'm sure." She rummaged through her medical kit, pulling out bottles and supplies. "I'll give you plenty of aspirin for the pain and inflammation. Just make sure not to overtax your right hand within the next few days, sir."

Murdoch nodded in silence, observing Esther as she reached for the ice. She wrapped one of the largest chunks in the tea towel and pressed it lightly against his swollen wrist. He breathed deeply at the cold touch, closing his eyes.

"This would have been much easier if you'd come to me sooner," Esther said. "You realize that, don't you?"

His reply was soft. "I do." Murdoch sat up straighter, opening his eyes to meet her sullen gaze. "It was my mistake. I was arrogant, to say nothing of idiotic. And I apologize."

"You apologize," she echoed flatly. "But do you actually mean it?"

"Of course I do, Miss Bailey."

But when she remained silent, he cocked his head to one side, his expression softening with concern.

"Miss Bailey?"

Still holding the ice against his hand, Esther traced one thumb along the skin of his wrist. "You've apologized before, Mr. Murdoch," she said quietly. "You said we needed to be on 'agreeable terms' for the interests of our work relationship. But that never happened."

Her breath hitched, and suddenly the words came flooding out, spilling from her lips in a messy, uncontrollable torrent of emotion she'd been holding back from the start.

"You've never once treated me with the same respect and patience you show for Moody or Pitman. You've saved my neck more than a few times, and yet you scold and belittle me afterwards, until I feel like I'm a—a nuisance, or some sort. I know we've been at odds with each other for some time now, sir, and I know that we're both to blame. I'm no saint, Mr. Murdoch, I've behaved poorly and spoken out of turn more often than I should. But…"

She drew in a sharp breath, her pulse thundering in her ears, struggling to fight back against that strange, unexpected emotion welling inside her. "But the difference between the two of us is I actually want to move past all that animosity. You seem perfectly content to make sure it still exists between us, and I just wish I knew *why*."

Her voice cracked on the last syllable, and she silently cursed herself. *Keep it together, why don't you?*

Murdoch heaved a sigh, his shoulders sloping. "Forgive me," he said, his voice dropping to a low murmur, the words catching Esther by complete surprise. "I don't mean to be hostile, Miss Bailey."

"I don't understand. Then what is the issue here?"

"The issue is I've never met someone like you before. And I still don't know what to make of you. I can't quite figure you out." His lips barely moved, while his seawater-blue eyes never left her face. "I wish I could. But I can't. And that makes me nervous."

Esther stared at him in disbelief, at this strapping senior officer who had seen more than twenty years at sea, and she scoffed, "I make you nervous?"

"In some ways, aye."

Esther wanted to ask, *What ways?* but Murdoch was already speaking again.

"I know that's no excuse for how unreasonable I've been, and for how poorly I treated you since the day you boarded this ship. I was a bitter man who thought you were to blame for my demotion, and I regret my actions every day. So please, if there's any way I can make it up to you, any way at all—"

"Teach me how to tie a tie."

The words went flying from her lips within seconds, startling even herself. Both subordinate and superior stared at each other before Murdoch arched a single brow.

"Is that all, then?"

Esther nodded earnestly. "It is. I can't keep relying on others to fix up my tie, sir. I want to learn how to do it on my own."

"How practical." Murdoch regarded her with amusement, a smile pulling at one corner of his mouth. "And here I thought you'd demand that I become your own personal valet, Miss Bailey."

She shot him a sly grin. "Careful. I might change my mind."

He let out the bellow of a laugh—a real, warm, hearty laugh—and she laughed along with him, her grip tightening on his hand a little. This touch seemed to momentarily distract him, and he looked down at her long fingers in a thoughtful manner.

"Before our watch tonight," he said, "come back to my cabin and bring a tie."

"Sure thing." Esther was smiling at him. But now she was looking down at their hands, too, and she started to trace the callouses along his palms, exploring their crevices and roughened surfaces with a soft, feather-light finger.

"So coarse," she murmured, almost to herself.

He didn't pull away. "Seafarer's hands, remember?"

She nodded, fingers now charting a course across his knuckles. "I like them."

Though Murdoch's expression was carefully neutral, his ears still reddened. Clearing his throat, he quickly changed the subject.

"By the way, I never had a chance to properly thank you for coming to my rescue earlier. Throwing tea wasn't the most graceful of methods, but it did the job."

"That was a mistake." Esther smirked. "I was actually aiming for you, sir."

He laughed again; boy, she was on a roll with humoring him this evening. "You know, I had a fair feeling that was the case," he snorted. "But at least your lousy aim allowed me to walk away unscathed. Can't say the same for that dafty of a passenger, however."

She shrugged. "He deserved it. I know it's unprofessional to say so, sir, but he really did. I have no patience with drunks, and I wasn't about to put up with the likes of him, by God. I was just lucky Harry gave me that tea in the first place."

"Forgive my prying, Miss Bailey, but why did he offer you tea, exactly?"

"He said something a bit tactless, that's all. But he wanted to make up for it, and so he brought me a cup."

"I see," Murdoch remarked coolly. "And are the two of you...on agreeable terms now?"

"We are, sir." Esther was smiling at the inquisitive look in his eyes.

"And that is all, then? Nothing more than that?"

"Well, I don't fancy him, if that's what you're asking."

Murdoch looked skeptical, so she continued to caress his hand, grazing her finger down to the pale, smooth underside of his wrist.

"Look," she said quietly, "I won't deny that he's handsome. He's funny, and he's about my age. But none of that matters, sir. Because I'm interested in someone else."

A soft silence filled the room as the two officers stared at each other. Esther felt the warmth in her cheeks, and she hoped to God she wasn't blushing. She didn't know what to make of this. Their relaxed postures, the complete breach of rank and etiquette between them—it was wrong, against all protocol.

And yet, she didn't want it to stop.

Murdoch couldn't seem to look away from her now. He leaned closer, curious, his eyes flicking down to study her lips.

Her pulse stuttered, suddenly haywire, and Esther drew closer to him in return, caught in the blue of his gaze and the inviting smell of his aftershave, *longing* for the distance between their lips to close once and for all—

But then Murdoch sharply pulled away, his face a wild shade of scarlet, his hand quick to leave hers. As if by habit, he reached for his pocket watch and clicked it open to inspect the time.

"It's already seven o'clock, Miss Bailey," he said swiftly, returning to protocol at once, "and our shift starts at ten. I suggest you get another hour or two of sleep, if you can. We've another long night ahead of us, unfortunately."

Esther didn't want to leave him, but she knew he was right. She'd be no use to anyone if she was stumbling around the bridge in a sleep-deprived stupor. So it was with great reluctance that she passed Murdoch the bundle of ice and rose to her feet. He stood with her, avoiding her eyes, the flush fading from his cheeks.

"You'll be okay, then?" she asked.

He snorted. "I'm injured, not helpless, thank you very much. I think I can manage."

She nodded and started for the door, trying to keep to professionalism while her thoughts were ablaze with something else.

"I'll leave you to it, then, sir."

Esther could feel his eyes on the back of her neck as she took her leave. And by the time she was tucked into her bed once more, drifting along the hazy rim of slumber, she was still thinking of him—still recalling his laughter, and the feel of his coarse palms beneath her fingertips.

20:30

Esther felt as if she'd barely closed her eyes before the alarm clock shocked her from sleep.

But she wasn't the least bit groggy as she climbed out of bed and readied herself for her watch. In fact, the seventh officer was a bundle of energy, skipping around the room and humming merrily as she stood before the washbasin. She spent a little extra time brushing the knots from her hair and making sure her collar was perfectly straight. Then she reached for a tie, slinging it loosely around her neck before tugging on her greatcoat and heading out the door.

She decided to make her way to the mess for some food, but the hunger was nearly driven from her mind when she stepped out onto the boat deck. Esther gasped at the cold, cursing aloud, the glacial wind chilling her straight down to the bone.

Christ, she thought, shivering. *Keeps getting colder, doesn't it?*

She hurried aft, nose swollen and pink with the chill, and almost sighed with relief when she scrambled inside the mess hall.

The room was nearly empty at this hour, its teakwood tables sparse beneath patches of amber lamplight. Esther spotted Lowe and Murdoch sitting in one corner, chatting quietly over what looked like plates of roasted lamb, mashed potatoes, and kedgeree. As she approached, Lowe was the first to greet her.

"Evenin', Esther," he said drowsily.

"Evening."

Esther settled beside Murdoch, who nodded at her and wordlessly slid her a cup of coffee. He was wearing his gloves again, the dark leather obscuring the swelling along his wrist. She wanted to ask how he was feeling, or whether the aspirin had helped, but Lowe was present, so she held her tongue.

Her stomach grumbled, and she dug into a plate of kedgeree with abandon. As she ate, she couldn't help but notice how exhausted Lowe looked, yawning widely and blinking red-rimmed eyes.

"You all right?" she asked him. "You look half-dead, there, Harry."

"Didn't get a lick of sleep," Lowe moaned. "Ended up spending the entire bloody evening playing poker with Bert and Jim after you left."

Esther stared at him in amazement. "You played poker for almost four hours?"

He yawned again, smacking his lips. "Just about, yeah."

She laughed. "Jesus. Well, that's pretty darn impressive. You have some good wins, then?"

"They're a ruthless pair, they are," he sighed. "I lost every round."

"What? What on earth did you lose? Not money, I hope?"

"No." Lowe dropped his forehead upon the table with a dull thud. "My dignity," Esther heard him mumble against the wooden surface. "And about ten shillings," he added as an afterthought.

Murdoch regarded him with amusement. "Could've been a lot worse, lad."

Lowe lifted his head from the table, rubbing tired eyes. "S'pose that's true. At least I know to never play with those gits again, so long as I live and breathe." He heaved another sigh before blinking at Esther, nodding to the loose ends of the tie hanging from her neck.

"You need a hand with that?"

Esther shuffled her fork across her plate. "Mr. Murdoch is teaching me how to knot a tie this evening," she explained, "so I'm keeping it undone for now. But thank you for the offer, Harry."

She spared a cursory glance at her superior officer, and although he was idly sipping from his teacup, gazing at nothing in particular, she didn't miss the subtle way his lips hitched into a small smile.

At a quarter to nine, she and Murdoch bade goodbye to Lowe before returning to the officers' quarters, walking side by side down the freezing boat deck. The silence between them was not quite awkward, but not quite companionable, either, and Esther wished she could think of something witty to say. But she kept quiet, and it wasn't until they reached his cabin that she pulled the tie from her shoulders, bundling it in her hands.

Once again, Murdoch made sure to keep the door cracked open when she stepped inside. Her eyes fell upon the large map sprawled above the desk, and this time, he noticed her curious gaze.

"Are you going to ask what it's for," he said evenly, "or are you just going to keep ogling with your mouth wide open?"

Esther snapped her jaw shut, resisting a snippy response as she merely said, "Jesus, okay. What's the giant map for, then?"

He stepped to her side. "I use it to mark the places I've traveled. And those I still have yet to visit."

Esther held back a smile. She'd almost forgotten his penchant for travel and the seas; she and Murdoch argued so often that their shared interests seemed to slip right through the cracks.

She was quiet as she studied the map, inspecting the blue push pins speckling enormous stretches of land and ocean and island. They were scattered all along the San Francisco Bay she had once called home, the sweeping coasts of Japan, the scattered archipelagos of Hawai'i and French Polynesia. She could see a few darker pins dotting those cities he'd already visited and told her about, from bustling Shanghai, all the way to little Valparaíso, tucked away on the other side of the world.

It was *incredible* to think he had seen all these wonderful places in his lifetime, and Esther couldn't help but envy him.

"Where do you want to go the most?" she asked eagerly. "Out of everything you've marked on this map?"

Murdoch looked thoughtful as he weighed her question. Then, after a long pause, he admitted, "San Francisco, I suppose. There's something that makes me want to visit again, far more than any other city. Not sure why, though. Perhaps I have you to blame for it."

Esther laughed. "Probably. I'm sure I've yapped about my hometown too much. But I'm glad it made you want to go back, at least." Her eyes traveled back to the map, and she added, "And who knows? Maybe I'll be there by then, to show you around."

Murdoch looked as if he wanted to say something more, but her attention shifted to the brass compass lying on the bedside table.

"May I?" she asked.

When he nodded, Esther scooped up the instrument and held it up to the light. She could see the sweeping cursive of his initials etched on the back of the casing. It glimmered beneath the lamplight, surprisingly heavy in her hand, its thin needle stuttering as she shifted it around.

"I owe my life to that thing," he murmured. "Wouldn't be here today without it."

Esther looked up at him, thinking of the wreck he had narrowly survived. Softly, she asked, "Were you scared?"

"'Course I was," Murdoch confessed, without skipping a beat. "But I was more concerned with my crew. They were my priority. The fear was there, aye. But it was also the last thing on my mind." His eyes grew unfocused for a moment, clouded in thought, and Esther wondered what he might be thinking. But then he purposefully cleared his throat, as if remembering why they had come to his cabin in the first place.

"Well?" he demanded. "This might come as a bit of a shock, Miss Bailey, but I think we have some tie-tying to attend to."

"Yes. Sorry." Esther had almost forgotten, too; she returned his compass to the bedside table and stood at attention.

"Right, then," Murdoch said, standing before the mirror above his washbasin, his tone suddenly businesslike. "Come here."

She did as she was told, moving closer to him and trying to ignore the wild fluttering of her heart. *Steady, girl,* she told herself.

Murdoch unloosed his tie and held it taut around his neck. "Watch my hands," he told her. "Keep the wide end twice as long as the narrow one, firstly. Like this, aye? Then take the wide end and wrap it 'round the narrow till it's facing forward. See?"

He demonstrated, his hands moving patiently, slow enough for her to follow. Esther hung on his every word, watching in fascination as he worked, his roughened fingers expertly looping and tightening until the shape of a knot began to form. She wondered about his sprained wrist, but it didn't seem to bother him; perhaps the aspirin had done its job.

"And there you have it," he said, sliding the knot upward until it rested perfectly against his throat. "The art of tying a tie. Fascinating, I'm sure."

She grinned. "Doesn't seem too difficult."

"Cocky, aren't you?" Murdoch was smirking. "I'd like to see you get it right on your first try." He gestured toward the washbasin with one hand. "Go on, then. Have at it, lass."

Esther shot him a challenging look, stepping smartly before the mirror with the silken tie pinched between her fingertips.

She started off well enough, managing her first loop with ease. But then she was utterly lost. She fumbled around, frustrated, clumsy hands only making the knot that much messier. It didn't help that Murdoch was distracting her. Inadvertently, of course, but a distraction nonetheless. He stood at a respectful distance with his hands behind his back, but close enough that she could still catch the smell of his aftershave. His blue eyes met hers in the mirror, and he shook his head with a laugh. He was being good-natured, but Esther still scowled; she hated being laughed at, especially when she was in the midst of a struggle.

"Having some difficulties?" Murdoch asked smoothly.

Her tone was sour. "You noticed?"

"Here," Murdoch said, stepping before her. His hands reached out to take hers, surprisingly gentle as he guided them through all manner of loops and twists. Esther swallowed, her chest barely rising with each shallow inhale, keeping desperately still despite the electrical storm of adrenaline sparking inside her.

She liked the feel of his weathered hands on hers. Perhaps a little too much. And by the time he'd helped her tighten the knot at the base of her neck, she was disappointed when he moved away.

"So," the first officer said nonchalantly, "what was that you were saying about this not being too difficult?"

"Oh, be quiet."

He smirked. "A wee child could do better." When she merely glowered at him in response, he encouraged, "Remember what I told you. And don't let your frustrations get the better of you."

Esther tried again and again, determined to get it right. Murdoch stepped in only when necessary, instructing her through the process with words or with his coarse, seafaring hands. He made a handful of sarcastic comments from time to time, but he was agreeable otherwise, and almost friendly. *Quite the reversal from earlier today,* she couldn't help but think.

By the time she'd managed to knot her tie without his help, Esther was about ready to jump with joy. She swung around to face Murdoch, grinning, bouncing on the balls of her feet.

"Sir, I did it!"

"Congratulations." Murdoch's voice was wry. "And it only took you damn near fifty tries."

Esther ignored him. "Oh, come on. Don't be a spoilsport. What do you think?"

He tilted his head to one side, scrutinizing the knot.

"Fair-to-middling," he concluded. "Loads better than before, obviously. But there's still room for improvement."

"I'll keep trying, then," Esther said. "Practice makes perfect, after all."

"Indeed it does."

She hesitated, feeling nervous as she toyed with the end of her tie, a question lingering on the tip of her tongue.

Don't do it, all instincts seemed to shout. But she ignored that side of her—the good, respectable, appropriate Esther Bailey, the Officer Bailey who was supposed to behave—and boldly asked, "So, may I practice on you, sir?"

A flicker of surprise crossed his face before he smoothed it away again. "If you'd like."

Wordlessly he unloosed his tie a second time, and Esther stepped forward, grasping the silken ends between her fingertips.

The space between them was minuscule; she knew she ought to take a step back. Keep a proper distance. But she *liked* being this close to him, twirling his tie and breathing in his heady aftershave.

She glanced up at him once, hoping to catch his gaze with hers. But his eyes were glued to the careful motions of her hands, observing in silence.

It wasn't until she'd slid the knot up to his throat that he finally looked at her.

Her cheeks pooled with heat when their eyes met. Her heartbeat quickened, hammering wildly in her chest.

And then, before she could stop herself—before she could consider the consequences of what she was doing—Esther twined her fingers around his tie and yanked him closer, pressing her mouth against his.

She kissed him softly, hands still clutching his tie, unwilling to let go.

It was a pure impulse she couldn't have resisted—not even if she'd tried. And as her lips found his, Esther could feel a distant pinprick of caution in her mind, warning her of the risk, reminding her of their ranks.

She was his subordinate. She wasn't supposed to be doing this.

But she didn't care.

This was something Esther had wanted for a while now. Something she had yearned for in some small, secret corner of her heart. The tension building between them these last few days had finally burst, like a dam buckling beneath heavy storm waters, flooding her with an array of emotions she didn't know she had.

Gone was the line dividing subordinate from superior. Snapped to pieces—just like that. The sudden immediacy of it all was nearly overwhelming. But the relief and sheer desire were even better, sweeter, flowing thickly through her veins like molasses as their lips met, and her hands slid up the column of his neck to course through his short hair.

After what felt like a lifetime, Esther pulled away, wondering if she made a mistake.

But she didn't get very far.

She only saw the blaze of Murdoch's blue eyes before he hastened forward, catching her face between his hands and kissing her right back.

He was gentle at first, his warm lips brushing hers, his tongue exploring the depths of her mouth in ways that sent sparks everywhere—fizzing across her skin, spiking through her veins, throbbing between her thighs. His smell of aftershave was wonderfully enticing, flooding her with a thrill she almost couldn't control.

She grasped a fistful of his coat lapels and tugged him closer, sinking into their kiss. He grew bolder at her insistence, one of his hands winding deep into her hair, the other cupping her chin, gently holding it in place.

But even beneath his tenderness, she could still sense something more.

She could taste it in his kiss, even—a thirst, a want, a *need* that he was barely holding back.

And she wanted to chase it.

Esther kissed him harder, longing to coax this need out of him and not caring what she might find. She was rough with him, letting him know what she wanted without words, nipping hard at his lower lip, roaming her palms across the muscles of his arms, dragging her nails down the expanse of his strong, sturdy back.

His grip on the sides of her face tightened, and his kiss grew deeper, fiercer—until his restraint snapped to pieces.

All at once, Esther found herself being pushed backward until her shoulders struck the wall behind them. Murdoch pinned her there in his fervor, lips never parting from hers, with one hand slipping down to clutch at her waist, greedily tugging her closer to him.

Her head was spinning; she was breathless, insatiable, longing for more of him. She broke her lips from his to start kissing his neck—tasting and teasing him, listening to his pulse skyrocket.

His groan filled her ears, rumbling up from his throat. She liked the sound of it, so she kissed lower, her lips and tongue trailing across the salt of his skin. But it wasn't until she started unfastening the buttons of his greatcoat that he finally spoke.

"Esther," he breathed. He'd never used her first name before, and she loved the sound of it on his tongue. "Esther, we shouldn't be doing this."

She stood on tiptoe, roaming her palms across the thick wool of his coat until she was clutching at his lapels once more.

"Shouldn't we?"

Her expression was one of amusement, but there was still a longing in her gaze, a sinful mischief he seemed to like. He brushed a strand of hair from her eyes, his breath hot as he spoke against her lips.

"They'll find out, lass…"

"They won't know," she murmured, pulling him closer until his body was flush against hers. "No one has to know, sir."

Her lips brushed against his ear as she spoke, and he closed his eyes, sighing with pleasure. It was enough to keep his restraint at bay, scattering away any second thoughts and letting his thirst run wild.

Murdoch kissed her again, long and hard and full of searing heat, hands sweeping through her hair first, then down the length of her entire body. She leaned into him, letting him explore every last inch of her, smoothing his rough, weathered palms over the curve of her hips and the swell of her breasts, every touch leaving a trail of fire in its path.

The friction between their bodies was burning, all-encompassing, hotter than flame. His lips soon found the hollow of her throat, and she couldn't stop her soft gasp as he kissed her there, marking her, making her his.

Esther felt his hands tighten at her work skirt, bunching up the fabric in his fists, ready to yank it away. Christ, how she wanted him to do it.

She was aching now, wild and full of want, breathing heavily until she was silenced by another raw, hungry kiss.

Her fingers scrabbled at the button on his trousers and his hands fumbled with her blouse; they were wearing far too many clothes, she realized. She wanted to know the heat of his skin, the feel of him between her legs, the taste of something other than just his mouth. She wanted him to fling her down on his bed—to roll around with him until those tidy sheets of his were all twisted and tangled and she was barely gasping his name.

And even as she kissed him, and roved her hands across his broad chest, the seventh officer knew in some small part of her mind that what they were doing was wrong.

But she would do nothing to stop it. And neither would he.

SIXTEEN

THE VALET

April 12, 1912 | 21:25

L IGHTOLLER WAS EXHAUSTED as he stood in the blue darkness of the bridge, waiting for his watch to come to an end.

It was half-past nine, and nearly time for Murdoch and Bailey to relieve him. Despite the intolerable cold, he was pleased to note that everything had run smooth and steady this evening.

There had been nothing out of the ordinary. Nothing that might have set him or his crew on edge. The sea had kept remarkably calm, still as gleaming glass, and the captain had ordered Lightoller to maintain speed and heading before retiring to his quarters.

They'd received a single ice warning, most fortunately—a notice from the SS *La Touraine*, which Mr. Bride delivered to the bridge around seven o'clock. Given how commonplace North Atlantic ice was this time of year, Smith found little cause for alarm. Lightoller, however, felt uneasy nonetheless. *Titanic* was already speeding fairly fast in her journey west, and it certainly didn't help that the only binoculars were still missing, rendering proper sights of growlers and bergs almost impossible.

He was just wondering whether he should order Pitman to search for another pair when a staccato of hasty footsteps made him turn.

"Mr. Lightoller, sir!"

The second officer glanced up to see Lowe sprinting along the promenade, his face twisted with shock, his greatcoat billowing in the wind behind him.

He skidded to a halt once he reached the bridge, winded and babbling some incoherent nonsense, but Lightoller stopped him with one hand.

"Steady on, Harold! What on earth is the matter with you?"

Lowe was almost too breathless to speak.

"It's—*Christ*—a woman, sir, a woman almost fell overboard—!"

Lightoller stared blankly at him. "You're not bloody serious."

"Wish I wasn't, sir. By the sound of things, she got too close to the railing on the starboard side and slipped. Damn near almost went over."

Lightoller stared at him for a split moment, his shock dissolving into flat-out fury.

"*How?*" he hissed. "How did this happen? Was there no one on duty who might've seen her?"

Lowe shook his head. "No, sir. Seems Wireless Operator Harold Bride was first on the scene. Was having a smoke, he said, when he heard her screams. Her shawl was all tangled around the rail, but he managed to free it and haul her back up in the nick of time."

"Good grief. And is she well? She wasn't hurt, was she?"

"No, she wasn't injured. Bit shaken, but I reckon she'll be all right."

"The captain will have to be notified," Lightoller murmured. Though he longed for a cigar and a warm bed, he started for the wheelhouse at a near half-sprint. He paused at the doorway, glancing over his shoulder to ask, "And do we know her identity?"

Lowe hesitated. "I dunno. She was definitely first-class, though, and I think she might've been the wife of Mr. Lockerbie."

Lightoller nodded, thinking of the pretty blonde he'd seen taking the air with Callum Lockerbie from time to time. "I see. I'll return shortly. Please keep an eye on the bridge in the meantime."

He waited until Lowe saluted in acknowledgment before starting down the corridor, shaking his head with a sigh. He could already envision the captain's outrage, and he held his breath as he rapped his knuckles on the door.

Smith appeared after a few moments, looking disheveled in his dressing robe but still sharp-eyed and alert all the same.

"Yes, Mr. Lightoller? Is everything all right?"

Lightoller wasted no time in explaining the situation, speaking in a hushed undertone, and he watched the captain's puzzled expression tighten to a mask of stern authority.

"Mr. Lightoller," Smith said, his voice suddenly hardened to steel, "please round up the rest of the officers and have them assemble in the chart room. I will telephone the Master-at-Arms to see if he can explain the situation. We will need to discuss the events that transpired tonight and ensure something of this nature never happens again. Is that clear?"

"Certainly, sir. I shall rouse them at once."

"See that you do. That will be all for now, Mr. Lightoller."

While Smith disappeared inside his cabin, Lightoller hastened to the officers' quarters to rouse his colleagues. He knocked on Wilde's door first, biting back a grumble. The chief officer appeared after what felt like a century, donned in a ridiculous dressing robe of lavender velvet with his eyes still thick with sleep.

"Time is it?" he mumbled groggily.

"Nearly ten."

Wilde scowled. "Then why the *blazes* are you waking me up? Don't you know a man needs his ruddy beauty sleep?"

Lightoller sighed, impatiently tapping his shoe. "We have an emergency, Mr. Wilde. A woman nearly fell overboard. Smith's called a meeting because of it."

"*What?*" Wilde's tired eyes flew open. "Blimey, is she all right?"

"She's fine, according to Lowe. No doubt shaken, I'm sure. Must've been quite the scare." Lightoller stole a brief glance down the corridor, peering down the long line of cabins and wondering which of his colleagues he needed to wake next. "But no use standing about," he urged his superior. "You'd best get dressed. Chart room, five minutes."

Wilde grunted his assent, too exhausted to offer a usual mocking quip, and shuffled inside his cabin.

Lightoller started for Murdoch's quarters next, only to find his door open just a crack, sending a slat of golden light falling upon the carpet.

So the first officer was awake, then.

Murdoch's watch would begin within minutes, after all. Lightoller figured his colleague was pulling on his greatcoat or knotting up his tie, so he didn't bother tapping his knuckles on the open door before swinging it wide open.

"Good, you're up—" he started to say.

But he stopped abruptly in his tracks at the sight before him.

Murdoch was in his cabin, all right. But he wasn't alone.

He and Miss Bailey—yes, Seventh Officer Esther Bailey—were locked in a tight embrace, kissing fiercely and senselessly, their hands roaming across each other in wild earnest.

Murdoch had the girl pressed up against the wall, self-control clearly forgotten, lips holding fast to hers. Her blouse was unbuttoned, revealing a lace brassiere underneath, and her fingers were steadily inching out of sight, slipping beneath the waistband of his trousers.

Lightoller blanched; his colleagues hadn't even noticed him standing awkwardly at the door. They were preoccupied, gasping and breathless, heedless of anything but each other.

The second officer could do nothing but stare, flabbergasted, gloved hand gripping the door handle so tightly, he thought it might crumple beneath his fingertips.

Whatever Lightoller had expected to find in Murdoch's cabin, it certainly hadn't been this. He'd suspected Murdoch of harboring hidden feelings for Bailey; it could not have been plainer in his actions and attitude regarding the girl. And naturally, he had seen the keen glances the girl had snuck at her superior officer from time to time.

But Lightoller had never expected it to come to this. Never once thought Murdoch would risk his entire maritime career for some fleeting, shortsighted lust. He was a better man than that. Or so Lightoller had thought.

It wasn't until Murdoch gripped Bailey by the waist and started easing her toward his bed that the second officer found words, his voice sizzling with disgust.

"Good *God* in Heaven."

The officers broke apart, stumbling away from one another in half a second.

Bailey scrambled to fasten up her blouse, her long fingers working hastily, her cheeks a rosy pink. Murdoch redid the top button of his trousers before stepping further away from his subordinate, hands linked behind his back. His expression was stone-faced, but his chest still heaved as he struggled to regain his breath, tie and collar both in disarray.

"Have you finished?" Lightoller spat. "We have an emergency meeting. Chart room. Five minutes. That should be enough time for you two idiots to get your act together."

He swung around and stormed down the hall, swallowing back the urge to start shouting questions at the pair of them, demanding to know what they were doing, and how they could be so damn foolish. But there were more important matters to attend to first, so he hurried to the chart room with his anger at a low simmer.

His footfalls were so heavy in the empty corridor that he didn't realize Murdoch trailed soundlessly after him, slinging a greatcoat over his broad shoulders. The two senior officers walked together in silence, with Lightoller seething and Murdoch looking astonishingly indifferent.

"Well?" the second officer said dully, when he could take the quiet no longer. "Where is she?" He didn't bother voicing Bailey's name.

"She went to her cabin to fetch a coat."

Lightoller snorted. "Oh? Given the two of you are so friendly, I'm simply astounded she didn't borrow one of yours."

"Have you seen the lass? She's too short. Wouldn't have fit, obviously."

The second officer shot Murdoch a scathing look, still trying not to think of the ravenous way the first officer had been kissing his subordinate.

"Have you no decency, Will?" he hissed. "No common sense at all?"

Murdoch ignored the question. "Spare me the lecture, Lights. We'll discuss this later. Tell me what's going on first."

"A passenger almost fell overboard. Female, first-class. I don't know all the details, but I'm certain the Master-at-Arms will fill us in."

Murdoch looked sharply at Lightoller, his attentiveness nothing short of immediate. But he asked no further questions as they entered the chart room. The officers gathered inside looked weary, clutching mugs of tea or pitch-black coffee. Wilde stood quietly in the far corner of the room, leaning against the wall with his arms folded across his chest. Pitman and Boxhall were present as well, while Lowe came strolling through the doorway with a bleary-eyed Moody at his side.

"Captain's on his way—" the fifth officer started to announce. But his strained expression lightened when Bailey shuffled inside the chart room.

She was quiet, refusing to meet the eye of any colleague—especially Lightoller. Her complexion was still tinged pink, and it was clear she was embarrassed.

As she damn well should be, Lightoller thought sourly, glowering at her until she assumed her place at Murdoch's side.

Smith appeared not long after, accompanied by the Master-at-Arms and a slightly dazed-looking Harold Bride. The officers listened in silence as they were briefed on the incident at hand—everything from the names of those involved to the steps the crew would take to avoid a similar mishap in the future.

But while Lightoller wished he could remain attentive, his mind was elsewhere, consumed by the overwhelming shock of what his colleagues had stupidly done.

Questions raced through his head, spreading like water upon the mess of his thoughts. How long had this…affair been going on between the pair of them? And did Murdoch have even the slightest idea of the consequences he and Bailey could face, should their dalliance come to light? Besides being sacked by White Star Line, they'd be shunned from the maritime industry, never to work at sea again.

Seafaring was Murdoch's life. How could he have risked something like this, when all he ever talked about was working his way up to captain? When he had forsworn his own marriage to pursue his ambitions? It didn't make any bloody sense.

Lightoller's fretful thoughts could not settle, and he was relieved when the meeting came to a close. As they filed out into the wheelhouse, he nudged Murdoch with one elbow and gestured toward the navigating room. The two senior officers slipped inside, and it wasn't until the door closed behind them that Lightoller rounded on Murdoch in a fury.

"I simply cannot believe you," he said, long legs pacing across the hardwood floor. "I really can't. Do you not realize the position you have put both yourself and Miss Bailey in?"

Murdoch's reply was stiff. "I do."

"Then what in God's name are you thinking? Fooling around with a subordinate? You must be mad!" Lightoller's eyes were blazing; he longed to grasp Murdoch by the shoulders and shake some sense into that thick skull of his. "What next?" he demanded furiously. "Will you be *shagging* her? Or have you already gone and seen to that?"

"Of course not. Calm down, Lights, let me explain—"

Lightoller snorted. "Oh, this should be rich," he said dryly. "Go on, then. Please justify why you thought it acceptable to get cozy with our first female officer and put both your jobs in peril. I'm dying to hear it."

"Shut your mouth," Murdoch snapped, his cool demeanor finally splintering apart. "You know nothing of this. You've no idea what I've been through. How hard I've fought to keep myself from actually feeling something for that girl—"

"So what are you saying? You're enamored with her, is that it?"

Murdoch looked away, glowering through the window at the deep gloom of night. "I can't answer that," he said curtly. "I've only known her for a week, now, haven't I? But I care dearly for her, Lights. I really do. More than anything."

"If you truly cared for Miss Bailey," Lightoller reasoned, "you wouldn't have kissed her. You would have snuffed out those inappropriate feelings at once. You would have done the sensible thing and remembered your boundaries. I mean, bloody hell, Will. When I said give her a chance, I didn't mean have a romp with her, for Heaven's sake!" He shook his head, the concern slipping through his disapproving gaze. "If anyone gets wind of the two of you being together, don't you realize what will happen to you? To her? She'll be seen as a floozy, no doubt, sleeping 'round with her superiors just to get ahead. She'll never find work aboard a commercial ship again. And neither will you, I'm afraid."

Murdoch was quiet, studying his gloved hands with a crease upon his brow. His silence unsettled Lightoller, who spoke his name aloud.

"Will?"

But Murdoch scarcely heard or even acknowledged him.

"I should've kept my distance from the start," he murmured, as if speaking to himself. "Should've kept pushing her away." His gaze traveled to Lightoller. "Will you be telling the captain about all this, then?"

Lightoller was almost scandalized.

"Honestly, Will. If you think I'd rat you out for something like this, then you clearly don't know me very well. I'll always have your back, my good man. Even when you make foolish decisions such as this one." He clapped one hand his colleague's shoulder, the heat of his voice softening. "What I don't agree with is the two of you slinking around the ship in secret trysts, however. I'll turn a blind eye, of course, if it comes to that. But I'm certain it'd only be a matter of time before someone else catches you. You need to consider her career as well as yours, Will. Don't make the mistake of throwing it away on a whim."

Murdoch stood remarkably still, staring distantly across the room as if lost in thought. His blue eyes were sightless, any emotion in their depths carefully shuttered away once more.

"I won't, Lights," he swore. "You can be sure of that."

He left the room without another word, and Lightoller stared after Murdoch's retreating back with a sigh, regretting his callous words and wondering if he should have said anything at all.

21:30

Although Murdoch stepped on the bridge with purpose, readying himself for the role as Officer of the Watch, it took every bit of strength he had left to hold himself together.

The first officer was in a right state, but no one would know just by looking at him. Beyond his collected composure, Murdoch gave nothing away. He was as professional as ever, nodding in greeting at Quartermaster Hichens and the crew before scribbling a note in the log.

But it wasn't until his eyes swept over Bailey that he felt his calm begin to waver, crumbling away like seawater wearing against stone.

Lightoller was right, though Murdoch was loath to admit it. As a senior officer, he needed to consider not only his maritime career, but Bailey's career as well.

Engaging in any sort of dalliance with the girl was too great of a risk. Too much of a detriment to their lives at sea. And that was the honest truth of it.

Murdoch gritted his teeth, struggling to get a hold on his emotions. But they were damn near uncontrollable, pouring through him in an undercurrent of bitterness and shame, longing and regret. He'd have to make a choice, just as he had done with Ada more than a year ago. It was either resign from his position at White Star Line to be with Esther Bailey—or else give up the girl altogether.

And as a man who had always known seafaring—who had come from an honorable lineage of accomplished captains, and regarded the ocean with an immeasurable degree of kinship and familiarity—Murdoch knew his decision, painful as it was.

He only wished he'd known it moments before he'd kissed her, and pinned her up against his cabin wall, and let her hands slip beneath his trousers to find his crotch.

Christ in Heaven, Murdoch couldn't help but think.

What had he done?

It was his own damn fault for letting their harmless flirting get this far. His own shameful lack of responsibility. Something else had clearly lingered beneath their snarky banter and animosity. Some quiet, pent-up tension that had simmered quietly between them, waiting to combust like oil to flame.

Murdoch knew he should have stopped it sooner. But he had been content to watch the spark grow, blazing brighter until it culminated with the two of them fumbling around in his cabin, hands and mouths exploring where they shouldn't.

Now he had no choice but to stamp out that spark, dousing it before their careers went up in flames entirely. But still, Murdoch would be lying if he said he wasn't upset...and he couldn't stop worrying that he would hurt her.

Quiet footsteps dragged him from his thoughts, and he turned to see Bailey stepping toward him with a smile. Her cheeks were still pink, though whether it was from the cold or because she was blushing, Murdoch couldn't say. He tried not to think of how beautiful she looked beneath the starlight. How he could still catch the taste of her on his lips. And how desperately he wanted to seize her and kiss her again and again, until they were breathless and wanting more.

She's not yours, he reminded himself. *You've made your decision.*

Bailey joined him at the bridge wing, close enough that their coats were brushing.

"I saw you speaking with Mr. Lightoller," she said curiously. "He's not going to...you know...tell anyone what he saw, is he?"

Murdoch shook his head and laced his gloved hands together, watching the stars glimmering above a pitch-black sea.

"Phew." Bailey laughed, soft and good-natured. "That was so stupid. How the hell did we forget the door, for Christ's sake? I'm blaming you, sir." Her eyes flashed with mischief, and she leaned closer with a smirk. "But at least now we'll remember to keep it locked in the future, right?"

Murdoch remained silent, his eyes fixed upon the night sky, and

Bailey regarded him with a frown.

"You're awfully quiet. I was expecting you to make some kind of sarcastic comment by now."

"So sorry to disappoint."

"There it is." Bailey grinned at his wry tone before nudging him with her elbow. "Say, after our rounds this evening, is there any chance you'd like to continue where we left off? I can do without sleep for one night."

She bit her lip, eyes sparkling as she looked him up and down.

Murdoch knew what she wanted; he wanted it, too. He'd never craved anything more. Even now, he couldn't stop thinking about it: the sight of her lying fully naked upon his sheets, clothing strewn all across the floor; the softness of her slender legs as his hands explored between them; the smooth, lovely curve of her spine as she arched her back and knelt on her hands and knees, letting him take her from behind.

That carnal need was overwhelming, and he sighed, running a hand over his face to collect himself.

"The bridge is a place of business, Miss Bailey," he said quietly. "Not of personal matters. So would you kindly make yourself useful and go fetch the ice report from the chart room, please?"

Her smile faltered. But she seemed to sense the edge in his voice, so she didn't pry. She offered a quick salute before obediently turning to the wheelhouse.

"Yes, sir."

It wasn't until her footsteps faded away that Murdoch heaved a sigh.

He'd have to talk to her sooner or later, he knew. But he wasn't even sure where to start.

His thoughts began to race again, fraught with ice-cold uncertainty, and he tried to calm himself by watching the sights before him: ocean water black as ink, stretching as far as the eye could see; glowing constellations sprinkling the heavens; telegraph lettering beaming white in the darkness of the bridge.

These images once might have soothed his frayed nerves. But now they were meaningless to him, and Murdoch found himself only longing for the solitude of his cabin.

For someplace far away from Bailey.

She returned to the bridge much too soon, bringing an ice report from the SS *La Touraine* along with her. Murdoch scanned the document and its coordinates quickly before ordering her to watch the helmsman. There were more errands he could have ordered her to run, of course. More tasks she could have fulfilled at his side. But he couldn't bear to speak with her for another moment, let alone look into her lovely green eyes. So he sent her along to the wheelhouse, while Moody assisted him with celestial sights and other minuscule tasks throughout the evening instead.

It wasn't until Wilde arrived at the bridge to relieve him from duty that Murdoch made his way toward his subordinate.

"Finally," she groaned when he came into view. "Can we take our rounds now? Because I think I'm gonna keel over if I don't get these legs moving." She shot him a sullen look before adding pointedly, "Though it's a wonder I didn't die from sheer boredom after you stuck me in the wheelhouse for four hours. *Sir.*"

Murdoch fiddled with the lapels of his greatcoat, unable to look her in the eyes. "Actually, I was thinking you would accompany Mr. Boxhall for your rounds on the starboard side of the ship tonight, while I'll take the port side."

Bailey was rubbing her hands together to warm them from the chill. But now she was motionless, staring at him in shock. "What? But we always take our rounds together, Mr. Murdoch."

"Exactly. Which is why a bit of variation won't kill you, Miss Bailey."

"Yes, it will," Bailey said stubbornly, and Murdoch sighed. "Besides, you do realize that Boxhall would rather jump ship than spend more than five minutes in my company? We aren't exactly the best of pals."

"All the more reason for you to spend some time getting to know each other, then."

Her eyebrows rose in disbelief. "You can't be serious. Whatever will we talk about?"

"The weather?" Murdoch offered, impatience finally creeping into his voice. "I don't know, and I don't rightly care. I've a bit of a headache, Miss Bailey, so I'm keeping my rounds short before retiring to my quarters." Although the lie was smooth, it still rasped his throat as if he'd swallowed sand, and he wanted nothing more than to take it back.

"Oh." Bailey's frown softened, replaced with sincere concern for her superior officer. "Are you feeling well?"

"Aye, fine. I just need to rest, is all."

"I can check you for fever—"

She reached out to brush her palm against his forehead. But Murdoch was swift, gently catching her by the wrist and drawing her hand away.

"No, lass. Please see to your rounds with Mr. Boxhall. I believe he's waiting for you on the officers' promenade as we speak."

Bailey stared uncomprehendingly at him. A flicker of hurt crossed her face, but she said nothing more as she turned and hurried away, heading for the starboard promenade where an unenthused Boxhall awaited her.

Murdoch watched her go, his heart flooding with guilt, before heading in the opposite direction to begin his cold, lonely rounds.

Coward, the voice in his head sneered.

He shouldn't have lied to her. He should have taken her aside and told her the truth—that their brief, fleeting intimacy was a mistake. That they would not, in fact, continue where they'd left off that earlier evening. And that he was a man who would always choose his career and ambition over anything—even a girl he cared so deeply for.

Murdoch should have been able to tell her these things outright.

But he chose to push her away—to bottle up his thoughts and emotions like the bleeding *coward* he was—and he despised himself for it.

April 13, 1912 | 10:05

Esther was usually in high spirits for her mid-morning watches.

She loved the way sunlight shone upon clear, glittering waves and wisps of foam before spilling its way onto the bridge. She loved the empty, peaceful quiet of the boat deck at the early hour, and she relished in how much warmer the salty air felt in comparison those long, late, chilled nights—warm enough to trade her greatcoat for her reefer jacket for once.

But most of all, she enjoyed sneaking glances at her superior officer, who always seemed so relaxed after a short breakfast and a cup of hot tea, his calm gaze fixed on the distant horizon stretching before them.

This morning, however, Esther was a far cry from being in high spirits.

She kept her head down and said very little. She fulfilled her tasks without pause. Where she once might have smiled at her crewmates, she now only offered polite nods and cursory words of greeting. And when it came to Murdoch, Esther was even more taciturn, mumbling a short "Good morning" before hurrying to her post. There was nothing more she could say to him. And clearly, nothing he had to say to her, either.

It was obvious Murdoch was keeping his distance from her, but Esther didn't know why. He certainly hadn't been *distant* with her last night, in the moments before their evening watch. His hands and tongue and mouth had claimed her body comfortably, and she was certain he would've ended up screwing her senseless had Lightoller not walked in on them.

But something had changed since last night. Something had reinstated the line dividing subordinate from superior. And now it seemed as if Murdoch wanted nothing more to do with her.

Esther forced herself to keep a watchful eye on the waves as the sun rose higher, and the crisp morning stretched on. But she felt so tired, dulled and empty, like a reservoir drained of its water.

She couldn't stop thinking about the night before. The way Murdoch had clutched her face between his hands and crashed his lips against hers. The blazing need she'd seen in his eyes, visceral enough to shred his self-control apart. The way he'd spoken her name aloud—*Esther*, just like that, not Miss Bailey—and how much she had liked it, wanting more than anything to hear him say it over and over again.

Even now, she could hear Murdoch conversing with the captain by the wheelhouse, and it was hard to believe that same raspy, Scottish burr had murmured her name with such longing, the sound soft and ragged against her ear. Her throat tightened at the memory, and she tried not to think of how she'd spent the morning staring up at her cabin ceiling when she ought to have been snoozing, kept wide awake by her scattered thoughts.

"All right, miss?"

A kind, warm voice filled her ears, and she blinked to see Lowe stepping to her side.

"I've seen better days, to be honest," Esther replied with a shrug. Not wanting to sound dour, she added, "At least the weather's warming up, though."

"Indeed. Still a bit nippy, yeah. But I no longer feel as if I'm going to die of hypothermia, so all in all, I'd say that's quite the improvement."

Esther wanted to laugh, but she could only manage a small smile as her dark, brooding thoughts continued to swirl about her mind like a cold rain. She fell silent shortly after, and Lowe cocked his head to one side, brows knotting together with concern.

"I don't like seeing you so blue, miss," he said gently. "Why don't you join me for dinner before our watches tonight? I'll even brew you a good, bold cuppa. Guaranteed to perk you right up, it will." Smirking, he added, "Though I hear your coffee's real strong, so perhaps we can try that instead. Wilde said it just about killed him, but I think he's full of it."

Esther stole a glance at Murdoch, who strolled past them to the starboard bridge wing. But he wasn't even looking at her; he only had eyes for the sea, and the billowing clouds piled high above it. She turned to Lowe—the one officer besides Moody who had been so sweet and welcoming from the beginning. The officer who had never once shouted at her, or snapped at her, or vexed her in ways Murdoch had.

And so she nodded, a sliver of hope bringing warmth back to her veins. "I'd like that very much. Maybe even a round of poker as well?"

Lowe looked sheepish. "After what happened with Jim and Bert last night, I think I'll have to pass."

Esther couldn't help but tease him. "Whatsa matter?" she said breezily, woes regarding Murdoch momentarily forgotten. "Scared I'll beat you?"

He seemed to like her playful nature, stepping closer with a crooked grin at the corner of his mouth.

"Please. If anything, you ought to be the one running scared. I might not be able to take on Jim and Bert, yeah, but I'm proper certain I can handle the likes of you, Esther Bailey."

She snorted. "We'll see, won't we? I don't mind a challenge."

"And neither do I."

His eyes held hers before flicking down to study her lips, and Esther took a step back in alarm, suddenly realizing what happened in that short, meaningful moment.

A single thought crystallized in her mind, a realization she should have recognized long before—that Lowe might see her as more than a friend and fellow officer. The intent way he was looking at her was enough to confirm her suspicions.

Shit, Esther thought, biting her bottom lip in dismay. *Shit shit shit.*

While she enjoyed Lowe's company as well as his banter, she didn't feel that way about him. Not when she was already so keen on her superior officer. She shifted from one foot to the other, gloved hands fidgeting behind her back. Suddenly, Murdoch's foul temper whenever she was hanging around Lowe made perfect sense—the acerbic remarks, the cold shoulders, the narrowed eyes that might have been full of jealousy.

"Erm..." Esther struggled for words. "We should probably get back to work before Mr. Murdoch starts shouting at us."

But Lowe looked untroubled. "Eh, he's not even looking over here. I think he's been out of sorts all morning, though, same as you. Was everything okay last night?"

"Yes, of course," Esther lied a little too quickly, and although Lowe still looked curious, he tipped his cap and started for his post.

The rest of the watch dragged on, with Murdoch almost determinedly ignoring his subordinate. He kept Esther rooted in the same spot for the entire day, and she was forced to watch—silent and fuming—as he assigned *her* tasks to other crewmen instead. She was livid, more than ready to give him a piece of her mind, but it wasn't until two in the afternoon that Murdoch made his way toward her. His face was expressionless, eyes indifferent in the bright sun, and she knew exactly what he was going to say before he opened his mouth.

"We're not taking our rounds together," she said flatly, "are we?"

Murdoch shook his head. "'Fraid not. You'll be taking the starboard side with Mr. Pitman today." He nodded over her shoulder, and Esther turned to see the third officer standing in the starboard bridge wing, whistling merrily as he faced the open sea.

"Swell." She glowered at him. "So what's the excuse this time? Another headache, Mr. Murdoch?"

"Never you mind," Murdoch said shortly, glancing down at his pocket watch before nodding at her in dismissal. "Go on, lass. You mustn't keep Mr. Pitman waiting."

He started for the chart room, presumably to record the ship's navigation on a chit for Wilde. Esther watched him go, chest heaving, only distantly aware of Pitman waiting for her in the bridge wing.

You have to talk to Murdoch, she told herself. *It's now or never.*

With her mind made up, Esther slipped inside the chart room after her superior officer and quietly closed the door behind her.

Murdoch didn't even turn around; his back was to her as he marked the sprawling map on the adjacent wall. Esther stood still, not sure how to proceed next. But then he spoke, turning his head slightly to one side but keeping his hands busy with the map.

"Shouldn't you be making your rounds, Miss Bailey?"

Clearly, he'd heard her soft footsteps. Perhaps he could hear the wild hammer of her heartbeat as well.

"To hell with rounds," Esther snapped. She'd hoped to remain civil, but like usual, her short temper seemed to get the better of her. "I want to know why you're acting like this. You've had us take separate rounds twice now, when we always walk the decks together. You won't even *look* at me, for God's sake, and I don't think you've said more than two sentences to my face since last night. You're avoiding me, and I damn well want to know why."

Murdoch finally turned around to face her. "I have my reasons," he said quietly. "But I'm not sure they're the ones you want to hear."

Esther hesitated, her throat suddenly dry. She opened her mouth to speak, but the words came out muddled, weighing heavy on her tongue like molasses. So she swallowed and tried again.

"Are you angry at me?"

He stepped closer, his face smoothed into an indecipherable mask.

"No," he said. "I'm angry at myself. For letting last night happen. For letting it get that far."

His words were a flat, simple statement, as if they were discussing the Atlantic weather, not the ruins of whatever affair crumbled between them. There was nothing in his voice. No anger or sarcasm. Just a hint of weary resignation that only made it that much worse.

"I don't remember you telling me to stop." Esther could feel herself trembling, though whether it was from anger or hurt, she couldn't say. "You kissed me back, Will. You wanted it, too."

"Aye, I did. I'll not deny it, lass." His voice was soft in its bitterness. "But I recognize my place well enough to know that what happened between us was a right mistake. And I blame myself for not stopping it sooner. I'm supposed to be your superior officer, for Christ's sake. And I couldn't even do that properly."

Esther opened her mouth to protest, but he lifted one hand to silence her. "Don't. What we did was wrong, and I won't hear a word otherwise. Do you even understand what might happen should anyone find out? We'd both lose our jobs, to say nothing of our reputations."

"I don't care, sir—"

"But you should," Murdoch implored. "This work suits you. You're driven, hardworking and clever; you have a great deal of potential as White Star Line's first woman officer. Don't squander it."

Esther stared blankly at him, at a loss for what to say. He'd never spoken about her like that before, and it took her several seconds to regain her thoughts—to realize he was praising her.

"I'm not squandering anything," she said firmly. "We could keep it quiet, you know. We could make it work. If we were careful—"

"What difference would it make?" Murdoch demanded, running one hand through his short hair. "We already weren't careful enough. Mr. Lightoller knows, and if we keep at it, he won't be the only one, now, will he? It would be best to move on. Forget all of this."

Anger ripped through her mind like lightning, vicious and shivering with sparks.

"That's *bullshit!*" she shouted, finally losing all control. "You can't pretend like nothing happened! You can't just *forget* about it. It doesn't work that way, Will. I'm a goddamn human being, you ass. I have feelings. And I know you try to hide it, but so do you!"

"Lass, the difference is I don't let my feelings interfere with my work." There was a definite edge to his words now. A flint to his dark blue eyes. "Perhaps you should learn to do the same."

"I can't," Esther insisted. *Because I like you,* she longed to say. *I'm crazy about you, Will.*

But Murdoch was staring hard at her, his jaw set.

"Then allow me to put this plainly for you," he said shortly. "I've known seafaring all my life. I've known you for only eight days. I'm sorry, Miss Bailey, but I won't risk my entire career on a brief affair. And if you have any sense, then neither will you."

Esther felt the hurt well up inside her. She longed to shout, to scream, to snag him by the lapels of his jacket and kiss him, hard and searing. But her anger was stronger, claiming her heart in an instant.

"Is that your decision, then?" she demanded.

"Aye." His voice rang out with curt finality. "It is."

Esther drew in deep breath. But her eyes were dry, her voice steady as she shrugged and said, "Then we have nothing more to say on the matter."

And with that, she straightened her collar and strolled for the door, not even daring a glance over her shoulder.

Cold, salty air stung her lungs as she returned to the bridge, where Pitman was waiting for her. He started forward, waving a hand.

"*Hoi*, 'bout time!" he called. "Let's make these rounds quick, eh? I won't beat about the bush, there's a marvelous cold-cuts sandwich waiting for me in the mess hall, see, and I'd rather not keep it waiting any longer."

Esther nodded distantly. "Sure, let's get going."

"By the by, what were you and Mr. Murdoch talking about?"

"Oh, nothing important. Just the usual business."

Esther was quick to change the subject, and she and Pitman dissolved into friendly conversation as they pursued the starboard decks, weaving through first-class passengers and blue-suited stewards carrying silver teaware. Esther tried to laugh and smile at her colleague's jokes. But she was struggling piece herself together, fighting back the sting of unshed tears. The roar of ocean water was soothing, at least, offering a shred of calm. But she was still aching, the pain a deep, lingering throb she felt not only in her heart, but in her bones as well.

"Now there's something you don't see every day," Pitman said abruptly.

Esther followed his gaze to see a lovely woman standing on the boat deck ahead of them. Donned in an embroidered dress of water-blue, she wore a tortoiseshell comb in her hair with a sash of silver tied around her corset-tightened waist. The seventh officer recognized Fay Harlow at once. But she was not alone; Wireless Operator Harold Bride was with her, and something about the young man seemed to intrigue Fay. She kept smiling at him as they spoke, observing his shy grin and eyes of bright blue, and Esther noted this was the happiest she'd seen Fay since she had boarded *Titanic*.

Esther didn't blame her, though. She'd be miserable, too, if she were engaged to a swine like Callum Lockerbie.

Pitman was staring, baffled by the sight of a first-class lady casually strolling the deck with a wireless operator. Esther tapped him on the shoulder. "That's Miss Fay Harlow."

His brows arched in surprise. "The woman who almost fell overboard last night?" When Esther nodded, Pitman remarked, "Blimey, she's beautiful."

"That she is." Esther studied Bride and Fay, looking thoughtful. "They seem pretty comfortable with each other, don't they?"

She watched as Fay snatched some kind of wireless instrument from Bride's hands and plopped down on a deck chair. He joined her, and the two of them were quiet and smiling as he showed her the equipment, pointing out all manner of circuits and coils. Pitman was still gaping, and Esther hissed good-naturedly, "Cripes, Bert. Stop staring, will ya?"

By the time they finished their rounds, Esther was weary and exhausted, longing for the haven of sleep. Pitman started for the mess hall, no doubt thinking of that sandwich of his, while she retraced her steps to the officers' quarters. She was heedless of anything but her grim thoughts, not even noticing the tall gentleman emerging from the First-Class Entrance until she collided right into him.

"Careful, you filth!"

Esther straightened up to see Lockerbie standing before her, looking annoyed as he smoothed out his fancy suit. But when he recognized her in the brilliant sun, his irritation dripped away at once.

"Goodness, Esther. I didn't realize that was you. I've not yet grown accustomed to seeing you so…mannish. It's horribly jarring, you know."

"Boy, I'm sure it is." Esther rolled her eyes before starting down the boat deck again, praying Lockerbie wouldn't follow. But he did, much to her disgruntlement, sauntering along with his stupid walking stick in hand. She stopped short, demanding, "Can I help you with something?"

"Indeed, you can. I need you to stand right there—without any cheek, preferably, thank you—and allow me to apologize."

"Oh?" Esther folded her arms across her chest. "I'm just surprised you actually know what an apology is, Mr. Lockerbie."

"I said no cheek."

"Whoops. So, to what do I owe this great honor?"

Lockerbie stepped closer, his emotionless hazel eyes searching her face. "I simply wanted to atone for the way I behaved at dinner the other night," he said almost lazily. "Had I known your former fiancé was an abusive drunk, I would have refrained from goading you as much as I did. I made a mistake, and I want you to know that I am sorry."

"Oh, *please*. You're only sorry because Booker chewed your damn ear off, I'm sure."

Lockerbie chuckled. "I won't deny it," he admitted, looking amused. "But he had every right to do so. He's one of my oldest friends, as are you, Esther. I'd never do anything that might hurt you. You know that."

Esther snorted. "Yeah? That's news to me."

Lockerbie shook his head at her, his expression almost chiding. "Esther, Esther. If this is because you're still bitter about my decision not to marry—"

"It's not." She scrunched her nose in disgust. "Trust me, it's not."

But Lockerbie still looked disbelieving. "You know," he said smoothly, "it's almost a pity I didn't marry you. Might have saved you a bit of headache from that drunk."

Esther clenched her fists tight, wanting nothing more than to slap him with all the strength she could muster. She stared hard into his filthy hazel eyes, ready to tell him with fierce words that she would have braved a drunk a thousand times over than marry a swine like him.

But before she could summon up a scathing retort, her attention drifted elsewhere, and she froze when she spotted her superior officer in the distance.

Like her, Murdoch must have finished his rounds. Only he wasn't alone. He was strolling alongside a beautiful woman in a day dress of sheer, flowy teal chiffon and sequins, her glossy hair piled up high with diamond-studded pins and a single butterfly comb. Esther recognized Miss Allen at once, and the breath whisked right out her lungs.

Where her jealousy for this woman had once been a mild twinge in the back of her mind, it was now overwhelming in its intensity, ruthless and white-hot as it pierced her like a bullet to the gut. Her throat tightened as she watched Miss Allen stroll alongside Murdoch, chattering away with her expensive, floaty dress swirling behind her.

Although the first officer looked weary, he still gave Miss Allen his undivided attention, matching her pace with his hands behind his back. Whether he was being respectful or truly interested in keeping her company, Esther couldn't say. But all she could think of was how stunning Miss Allen looked, and how deeply Esther wished *she* was the one walking the decks with Murdoch instead.

What was he even doing strolling around with a first-class passenger, anyhow? Perhaps they were merely talking, but Esther didn't care. The jealousy in her stomach knotted up tight, tugging at her temper and—worse even—her feelings.

"Are you even listening to me?"

The icy voice dragged her eyes away from Murdoch, and Esther rounded on Lockerbie, hating him, too. Christ, she was so tired of everyone. She just wanted to crawl into bed, so she snapped, "What do you think? I'd love to stick around and listen to your touching apologies, but I'm tired. I've been on duty since ten. I need my sleep."

He shrugged. "Suit yourself. Just know that I am truly sorry, Esther."

Truly an asshole, more like, Esther thought, irritable.

Before she could march away, Lockerbie spoke once more.

"A moment. You haven't seen my fiancée by chance, have you? She left our luncheon early. Said she was headed out to take the air." He hesitated, a troubled look in his eyes. "Ever since the mishap last night, I've been rather…hesitant to let her out of my sight. Perhaps I'm being too overprotective, but she is my future wife. I don't know what I would do without her."

Esther stared at him, stunned by his concern and wondering if he wasn't as heartless as she'd thought.

But then she thought of Fay sitting on the boat deck, her eyes bright and curious as she chatted with Wireless Operator Bride. The young woman had looked so different. Content, almost. Nothing compared to how she had been at dinner, sitting there with her eyes glazed and empty, her lovely face as lifeless as marble. It was a mask Esther knew all too well. A mask she herself had worn during the long weeks and months of her ruined engagement with Muir.

Part of her knew she ought to placate Lockerbie and tell the truth. But Esther refused to ruin whatever shred of happiness Fay had found with Bride, so the lie bubbled swiftly at her lips.

"I think I saw her making for the Grand Staircase on A Deck," she told Lockerbie. "Perhaps you'll find her there."

Lockerbie smiled. "I had better, my dear."

His reply was soft, measured. But something else lingered behind the smoothness of his voice. Something faint and menacing, something that carried the quiet implication of a threat—and Esther didn't like it one bit.

Suddenly, she found herself wondering how, exactly, Miss Fay had almost fallen overboard, and it occurred to her that Lockerbie might know more than he'd let on.

She threw him a sharp look, regarding him with caution as the former softness in his gaze hardened to steel. But Lockerbie had already turned to leave, straightening his bowler hat and smiling at her in a manner that did not meet his piercing eyes.

"Good day, Miss Bailey," was all he said over one shoulder.

"Good day, Mr. Lockerbie."

20:00

Esther awoke in the sleepy darkness of her cabin some hours later, tucked away in the depths of her bed.

She rolled over on her side, blinking in the thin moonlight filtering through the frosted-glass window. Her hands fumbled with the clock on her bedside table, dragging it toward her to inspect the time.

8 o'clock, Esther read through blurred eyes.

Still enough time to fall back asleep. Still another blessed hour before she had to drag herself out of bed and onto the bridge once again.

Esther shoved away her pillow, which was wet with the tears she'd shed crying herself to sleep. Muted voices and soft footsteps echoed beyond the door, as if officers or crew were crossing to and from the bridge. Briefly, Esther wondered who was trading shifts at this hour. But then she decided she didn't care. She smashed her face into the mattress, trying to blot out all the useless noise. She wanted everything to go away. She wanted to drift into slumber rather than wade through an ocean of unpleasant thoughts. So she burrowed herself into her blankets, wishing they were like water she could sink into, deeper and deeper until she was gone from the world and her woes entirely.

She wasn't sure how much time passed until her alarm went off.

Esther groaned, silencing its shriek and clambering to her feet.

Her cabin was in disarray after losing her temper before bed; she'd stormed around the room in a fury, cursing and crying, shoving books to the floor and flinging clothes everywhere in her distress.

But now that Esther had slept on her emotions, she realized how foolish she'd been.

She knelt to pick up the overturned lamp dumped on the floor, returning it to the desk with shame in her heart. She'd tidy up later, of course. But for now, she needed to prepare for her watch.

Esther was quiet as she readied herself, running a comb through her hair, tugging on her work skirt and struggling not to think of William Murdoch. But no matter how hard she tried, she couldn't scrub the man from her mind. Her superior officer kept flooding back to her and she hated it, wanting nothing more than to forget him and his lousy blue eyes altogether.

He had chosen his job over her. He had sacrificed any sort of intimacy between them to protect his career and respectability, as well as her own.

It had been for the best, of course. A decision as painful as it was practical. And now there was nothing else to do except move on, difficult though it was.

Esther swept her tie around her neck and began to knot the silk fabric, moving her fingers just as Murdoch had taught her. Her thoughts turned to his hands, thinking of how coarse and calloused they were, and yet how gently they touched and explored...

She fumbled with the tie, hating these memories and hating herself for dwelling on them. Why was she even pining after the man in the first place? She had her own priorities to worry about. As the first female officer in White Star Line history, she was the one responsible for paving the way for those women ready and willing to join the maritime industry. She was supposed to be setting a good example. But how could do that if she was fooling around with a superior?

I won't squander it, she swore to herself, recalling Murdoch's words as she buttoned up her blouse. *I won't.*

By the time she was fully dressed, gloves and greatcoat pulled on for the chill no doubt awaiting her outside, Esther made her way to Lowe's cabin.

"Harry?" she called softly, tapping her knuckles on the door.

Silence answered her, much to her surprise. But Lowe wasn't the kind of person to carelessly snooze through his alarm; he was far too steadfast a sailor for that. She figured he was brewing up a batch of tea in the mess hall, no doubt waiting for her, so she started there at once.

The boat deck was wickedly cold, and she shivered, her breath misting the air to white. She passed Boxhall, who was smoking at the end of the officers' promenade, a glow of amber flaming from his cigarette in the darkness. They exchanged stilted nods—a slight improvement from the cold shoulder she usually expected from him—and Esther wondered if Murdoch's order to conduct rounds with the quiet fourth officer had helped lessen his contempt for her after all.

She continued aft, crossing through the gate dividing the officers' promenade. But Esther had barely closed it behind her when a dark, slender figure emerged from the shadow of a lifeboat and stepped forward, blocking her path.

It was a man who looked strangely familiar to Esther, though she couldn't place where she might have seen him before.

He was an older, hatchet-faced gentleman with smooth graying hair, dressed smartly in a pressed suit and tie. His thin lips were pressed into a grimace, and his gunmetal eyes—which were hawkish sharp and just as unblinking—stared at her from a pool of deep wrinkles.

"Are you Miss Esther Bailey?" he asked in a crisp voice.

Esther hesitated. "I am," she answered, appraising the man with a wary gaze. She studied his thin hair and grimacing mouth, recognizing him in the dim light: Gideon Slate. Lockerbie's valet.

"I'd like for you to come with me," the valet said. "Mr. Lockerbie has taken ill, and he is in need of your assistance immediately."

Esther arched an eyebrow. "He's ill?" she snorted, skeptical. "What a load of bull. I saw him not even that long ago, and he was perfectly fine."

Slate answered her with a tight-lipped, condescending smile. "Yes, and that was then, obviously. But things happen, and I regret to say he fell sick shortly after dinner this evening."

"Can't he call upon Dr. O'Loughlin?" Esther demanded.

"No. He can't." His austere eyes swept her up and down, jaw tightening as if annoyed by all her questions. "He's asking specifically for you. And as a former nurse, surely you're more than capable of lending a hand."

Esther glowered at the valet, folding her arms across her chest.

"Lockerbie told you I was a nurse, did he? Well, did he also tell you that I'm an officer? And that as an officer, I have work to attend to?"

"What work?" Slate drawled. "Your shift doesn't begin for another hour. I daresay that's more than enough time to see to him."

"How—?" Ether started to ask. But then she stopped herself, deciding she didn't care to know how the valet knew her schedule. Perhaps Lockerbie had spoken with a purser or passing deckhand at some time or another.

Sighing, she shoved aside her misgivings and grumbled, "All right, fine. I'll help him. I've no reason not to. Let me get my medical kit—"

"That won't be necessary," Slate cut in smoothly. "We'll have everything you need in his suite."

Esther blinked warily at him for a moment, unable to stem the suspicion from slithering through her veins.

There was something odd about all this. Something very peculiar. Lockerbie's manservant wasn't making the situation any better, either. She didn't like him—or his cold, ugly eyes that reminded her of empty tunnels. But it seemed as if Lockerbie needed her help, so Esther glanced over her shoulder to where Boxhall stood, puffing idly on his cigarette.

"Hey," she called, "if you see Mr. Lowe, would you please tell him there's been a bit of an emergency, and that I'm sorry I couldn't make it to dinner?"

Boxhall shrugged, but thankfully he didn't give her any attitude as he said, "Sure."

"Thanks." Esther smiled at him before turning to the valet, who gestured down the boat deck with one hand, gray eyes boring into hers like sharpened steel.

"After you, miss."

SEVENTEEN

EMBRACE

April 13, 1912 | 21:15

ESTHER WASN'T ENTIRELY sure what she was doing as she followed Slate down the corridors of B Deck, crossing the long sprawl of carpet running endlessly beneath their feet.

Lockerbie's valet hadn't said a word since leading her away from the boat deck, and Esther could feel her uneasiness grow as she trailed after him.

She fidgeted with the edge of her leather glove and wondered if she was making a mistake. But she did want to help Lockerbie—and not only because her old nursing habits had driven her to offer immediate aid.

It was because underneath his stupid, pompous disposition, Lockerbie was her childhood friend.

Esther had grown up with him. Cared for him. Witnessed him shed his youthful charm to become an oil heir shaped and molded by high-class society. She'd spent summers with him on his family's Sausalito estate, exchanging flirty glances and oftentimes curling up on his lap when they'd thought no one was looking. He'd let her sob and scream in his arms when they'd found Brighton after the Great Earthquake, buried beneath the rubble of singed bricks and charred cinders. Esther had even kissed the bastard, God help her, during a time when she'd been a foolish girl chasing after his affections.

Their pasts were entwined and always would be—no matter how hard she tried to forget it.

Esther still loathed the man, of course. Lockerbie was an insufferably arrogant swine who deserved a good punching to the nose. But her compassion was stronger than her hatred, so Esther was willing to set aside her grievances and help.

And yet…something about his sudden illness didn't sit right with her.

Why even call for her when there was a perfectly capable doctor and his assistant a mere deck below?

It was all very odd, and Esther was feeling ill at ease, wishing she'd refused the request in the first place.

She could have been dining with Lowe in the mess hall right now. She could have been snorting at his jokes, sipping hot tea and wiping the floor with him in a round of poker. It sounded all too desirable as she trudged reluctantly down the long white corridor, passing the rows of parlor suites and trying not to scowl at the back of Slate's graying hair.

They stopped at a gleaming door with a plaque reading *B-52-56*. Slate ushered her inside, and Esther found herself standing amidst a ridiculously ornate sitting room. The walls were swept in dark mahogany wood, each panel edged with gilt embellishments and dotted with golden sconces. An exquisite marble fireplace sat across from her, its smooth surface inlaid with mother-of-pearl, its electric light glowing behind a metal grate. Floral patterns swirled along the satin chairs and lone settee, while a handful of unique paintings were propped up on a chaise lounge.

Esther cocked her head to one side as she studied them, intrigued, marveling at their distinct colors and wild brush strokes. They were bizarre but enthralling, and she was so transfixed by their artistry that she didn't hear the valet slip soundlessly from the room.

For a moment, the only noise to fill the glittering, gilded parlor was that of the fire. Then the muffled rush of footsteps wearing across carpet filled her ears, and she turned.

Lockerbie came storming out of an adjacent room, his hair perfectly slicked back, his eyes dark with annoyance. He held a glass of champagne in one hand and a full bottle in another; he dumped the latter into the silver ice bucket on the table before pacing closer.

Esther figured he must have come from dinner, since he was still donned in his white tie, carrying the stench of cigar smoke along with him. But as her narrowed gaze swept him up and down, it became instantaneously apparent that there was nothing *ill* about him. She glared at Lockerbie, torn between disbelief and irritation as he plopped into one of the easy chairs and took a swig from his champagne glass.

"Good," he said idly. "You're here."

"Unfortunately." Esther crossed her arms over her chest, shaking her head. "You're looking real infirm there, buddy," she said dryly. "Practically on your deathbed as we speak."

"Don't be spiky. How else was I going to get you to come here?"

"Being honest wouldn't be a bad start."

He shrugged, swirling around his champagne glass with a faint smirk. "Perhaps," he drawled. "But where's the fun in that?"

Esther rolled her eyes, turning for the door. "That's it. I'm going."

But Lockerbie was quick, shooting from his chair at once.

"Don't," he said, his voice both a plea and sharp command. "Come, have some champagne." He gestured toward the heavy bottle sunken in ice. "It's *Bouchard Père et Fils.*"

"Champagne makes me sick to my stomach," she said flatly, striding across the room without a backward glance. "So…thanks, but no thanks."

"Esther."

Lockerbie crossed the parlor with an impatient stride, throwing out an arm to bar her path. "Can't you hear me out for a moment? I need to gripe to someone, dammit." His voice grew sour, and he added, "I tried asking your brother to come instead, but he was far too busy talking nonsense with that Thomas Andrews again."

She raised her brows. "Nonsense as in their work, you mean?"

"Exactly."

Esther made a noise between a laugh and a scoff. "Unbelievable. You're a real piece of work, Mr. Lockerbie. Tell me, have you ever once stopped to think that the universe doesn't revolve around you?"

Lockerbie strolled back to the champagne bottle and poured another glass. "Oh, pipe down. I'm in no such mood for your cheek *or* criticism tonight, Esther."

"Pity," she said dully. "You'd do well to take it to heart."

Esther shook her head and started for the door, wondering how she'd been so stupid to think Lockerbie needed help in the first place. But her foolish curiosity somehow got the better of her, and she came to a stop.

"You said you needed to gripe to someone," she said slowly, drawing her fingers away from the door handle. "Why? What happened?"

He swallowed another sip of champagne, eyes narrowing. "Do you even wish to know? You were halfway to the door."

Exasperated, Esther raised her voice at him. "Look, you already dragged me down here! Just tell me what's the matter. Christ's sake."

Lockerbie looked away, sulking, scowling into the amber glow of the electric fire. Then, in a sudden blaze of movement, he spun on his heel and started to pace the lavish room.

"It's my fiancée," he explained furiously, one hand sifting through his sleek hair.

"Fay?" Esther was surprised, but pressed on, "What about her? Is she all right?"

Lockerbie threw her a scathing look, still pacing the room with his coattails whipping out behind him. "Oh, she's perfectly *fine*," he snapped. "Smoking cigarettes and hanging around the wireless room as we speak, according to my man."

"Is she?" Esther asked with a smile, not even trying to conceal her amusement. "So what's the problem, then?"

"The problem?" Lockerbie echoed softly, turning a hard gaze on her.

For a moment, there was only silence.

Then his arm lashed out, knocking the champagne bottle and its bucket from the table.

It fell to the floor with a thud, ice skittering everywhere, sparkling liquid soaking into the carpet. Lockerbie rounded on her, bellowing out his rage.

"The problem, Esther, is that her behavior is nothing short of obscene! The problem is that she is making a mockery of myself and our engagement! And the *problem* is that she is engaging in all these indecencies with some filthy, worthless, working-class drudge!"

Esther held her ground as Lockerbie bore over her, looming nearly twice her height. A bit of spit from snarling mouth landed on her cheek, and she wiped it away with her palm.

"Drudge?" she echoed in disgust. "You've got a lotta nerve. How dare you talk about Mr. Bride like that. He saved your fiancée's life—"

"And does that give him the right to drag her below decks to his stinking wireless hovel?" Lockerbie demanded, slamming a fist upon the nearest end-table. "To indulge a lady of her stature in cigars? And to stay holed up with him in some room where he can no doubt put his dirty fingers all over her? I invite that riff-raff to dine with us this evening, and this is how he repays my generosity? It's insulting! Absurd!"

His chest was heaving as he spoke, hazel eyes sightless in their rage. "I wouldn't be surprised if she's already fooling around with him as we speak, given the way she kept making eyes at him over dinner, the little *slut*—"

"Stop that!" Esther hissed. "Now you're just being juvenile."

"Far from it," Lockerbie retorted. "She is *mine*. My fiancée, my future wife. I have given her everything. Cash, gowns, jewels, diamonds worth a fortune—and yet it's not enough to keep her from whoring around with a lowly gutter rat who makes a living tapping dots and dashes into a box."

Lockerbie dropped into a chair with a brooding glower before tossing down the rest of his champagne. He was like a petulant child, throwing a tantrum when he didn't get his way.

"She ought to be with me tonight," he said sullenly, crossing one long leg over the other. "Not him. *I'm* her fiancé, God damn it."

Esther rolled her eyes. "Good grief. Now I know why Booker wanted to keep to his work instead of coming here. Your level of insecurity is simply astounding."

"Excuse me?" Lockerbie's voice was colder than ice.

"You heard me. Be reasonable, will you? What makes you think your fiancée is being promiscuous? She's only having a good time with the man who saved her from almost certain death."

"By screwing him, you mean."

"Oh, get over yourself."

"It's a valid concern, *Esther*," Lockerbie scoffed. "She's been acting odd ever since we boarded this damn ship. She's ill-tempered, rude, difficult—and on top of all that, she refuses to come to my bed at night."

"How tragic," Esther said wryly, unable to hide the smirk forming on the edge of her lips. "But I'm sure she has her reasons. Perhaps your coital skills are lackluster."

Lockerbie stared at her, affronted. "Don't be ridiculous. I'll have you know I am perfectly accomplished at lovemaking. *She's* the one being problematic."

Esther snorted. "Right," she said breezily. "Whatever you say, Mr. Lockerbie."

Lockerbie said nothing in reply, strangely enough. She'd expected a retort, with a heated argument to follow. But now he was quiet, uncrossing his legs and lacing his fingers together in his lap, studying her in silence.

Esther didn't like the way he was looking at her. His eyes lingered, sweeping her up and down with careful, razor-thin scrutiny, and she backed away, grappling for the doorknob behind her.

"I should be going," she said quickly, trying to ignore the waves of uncertainty flooding across her skin. "My watch is starting soon, and if I'm late—"

"A moment."

She watched Lockerbie rise from his chair and draw closer, tall frame towering over her short, wiry one.

"I wonder…" he murmured thoughtfully, almost to himself.

His steps continued forward, and she backed away from him until her shoulders struck the door behind her. He pressed his palms flat up against the wood on either side of her head, framing her there, his voice softer, and slower, murmuring against her ear.

"I daresay if my fiancée is out having a romp, well…I'm damn well entitled to have one of my own. Wouldn't you agree?"

Pressed up against the door with her heart racing a mile a minute, Esther could only gape at him.

Christ, was he actually propositioning her? Where she once might have laughed aloud, there was something about this situation that held the laughter back. She didn't know what else to say, so she made a lame attempt at humor.

"Well, good thing Mr. Slate is in the other room, so…"

He smiled humorlessly. "Very funny, Esther."

Lockerbie was much too close to her now. His heavy breath tickled her hair, smelling of champagne and cigar smoke, and she wrinkled her nose. There was a glaze to his eyes as he stared her down, cross-examining her with a frightening intensity. He was clearly very inebriated. Or perhaps too consumed with his jealousy of Bride to even see straight.

He leaned in closer, hands still braced against the door, his voice smooth as silk. "We have a history, you and I," he said in a smug, amused voice. "We've been intimate before, have we not?"

Esther suddenly couldn't think. Her brain stumbled and chugged, like metal clockwork in need of oiling, and yet her words came out level as she reminded, "That was a long time ago, Mr. Lockerbie. It was one kiss, and we were young and stupid."

"But you liked it," he said almost lazily. "And I know you wanted more."

"Don't flatter yourself," she spat.

But Lockerbie wasn't listening. He smiled a little, but it was sinister— full of a dark, suggestive longing that had her stomach lurching and her throat swelling with bile.

"I can give you more, if you'll let me," he whispered. "I can be very, very good to you, my dear. Certainly far from lackluster."

Esther glanced away in repulsion, but Lockerbie snagged her jaw with his fingers, forcing her to look at him. She had no choice but to glare into his eyes—angry, trembling and defiant—as he breathed the words aloud.

"I'll have you moaning my name until I've finished, Esther. Make no mistake of it—"

Furious, Esther wrestled away from him.

"Get the hell away from me!" she shouted, her palm colliding against his cheek in a resounding *smack*.

The slap filled the room like the crack of a gunshot.

Lockerbie staggered backward, shocked and stricken by the force of the blow, clutching the bright pink welt now swelling across his cheek. Yet his eyes still scorched her, sizzling with outrage and a lascivious desire for more.

Esther whirled around, scrambling for the door, nearly knocking over a gilt vase of lilies in her haste. But Lockerbie was quicker, slamming her forward until her cheek dully struck the wood panel. He kept her there, one hand pinning her wrists together behind her back, the other twisting up into her hair, yanking it tight.

Esther could only manage a hiss of fear and rage as she realized what was happening. He was still reeking of champagne and cigars, and his grip on her wrists was like a vice, no matter how hard she wrenched and fought against him. She could feel him lean into her, grinding against her rear, his breath hot and filthy at her neck. It was like Muir all over again— claiming her, roughing her up, treating her no better than a toy—and she felt as if she were going to be sick.

The hand trapping her hair pulled away, and panic sliced through her chest when she heard Lockerbie fumbling with the button of his trousers behind her. Esther had to think of some way to get away from him—to escape his grasp before he could take it any further—so she gasped the first words to come to mind.

"*Wait*. The couch, Cal. Take me on the couch."

His hand tightened on her wrist, hard enough to leave marks.

"I want you here," he growled. She could hear the urgency seeping into his voice. "Es, I want you right up against the damn door—"

"And I want you on top of me, not behind," Esther gritted out, forcing herself not to spew vomit as the lie came spilling from her lips. His fingers snaked down the waistband of her skirt, reaching between her thighs, penetrating her, and she panted, "I—want to see everything."

The sickening appeal to his narcissism seemed to have worked; Lockerbie released his strong grip on her wrists but moved one hand to her throat, fingers clenching tight. It was as if he were claiming her, letting her know she was *his* plaything, his little distraction to keep him from thinking of his fiancée running rampant with another man.

His lidded eyes leered at her, sweeping down the length of her body before lingering on her breasts, and Esther figured that perhaps he'd mistaken her frantic breathing for that of passion. She felt his hand clench her throat even tighter, and she feigned a moan of soft, needy pleasure, hoping it would be enough to let his guard down.

It *was*.

He leaned in once again to kiss her, this time biting hard at her bottom lip, and Esther felt the repulsion jolt through her like a shock of lightning.

But it didn't matter. He'd released her wrists. Her hands were free. That was enough. That was all she needed.

And in those few, crucial seconds that Lockerbie was distracted, Esther seized the gilded vase of lilies by the door and swung it ruthlessly across his head.

Lockerbie went toppling down to the carpet in an instant, bellowing out in pain and anger, calling her an assortment of curses ranging from bitch to *whore*. But Esther could scarcely hear him over the blood thundering in her ears. She was blinded by her own fury as she stood above him, chest heaving, green eyes wild.

And then she snapped.

She broke apart, temper all but exploding and mind splintering beneath a hail of icy rage.

"Shit-eating *bastard*!" Esther snarled.

She flung the vase aside and started kicking and punching him with every bit of strength she could muster, striking his limbs, his groin, his stomach—anything within reach. It was if she were beating Lockerbie as well as Muir, taking all the misery and torment that slept within her heart for so long and channeling it into each striking blow.

There was no mercy. No second thoughts or hesitations. She would fight for herself, for the lost, scared, eighteen-year-old Esther Bailey who had once taken her fiancé's abuse without question.

But now she was older. Stronger. Braver.

No one would put their hands on her like that again, least of all the sick bastard lying at her feet.

The hit from the vase must have dazed Lockerbie, because he was doing very little to fight back. At most, he was curled over on one side, shielding his face from harm while spitting angrily for his valet. Less than a second passed before Slate came sprinting from the private promenade, cigarette hanging from his mouth, and Lockerbie twisted toward him, still grappling with Esther on the floor.

"Don't simply stand there!" he bellowed, hair mussed and face redder than flame. "Get this whore off me!"

Slate did not need to be told twice. Calmly, deftly, he slid back his jacket and drew his sidearm from its holster.

Esther saw the cold glint of metal catch the light before he smashed the gun across her face, pistol-whipping her into a dazed, dizzying shock.

Blood blinded her, spurting from her nose and dripping into the carpet, and she fell away from Lockerbie in agony, clutching her battered face.

Though Esther was no stranger to pain, the jolt of metal against flesh and bone was all but excruciating. But she forced herself to ignore it, her breathing ragged as she crawled for the door, her tongue tasting blood as it spilled from her nose and dribbled into her white undershirt.

Lockerbie rounded on his manservant, his furious shout barely discernible over the ringing in her ears.

"I said get her off me, your moron, not bash her face in! What the hell is the matter with you?"

Esther clambered unsteadily to her feet, swiping her sleeve across her damp nose until the cuff was stained crimson. Lockerbie rushed forward, his hands reaching for her, his face pale and pebbled with her blood.

"Jesus *Christ*, Esther, I—"

Shock and remorse lay heavy in his eyes, but Esther refused to hear another word from his sickening mouth. She shoved past him, trying to ignore the sharp throbbing in her nose and across her cheek.

Lockerbie let her pass in silence, and before she knew it, she was stumbling down the gloss-white corridors of B Deck, leaving a trail of blood in her wake.

22:25

Quiet flooded the bridge as Murdoch reported for duty, fulfilling his place in the starboard bridge wing with his gaze fixed upon the pitch-black sea.

It was a quarter-past ten, and Bailey had yet to report for their watch. Murdoch kept snapping open his pocket watch to check the time, his eyes roving the bridge in hopes of some sight of her.

But she was nowhere to be seen.

The girl had been tardy before, of course. But in those instances, she'd been no more than five minutes late to the bridge—*not* twenty-five. It was unusual, and Murdoch wondered if her absence was because of their argument earlier that day.

He had never meant to hurt her when he'd put an end to their…affair, intimacy, spur of the moment lust—whatever it was. Murdoch had only wanted to protect her career as well as her own. To ensure they both wouldn't risk everything on the whim of some dalliance.

It was a heavy price to pay, and he knew it.

There was no woman quite like her. No woman who could counter his sarcasm and wit, let alone match his adoration for seafaring. She wasn't like Ada, or any of the other women Murdoch had once courted or taken to bed in the past. There was something *else* about her. She was rough around the edges, he had to admit. Reckless and short-tempered and stubborn more often than not. But she was also clever and caring in her own right, and Murdoch could not stop thinking about the lass.

He wished they could be together. Truly, he did. But life could never be that simple. Not when their ranks were a deep, perilous sea he dared not cross.

Subordinate and superior, he thought bitterly. That was all they were to each other. And that was how they would always be.

Murdoch sighed as he watched the bridge, his thoughts dark and miserable. His wrist still ached, but the aspirin he'd swallowed earlier made the soreness tolerable. He checked his watch again and again as the minutes slipped past, wondering if he ought to send someone to check on Bailey's cabin after all. But the sound of footsteps caught his ears, and he turned, hopeful—only to see a weary Boxhall returning from his rounds.

The fourth officer entered the wheelhouse and went straight for Lowe, who emerged from the officers' quarters with a chit in hand. Murdoch could see the pair of them talking through the glass windows, with Lowe looking disappointed for some reason. Curiosity got the better of him, so he strolled into the wheelhouse to have a listen.

"—was looking for you," Boxhall was saying. "She had some sort of emergency, I think. Told me to tell you she's sorry she missed dinner."

Lowe nodded glumly. "Least now I know where she ran off to," he sighed. "Thought she might a' stood me up or something."

Murdoch stepped forward, hands gripped behind his back, blue eyes glancing from one colleague to the other.

"What's all this, then?"

"We were discussing Miss Bailey," Lowe explained. "She was supposed to meet me for dinner this evening, but Mr. Boxhall here says she left to help with an emergency."

"Emergency?" Murdoch looked sharply to Boxhall. "Of what sort?"

The fourth officer shrugged. "Search me. She left the boat deck with some older chap, though. First-class, by the look of him. Ugly, too," he added as an afterthought, making Lowe chuckle.

Murdoch, however, didn't seem to acknowledge the slight. He was lost in thought, mind swirling with misgivings of his subordinate.

"Odd," he remarked with a frown. "It's no wonder she failed to report for duty, then. Though she might've telephoned the bridge, aye? Would've been nice to know she'd be late."

Boxhall stifled a yawn. "Perhaps she didn't know it'd take this long," he pointed out. "Whatever it is she's doing."

"Perhaps," Murdoch echoed distantly. With a cursory nod, he added, "You're free to retire for the evening, Joseph, thank you."

Once Boxhall had disappeared, Murdoch left the wheelhouse and made for the starboard bridge wing, motioning for Lowe to follow. The two officers stood side by side for a moment, with only the gliding rush of water filling the silence between them. Then Murdoch spoke.

"So, you were to dine with Miss Bailey this evening, then?" he asked coolly.

Lowe nodded, his eyes soft. "Yeah, I was. She was upset about something, so I'd wanted to buck her up." Murdoch felt his heart sink, but he said nothing as his colleague continued, "We were supposed to play a few rounds o' poker afterwards, and then I was going to—"

He broke off with a hard swallow, embarrassed. But Murdoch wasn't about to leave it alone. Something in Lowe's voice caught his attention, so he pried, "To what? Let's hear it, lad."

Lowe hesitated. Then the words came spilling out, sloppy and full of earnest. "I was going to tell her how I feel about her," he admitted, a flush coloring his sheepish face. "I know Mr. Lightoller said relationships between crew are forbidden, and I get it, but I can't rightly keep this bottled up any longer, sir. I just want her to know."

Murdoch heaved a long sigh. Surprisingly, he felt little jealousy as he weighed Lowe's confession. Only pity. Pity for Lowe or pity for himself—he wasn't entirely sure. But he clapped his good hand on his colleague's shoulder, his voice dropping to a soft, resigned undertone as he explained the honest truth.

"She's not meant for you, Mr. Lowe. There will be other lasses you can pine for. Others you can cherish."

"None like her, though."

No, Murdoch thought wearily. *None like her.*

There was more Murdoch wanted to say, but he and Lowe were on duty, after all. There was work to be done. Besides, Murdoch couldn't guarantee that he could control his emotions any longer. Already they threatened to crack right through his resolve like waves pummeling against breakwaters, wearing him down to the bone.

With professionalism cemented in his mind, Murdoch sent the fifth officer along to observe the compass while he shuffled back into the wheelhouse, trying not to think of Bailey as he went.

He was just reaching for the telephone to give the crow's nest a quick ring when he heard a door slam behind him.

Bemused, he glanced over one shoulder at Hichens, who merely shrugged. The noise had almost certainly come from the officers' quarters, and while Murdoch should have thought little of it, Bailey's unusual absence made him all the more inquisitive. He called out to a quick order to Pitman, commanding the third officer to man the bridge before hurrying down the corridor to investigate.

The hall was dead silent, save for his footsteps and the distant rumble of engines working far beneath him. Murdoch was hopeful he'd find Bailey in the corridor, thinking she might've returned from whatever issue she'd been sorting out. But when he knocked on her cabin door, he was met with empty silence.

Murdoch sighed, trying not to feel irritated with the girl. He knew she'd been called away to assist with some issue, but still. Why even lend a hand if she couldn't be responsible enough to inform the bridge where she was running off to? And why hadn't any other crew or officers been notified yet? It was all very odd, and Murdoch didn't like it one bit.

He turned, about to head back to the bridge when something caught his eye further down the hall. His brow tightened, and he squinted to see better in the low lamplight.

Dark liquid mottled the wooden floorboards, winding in a trail from the door of their promenade to the nearest lavatory. And it was only when Murdoch stepped closer that he realized what it was.

Blood.

Panic seized him, stinging in his chest like a knife wound and sending his pulse stuttering wild. But Murdoch fought against his emotions, resolving himself to keep a cool, level-head as he moved closer to the lavatory.

Blood was smeared across the brass handle, with crimson fingerprints dotting the white wood. He listened hard, noting the hiss of a faucet running beyond the door. It was clear whoever was in the lavatory was injured, and Murdoch, praying it wasn't Bailey, gave a sharp knock.

"Everything all right in there?"

There was no reply. Murdoch tried the doorknob, but it refused to yield to his hand. The gush of water grew louder, and he raised his voice.

"Miss Bailey, is that you?"

Still, he was met with silence.

Murdoch felt the panic return, ruthless and profound as it sunk deep within him, freezing his lungs and chilling his blood, his bones. His eyes lingered upon the pools of crimson splattered across the floor, the breath catching in his throat—and suddenly he was racing to the wheelhouse, his face a tight mask that could scarcely cloak his turmoil. He flung himself into the chart room, ignoring the startled looks from Hichens and Pitman. His hands rushed through the drawers of the nearest desk, yanking out papers and blueprints and spare gloves, frantically searching and *searching* until he found what he was looking for.

The master key to the officers' quarters.

Barreling through the wheelhouse and back down the corridor, Murdoch staggered to a halt before Lightoller's cabin. It took all his strength not to pound his fists upon the door, his desperate panic swelling like the tide. Relief coursed through him when his colleague appeared after a few brisk knocks, looking as if he were still undressing, suspenders draped from his trousers and tie hanging loose around his neck.

"Will?" he exclaimed in surprise. "What in the world are you—?"

But Murdoch was already speaking over him. "I need you to fill in as Officer of the Watch."

Lightoller raised his brows, looking utterly baffled. "I beg your pardon? I've only just finished my rounds, and you want me back on the bridge? You must be mad."

"Please, Lights," Murdoch begged, desperation turning his voice cracked and broken. "I can't perform my duties this evening. It seems there's been an accident, and I—" He fumbled for words as his nerves got the better of him, sparking through his mind like an electric shock. "I think Miss Bailey is in trouble. I must see to her immediately."

It was a measure of their trust and friendship that Lightoller said, "I see. Then don't you worry, Will. I shall fetch my coat and be out on the bridge at once."

There were no further questions or qualms on the matter; Lightoller simply grasped his colleague's arm tight before turning into his cabin to dress, and Murdoch breathed a sigh of immeasurable gratitude before hurrying down the corridor.

When he reached the lavatory, he did not hesitate to jam the brass key into its lock. There was a merciful *click*, and he yanked the door open, heart hammering, not entirely sure what he might find.

It was Bailey. Of course it was Bailey.

She stood hunched over the washbasin, blood dripping from her face, staining the marble to scarlet.

Murdoch felt the breath leave his lungs when he saw the deep purple bruise blooming across her cheek, as if she had been stricken by a heavy blow. She looked so horribly pale beneath all the blood, her eyes sightless and unseeing. Her hands were caked in crimson, shaking, gripping the rim of the sink as blistering water torrented from the faucet and wreathed her in steam.

Murdoch stood frozen in the doorway, staring at her in horror. But then he closed the door shut behind him—protocol be damned—and hurried to her side.

There were so many emotions whirling inside him that he almost couldn't think straight. Fear, panic, anguish, *anger*. It was clear this was no accident; someone hurt her, and Murdoch wanted nothing more than to find them and break their neck with his bare hands. But he pulled back his rage, saving it for another time.

For now, all that mattered was her.

He moved closer, keeping his steps slow and cautious on the blood-flecked tiles, not wanting to scare the poor girl. But she wasn't even looking at him. Her trembling fingers clutched a damp washcloth, which she used to wipe the blood from her freckled face.

Murdoch didn't know what to do or say. But he wanted to help, so he eased the cloth from her shaky hands.

"Let me," he said gently.

She was the nurse. She could probably do better. But he didn't care.

Murdoch took the washcloth, placed it beneath the glistening jet of hot water, and brought it to her battered face. Bailey winced a little at his gentle touch, yet she did nothing to keep him away. Quietly, tenderly, he swept away the blood staining her skin, rinsing the washcloth again and again until the water in the sink swirled red. She stood remarkably still, her eyes clouded, staring down at the floor.

With most of the blood cleared, Murdoch could see the severity of her bruise. It formed a ridge down the length of her freckled cheek, swollen and purple, the sight of it cracking his heart in two. Though she didn't show it, Murdoch knew she had to be hurting. Christ, with a bruise like that, how could she not be?

He had so many questions he wanted to ask her. So many misgivings that tore him to pieces. But Murdoch wasn't about to pry—not until she was fully rested and had her bearings once more. So he kept silent, wordlessly cleaning the blood from her hands before crossing the room to run a bath.

It wasn't until the tub filled with steamy water that he cranked off the faucet and finally turned to her.

"Go ahead and get yourself cleaned up, lass," he said quietly, struggling to keep his voice from breaking. "I'll fetch you some fresh clothes."

She was still staring at the floor, unwilling to look at him. Though most of her blood had been wiped away, it mottled the white of her collar and undershirt—a grim reminder of what she must have endured.

Murdoch stepped closer to her, longing for some sign of life. Longing to know she was okay. A sudden thought plummeted through his mind before he could stop it—a fear that she sustained wounds deeper than her busted nose and bruised face. That whoever did this had thought to put their hands on her in a different manner.

Christ, no, he thought desperately, his frantic eyes lingering on her wrinkled skirt and tangled hair. *Please, no.*

The panic within him reached a near boiling point, roaring over his head like a violent tide, but he fought to keep calm as he murmured softly, "Esther?"

Her bottom lip trembled when he spoke her name, and suddenly the tears she seemed to have been holding back broke loose from their confines entirely. They poured down her cheeks in floods and rivers, dripping into her bloodstained shirt.

Murdoch had never seen the girl cry. He'd seen her eyes turn watery on occasion—once, after that wretched first-class dinner, and again when he admonished her for her tardiness. But nothing could have prepared him for this—for seeing this confident, stubborn, spirited girl so broken and vulnerable, the tears raining down her face, the sobs tearing at her throat.

He moved toward her without a second thought, wrapping her in his arms and pulling her tight to his chest.

She didn't push him away. She merely buried her face into his greatcoat, shaking, sobbing her heart out against him.

Murdoch said nothing. He simply held her close, his hands firm but gentle, hoping to draw out every last drop of sorrow and pain. Her fists bunched up the fabric of his coat, clinging to him, and he gripped her even tighter.

Some small part of him knew he was crossing the line with this behavior. He knew the trouble they might find themselves in, should anyone stumble in the washroom and find them embracing.

But Murdoch did not care. He just wanted to be with her, to ache with her, to let her sink into him and cry against his chest. Her hurt was a wound of its own—a deep chasm laid cold and bare before him. He didn't know if he could make it right again. But he was certainly going to try.

He buried his face deep into her hair, holding her with all his might and fighting to keep back the emotions of his own. Seeing her dripping in blood had filled him with a ruthless terror unlike anything he'd never known. He was a seasoned sailor; he'd experienced his fair share of fears throughout his career. But those fears manifested themselves into the form of violent hurricanes and devastating shipwrecks, narrow collisions and near-disasters at sea. Those fears always yielded to his cool, quick-thinking professionalism.

They were *nothing* like this.

Nothing compared to finding Bailey bruised, bleeding and clearly hurt. Murdoch was bloody terrified. He needed to hold her just as much as she needed to hold him.

He wasn't sure how much time passed before her muffled sobs subsided, and they finally broke apart. Bailey stumbled away from him with a hiccup, cheeks tear-stained and eyes horribly bloodshot. But now that there was distance between them again, Murdoch couldn't help himself. He reached out unthinkingly, wiping away the tears beneath her eyes and cradling her chin in one heavy palm.

"Esther," he said again. Only this time, his voice was hoarse.

"You should go." She swallowed, reaching up to pull his hand away. Her eyes traveled to the closed door, and she added quietly, "Before anyone wonders where we are."

She was right, and Murdoch silently cursed himself for letting his barriers down once again. He cleared his throat, keeping a respectful distance from her with his hands gripped behind his back.

"I'll bring you a robe once you've finished bathing," he said, starting for the door. "Will you be needing anything else, love?" He froze for a moment, face beet-red, and corrected swiftly, "Lass?"

But she paid little mind to his mistake. "Aspirin, please. As much as you can carry."

He nodded. "Of course."

Silently she stepped toward the crystal-clear bathwater, not even acknowledging him as she kicked off her Oxfords and loosened her tie. Her trembling hands unbuttoned her greatcoat, letting it drop from her shoulders until it pooled to the floor at her feet.

Murdoch quickly glanced away, his breath short, his heart beating wild. Then he left the lavatory without a backward look, clenching his teeth to reel in his emotions as her sobs burned in his mind.

23:50

A right mess greeted Murdoch when he entered Bailey's quarters, crossing a cabin almost unrecognizable beneath heaps of clutter.

It was as if a whirlwind had swept up her room, ravaging her bed and wardrobe, scattering books and clothes and papers across the floor.

Murdoch, who knew all too well of her temper, tried not to think of her storming around the room in a fury, no doubt cursing him, hating him for what he had done. But the thought of her vicious anger was secondary to his overwhelming concern, and he hurried around the room even faster, stumbling over discarded tomes and strewn skivvies in his haste.

Eventually he found her dressing robe hanging haphazardly over the desk, sprawled over an assortment of framed photographs. He knew Bailey was still bathing, so he studied the pictures a moment longer, curious to see a small sliver of her life.

There was Booker, standing with a handsome, near-identical man who was almost certainly his twin. And there was also a beautiful woman who looked to be Bailey's mother, given her wild freckles and sleek, dark hair.

But as he bundled her robe in his hands with care, another photograph caught his eye.

This one was older, bent and wrinkled, as if a hand had once crumpled it up and thought better of it. Booker and his twin were at the forefront. But they stood with another gentleman in the picture, and it took Murdoch a moment to realize he was looking at a younger Callum Lockerbie.

Murdoch arched a brow. He kept forgetting that Bailey and Lockerbie were childhood friends. He had trouble imagining it. She was a bit of a handful, fiery but compassionate at heart...whereas Lockerbie was as about as far up on his high horse as one could get. Before this voyage, Murdoch had only heard of him through secondhand gossip and newspaper headlines. But his first impression of the oil heir aboard this ship had been less than memorable.

Even now, Lockerbie's sly taunts and lofty attitude at the first-class dinner irked him, filling him with a deep well of cool anger. But Murdoch knew they would never share in each other's company again, thank Christ, so he didn't trouble himself further with Lockerbie, and left the room.

While Bailey washed up, Murdoch spent a few moments cleaning her blood from the corridor, relieved none of his colleagues had stumbled upon it. Only after the last drop was wiped away did he knock on the door to check in on her.

"Lass?" he called quietly. "I've your robe, if you're finished."

"Thank you, sir."

The door cracked open; a slender, freckled arm appeared through the gap, and Murdoch passed the soft, silky fabric into her waiting hand. He could hear her fumbling behind the wood panel as she dressed herself, and he tried not to think of how desperately he wanted to sweep her back into his arms, longing to hold her close again.

She appeared moments later, smelling of soap and lavender, cradling her bloodied uniform, her damp hair framing her face. Despite her grisly bruise, Murdoch was pleased to see she was no longer the dazed, trembling woman he'd found in the lavatory. Her eyes were clear and bold, her strength sewing itself up again. Relief spread through him, as warm and rich as melted honey as he drew closer to her.

"How are you feeling?"

"Better," she admitted.

His eyes swept over her battered face. "Nothing broken, is there?"

She shook her head. "No, sir. But I—I won't lie. My nose hurts like a sonofabitch. Could use a little something for the pain." Her eyes lingered on the pockets of his greatcoat. "You wouldn't happen to have that aspirin, would you?"

Murdoch slid a hand through his hair, annoyed with himself that he'd forgotten. "I'll fetch it," he swore. "Go and rest, aye? I'll be back in a mo'."

Something peculiar flickered in her eyes at his words. Some lingering hesitancy that suggested she was reluctant to keep his company and wanted to be rid of him right then and there. But Murdoch pretended not to notice, waiting until she disappeared inside her cabin before crossing the hall to his own.

The aspirin was right where he'd left it, sitting on his washbasin to treat his sore wrist. He pocketed the bottle and made his way to the mess afterwards, where he nicked several chunks of ice, a tea towel, and a canteen filled with fresh drinking water.

As he made his way back to the officers' quarters, he found himself thinking of Bailey. How he was retracing her steps from last night. How she, too, rushed around the ship for ice and medicine to treat his sprained wrist. She had not hesitated to help him—not even after his foul attitude earlier that day. He was grateful for her compassion, and damn well determined to care for her just as she'd cared for him.

Murdoch knocked softly on her door once he was back in their quarters. Although her voice was faint, he heard her call, "Come in."

Murdoch hurried inside, moving quickly before anyone could spot him hovering before her cabin. He found her lying in her bunk, tucked away beneath the covers with her back propped up against a pillow. Her bruise was as heartbreaking as ever, marring the beautiful freckles he adored so much, and he couldn't bear to look at it as he passed her the aspirin bottle and canteen. He waited until she'd swallowed down the pills with a swig of water before walking to the door and closing it shut with a snap.

Her eyes widened with shock. "Sir?" she said looking distinctly uncomfortable. "We ought to leave it open, sir, so we don't—"

But Murdoch shook his head. "No. Not tonight. Not for this."

He settled on the edge of her bed, bundling the ice in the tea towel and holding it gingerly against her bruise. She sighed, her eyes fluttering shut, and the two officers were quiet until Murdoch broke the stillness with a single question.

"Who did this to you?"

Esther didn't answer him for a long moment. She opened her eyes, but they remained downcast, long lashes sweeping across her cheeks. "It doesn't matter, Mr. Murdoch—"

"It does matter, lass." Murdoch leaned closer to her, gentle as he held the wrapped ice against her cheek. "It matters very much. Whoever did this isn't going to get away with it. I can promise you that."

The blankets shifted as Bailey drew her knees up, hugging them tight to her chest. "That's the thing, sir. I'm afraid he will get away with it." Her breath hitched, and she buried her face from sight, dropping it against her kneecaps. "Because I was the one foolish enough to go to his suite. To trust him."

Murdoch felt something icy flood his chest, as if he'd swallowed down a freezing mouthful of Atlantic seawater. That fear he'd felt earlier—the one that made him question whether she'd been abused in a different manner—was overwhelming now, merciless, cold enough to hurt. His voice became low, teetering on the edge of calm as he asked, "Did you know this man?"

Bailey didn't lift her head. "Yes," she mumbled against her blanket, her voice soft and weary. "I did, sir. He and I were childhood friends. I always knew he was an arrogant bastard, but I never thought he would…" Her voice trailed away. But as Murdoch weighed her words, a sudden, horrid thought occurred to him. He thought of the photograph in her cabin—the one of Mr. Lockerbie with her twin brothers in particular— and recalled the smooth words the oil heir had spoken during dinner.

Miss Bailey and I have been family friends for a long while…used to talk about nothing but boats when we were young…

Murdoch did not remember shooting to his feet. But he found himself rising from her bed and pacing across the room, his collected composure broken, lying in shambles at his feet.

"It was Lockerbie." The words quavered in his anger. "Callum Lockerbie. I should've bloody *known*."

"It wasn't only him, sir. It was his valet as well." Her voice turned cold, her eyes dark and baleful as she growled the name through her teeth. "Gideon Slate."

"Then allow me to telephone the Master-at-Arms, lass, and we can have them arrested in their damn beds—"

"It won't make any difference," Bailey said flatly. "There were no other witnesses, and I entered his stateroom on my own accord." She shook her head. "It would be so easy for him and his manservant to twist the truth, sir. To say I attacked him, or seduced him, or that I've been his mistress this entire time. He's a good liar with a great deal of money. And that is a dangerous mix to go up against."

But Murdoch scarcely heard her, still roaming back and forth in the tiny space of her cabin, footfalls heavier than thunder.

"I don't care," he shot back. "That man *hurt* you. I have half a mind to throw him off this bleedin' ship, lass."

He was livid; the idea of someone putting their hands on her was almost too much to bear. Anger drenched him like a sheet of molten metal, lacing his mind with a fierce desire to protect the woman sitting before him. He settled back on her bed, keeping close to her as if his life depended on it, hands bracing the ice against her injured cheek. As the moments passed, Murdoch felt his anger cool. She calmed him, as if she was a fixed point in a stormy wrath of turbulent sea.

"How did all this come about?" he asked. "How did you even end up in his room in the first place?"

She looked away, shamefaced. "I was lied to, sir. Lockerbie sent his manservant to fetch me tonight. To tell me that he had taken ill. And I went off to help."

Murdoch was disgusted. "This was the emergency Boxhall was referring to, I take it?"

Bailey nodded. "Lockerbie tricked me into thinking he was sick, when it was all just a stupid ploy to bring me back to his suite." Her eyes grew clouded, staring into her own distant recollections. "It was harmless at first…he was lonely, I think. He wanted someone to talk to. But then he seemed to lose himself. He had had too much champagne, and then he…"

She was struggling for words again. It was as if she couldn't quite touch the truth of what happened, tiptoeing around it instead. Murdoch swallowed down the bile in his throat, clinging to every last scrap of sanity he had left as she finally spoke the words aloud.

"He tried to have his way with me, sir."

Murdoch slowly closed his eyes, pressing one hand against his temples to keep from thinking about it—from imagining all the wretched things Lockerbie might have done to her. He felt as if he were going to be sick. "And…and did he?"

"He didn't," Bailey said strongly, and this time, there was a bold note of pride in her voice, burning away her timidity like a moth to flame. Murdoch glanced up, stunned to see her grinning. "Because I beat the ever-living crap outta him. He ended up crying for his valet like a bitch, pardon my French, so Slate pulled out his gun and hit me in the face. That's how I got this, sir."

She pointed at the bruise, deep and purple against her golden skin.

"Stings something awful, but it was worth it."

Silence fell between them as Murdoch gaped at her, completely at a loss for words. But as his shock turned to profound relief, he suddenly found himself dissolving into a fit of deep, husky, uncontrollable laughter.

Bailey wasn't offended by his reaction; she was laughing along with him, too, that lively glint returning to her eyes. They laughed and laughed, sharing in the giddiness of the moment together, with Esther's hysterical snorts making them laugh even harder.

By the time the officers managed to compose themselves, Murdoch turned to her with a genuine smile. His eyes were warm as sunlit seas, glowing with all manner of emotions he didn't try to hide this time: mirth, pride, tenderness, delight.

"I'm so sorry, Esther," he breathed. "I know this is a right serious matter. But the thought of you kicking that man's arse to high heaven brings me more joy than you can possibly imagine."

Bailey wiped the tears of laughter from her eyes. "Bastard had it coming," she told him. "I've endured enough shit in my life, sir. I didn't need any more of it from him."

Murdoch was silent, his smile fading as he looked down at her scarred forearms, studying the markings rippling across her speckled skin. There were other bruises on her wrists, he noted, but these were recent—as if a strong grip had wrenched and yanked her around. The anger returned, nearly blinding him with a senseless desire to throttle, to maim—to put an end to the man responsible for tonight. Bailey must have seen the vindictive thirst darkening his eyes, because she spoke softly to him.

"Please don't speak a word of this, Mr. Murdoch. Not to the captain. Not to anyone."

He stared at her in disbelief. "Surely you don't intend to let this go?"

"I don't have much of a choice. Even if you back my word, Mr. Murdoch, you're forgetting I'm a woman." Her voice fell to a soft, resigned snarl. "Any repercussions—good or bad—would soil my reputation either way. Even if I'm not to blame, it's still a scandal. They would shun me from maritime work for it. You know they would."

"But *lass*—" he pleaded once again.

Her sharp green eyes bore into his. "Do I have your word, sir?"

Murdoch almost wanted to refuse. But he knew he had no choice but to respect her wishes—no matter how strongly he disagreed with them.

"Aye, lass," he promised. "You have my word. You always will."

He shifted the bundle of ice to his other hand, pressing it to her cheek, and she breathed a grateful sigh. His eyes lingered on her arms again, mapping her bruises and scars. "Everything that happened tonight…it reminded you of him, didn't it? Your fiancé."

She nodded. "Yes, sir. That's why I was so upset. It brought out everything I tried to run away from for so long. Bad thoughts, feelings, memories…they all came flooding back. It sort of…overwhelmed me. And I didn't know what else to do except cry, I suppose."

A pink blushed rushed into her cheeks, swirling a bit of color around the rough edges of her bruise, and she mumbled, "I didn't mean to lose my head like that in front of you, sir. I hope I didn't embarrass you."

But Murdoch's voice was firm. "Don't think for a moment that you did, lass. You have my permission to cry on me whenever and wherever you please." He laughed softly, the ghost of a teasing smirk on his lips as he added, "So long as you don't use my coat as a handkerchief, mind."

Bailey neither laughed nor smiled at his jest. She merely stared down at her hands, avoiding his gaze.

"That's mighty kind of you, sir. But if something like that happens again, I won't trouble you."

"Esther." Murdoch spoke her name quietly as he shifted closer to her on the bed, his hand falling upon her forearm, her scars and bruises. "I want you to trouble me."

And before he could stop himself, Murdoch reached out to smooth a stray strand of hair away from her face, tucking it behind the curve of her ear.

Wide, pale green eyes finally looked up at him, no longer reluctant to meet his gaze. His hand delicately skimmed the purple welt of her bruise before cupping her chin, one calloused thumb lingering on her bottom lip, tracing its soft outline.

Christ, he had to stop this. He had to stop touching her.

But it was damn near impossible, when all he wanted to do was hold her close—to let her know that no man would ever hurt her again. Including him.

He couldn't look away from her lips now. His hands moved to trace the curve of her jaw and the sweep of her freckles before slipping into her dark hair, cradling the nape of her neck. She smelled like lavender, like the sea. Like home.

Murdoch could hear her pulse thrumming in his ears, mingling with the nervous thud of his own. He shifted closer to her on the bed, his nose brushing hers, his other hand cradling her good cheek in his palm.

And then he did something so instinctive and yet so very foolish.

He leaned forward and pressed a heartbreakingly soft kiss against her forehead, savoring the warmth of her skin beneath his lips, and wishing he could explain with words how much *he* needed *her*—

"Please don't."

Her quiet plea had Murdoch wrenching away from her at once. Bailey was staring sadly at him, her fingers twisting together in her lap.

"I care about you, Mr. Murdoch," she admitted. "But I've thought long and hard about our conversation earlier, and I've come to agree with your decision. I let my feelings for you cloud my judgment, sir. I lost sight of myself and of how hard I've worked to get here."

Though her eyes were glazed with tears, her voice still came out level as she went on, "I'm fortunate enough to become one of the first female officers in maritime history, sir, and…it's just as you said. I—I shouldn't squander it. And I shouldn't try and jeopardize your position, either." She drew in a deep breath, her eyes straying to the door. "So that's why I think it would be best if you were to leave now. Before we end up doing something we shouldn't."

Murdoch tore his gaze from hers, swallowing against the lump in his throat. Though he was a grown man hardened by a great many years at sea, he had never felt so wretched in his life.

But he knew Bailey was right. She was the one being sensible now. Not him. He had no right to touch her and kiss her in such a familiar manner after rejecting the possibility of an intimate relationship. Murdoch had made his choice, so had she; he had to respect that. He had to own up to his decision like a man.

"I'm sorry," he apologized, the words rasping and remorseful against his dry lips. "You're absolutely right, Miss Bailey. I'll leave you be."

Murdoch rose to his feet and shuffled for the door, painfully aware of her eyes following him as he went. But then he stopped short, looking anywhere else but her as he added swiftly, "They'll ask about the bruise tomorrow. We can say you were attacked by some nameless passenger during rounds. Or struck during a brawl below decks, perhaps. I can vouch for you, and so can Mr. Lightoller."

"Thank you, sir. But that won't be necessary. I've something to cover the bruise so no one will know it's there."

"Very well, then."

Murdoch could think of nothing more to say, so he merely nodded in farewell before starting down the corridor in silence.

But it wasn't until he reached the darkness of his cabin that he sank onto his bed and buried his face in one hand, bowing to his emotions and wishing with all his might that things were different—that he was different—and that in some way, he and Bailey could be together.

EIGHTEEN

WARNING

April 14, 1912 | 02:00

AS HE STOOD in the deep, frozen shadows of the early morning, Lightoller found himself longing for a damn good cup of coffee. Although he had tossed down plenty of tea during the last few hours, Lightoller was now in need of something far stronger— something to keep him up and on his toes. Coffee seemed like it might do the trick, and so he'd sent Lowe off to brew a batch in the mess, hoping its rich, bitter taste might shock him back into wakefulness.

A quick glance at the wheelhouse informed him of the time.

Two o'clock, the tiny brass clock read.

One more hour until his watch would come to a close, and he could finally retire from this godforsaken cold. He'd kept his position on the bridge for hours now, blinking wearily into the starlit darkness and stifling a myriad of yawns. It had been ages since he had worked a double watch; even with years of seafaring experience under his belt, it was no simple task. Lightoller was tired, cold, running on scraps of energy—and the harrowing realization that he'd be reporting back on the bridge in another four hours certainly didn't help the situation any.

But he had no other choice. Murdoch had needed his help, and so Lightoller stepped in to assist—no questions asked.

In the late hours of last night, the crew had been stunned to see the second officer strolling onto the bridge in place of the first, tugging on his gloves and going about business as usual. But they'd been even more curious to know why Murdoch had come barreling out of the officers' quarters like a madman before disappearing from sight.

Lightoller had kept his explanation simple: a saltwater pipe burst in one of the boat deck lavatories, and Murdoch had hurried off to see it fixed. It had been a poor lie, but it had done its job, and the crew had returned to their duties with no further qualms or curiousness on the matter.

But as Lightoller stood vigil in the quiet solitude of the bridge wing, struggling to cast away the drowsy ache of fatigue, he kept recalling the sheer, senseless panic he'd seen in Murdoch's eyes.

It was clear something terrible happened to Bailey, and now Lightoller couldn't help but fret over the girl himself.

He studied the smooth precision of the bow before him, watching as *Titanic* drifted onward, hanging between stars and sea.

Although his watch had been an exhausting blur, with worried thoughts of Murdoch and Bailey meshed in between, Lightoller had attended to the bridge with as much decorum as ever. He'd kept his eyes trained upon the waves of glassy black, periodically scouring the horizon for signs of trouble. A single ice warning had reached him around eleven, this time from the SS *Rappahannock*, which had found herself crippled by ice not far from their course. Barely an hour had passed before Lightoller spotted the steamer abeam in the distance, stopped for the night and surrounded by glistening, blue-gray floes. It had merely flashed a brief acknowledgment as *Titanic* continued due west, maintaining a speed of twenty-one knots through a path unencumbered by ice.

Other than crossing paths with the *Rappahannock*, there had been little activity on the bridge since then. The men around him were weary, breathing into their hands and rubbing them together for warmth. Lightoller, too, was fading fast. But his thoughts were still fraught with worry for his colleagues, and he hoped Wilde would hurry along to relieve him. The sooner he could speak with Murdoch, the better.

Lightoller was just glancing around for his coffee when a deep, all-too-familiar voice struck the air.

"Well, this is a marvelous surprise."

Heavy footfalls echoed across the deck as Officer Wilde joined him on the bridge. But Lightoller didn't even look at him, keeping his eyes fixed upon the sea instead. It was easier to ignore the chief officer more often than not—to tune him out before those sly, underhanded comments could get underneath his skin. So he remained tight-lipped and silent, staring straight ahead until Wilde promptly cleared his throat.

"Aren't you going to greet your superior officer, Mr. Lightoller?"

Lightoller turned to him with a sigh. "Hello, Mr. Wilde."

"Hello, darling." Wilde studied him with interest. "My, I wasn't expecting to be graced by your charming blue eyes so early this morning. To what do I owe this pleasure?"

"Will asked me to cover his shift," Lightoller replied, biting the inside of his cheek to suppress his annoyance. "So here I am."

"Indeed? That jolly well doesn't sound like our first officer. I don't think he's ever skived off in his life."

"There's a first time for everything."

"Right enough." Wilde snorted. "Where'd he run off to, then?"

Lightoller hesitated. Although he was aware of Wilde and Murdoch's friendship, he wasn't sure how much the chief officer knew about Bailey. Perhaps he knew every last detail. Perhaps he knew nothing at all. But whatever the case, Lightoller wasn't willing to expose Murdoch's secret to the oaf before him. He remained guarded, fixing Wilde with a cool gaze and skittering around the truth instead.

"Can't say. Will came to my door last night. Said he had some kind of incident to attend to."

"Incident?" A flicker of concern crossed Wilde's face. "Is he well?"

"I believe so," Lightoller lied swiftly. "It sounded as if someone else was in trouble—a passenger, perhaps—so he went off to help. But that's all I know, I'm afraid."

Wilde, however, looked less than convinced. He frowned at Lightoller, gray eyes dark with suspicion. "Why do I get the feeling you know a lot more than you're letting on?"

Lightoller shot him a withering look. "I haven't the faintest clue, Mr. Wilde. But if you have any other questions or concerns, then perhaps you ought to take them up with Will once he's awake."

"Oh, undoubtedly," Wilde said in a smooth voice. "Since you seem to be quite...ah, *incapable* of telling me the full story, Mr. Lightoller."

"And you seem to be quite incapable of minding your own business, Mr. Wilde."

Wilde didn't seem bothered by the snarky retort; in fact, his eyes glittered with amusement as he appraised his colleague.

"Oh ho. High praise coming from a prissy old tosser. Sun hasn't even risen yet, and already you've got your knickers in a bunch."

"Comes with the territory of working a double watch, I'm afraid."

"Then perhaps you ought to see to your rounds, Mr. Lightoller. Don't want your foul attitude rubbing off on me anytime soon, thanks."

Lightoller scowled, biting back some of the choicest words he longed to snarl. His attention was diverted when Lowe came trotting across the deck with a coffee mug, and he almost breathed a sigh of relief as the hot drink was passed into his freezing hands.

"Excuse me?" Wilde demanded, indignant. "Where's mine?"

Lowe laughed as he started across the bridge, calling over his shoulder, "I'll fetch you a cup, too, sir, not to worry."

As the fifth officer disappeared into the wheelhouse, Lightoller blew steam from his coffee and downed a deep gulp, ignoring the way it scalded his mouth. He was aware that Wilde was studying him with a curious expression, and he regarded the chief officer warily as he paced closer, towering over Lightoller with his unmatched height.

"Before you go on your merry way, Mr. Lightoller, I've a question for you. Do you recall the other night, when that poor woman almost fell overboard, and we all had a chat in the chart room not long after?"

Wilde waited until Lightoller nodded before continuing on, "Well, I couldn't help but notice that Will was looking a bit...ruffled that evening. Which is saying something, considering our dear Scottish friend is never ruffled. The man's a blank slate, more often than not. But this..." He swept a sharp, scrutinizing gaze over Lightoller, no trace of warmth or humor in his eyes. "This was fairly unusual. Especially since the two of you snuck off to have a word in the navigating room afterwards, curiously enough."

His voice was casual, as if they were old mates chatting over tea, and yet it carried a note of steely authority that made Lightoller stiffen.

"If you can't tell me about his goings-on this evening," Wilde continued, "then perhaps you might be kind enough to tell me what the pair of you discussed that night. Because it's damn clear something did happen. And I'll be honest when I say neither of you looked too thrilled about it."

Sighing, Lightoller removed his cap and brushed a hand through his sandy brown hair. For the last two nights, the realization his close mate was dallying with a subordinate had been almost too much for him to bear. The second officer was torn between loyalty to his friend and loyalty to maritime law, and the moral consequences of choosing one over the other weighed like steel upon his shoulders.

But something else was needling Lightoller now. Something far worse than his own personal quandaries.

He couldn't stop thinking of Murdoch sprinting to his cabin, banging on his door and begging him to man the bridge. There had been fear buried in his eyes. Lightoller had never seen Murdoch bow to his emotions like that, in all the years they had come to know each other. The Scotsman was usually able to control that side of him, sealing his own feelings behind a mask of professionalism to fulfill his duties at sea. But something had changed in him last night. And now Lightoller was left wondering whether Bailey meant more to Murdoch than he initially thought.

Lightoller finally met his colleague's unwavering gaze. But this time, he didn't hold back as he explained, "We had a bit of a row that night, Mr. Wilde. Will..." He swallowed, choosing his next words carefully, not wishing to give his friend away. "Will has been involved in something I don't necessarily agree with, and I'd no choice but to try and reason with him. But looking back now, I worry the things I said to him may have been...misguided."

Wilde was silent for short moment, frowning out at the void of the dark sea. And when he finally spoke, his voice was cautious. "This...wouldn't have to do with a lady, now, would it?"

Lightoller froze as the breath whisked from his lungs. But he gave nothing away as he faced his superior, composing himself with a quick-tongued lie. "Indeed it does," he said. "With a...passenger, in fact."

"A passenger?" Wilde was boggling at him now. "But I thought he fancied Miss—?"

"Who?" Lightoller demanded sharply. "Fancied who?"

Wilde shrugged, standing even taller with his hands folded behind his back. "Nothing," he grunted. "Nobody. Ignore me."

But Lightoller wasn't about to quit. Not when his colleague was so obviously informed of the affair between Murdoch and Bailey. He needed to raise his concerns with someone, damn it—especially after everything that had happened tonight, and he hissed, "Spit it out, Mr. Wilde!"

The two senior officers went on staring at each other in silence, gauging what the other knew. But Wilde was the one to finally give in, leaning close to Lightoller's ear.

"Miss Bailey, all right?" he muttered. "I'm talking about Miss Bailey." His wary eyes swept his colleague up and down, and he added, "Though something tells me you already knew that."

Lightoller almost breathed a sigh of relief. Finally, another person he could confide in—albeit a complete oaf.

"Unfortunately so, Mr. Wilde."

"I gather she was the nature of your row, then?" Wilde snorted. "Rather unnecessary, don't you think? It's only a harmless little infatuation. Surely you wouldn't be so cruel as to deny William that."

"Harmless?" Lightoller echoed. He stalked forward, keeping his voice low as he explained, "Henry, you've no idea. We weren't quarreling that night because of his keenness for her. We were quarreling because I walked into his cabin and found the two of them all over each other."

His words didn't have the desired effect he'd wanted. Rather than stare in shock or outrage, Wilde broke into a white-toothed grin.

"Really, now? You don't say?"

"It's true. They were kissing, groping—the whole damn lot of it. I'm fairly certain they would've been shagging in another second or two, had I not stumbled upon them."

"Well, well." Wilde looked amused. "I didn't think our dear William had it in him. I must say, I'm impressed."

Lightoller scowled. "You're taking this surprisingly well, Henry."

"Why yes, Charles, I am. Because I see the way he looks at that girl, and the way she looks at him. And while it's true they're in a bit of a tricky situation that could cost them their jobs, I reckon Will wouldn't risk it all on some shortsighted lust. She clearly means more to him than we know. More than his position, even."

"Well," Lightoller muttered, "that's what I've been wondering myself as of late. See, it was Miss Bailey he ran off to help this evening, and—"

The words caught in his throat as Wilde pounded a triumphant fist into his shoulder, the blow like a wrecking ball to his bones.

"I bloody well knew it," the chief officer said smugly, a smirk crooking up one corner of his mouth. He chuckled at the disgruntled look on Lightoller's face, waving an idle hand. "Carry on, Charles, carry on."

"As I was saying," Lightoller continued irritably, brushing off his coat and rolling his sore shoulder, "Will went to assist Miss Bailey tonight. Something awful must have happened, because I've never seen him so panicked. Scared, even. I truly think he cares for her, Henry, and I've been thinking that perhaps...well..."

"We should let them carry on." Wilde nodded. "I told Will from the beginning that I'd look the other way, and I damn well meant it. If we took precautions when they were together, Mr. Lightoller...covered for him from time to time...made some scheduling adjustments on occasion, just to make sure they have some time to themselves...it could work. He'd have the pair of us on his side, in any case. Two senior officers who could vouch for him and for her, should anything happen."

"And if something does happen? If someone else finds out?"

"He's not stupid," Wilde reasoned. "He knows the consequences. But it's obviously a risk he's willing to take."

His gaze softened as he stared up at the stars and swirling constellations high above, and the quiet, thoughtful sadness of his voice caught Lightoller by surprise.

"I lost my wife and my twin boys well before their time, you know. Nothing I could do once their scarlet fever turned worse."

Wilde studied his thick hands and weather-beaten knuckles for a moment, and Lightoller kept silent, waiting for him to continue.

"They say the grief gets better in time. But that's a load of bollocks. It never really does. Not for me, at least." He smiled sadly, his eyes wandering the stars, trailing those distant giants in their oceans of glittering nebulas and deep darkness. "My wife, my sons...I can't go a day without thinking of them. Without cherishing what little moments I was able to spend with them. We're not bleedin' gods, mate. We only have so much time to love and laugh and shag and cry and grow old together as that ruddy clock keeps ticking away. So I won't deny Will a bit of happiness if I can help it. Not now. Not in this life, I'm afraid."

Lightoller didn't know what to say. He was stunned and admittedly touched that his superior officer—whom he'd once loathed more than anyone aboard this ship—trusted Lightoller enough to spill out his deepest wounds, his darkest emotions. He dropped a hand on Wilde's hard shoulder, all animosity forgotten, and gripped it tight.

"Listen, let me talk to Will," he insisted. "Find out what happened with Miss Bailey. Tell him we're on his side. And who knows? Perhaps it'll be enough to make things right again."

When Wilde nodded his approval, Lightoller downed the last of his coffee and turned to leave. But something stopped him in his tracks, and he eyed his colleague with a curious stare.

"And thank you, Mr. Wilde."

The chief officer raised his brows. "Whatever for?"

"For lending me your ear." Lightoller suddenly felt hot underneath his greatcoat, almost wishing he'd never spoken in the first place. "And for not being too much of a prat about it," he added.

Wilde smirked. "Why, you're very welcome. Now get off my bridge, you old codger. You were off duty ten minutes ago."

Lightoller couldn't fight back a grudging smile. "Right you are, sir."

He was quiet as he slipped into the wheelhouse, nodding at Quartermaster Rowe as he passed. The corridor to the officers' quarters was empty, silent. When he reached Murdoch's cabin, he brushed his knuckles softly against the door.

"Will?" he called into the quiet. "Are you awake?"

Lightoller expected to knock again, thinking perhaps Murdoch was fast asleep. But he'd barely lifted his hand when the door cracked open, and the first officer appeared.

He was donned in a blue dressing robe, his eyes weighing heavy with exhaustion. "Yes, Lights?"

"I was wondering if I might have a quick word. May I come in?"

Murdoch nodded wordlessly, stepping back to admit his colleague inside. Lightoller waited until the first officer closed the door before settling on the bed, crossing one leg over the other.

"Well? What on earth happened last night? Is Miss Bailey all right?"

Murdoch did not answer right away. His hands fiddled with the sash of his dressing robe before he quietly explained, "She was attacked by Callum Lockerbie, Lights."

Lightoller sucked in a sharp breath, his wide eyes scouring Murdoch's face as the first officer continued, "He lured her into his stateroom. Forced himself on her. She fought back, until Lockerbie's valet struck her with his pistol." His voice was level, but Lightoller could still hear the barely-controlled fury lingering in every word. "I found her bleeding in the lavatory and had no choice but to help."

Lightoller was shocked. He swallowed, utterly at a loss for words, lacing his fingers together until his knuckles were white. A sudden, unbridled concern for Bailey overwhelmed him, and he asked softly, "How is she? Will she be all right?"

"She will." Murdoch's voice was firm. "She's strong, Lights. Nothing broken, either, thank God. Just a good amount of pain and a right awful bruise to show for it."

"And Lockerbie?" Lightoller asked, disgusted. "I hope you raised the alarm on the bastard."

Murdoch clenched his jaw. "No. Miss Bailey refused to consider it."

"*What?*" Lightoller nearly catapulted himself to his feet. He gaped at his colleague, stunned and angry and grasping for reason. "Why ever not? We can't have a fiend of that sort walking freely aboard this damn ship!"

"Aye, and I agree with you, Lights. I'm only respecting her wish to keep it quiet. She wants to avoid a scandal. Seems to think Lockerbie would use his money to weasel his way out of it, or else invent some vile lie to stain her reputation entirely." Acid seeped into Murdoch's voice, brutal enough to melt steel. "Trust me, Lights. I'd go to the Master-at-Arms in a heartbeat if I could. Christ above, I'd snap his bleedin' neck in two if I thought I might get away with it."

"As would I, to be honest." Lightoller heaved a sigh. "We'll find some way to get this sorted."

Though Murdoch nodded, his blue eyes were deep and dark with rage. "Boxhall might be a witness," he explained quietly. "He was on the boat deck when that wank of a manservant led her away." He brought a hand to his temples, the cold anger in his voice easing as he added, "If anything, at least she managed to kick his arse good and proper. I'm proud of her for that."

They were quiet for a moment, the distant hiss of ocean water and hum of engines filling the silence between them. Then Lightoller sighed, gathered up his wits, and finally spoke.

"I've been meaning to talk to you about her, Will. I was speaking with

Mr. Wilde a few moments ago, you see, and I've come to reconsider what I said before. About your involvement with Miss Bailey."

Murdoch glanced up at him, but his face was carefully impassive as Lightoller continued, "I must be daft, but I think you should continue to see the girl. It's clear she means a great deal to you, so Mr. Wilde and I will do everything in our power to ensure your relationship remains secret. You need only be discreet and take proper measures, of course—such as closing and locking your damn door, for example," he added sourly.

Murdoch cracked a small smile. But it was momentary, disappearing beneath a defeated grimace. "It's too late for that now," he sighed. "She won't have anything to do with me. Not after what I said. Not after she realized what this job means to her."

"Talk to her," Lightoller encouraged. "Explain things have changed. Tell her what she means to you. Show her, if you must."

"It won't help." Murdoch was shaking his head. "None of it'll help. She's already made up her mind, Lights. And besides," he added wearily, "I can't possibly subject her to such a risk, now, can I? Let alone watch her throw her career down the gutter for the likes of me."

Lightoller rose to his feet, dropping a firm hand on his friend's shoulder and clutching it tight.

"Give it some thought, Will. And just know that I'll always be here for you. Same as Henry, of course."

He crossed the room in silence, stealing one last, lingering glance at the first officer and willing everything to be right again.

07:30

Daylight crept through the cabin window, washing his room in soft, gleaming white as Murdoch readied himself for the morning.

He was mechanical as he shaved, exhausted from what little sleep he'd gotten, and dreading the long day ahead of him.

While his ten o'clock watch wouldn't be much of an issue, it was the church service in the dining saloon he kept grimacing about. Murdoch had nearly forgotten the damn thing until he'd spared a glance at the calendar and remembered today was, in fact, Sunday—and like Smith and Wilde, he would be expected to attend.

Bailey would join them at the sermon as well, and Murdoch tried not to think of her as he drew the straight-razor across the stubble of his jaw.

But it was useless; the girl was everywhere, flooding his thoughts, his head, his heart. She was an ocean, and he was just a sinking man lost in her waves.

He couldn't stop thinking of last night. How she had stood hunched over the washbasin, blood dripping from her nose. The way he'd let her cry in his arms, cradling her, clinging to her like a drowning man thrown a rope after being pitched out to sea. And the soft sadness in her eyes after he'd braved a kiss against her forehead and she'd told him to stop.

Even now, his stomach rolled when he imagined the poor lass readying herself in her own cabin, dabbing some kind of cosmetic over the bruise. She was willing to keep her abuse a secret.

But Murdoch wasn't.

He was only keeping quiet for her sake. But still, he knew the truth of what happened. He knew who was responsible. And he could not stop dwelling on it.

He didn't see Bailey as he crossed the hall, though his eyes lingered on her cabin door as he passed. A chilly wind brushed his skin when he emerged from the wheelhouse, and he paused for a moment, breathing deeply, feeling soothed by the saltwater air and glistening sea. As he gazed out across the calm expanse of water, a voice spoke behind him.

"Ah, Mr. Murdoch. Just the man I was hoping to see."

Murdoch turned to see Smith striding toward him. The captain's eyes were clear in the early morn, and his frost-white beard was neatly trimmed as usual. His medals glistened from the pocket of his jacket—the first awarded for fifteen years in the Royal Naval Service, the second marking his efforts during the Boer War.

Squaring his shoulders, Murdoch swept his hand to his temple in a prompt salute.

"Sir," he greeted.

Smith tipped his cap in return. "At ease, Mr. Murdoch," he said calmly. "I was wondering if perhaps you might join me in the chart room? I'd like to have a quick word before the sermon."

"Certainly, sir."

Smith led him away from the briny cold of the bridge and inside the cozy warmth of the wheelhouse, nodding at Quartermaster Hichens as he passed. Once inside the chart room, he settled at the mahogany desk while Murdoch remained standing, hands behind his back, waiting patiently for his captain to speak.

"I have splendid news to share with you today, Mr. Murdoch," Smith said with a smile. "As you know, I was not entirely pleased with having to reshuffle ranks for the extent of the crossing. Given your extensive maritime history and dedication for seamanship, there was no doubt in my mind that you were well-suited for the role of chief officer, and I sorely regretted having to bump you to first. That being said, I received a wire from White Star Line earlier this morning an am pleased to announce that they would like to offer you the position of chief officer aboard *Olympic*. Should you choose to accept, you will remain at Chelsea Piers when we make berth in New York and await *Olympic*'s arrival on the twenty-fourth."

A stunned silence followed as Murdoch struggled to wrap his head around the news.

"Chief officer?" he echoed. Where he once might have been elated, now there was something holding him back, dousing his excitement as if he'd been drenched in cold seawater.

"Who would take my place as first officer, sir?" Murdoch asked numbly. "Mr. Lightoller?"

Smith gave a stout nod. "Correct, Mr. Lightoller would become first officer. It's a messy business, you understand, but White Star Line thinks it's for the best. And they would quite like to reward your impeccable skill and maritime prowess by offering you this promotion, Mr. Murdoch."

Murdoch could think of nothing to say. Any words that came to his tongue felt thick and useless, as if he'd swallowed a mouthful of mud. But the captain was watching him, so he forced himself to speak.

"May I have some time to think it over, sir?"

"Of course, Mr. Murdoch. And remember: you do not have to accept. You are more than welcome to remain *Titanic*'s first officer. Though the increase in pay aboard *Olympic* is a hard thing to pass up, I imagine. I will be sorry to see you go, but it's ultimately your decision, as it were."

"And what will happen to Miss Bailey, sir?"

Smith seemed mildly surprised by the question.

"Well, Miss Bailey is the responsibility of the first officer until she's properly trained," he said. "So she'll become Mr. Lightoller's charge if you choose to depart." A thoughtful look crossed his face as he added, "I've been meaning to ask about her, as Mr. Bailey would like some idea of his niece's performance thus far. Has she been up to the mark since we set sail, Mr. Murdoch?"

Murdoch was quiet as recollections from the past week rushed across his mind, quick and constant as waves spreading themselves along the shore: the giddy excitement in his subordinate's eyes the day he'd introduced her to the bridge, and how she'd dismissed his patronizing remarks by listing off every piece of equipment in sight. The peaceful moment they shared at the stern on sailing day, when the wind swept her hair around, and she'd told him it was the happiest moment of her life. Those long, late watches she endured without complaint at his side. The quiet intensity in which she fulfilled her daily tasks, whether that be assisting with lifeboat lines or running an errand to the wireless room. And the compassion in her eyes when she'd knelt before him in his cabin, tending carefully to his injured wrist.

A soft, proud glow came to his eyes, and he had to fight back a smile as he admitted strongly, "She has, sir. I had my misgivings at first. But she has proven herself to be an exemplary officer."

Smith nodded, though his eyes were curious as they appraised his first officer. "Very good, Mr. Murdoch. I suppose having her here wasn't such a complication after all." He stole a quick glance at the brass clock before rising to his feet. "I daresay we'd best be getting on. There's no need to rush your answer, Mr. Murdoch. Take all the time you need to decide, though preferably before we make berth in New York."

"Of course, sir."

They fell into step together, chatting amiably about the voyage and the clear weather until they reached the Dining Saloon. The entire room had been transformed into a place of worship, the tables all drawn away and the chairs set in rows before a makeshift altar. First-class patrons were milling about, exchanging pleasantries in their posh clothes and jewels. But Murdoch paid no notice to any of them. He was bewildered, lost in his delirious thoughts as Smith's offer continued to swirl and eddy through his mind.

Chief officer?

Murdoch couldn't shake the words from his head as he stepped up on the altar, paying little heed to the proceedings around him. Wilde was already present for the sermon, and judging by his brooding scowl, he looked none too happy it. Bailey was still missing, while the remaining officers were unable to attend due to their conflicting watches. Murdoch damn near envied them. He sighed as he glanced around the room for Bailey, wondering if she would even attend the morning sermon at all.

And then he saw them.

Callum Lockerbie and his entourage had entered the dining saloon, donned in their finery of cashmere and silks, with Callum flashing smiles and handshakes and lofty how-do-you-dos to the nearby patrons.

His pretty fiancé clung to his arm, wearing a bored expression and ignoring her sister twittering at her side. And trailing after them all was their filthy valet—the one with the pointed nose and sallow skin. The one who had dared to harm Bailey last night.

An ocean of dark, unrestrained rage cut through Murdoch as he swept his cold gaze over them—a rage so terribly profound that it nearly blinded him, rendering all rational thought useless.

His blood was boiling, his hands clenching into shaking fists, and it took every last bit of self-control he had to reign himself in, to shift away from his vindictive anger and trade it for calmness instead. He spared a glance at Wilde, who was glaring daggers at Miss Florence at his side; clearly, the chief officer had not yet forgotten her heartless ridicule of Bailey. Murdoch certainly hadn't, either. But his loathing for that twisted wench was insignificant compared to the deep-rooted hatred he felt for Lockerbie and his manservant. It was a raw, ruthless, unstable sort of hate, harsh enough to make him see red. He almost couldn't stand it.

"Will?"

He turned to see Wilde staring at him. "Blimey," the chief officer murmured. "And I thought I was out of sorts this morning. You all right there, mate?"

"Pure dead brilliant, Henry," Murdoch gritted through clenched teeth. "Never better. But if I wind up subject to court martial for involuntary manslaughter by the end of the day, don't be rightly surprised."

Wilde shot him a questioning look, his needle-sharp gaze sensing something darker beneath Murdoch's sardonic tone. But he didn't dare pry in front of the captain, and the two officers lapsed into silence.

Cream-colored hymnals were passed around, and as Murdoch had one of the songbooks shoved into his hand, he glanced up to see Bailey and her brother entering the dining saloon. The first officer found himself staring at her for longer than appropriate, shocked by the sight before him.

Her bruise was nearly *gone*.

Or rather, it was expertly hidden behind cosmetics, her cheek smooth and flawless as if she'd never been struck in the first place. A few freckles were lost beneath whatever cream she applied, and there was still some light swelling, but it wouldn't raise any eyebrows.

For a brief moment, Murdoch couldn't help but admire her handiwork. But that admiration snapped to pieces as he watched her pass her abusers and make for the altar. Her chin was raised, her eyes glittering with cold defiance. She assumed her place beside Wilde without so much as a glance at Murdoch, while her brother assumed a seat next to Lockerbie, of all people.

Murdoch was almost beside himself with frustration. *Hasn't she told him yet?* he thought.

Surely she wouldn't keep something like this from her own brother?

The first officer could scarcely focus on the sermon once it began, blotting out the choral voices and piano song that grated on his nerves. His mind was elsewhere, the flood of his thoughts fixed upon Bailey and only Bailey, as she sang quietly from the hymnal in her hand:

> *Eternal Father, strong to save*
> *Whose arm hath bound the restless wave.*

She hadn't even looked at Murdoch since entering the room; perhaps she was still upset with him.

> *O Christ, whose voice the waters heard*
> *And hushed their raging at Thy word.*

But Murdoch knew she had every right to be upset. Especially after the way he'd behaved last night. The kiss he'd placed on her forehead had been so careless. So bloody inappropriate. But he'd been so worried about her—and so grateful she hadn't been seriously hurt—that his emotions had gotten the better of him.

From rock and tempest, fire and foe
Protect them wheresoe'er they go.

Nevertheless, the damage was done. And now Murdoch could only hope his rash mistake hadn't ruined whatever amiability remained between them—if there was any left at all.

O hear us when we cry to Thee
For those in peril on the sea...

When the service was finally called to a close, Murdoch wasn't sure who looked most relieved—Wilde, Bailey or himself. The officers weren't expected to mingle afterwards, thank Christ, so they made their way topside for breakfast, with Wilde charging out of the saloon as fast as his long legs could carry him.

They joined Lowe and Pitman in the mess hall, piling their plates with an assortment of bacon, eggs, kippers, toast, and scones. Bailey wasn't eating much, Murdoch noticed. She merely picked at a sultana scone in between sips of coffee, her distracted eyes fixed upon the book she'd brought along with her. It was a heavy leather tome thicker than Murdoch's arm, and when he tilted his head to one side, he could read the title in silver lettering: *The Atlantic Ocean and Northernmost Seas: A Maritime History.*

Lowe kept glancing at Bailey throughout breakfast, his brown eyes soft in a way that made Murdoch irritable, until eventually the fifth officer asked, "Did you get that issue sorted last night, miss?"

She looked up from her book with a pearly smile. "I did, Harry. And I'm terribly sorry I was unable to make it to dinner."

"Perhaps you'd like to make it up to me this evening, then?" Lowe grinned at her. "We've a few rounds of poker planned in the smoking room tonight. Even Wilde is joining in, and he's a ruthless player if I've ever seen one. Be real entertaining to watch him humiliate Bert and Jim, it will."

Pitman scowled at him from across the table, and Lowe smirked, adding blithely, "No *offense*, sir."

Bailey hesitated, biting her lower lip. "I'll see how I'm feeling," she told him. "But I've been neglecting my brother lately, and...well, I figure I ought to spend some time with him this evening."

She quietly returned to her book then. Murdoch found himself staring at her cheek, thinking only of the purple bruising hidden beneath God knows how many layers of cosmetic cream. Some part of him wondered if she'd become an expert at disguising these marks after enduring so much abuse from her fiancé. It was a sick thought, sick enough to make his chest ache, and Murdoch shoved away his plate, appetite lost entirely.

While the rest of the officers laughed and chatted over their breakfast, Murdoch remained silent, his hands absentmindedly toying with the compass and silver whistle buried in his pocket. His eyes lingered on Bailey's bruise again, and he thought of Lightoller's words, spoken in the darkness of his cabin last night.

Tell her what she means to you. Show her, if you must.

But how? he wondered, over and over again.

How on earth could he show Bailey how much she truly meant to him?

Murdoch didn't realize how long he'd been staring at her until she suddenly looked up from her book, sensing his gaze.

Green eyes fell upon deep blue, and for one brief, heart-wrenching moment, Murdoch felt as if they were the only ones in the room—the only two people on this damn ship, even—

"Sir?"

A voice dragged his attention away from Bailey, and he turned to see Lowe looking expectantly at him. "Sorry?"

Lowe chuckled. "Honestly! I was asking if you're gonna take the job!"

"What job?" Pitman asked curiously.

"He's been offered the position of chief officer aboard the *Olympic*," Lowe explained. "Mr. Wilde's former ship. Jim told me this morning."

Bailey went very still, her blank eyes studying the coffee mug nestled between her hands. Wilde was watching her closely as he puffed on his cigarette. But before Murdoch could speak another word, he found himself besieged by compliments and congratulatory words from the rest of the table.

Pitman gave him a cheerful pat on the back, exclaiming, "Congrats, Will!" Turning back to Lowe, the third officer added, "You off your rocker, son? 'Course he's gonna take it! He's no reason not to. And besides, it's one step closer to becoming captain, eh?"

Murdoch quietly shifted his fork around his plate, avoiding the eyes of everyone at the table. "Aye. That's true."

But he said nothing more on the matter, and he was glad when no one else pried.

At length, Wilde slunk away to his quarters to have a kip, while the rest of the officers headed to the bridge to report for duty. Murdoch wanted to talk with Bailey, but Lowe held her attention with all his jokes and charming banter, so he fell into conversation with Pitman instead, trying to ignore the bitter knot of jealousy in his stomach.

By the time they reached the bridge, Murdoch was once again made calm by the ocean of endless blue, the brine of saltwater, the rumble of wind and waves. Lightoller was waiting for him in the port bridge wing, looking downright haggard after working his own shift and Murdoch's in the span of twenty-four hours. His eyes were red-rimmed, heavy with exhaustion, and Murdoch felt a stab of guilt mixed with gratitude as he leaned close to murmur, "Thank you, old friend."

Lightoller nodded, offering a tired smile, and Murdoch relieved him from duty before assuming his place on the bridge.

The watch ran smoothly, as per usual. Clear skies, calm seas, and a bracing wind that grew surprisingly tame by mid-morning. Murdoch was attentive to Bailey rather than ignoring her this time, making every effort to assign the proper tasks and duties allowed to her. But a distance still lingered between them, made all the more apparent by the way she avoided his eyes and kept her responses curt. It was as if a gulf had appeared between the two officers, and Murdoch was fretful by the cool distance separating them, keeping them poles apart. But he tried to push her from his mind, toying with the compass in his pocket from time to time and letting work and routine distract him.

Around noon, he was met with a rather unfortunate surprise. Thomas Andrews and Booker Bailey were giving first-class passengers a tour of the boat deck, and Murdoch was disgusted to see Callum Lockerbie among them. They were exploring the bridge, with Andrews gesturing proudly at the equipment, pointing out this and that. Murdoch glanced at Bailey, who stood before the logbook in the wheelhouse, watching Lockerbie with a narrowed gaze. Their eyes met for a half second before the oil heir stalked off to join Booker, and Murdoch caught the gist of their conversation as he strolled past.

"I daresay your sister fits the sailor role rather well," Lockerbie drawled. "Perhaps she'll even grow a beard by the end of it."

But Booker didn't seem to hear him. He was distracted, studying his sister through the wheelhouse windows. "You wouldn't happen to know what's the matter with her, would you? She won't talk to me. Hasn't said a word all morning. I can't imagine why, though."

Lockerbie shrugged, looking indifferent. "Haven't a clue, I'm afraid…"

Murdoch was done. He had to purposefully remove himself from the bridge before his fist could connect with Lockerbie's mouth.

Years of discipline were his only saving grace; for the sake of his job and for the sake of keeping his word to Bailey, he had no choice but to keep his anger at bay, no matter how hotly it burned him to the core.

He went to Bailey at once, crossing through the wheelhouse with a nod at Quartermaster Hichens before leaning close to her ear.

"You don't have to stay here," he said quietly. "I can send you off on an errand, if you'd prefer to be away from him."

"No, sir." Her voice was firm. "I'm fine right where I am."

"Lass—" Murdoch tried to protest.

But he suddenly found himself flabbergasted as she rounded on him, her eyes like fire, blazing something fierce.

"I said I'm fine, thanks," she snapped.

Murdoch couldn't help but bristle. "Perhaps you haven't noticed, Miss Bailey, but I'm only trying to help."

"You could help by leaving it alone, Mr. Murdoch," she retorted. "It's none of your concern, anyhow."

Stealing a wary glance around the wheelhouse, Murdoch made sure their crewmates were otherwise occupied before quietly reminding her, "Well, I hate to be the bearer of bad news, but it most certainly is my concern. So long as you're in my charge, you're my responsibility."

"Oh, *goody*. Just my luck." Her voice was dull, carrying the bite of sarcasm. "You know, I liked you better when you were ignoring me, Mr. Murdoch."

"So did I," he shot back, before he could stop himself.

"Yeah?" He could see the heat rising in her cheeks now. "Then maybe you ought to make a habit of it, *sir*. Starting now."

"Not a bad idea, *lass*. Less time spent listening to you mouth off, that's for damn sure."

And with that, Murdoch stalked away before he could say anything else he'd end up regretting later. He didn't want to fight; fat lot of good that would do, anyhow, besides deepen the rift between them. So he stepped out onto the bridge with a brooding look, arriving to catch the end of Miss Florence's question.

"And why the need for two steering wheels, Mr. Andrews?"

The shipwright gestured toward the bridge helm with a smile. "Well, we only use this wheel near the shore—"

Quiet footfalls echoed across the bridge, and everyone turned to see Bride emerging from the wheelhouse. The young wireless operator was smartly dressed as usual, his reefer jacket ironed straight and sleek hair combed to one side. Murdoch couldn't help but notice the familiar way his eyes lingered on Fay Harlow, who was clearly trying to hide her smile.

"Excuse me, sir," Bride said, finally wrenching his gaze away from Miss Fay and holding a marconigram out to the captain. "We've another ice warning. This one's from the *Noordam*."

With a mild gaze, Smith gave the marconigram a once-over. "Thank you, Bride," he said, and Bride inclined his head before smiling at Miss Fay and taking his leave.

The passengers had gone quiet, studying Smith uncertainly, but the captain met their worrisome expressions with a reassuring smile.

"Oh, not to worry," he said with a merry smile. "Ice warnings are perfectly normal for this time of year. There's no cause for alarm; in fact, we're speeding up. I've ordered the last boilers lit, and we should arrive in New York within no time."

While the passengers seemed placated by his untroubled demeanor, Murdoch still felt ill at ease. Smith wasn't wrong, of course; pack ice and growlers were common in this freezing weather. Even the larger bergs could be spotted from time to time, rising from the sea like glistening giants of smoothed ice. But they were of little concern; a crew could spot them over a half a mile away, so long as the conditions were decent, and the swells sent water breaking along the iceberg's base. Murdoch knew there was no need for caution, just as he knew Smith was an experienced shipmaster who knew these waters well. There was no reason to question the matter, no matter what his gut was telling him. He turned a level gaze to his captain, hoping his mask of professionalism would be enough to cloak his true misgivings.

"Shall I post the ice warning and its coordinates in the chart room, sir?"

With a shake of the head, Smith tucked the marconigram into his breast pocket. "No, no, that won't be necessary Mr. Murdoch. I'll see to it later once I've sent back a response."

"Aye, sir."

While Andrews and his retinue of passengers continued with the tour, shuffling their way aft toward the gymnasium, Lockerbie made no effort to join them. He hovered near the wheelhouse, hazel eyes narrowed at Bailey as if debating whether to approach her. But Murdoch was more than happy to make that decision for him. He stalked forward, crossing through the wheelhouse and barring the doorway to prevent Lockerbie from going any further.

"Shouldn't you be on your way, Mr. Lockerbie?" he demanded curtly.

Lockerbie stood straighter, flashing a thin, cold smile. "Actually," he drawled, "I'd like a quick word with Miss Bailey, if you don't mind."

"I do mind, actually." Murdoch knew he was overstepping the mark, but he didn't care. He was past caring at this point. Lockerbie could rot in hell, as far as he was concerned. He couldn't stop thinking of the sick bastard luring Bailey into his cabin, hurting her—violating her—and almost getting his way, had she not fought back.

Rage slipped through his guise, hot enough to burn away the midday chill. He could hear the blood roar in his ears, and it took every fiber of his being not to throttle Lockerbie until he turned blue.

"I think you'd best stay away from her," Murdoch warned, "if you bloody well know what's good for you."

The threat was quiet, mild—and yet it sizzled the air as the two men appraised each other.

Lockerbie pursed his lips, his expression snide but strangely inquisitive, as if gauging how much the first officer knew. Murdoch raised his chin, daring him to protest, hoping his eyes could convey enough of his hate. But Lockerbie seemed to have enough sense to let well enough alone. He gave a sharp turn on his heel and slunk his way back to the group, scowling darkly at the first officer as he went.

Murdoch waited until the bastard disappeared before stealing a glance at Bailey. Standing in the bridge wing with her eyes on the sea, she hadn't even noticed the tense exchange. But he figured that was for the best. Bailey wasn't the type of girl to be protected or coddled; she seemed determined to hold her own against Lockerbie, as if to prove the filthy things he'd done to her hadn't hindered her in the slightest. The lass carried herself with a strength harder than marble, and it was just another one of the many reasons why Murdoch respected her.

He could hear Lightoller's words flowing through his head once again, spilling across his thoughts like water without a path.

Show her, if you must.

The sudden realization struck him like a lightning bolt—a realization so obvious, so he wondered why he hadn't thought of it before.

Murdoch set off for the chart room at once, knowing exactly how to show Bailey his change of heart and hoping it might be enough to convince her.

NINETEEN

DAYLIGHT

April 14, 1912 | 14:05

ESTHER WAS DRAWING back the lid of the wheelhouse binnacle when Murdoch made his way toward her.

She hesitated, feeling terribly nervous as she closed the window lid and stood at attention. Whereas she once might have been pleased to see her superior officer, she was now withdrawn, and not entirely sure what to make of him.

Her head was swirling with thoughts of last night. How he'd cared for her, and kissed her forehead, and held her while she'd cried. It was a soft side she'd never seen from Murdoch before. Not from any man, for that matter.

But while she was deeply grateful for his help, Esther was now more confused than ever.

Murdoch had already made the extent of their relationship quite clear. They were subordinate and superior, nothing more. There were supposed to be *boundaries* between them—and yet his behavior last night had clearly suggested otherwise. The concern in his gaze, the brush of his lips against her forehead….it was enough to make her wonder if Murdoch cared for her more than he was letting on. Than he had ever let on, honestly.

Esther wasn't foolish, however. Even if there was the tiniest, smallest chance that Murdoch still had feelings for her, she couldn't act upon them. She couldn't be that reckless girl who'd let herself tease and flirt with a superior officer who couldn't even keep his emotions straight. Her career would always—and should always—come first.

If that's the case, she thought heavily, *then why do I feel so awful?*

With a deep breath, Esther watched Murdoch enter the wheelhouse.

He came to a halt before her, his expressionless gaze sweeping over her salute and stiff posture.

"At ease, Miss Bailey," he ordered.

Her muscles relaxed, stiff shoulders losing some of their tension, and Murdoch addressed her once more.

"Rounds await us, I'm afraid," he said. When she said nothing in response, he took one look at her flat expression and deadpanned, "Try to contain your excitement, lass."

It was a small attempt at dry humor, but Esther couldn't even force a smile. She kept her eyes on her feet, and Murdoch awkwardly cleared his throat before opening the wheelhouse door.

"Well...come along, then."

They fell into step together, moving aft with the cold blue sky above their heads and a crisp wind carrying the smell of sea salt behind them. The temperature had taken an incredible plummet; passengers and crew had cleared the boat deck and retreated inside the ship, seeking refuge from the bitter chill.

Esther rubbed her hands together for warmth as she walked alongside her superior. She was quiet, so it was Murdoch who finally broke the silence.

"I know you're angry at me," he said. "Not only for last night, but for earlier today. I didn't mean to upset you. I merely thought it would be better if you were away from Lockerbie."

Esther avoided his gaze, studying the blue swirls of ocean and letting its ebb and flow calm her flittering nerves.

"I'm not angry," she admitted. "And I'm sorry I snapped at you. I know you meant well, Mr. Murdoch. But running away from him wouldn't solve anything. It would only make things worse."

She hesitated, toying with the edge of her cuff as she added, "Also...I never properly thanked you for helping me last night. It was mighty kind of you, sir. And even though things...um, got out of hand..." His ears reddened a bit, and she knew he was remembering the kiss against her forehead. "I'm grateful for what you did for me. Truly, I am."

Murdoch stood straighter, his voice surprisingly casual as he replied, "I was glad to have helped a fellow officer. No matter how insufferably cheeky she might be."

Esther snapped a cold, angry gaze on him, ready for an argument—but the fight within her vanished when she saw the amusement sparkling in his eyes. He wasn't criticizing her. He was teasing. And Esther couldn't help but tease him back.

"Cheeky?" she demanded, unable to stop the faint smile curving on her mouth. "Oh, please. You're one to talk, Mr. Murdoch."

"I'm pleasantly sarcastic. There's a slight difference."

Esther let out a bellow of hearty laughter. It had been a while since she'd felt this relaxed and good-natured. She grinned at her superior.

"'Pleasantly sarcastic'?" she snorted. "This might come as a shock, Mr. Murdoch, but there's a point where sarcasm actually ceases to be pleasant."

"Is there?" He smirked a little. "I hadn't noticed."

Esther almost laughed again. But something unpleasant prickled at the back of her mind, cold enough to send the smile dripping from her face. She looked away from him, rolling back her in a nonchalant manner.

"Gee. I almost feel sorry for your new shipmates. All that dry humor they'll have to contend with day after day…they won't even survive it."

"Come again?"

"Well, you're taking the position aboard the *Olympic*, aren't you, Chief Officer Murdoch?"

His voice was remarkably calm. "Not exactly. I haven't decided yet."

Esther didn't respond immediately. Small sparks of joy danced within her chest, but she tried to stamp them out, keeping her expression neutral and her emotions guarded. "I'm surprised at you," she said coolly. "I thought you would've leaped at the chance."

"Aye. I thought so, too." He cocked his head to one side, looking curiously at her. "But I wouldn't mind hearing your thoughts on the matter first."

Esther felt her heart shudder to a stop. She gaped at Murdoch, the shock cascading through her bones as she fumbled for words. "I—I don't have any thoughts," she stammered. "It's your decision, Mr. Murdoch."

"It most certainly is," he said evenly. "But I'd still like to know what you think. Consider it a healthy curiosity of sorts."

They stopped on the port side of *Titanic*, rounds all but forgotten, standing near the lifeboats with no one else around them. Esther bit her lip, looking everywhere except Murdoch—the calm sea, the barren deck, the davits arching high above her head. Her heartbeat was erratic, hammering wildly in her chest, and she prayed he couldn't hear it over the roar of splitting seawater.

Christ, she thought. What could she say?

Of course she didn't want him to take the job. She wanted him to stay right here, to remain as her superior officer for as long they were working *Titanic*. Even after all the nonsense they had been through—all the bickering, the pent-up tension and inappropriate lust—she still enjoyed his company and seafaring experience. Hell, she even enjoyed his dry, sarcastic wit that irked her from time to time.

But deep down, Esther knew becoming a captain meant the world to him. And that joining the *Olympic* as chief officer was another small step leading up to his lifelong goal. It would be for the best, of course, if only to keep them apart before they could do something stupid. It would make things easier…painful, but far easier…

Esther finally looked up at Murdoch, meeting his steady eyes of sea-blue that carried the faintest hint of longing, the breath catching in her throat as she struggled to find the right words to say—

"Esther! Hey, I've been looking for you!"

The officers tore their gazes away from each other to see Booker crossing the deck, beaming, one hand tucking a polished watch inside his vest.

Murdoch tipped his cap. "Mr. Bailey," he said politely, but it was Esther he was still looking at.

"Mr. Murdoch." Booker kept his greeting swift, surprisingly bright-eyed and breathless with excitement. "I'm terribly sorry, but I was wondering if I might have a short word with my sister."

"Certainly. We were nearly finished with our rounds, anyhow, so we might as well stop here." Murdoch glanced at Esther before starting down the promenade. "I'll see you at ten o'clock this evening, lass."

He moved very close to her as he passed, gloved hand brushing against the wool of her greatcoat.

Esther felt a heavy weight drop into her pocket, but she didn't dare have a look. Not here. Not with Booker watching.

She kept a straight face instead, swallowing down the flame of curiosity flickering within her, urging her to check her coat pocket. Her eyes lingered on Murdoch for a long while, watching him disappear around a corner with his hands behind his back, and it wasn't until her brother spoke that she jolted back to her senses with a start.

"'Lass'?" he said, eyebrow raised. "Since when did he start calling you that?"

Esther gave a noncommittal shrug of the shoulders. "I don't know. For a while now, I guess."

Booker snorted. "Last time I checked, senior officers addressed their subordinates by their surnames."

Esther rolled her eyes. "He's Scottish, Booker. What do you expect? He probably calls every girl on this ship lass."

"Not exactly. I saw him taking the air with a first-class lady when I was out inspecting the davits the other day, and he didn't call *her* lass once—"

"Huh," Esther remarked casually. "Interesting."

She didn't dare meet her brother's gaze, but her mood was certainly more cheerful as they started down the boat deck together.

Booker started to complain about the cold, so she followed him inside the warm depths of the ship, making their way to his quarters on A Deck. His cabin was almost as messy as her own, the desk and floor coated in blueprints and littered with an assortment of compasses, pencils, and slide rules. Esther dropped herself into a chair while Booker remained standing, pacing the room in his excitement. But she only vaguely listened as he shared the news: Andrews had offered him the position of senior architect on Harland and Wolff's latest project, the SS *Pacific*. Together they would draft plans this summer and hopefully start laying the keel by early next year. Booker was elated, close to bursting with pride, and Esther found herself smiling despite her weary mood.

"Congratulations, Booker. You'll do wonderfully. I know you will."

"Thank you, but…" Her brother frowned, the wide grin dripping from his face. "Is everything all right? You've been acting odd all morning."

Her lie was too quick. "Just tired, I suppose. I had a late watch last night."

Booker snorted. "Come on. You're my sister, for Heaven's sake. I can see right through you—"

"Then you'll know there's nothing the matter," she retorted.

Her brother stared at her, clearly hurt, and Esther looked away to hide her guilt. She wasn't quite ready to revisit the events of last night. The memory of Lockerbie pinning her in place with harsh breath at her neck and his hands between her legs was enough to make her stomach roll.

But when she saw the wounded look in her brother's eyes, Esther knew she had to tell him the truth. Booker needed to know what Lockerbie was capable of, so she summoned up her courage, clinging to her bearings and letting those dark remembrances sift away like sand.

"You're right, Booker," she confessed. "There is something the matter. And it has to do with Callum Lockerbie."

"Callum?" Booker seemed surprised. "What happened?"

Esther drew in a deep breath before explaining everything. She told him how Slate had lied about Lockerbie being ill. She told him how the man she'd thought was her childhood friend had ranted and flung down glasses of champagne before trying to rape her against his parlor door. She told him how fiercely she'd fought back until Slate had smashed his gun against her face…how she'd staggered up to the boat deck with her nose bleeding out…how Murdoch had found her in the lavatory not long after, and done everything in his power to help.

And the more Esther told her brother of last night, the more heartbroken he seemed to become.

But there was one detail she chose to omit, and that was her forbidden intimacy with Murdoch. Booker still didn't know she had kissed the first officer, and Esther wanted to keep it that way. She would tell Booker the truth, of course…eventually. But after disclosing the sickening truth of Lockerbie, she didn't want to throw her dalliance with Murdoch into the mix, lest her brother have a stroke.

By the time she finished, tears glistened in her brother's eyes. He rushed toward her, grasping her hands so tightly she thought he might break her fingertips. "I'm sorry," he whispered. "Christ, Esther, I'm so sorry. You tried to warn me about him, and I didn't listen. I thought he was my friend. Our friend. And to have this happen to you, after dealing with that other wretched bastard…." His voice cracked, suddenly hoarse beneath layers of sorrow and shame. "It's my fault, Es, I should have stopped him, I should have been there—"

Esther squeezed his hand, glad to have her brother close. "It's okay. Stop blaming yourself, all right? You couldn't have known that jackass was capable of something like this—"

"But I *should* have known," Booker insisted angrily. "That's the point. And now look at what's happened. Look at what he's done." He shot to his feet, pacing in a murderous fury. "We'll have to do something, for cryin' out loud. Contact the Master-at-Arms, and the police once we're ashore—"

But Esther shook her head. "Booker, Lockerbie would ruin me."

Her brother rounded on her in disbelief. "How so?"

"Think about it," Esther reasoned. "He has money, influence, people to do his dirty work. It would be so easy to put the blame on me, Booker. To twist it so he's innocent, and I'm the whore bedding businessmen to get ahead." Her voice was a soft, angry hiss. "And even if we try to press charges, how could I continue working as an officer with this mess over my head? I'd never find a job at sea again. I'd be seen as another girl caught up in a scandal, bringing trouble wherever she goes."

Booker was seething, one hand diving through his dark hair. "Esther, listen to me. I don't want to see something like that happen, either. But I'll be *damned* if I let that miserable sonofabitch walk free after what he did to you. I won't even be able to look at him without wanting to beat him to a bloody pulp—"

"You don't have to worry about that," Esther assured him darkly. "I already gave him a decent ass-kicking. Might've bruised a rib, even. So I'm fairly satisfied."

"That certainly makes one of us," Booker muttered. "Bruised rib ain't enough for scum like him, Esther. The man deserves a goddamn body bag."

He settled on the bed across from Esther, still clinging to her hand as if his life depended on it. Gradually the anger in his eyes began to fade, and he whispered, "I'm sorry I wasn't there to help you last night. I wish you would've come to me."

"I know, and I should have. But Mr. Murdoch took good care of me, so don't worry." Her smile was wistful, and she dropped her gaze to her hands, hoping her brother wouldn't see her remorse. "He's a fine man," she said quietly. "I know I loathed him at first, but I've actually enjoyed having him as my mentor. I'll be sorry to see him go." When Booker frowned, she explained, "He's been offered a promotion aboard the *Olympic*. And I'm almost certain he's going to take it."

Something in her voice seemed to catch her brother's attention. He studied her for a long moment, his eyes narrowed.

"Is he, now? And do you want him to?"

"Well, I mean, it's what he's always wanted, isn't it? One step closer to becoming captain—"

"That doesn't answer the question," Booker said simply. "Do you want him to go?"

"I…" Esther hesitated. She suddenly felt lost, her thoughts running like watercourses with no end. Her voice dropped to a mumble as she twisted her fingers together. "No, Booker. Of course I don't."

"Then perhaps you should tell him that."

Esther finally glanced up, stunned, meeting her brother's meaningful stare and wondering if he suspected her true feelings for Murdoch after all. Her brother had always been able to see right through her, after all—clear as if gazing through glass. Perhaps he could see that there was something more between her and the first officer. But even if he did, it didn't explain why he was so open to the matter. Booker hadn't been this understanding the other day, when they'd stood on the boat deck, and he'd warned her not to get involved with a superior. He had been adamant about Esther keeping her relationship with Murdoch strictly platonic, focused on work and little else. So what could have possibly changed?

Before she could muster up a reply, a soft knock had them glancing at the door. Booker was swift, rising from his chair to answer it, and his demeanor brightened immediately when he saw Thomas Andrews standing in the hall. The shipwright looked as handsome as ever, his salt-and-pepper hair sleek and combed. A fountain pen was tucked behind his left ear, while he held a tiny black notebook in his hands.

"Sir," Booker greeted, and Esther didn't miss the faint pink blush creeping into his cheeks.

Andrews offered him a warm smile. "Afternoon, Booker. And Esther, of course." He nodded kindly in her direction. "How wonderful it is to see you again, miss. Has Mr. Murdoch been keeping you busy?"

Esther managed a polite nod, trying to drag herself from the slippery undercurrent of her thoughts.

"As always, sir," she replied. "He wouldn't dare do otherwise."

"I suppose not." Andrews looked amused. "The man lives and breathes his work, doesn't he? He's a proper sailor, that one." His gaze shifted to Booker, who stood somewhat taller, the flush still high in his cheeks. "I know this rather impromptu of me, Mr. Bailey, but would you care to review my notes from this afternoon? I've a few more improvements for *Titanic* in mind—nothing grand in scale, o'course, just the little things—and I'd quite like to hear your thoughts."

He looked full of energy, his eyes glittering, ready for work. Booker offered him a seat, and suddenly the two shipbuilders were poring over the little notebook, leaning unusually close to one another as they chatted away. Esther was all but forgotten, but she didn't mind; they were an amusing pair to watch as they rambled and swapped ideas.

"—was thinking we might consider installing back plates for the electric reading lamps in the suite staterooms," Andrews explained, finger skating across the inked pages of his notebook. "And sponge holders fitted in the private bathrooms on B and C decks…the Palm Court could use an additional four tables, I'm thinking, as it seems rather short on table accommodation …Smith also suggested protective windows with round bulls-eye lights for the bridge, similar to the *Arabic*, perhaps…"

Esther decided to leave them to it, politely excusing herself and rising to her feet. But she was only halfway to the door when she remembered the heavy weight in her coat pocket. She reached for it, surprised to feel something cool and hard graze her fingertips. Something metal.

Esther didn't care if her brother was watching. In a blaze of rashness, she yanked the object from the confines of her pocket. And when she realized what Murdoch gave her, she had to clench her teeth to keep her emotion from bubbling right over.

It was his compass.

The brass compass he'd carried with him throughout his maritime career, ever since his accident at sea.

There was a tiny note attached to the casing, penned in dark blue ink, and it took her a moment to discern Murdoch's scribbled penmanship.

For your travels.

Esther clasped the compass tightly, her bottom lip trembling, one shaky thumb skating over his engraved initials.

This was something Murdoch had kept on him for over twenty years. Something that had reminded him of the fears and hardships he'd managed to overcome. It wasn't just any old keepsake; it was something very personal to him.

But he had passed it to her without question.

It was a reminder that he wanted her to fulfill her wildest hopes and dreams. That he wanted her to go out and explore the oceans she'd always longed to see. And that no matter how far they might drift apart, she would always have something to remember him by.

As she held the compass in her palm, Esther found herself dreading the thought of Murdoch leaving *Titanic*—of exchanging stilted goodbyes with the man and not knowing when she would see him again.

She knew she had her own dreams and ambitions to worry about. She knew staying away from Murdoch was for the best. And yet, something inexplicably kept pulling her back to him, keeping him grounded not only in her thoughts, but in her heart as well.

Esther thought of the first time Murdoch had helped her, hurrying down to the tailor shop to come to her aid. The times he had stood up for her, and defended her, and fought for her place as a female officer. And then she recalled last night, when he had rushed to hold her in the lavatory, no second thoughts or hesitations in his mind…

There was a scramble of movement as Esther barreled out the door and into the corridor, ignoring the startled looks from her brother and Andrews as she passed. She felt as if something within her was going haywire; she could feel it crackling across her skin like static, turning her limbs restless and sending her heartbeat stuttering fast. But despite the lightning storm fizzing along her nerves, her mind was set, becoming an ocean of calm that drove her onward, convincing her not to be afraid.

Esther clung to her resolve as she set out to find her superior officer, thinking of the compass weighing heavy in her pocket and wondering what on earth she might say to him.

15:15

She knocked quietly on the first officer's door, not at all certain if he was sleeping. But he appeared within moments, looking weary, but awake all the same. He'd discarded his coat, cap, and gloves since she'd seen him last. His shirt was somewhat creased, suspender straps still hooked around his shoulders and tie hanging loose around his neck.

"Miss Bailey?" He seemed mildly surprised to see her.

"May I come in, sir?"

He merely nodded, holding open the door wider to admit her inside. Esther swallowed, suddenly feeling nervous as she entered his cabin. But she knew what she'd come here to say, so she waited until Murdoch crossed the room before she grasped the door, closed it, and locked it behind her. He raised an eyebrow at this but said nothing, his face inscrutable as he studied his subordinate.

Esther drew in a deep breath, not entirely sure where to start. She hadn't said a single word, and yet her confidence was already slipping, crumbling beneath a shyness she'd never known before. But she pressed on, still holding on to his compass and willing the strength back into her heart.

"I wanted to thank you, Mr. Murdoch. For giving me your compass. I know it means a great deal to you, sir. And I'll always remember that."

Esther waited for him to speak, but his only response was a wordless nod. It wasn't much of an encouragement, but it was enough. She found herself pacing the room, hands sweeping her cap from her head and wringing it tight, the words spilling from her mouth at long last.

"Sir, listen," she began, "I know you've worked at sea for over twenty years. I know how much experience and knowledge you have when it comes to seafaring. And I know you've been dead-set on becoming captain all your life, 'specially since you said you'd be following in your father's footsteps. Your grandfather's footsteps, even."

Esther felt sloppy and inelegant with her words, but she did not care. She just needed him to know, so she rambled on, "I saw how upset you were when they bumped you down from chief officer to first. Upset enough to take your frustrations out on me, even. It's obvious this is your life, sir. That seafaring means everything to you. So I know you must've been pretty darn pleased when you got the news today. And I don't blame you one bit."

Murdoch was silent, leaning against the mahogany desk with his hands braced against its edge, blue eyes following her every move as she flailed her arms and paced back and forth.

"I've no doubt you would make a damn fine chief officer, Mr. Murdoch, and an even finer captain someday. You're a bit of an ass sometimes, sir, and yet you're brilliant. Sharp as a tack and steadfast in ways I hope to intimate someday. But…you said you wanted to hear my thoughts on the matter, so I…" She stopped abruptly in her tracks, looking straight into his eyes and finding him looking right back.

"I don't want you to go, dammit." Her voice was small. "I want you to stay. And I want *more* than that. I want to be with you, Will." She hadn't meant to say those last words, but they spilled out anyway, and there was no going back. Esther studied the floor, her chest heaving, her heart fluttering like a trapped bird against her ribcage. "I know it's selfish and wrong," she admitted. "And I know we agreed to keep away from each other for the sake of our jobs. But that's how I feel, sir. Because there's no one else like you, who has cared for me and guided me and ticked me off. I'm sorry if I'm overstepping my bounds. I just needed you to know."

Murdoch stood motionless, gazing at her with an intensity she'd never seen before. But his silence was worrying, enough to make her regret her sudden rashness.

Esther bit down on her bottom lip, wondering if she had gone too far—and wishing she'd kept her mouth shut after all. Humiliation swirled hot across her skin, and she didn't know what else to do except hurry for the door, desperate to flee from her awful mistake.

But she had barely grasped the doorknob when a warm, calloused hand caught hers, gently tugging her back.

Esther turned, hardly daring to believe it, and the breath caught in her throat when she realized Murdoch was smiling. His blue eyes were shining and soft as they held hers, mirroring the feelings and emotions she'd laid bare before him.

"C'mere, lass."

Esther stepped closer to him, her cheeks blushing bright pink. He still hadn't released her hand, and she let him pull her part of the way, too shy to meet his eyes.

But Murdoch didn't look away once. He seemed almost mesmerized by her, his gaze lingering on her freckles, her lips.

He combed his fingers through her hair first, his touch sending shocks of electricity through her veins.

Then he gently tipped her chin up, leaning forward to press his mouth against hers.

He kissed her deeply, and something about this kiss was much different than the first one they had shared. It was soft and intimate and so very familiar, and Esther leaned into him, suddenly lightheaded, clutching fistfuls of his shirt.

Every little worry in her mind or ache in her injured face suddenly became meaningless, trickling away like grains of sand, and all that mattered in this world was William Murdoch—the feel of his tongue and the smell of his aftershave and the way his strong, warm frame felt so right against her own.

They were breathless when they finally broke apart, her fingers moving to clutch his suspenders, his reaching out to caress her cheek. He bent his head, pressing his forehead against hers for a long moment, and although Esther kept her eyes closed, she could still hear the smile in his voice as he swore, "I'm not going anywhere, you dafty. My place is here, with my men. With Lights and Wilde." He leaned closer, cradling her face between his coarse palms, lips barely grazing hers. "With you."

She opened her eyes, drawing back to meet his gaze. "And if we're caught?" she asked. "If we lose our jobs?"

"We'll be careful," he assured her, dropping a kiss on her forehead before twining his fingers with hers. "We have Lights and Wilde to help without question. And we'll take extra precautions, of course—both in port and at sea. We've already remembered the bleedin' door, at least," he added with a grin, "so I'd say we're doing proper well at this point."

She snorted with laughter, burying her face deep into his shirt to hide her embarrassment. "Christ's sake. I still blame *you* for that blunder, sir."

"Do you, now?" He wrapped her in his arms, his breathy laugh warm against her ear. "Pretty rich coming from a lass who can't even lock her door before havin' a bath—"

"That was one time," she protested hotly, and Murdoch laughed.

"It was enough, mind," he said, amused. "I daresay you're just as guilty as I am, lass, if not more."

She felt his fingers work around her tie as he spoke, slowly tugging the knot free. Her heart stuttered as the silk fabric came loose around her shoulders.

"But no matter what happens," Murdoch told her, his voice quiet, "I'm dead willing to make this work. Because I need you, lass." His hands swept down to grip her waist, pulling her body flush against him. A sensation like lightning gathered where he touched, sparkling hot across her skin. "It sounds right daft, but I do. More than you'll ever know."

He kissed her again, but this time it was hard and hungry and full of want, and she knew in that moment he desired something more. She could taste it in his kiss—that reserve of need she'd glimpsed once before, hidden beneath barriers of restraint and self-control.

Only this time, she knew he wouldn't hold back.

Rough hands grasped her hips, and she suddenly found herself being lifted up on the mahogany desk behind them, scattering pens and papers to the floor. Murdoch nudged her knees apart, standing between her legs as he leaned into her, deepening their kiss without hesitation.

Her fingers skated up through his hair before trailing across his strong back and broad shoulders, feeling the hard, solid expanse of muscle beneath her palms. She explored lower, smoothing her hand down to his trousers, and she nipped his lip with wicked pleasure when she found him already hard. Her touch was enough to make him groan through their kiss, and he unfastened the buttons of her coat in a fervor, yanking it from her shoulders and flinging it to the floor.

His hands slid across her legs this time, hitching up her skirt until the lace of her undergarments were visible. She knew he wanted her right then and there, flat on her back upon his desk with her skirt pushed past her thighs. The very thought was enough to send a coil of heat shooting between her legs.

But she didn't want to have him here. Not yet, at least. She wanted the bed first. She wanted to make it last.

She slid off the wooden surface with a smirk, kissing away his surprise as she eased him closer to his bed. She waited until the mattress was behind him before shoving her palms against his chest, sending him toppling down to the smooth white sheets. Esther laughed aloud at his look of mingled indignation and shock, which quickly turned to hunger as he gazed up into her eyes, wanting her. *Needing* her.

She didn't keep him waiting long.

Esther climbed onto his lap, straddling him, shamelessly enjoying the way he seemed unable to look away from her. He hurried to undress himself now that she was on top of him, yanking away his tie and peeling off his shirt and suspenders. He kissed her harder, and she let her hands roam across the plane of his bare chest, the heat of his skin soaking into her palms.

Murdoch leaned back and put his weight on his elbows as he pulled her down to the mattress along with him. Esther obliged, unwilling to break their kiss. She rolled her hips against his, grinding down on his hardness beneath her, craving to be full of him. His breathing grew ragged as he went for her clothing, the blaze of exhilaration and need in his eyes matching her own. She felt his hands fumble with the buttons on her blouse until he grew impatient and ripped it open entirely. He went for her brassiere next, struggling with the lacing until they were both laughing, and she had to guide his hand. The silk fabric fell away from her breasts at last, and Murdoch kissed up the soft space between them before sucking each of her nipples, hard enough to send a soft moan tumbling from her lips.

But still, Esther wanted more. She *needed* more. She needed him. Her hands pinned his wrists into the mattress as she moved lower, kissing feverishly down his abdomen and toying with the button of his trousers until she found what she was looking for.

His sharp intake of breath filled the room as she bent her head and took him in her mouth, tasting him and making him hers. She took her time, enjoying the way he clenched the sheets tight in his fists, his blue eyes dazed and rapt, locked upon her every move. Her tongue swirled around his tip before she went even deeper, lips wrapped tight around him, sliding up and down with the slick, rigid length of him grazing the back of her throat.

"*Christ*, lass," Murdoch choked out. The sound was almost strangled, soft in the darkness of the cabin.

There was a whirl of movement as he broke from her grasp, snagging her by the waist and rolling them around until he was straddling her this time, one knee on either side of her hips. He yanked off her skirt and stripped away her undergarments, no patience or finesse about it. Just burning, voracious, unrestrained want.

Her clothing went toppling to the floor, and his along with it. Esther was fully naked beneath him now, hair spilled upon his pillow, eyes wild and waiting. A look of wonder filled his gaze as he simply admired her sprawled out on his sheets, coarse hands trailing across the golden, freckled expanse of her bare skin and leaving blistering warmth in their path. God, how Esther loved his hands. He slid them across every curve of her body, mapping the smooth contours of her hips, her breasts, her slender legs. His palms were rough but soothing as they claimed her, exploring the tender places that made her mind stutter with dizzying bliss.

Esther almost couldn't think straight; she could feel the ache building between her thighs, that *need* growing by the second. She arched into his touch, craving more, and Murdoch didn't hesitate to trade his calloused hands for his mouth.

He kissed her neck before working his way down to her taut nipples, moving lower, and lower, until he was right between her thighs. She shuddered when she felt the first soft, long lick. Then came another, and another, until he found a rhythm with his tongue that nearly drove her senseless. Her head fell onto the pillows, back arching up high, toes curling up tight. She could feel a hotter sensation coiling through her body now, more like sparkling electricity than smoldering flame as she panted and writhed beneath his teasing mouth.

"*Will.*"

Her gasp was soft—a plea, a longing for more.

Murdoch stood at once, tugging her to the edge of his bed, strong hands gripping her thighs and spreading them apart. She heard a low groan work its way up his throat as he sank into her, and Esther found herself enveloped in thrilling heat as they were finally together at last.

He was gentle at first, cupping her breasts and dropping hot, searing kisses on her lips, her forehead, her collarbone. His hips worked carefully, letting her adjust to his thickness, the friction slow and steady between them.

But Esther wanted *more*. His restraint buckled when she wrapped her legs tightly around him, and the heat in her body became that of a wildfire as his pace quickened, each pounding stroke harder than the last.

She was gasping beneath him, her hips pressing deep into the mattress, her nails dragging down his solid, sturdy back and finding it slick with sweat. It was unbearable, almost, having to keep quiet when her body was ablaze with such overwhelming pleasure: the fullness of him inside her, the heat of his mouth, the feel of his thumb caressing her most sensitive spot right above where they were joined. Esther had never felt something like this before. That fire was spreading across every inch of her now, melting her, searing her—and *Christ*, she never wanted him to stop.

They weren't exactly silent; every hard thrust had the mattress springs creaking, bedframe thrumming a tempo against the bulkhead behind them. But the noises might as well have been nonexistent, for all they cared. They were heedless of anything but each other, breaths mingling and bodies moving in time, that fire still spreading and pooling between them.

Murdoch pulled out and effortlessly hauled her over top of him. His blue eyes blazed up at her, a silent invitation for her to take control.

Esther had only tried such a position once before, and although the angle seemed new and intimidating, she was more than willing to try it with him. She tossed back her hair and lowered herself over him without pause, giving him everything she had as she rode him hard. His hands clutched the small span of her waist as he bucked up into her, meeting her pace. Her body was scorching, alight with a fierce, fiery need as she ground against him, rolling her hips, drinking in the sight of him sprawled beneath her. Murdoch was marveling up at her, and she couldn't stop watching him, either. The heaving of his chest, the flex of his muscles, the sigh of ecstasy escaping his lips each time she slid down to the hilt, the sensation of him filling her almost too much to bear.

"Esther," he murmured, breath hot against her lips.

He hammered into her even faster, and she collapsed onto his chest with a whimper, hair falling into his face, nails digging deep into his skin.

She expected him to come like this, and her along with him. But Murdoch suddenly flipped her flat on her back again, standing as he took her from the edge of his bed once more. He hoisted her legs up higher this time, bracing against them, thrusting deeper, rougher—the angle so overwhelming she had to bite the pillow to keep from moaning aloud.

Her skin was shining with sweat, her hips aching beneath the tight grip of his hands, but Esther loved every single second of it. She reached out to run her palm across his chest, but he caught her wrist and pinned it into the pillow above her head, anchoring himself as his pace slowed to a steady grind.

She was so close now, she just needed him to keep going. And he did, leaning forward with his lips at her ear, telling her she was *his*, saying her name again and again until she could contain herself no longer.

Esther stifled a moan as she finally broke apart beneath him, her skin flushed with pink and her entire body shuddering as sheer, white-hot pleasure flooded every inch of her. He breathed her name once more, only louder this time, hips slamming against hers, hands knotting in her hair— until he buried himself deep and came right with her.

It was a while before their heavy breathing grew softer and slower in the cabin. Esther was quivering from head to toe, feeling the aftershocks ripple between her thighs. Murdoch collapsed beside her on the bed, panting and spent, and she curled closer to him, seeking his warmth.

They lay together for a long while, messy and glowing and wholly satisfied, touching and exploring each other in silence. She traced her fingers across his chest as it rose and fell, still glistening with sweat. He lifted one of her arms and rained kisses down her scarred skin. Then he ran his hand through her mussed hair again and again, the movement slow and affectionate, making her sigh.

She felt so content lying here with him, regardless of their separate ranks. That didn't matter any longer. Not now, and certainly not here, as they tangled their legs together and pressed lazy, exhausted kisses against each others' lips.

Esther was the first to speak, her amused voice filling the quiet comfort of the room. "If there was ever a time to write me up for gross misconduct, I think now would be it."

His raspy, tired laughter made her smile. "Don't tempt me, lass." He leaned closer to her, burying his face against her soaked neck as he breathed, "Good God, I can't tell you how much I've wanted this."

"Took us long enough, huh?"

"Aye, far too long," he agreed, pulling her deeper into his arms. "But now I have you, don't I? You are mine, cheek and stubbornness and all."

She wrinkled her nose up at him, and he laughed, adding, "I *like* that about you, lass. Just as I admire your strength." He kissed her nose. "And your compassion." He kissed the top of her forehead. "And your cleverness."

Murdoch finally smoothed her hair away from her face, gazing steadily into her pale green eyes. "You're different, Esther. And you're so lovely. I've never met anyone else quite like you." His voice was soft, his fingers gentle as they laced with hers. "I know I've not been good to you," he admitted. "I've hurt you. I thought that maybe, if I pushed you away, I could snuff out my feelings for you. Put our careers first and all that. But when I saw what happened to you last night, I just—I—"

Her heart softened as she watched Murdoch swallow and struggle for words, a shade of beet-red in his cheeks.

"I realized how much you mean to me, lass. And I simply can't be without you. I care for you far too much."

His hand reached out, dragging from her breast down to the soft plane of her stomach. Then he took her palm and kissed it, closing his eyes. Esther was almost beside herself with happiness as she studied him, tracing every last detail of this moment and committing it to memory. She loved how dark and blue his eyes were, their color like deep ocean water, their outer corners edged with wrinkles. She loved the speckling of pale freckles and moles across his face. The nickel-sized birthmark on the side of his thick neck. His bold jaw and round ears and sleek, dark hair that was beginning to gray.

She observed and memorized every piece of him, marveling that the man lying by her side was the same officer she'd once loathed and treated with a complete lack of respect. The same officer who'd belittled her and treated her with cold, unwavering indifference day after day.

But everything had changed between them.

They had worn away at each other, smoothing away all the jagged corners, sharp edges, and imperfections until she'd found the softness in his heart, and he'd found hers. Esther felt so right with him. So connected and so infinitely, wonderfully whole.

How different this was, compared to her other relationships in the past. Murdoch was nothing like Muir, who had gone out of his way to abuse and control her, crushing her spirit and stripping her of everything she had. And he certainly wasn't like the other gentlemen she'd dabbled with in the past, who'd left her and moved on to other women—women who were far less taboo, didn't boldly speak their minds, pour themselves into maritime books, or profess their unbridled passion for the sea.

But Murdoch liked those things. He liked everything about her. Admired her, even. It was enough to warm her heart, making her feel more adored and wanted and beautiful than she had ever felt before.

And where Esther once might have assumed her relationship with her superior was born from pure lust—that rough sex and a quick release were all they'd needed from each other—she knew it stretched much deeper than that. The evidence was right there, as he gazed into her eyes and threaded his fingers through her hair.

"You are mine," he said softly against the hollow of her throat, pulling her closer into his arms. "Mine, love."

And as she curled closer to him beneath the blankets, snuggling against his chest and listening to his soft breathing in her ear, Esther knew she believed him.

17:05

The two officers decided to bathe together once they finally crawled out of Murdoch's bed, taking a number of precautions to remain discreet.

Esther threw on her clothes and tiptoed to the lavatory first, running the bathwater in the deep clawfoot tub until it was steaming hot. She waited nearly fifteen minutes until a robed Murdoch unlocked the door and slipped inside, using the master key he'd kept from the night before. They kept the taps in the washbasin running at full blast, lest anyone might overhear their voices. Then they slid into the warm water together, working soap into each other's skin and hair, and the lingering curiosity they had once had—if the tubs could accommodate more than one person—was certainly answered.

They leaned back against the smooth rim of the tub after a while, content and comfortable, talking quietly across the soapy water between them. Their voices were low, drowned out by the gushing torrent of the washbasin taps, and Esther found herself learning so many things about him. How he'd always found her freckles charming. How deeply he missed

Dalbeattie summers and the taste of his mother's homemade whisky tablet. How he sometimes longed for the adrenaline of charting the rough, wild seas compared to the smooth crossings White Star Line vessels promised. And how eagerly he wanted to travel with her—to show her the dazzling coasts of Chile and beyond.

"We'll go there someday," Murdoch promised. "It might be years away, but we'll still go. I'll show you Valparaíso, of course. All its food and sights and ports…it's pure magic, it is."

He was chatty in a way that amused her. She could feel his hands absentmindedly caressing her legs beneath the water as he continued, "Perhaps we'll even make it north to San Francisco, aye? Wouldn't mind seeing it again, fog and all. Might even be willing to try that…thing with the breaded bowl you keep haverin' on about."

Amused, Esther lazily swirled her hand in the bathwater. "Clam chowder, you mean?"

"Aye, that." His smile was teasing. "I'm sure it's decent—even if it is American. Can't be any worse than your coffee, now, can it?"

She sloshed water right in his face. "Hey! What's the matter with my coffee?"

He raised his brows in an innocent manner, smirking, blinking the wetness from his eyes. "*Nothing*, lass…if you enjoy the taste and consistency of motor oil, that is…"

Esther smacked him with another wave of bathwater, and suddenly the two officers were at war, splashing the other as if no better than children. She had never seen this side of him—relaxed and lighthearted—and she loved it. Her laughter echoed off the walls of the room, rising above the running washbasin faucets, and Murdoch silenced her with a cautionary look.

"Right, that's enough," he urged, laughter fading beneath a serious tone. "Get ahold of yourself, won't you? We have to keep quiet."

He paused, watching her settle back against the rim of the tub. And then he swept one last splash of water directly in her face.

Esther gasped, coughing and spluttering, wondering how she could have been so foolish as to fall for his trick. "You sneaky Scottish bastard," she said, and he grinned before pulling her in for a slow, lingering kiss.

Once they were rinsed clean, the officers had to be just as discreet leaving the lavatory as they were entering it. Fortunately for them, Murdoch knew the schedules of his officers well. All were on duty at the moment, as far as he knew—save for Lightoller and Boxhall, who were likely fast asleep.

They decided Esther would leave the lavatory first, locking the door behind her, while Murdoch would depart at least ten minutes thereafter. It wasn't a foolproof plan, of course, but it would have to do.

Esther climbed out of the tub then, drying herself with a cotton towel. And when she turned back to Murdoch, who was still soaking in the bath, she found him looking up at her with a tenderness she'd never seen before. She smiled at him as she pulled on her robe.

"What?" she asked of him.

"Nothing," he said lightly. "Just having a look at you, is all."

Her laughter was hearty. "Is that so?" she teased. "How flattering, Will. I didn't realize I was such a spectacle."

He laughed along with her, sitting upright in the clear bathwater. "A pain in my arse, more like," he corrected. "And a very distracting one, at that." His eyes trailed down the length of her body, roaming from her dark, soaked hair to her slender legs peeking beyond the layers of silk. "I'm still debating whether to order you back in the tub with me. Although," he added thoughtfully, "I'm not so sure I'd be able to keep my hands to myself. So perhaps it's best if we vacate the washroom now, aye? Before one thing leads to another."

"What's so wrong with that?" she demanded, and Murdoch chuckled.

"*Later*, lass," he said, smirking. "Patience."

Wordlessly, she swooped down to kiss him again, catching him by surprise. It was soft and sensual—a reminder that she wanted more of him later tonight, even if she couldn't have him right here in the bath.

"Oh, fine," she agreed. "Care to join me for tea in the mess in say, a half hour, then?"

He was still admiring her, his voice soft as he said, "'Course."

Glowing with warmth and giddiness, Esther hurried for the door. She was breathless, grinning from ear to ear like some lovesick young girl again. Her lips were swollen from how hard she'd been kissed, and there was a newfound, satisfying soreness between her legs. But she didn't care about these aches in the slightest. She was too consumed by the wonderful, weightless sensation within her chest, her head, her *heart*. It was a happiness Esther hadn't known in years—or ever, come to think of it. She couldn't stop smiling, stunned by how far she and Murdoch had come—and delighted that her feelings for him were wholly reciprocated.

Whistling merrily, Esther skipped out into the deserted corridor. She closed the door behind her, about to lock it tight—but stopped cold when a familiar voice spoke behind her.

"Esther?"

Esther froze, the smile plummeting from her face. Panic sparked through her veins like an electric current, seizing up her limbs and tearing her nerves apart. But then she managed to collect herself, fumbling with the master key until she jammed it into the lock. It gave a soft click, and she pocketed the key before whirling around to see Lowe, of all people, making his way toward her.

The fifth officer wore a perplexed look, as if he hadn't expected to find Esther standing in the corridor with her hair still damp, and nothing but a thin silk dressing robe shielding her nakedness from view.

But there was something else in his eyes—a subtle captivation that suggested he was intrigued by the sight of her. She stumbled away from him, pressing her back flat against the door and thinking of Murdoch sitting in the bath right behind her.

Oh, Christ.

Heart fluttering madly, Esther raised her chin and forced a smile.

"Harry!" she said brightly. "How wonderful to see you. I thought you were supposed to be on watch this evening?"

"Oh, I am. Unfortunately." Looking weary, he stifled a yawn with the back of his palm and rubbed his nose, which was pink with cold. "Just needed to pass along a quick word from the bridge to Mr. Murdoch. He's not in his cabin, though, oddly enough. Haven't seen him, have you?"

Don't blush, for Heaven's sake, whatever you do.

Fighting to keep her voice nonchalant, Esther quickly lied, "No, not all. Last I saw of him, he was walking the starboard deck with Mr. Lightoller, I think."

Lowe stole a glance down the length of the hall, which was empty apart from the pair of them. "Ah well," he said with a shrug. "I'm sure he'll turn up soon enough." Nodding at the lavatory door, he added, "You all finished? Might as well pop in and seize the opportunity before I head back—"

Although the door was locked tight, Esther scrambled forward. "Don't!" she blurted.

Lowe stopped in his tracks, looking utterly bemused, and Esther felt her limbs lock up as she stood before his questioning stare, struggling to think of a ruse. She'd always been a poor liar, and it didn't feel right to deceive someone as sweet and friendly as Lowe. But Esther knew she had no choice. If Lowe were to try the doorknob and find it locked, that would raise suspicion—and possibly put her relationship with Murdoch at risk. She had to lie. It was her only option, shameful as it was.

She stood straighter, clinging to her bearings as the dishonest words came spilling out.

"I wouldn't go in there," she warned him. "I'm not usually the seasick type, Harry, but I fell terribly ill after my watch, and, well…" Esther held back a wince. She couldn't believe she was telling him this, but she pressed on, "It's a mess, Harry. I couldn't make it to the bowl in time, and it ended up everywhere. Please forgive me if this is too vulgar a conversation, but…at least now you know. I'd probably use the other lavatory if I were you, honestly. Probably for the best."

She expected Lowe to react with disgust, or even skepticism, perhaps. But what she didn't anticipate was the look of honest-to-God concern spreading across his face.

"Blimey, Esther." His soft, warm brown eyes held hers as he moved closer. Far too close. "What can I do to help?"

She forced a smile at him, heart running faster than a racehorse, sweating palms pressed flat against the door behind her. "Oh, don't you worry about me," she insisted. "I'm going to lie down in my cabin and have a bottle of seltzer water. You head back to the bridge, okay? I'll send Mr. Murdoch to you if I spot him."

"That's all very well," Lowe said, "but I'd rather not leave you like this. Not when you're unwell."

She watched as he stepped even closer, his coat brushing against her robe, and a different smell of aftershave washed over her. It wasn't anything like Murdoch's subtle scent. It was rich with heady spice, overpowering her with the scent of cloves. Esther wrinkled her nose, but

Lowe didn't seem to notice. He lifted one gloved hand, and for one brief, horrifying moment, Esther thought he was going to cup her cheek.

Oh, Jesus no, was all she could think, her thoughts suddenly useless, frozen solid.

But then her colleague seemed to think better of it, remembering his boundaries and taking a step back.

"I—" Lowe stammered, eyes wide. He seemed shocked by his behavior, but there was still a deep conflict in his gaze as he looked her up and down.

"Hey, I'll be fine," she assured him. "Really, Harry. Don't fret."

"Sure. Right." Lowe finally nodded. "But lemme know if you need anything else, you hear? I'm only a few footsteps away."

"Of course." Esther lowered her eyes to her feet, hoping her lashes might hide her awful guilt. "Thank you."

His eyes lingered on her for moment before he politely tipped his cap in farewell, and Esther watched him go, stunned but admittedly relieved he had swallowed her lie without question. She waited until he disappeared around the corner before scrambling back to the lavatory door, knowing fully well that Murdoch was standing right behind it, waiting for the all-clear.

"He's gone," she said quietly against the wood.

Murdoch gave no spoken reply, only a soft knock of acknowledgment against the doorframe, and Esther hurried to her cabin at once.

She dressed quickly, yanking on the components of her uniform and dabbing fresh cosmetic cream over her bruise. Exhaustion was beginning to settle over the seventh officer now that the long day had caught finally caught up with her, and she sighed when she remembered her nightly watch this evening. She'd squeeze in a few hours of sleep later this evening, of course. But for now, she wanted to be with Murdoch.

They met on the officers' promenade half an hour later, wearing their gloves and greatcoats to bar the evening chill. It was darker now that the sun had set, but a glimmer of light still edged the sea, shimmering across the endless expanse of water. Esther couldn't help but smile at Murdoch as he joined her at the rail. He looked handsome as always, a true gentleman in uniform, but there was a different glow to his blue eyes as he smiled at her. It was almost astounding to think they had been intimate a mere hour earlier, and her cheeks flared pink when she remembered all the things they had done in secret within his cabin.

Esther cleared her throat, hoping Murdoch would think the blush on her cheeks was from the cold, and nothing else.

"Good evening, Mr. Murdoch," she said, eyes glittering mischievously at him. "Fancy meeting you here."

He regarded her with amusement. "Indeed, Miss Bailey. I was just thinking the same. Especially since I've had a rather *fascinating* conversation with Mr. Lowe." His words were enough to make her groan. She hid her face behind her hands in embarrassment, peeking between her gloved fingers to see his taunting smile. "Seasick?" he snorted. "Really, lass? That was the best you could come up with?"

She shrugged, her grin sheepish. "Hey, it worked, didn't it?"

"Aye, though how it did, I'll never know. You're a right awful liar, you are. Which is a proper good thing for me, I s'pose." Shaking his head with a smile, he gestured down the length of the boat deck. "Well? I do believe I was promised some tea, Miss Bailey, and I don't think you should keep your superior officer waiting any longer."

"I changed my mind, actually." Esther smirked as she tried to mimic his accent. "How about a wee pot o' coffee, aye, lad?"

Murdoch shot her a look between scorn and amusement. "Is that an attempt at Scottish," he said dryly, "or are you simply having a stroke?"

"Oh, come on!" she chuckled. "It wasn't *that* bad, was it?"

"It was decent, aye, for someone recovering from extensive brain damage—"

Esther burst out laughing, startling a handful of passing crewmen. But she paid little notice to their alarm, clutching the rail as she doubled over. "Oh, shut it!" she managed to choke out. "Now come on, you ol' curmudgeon. Let's get some coffee before we freeze our asses off."

Murdoch winced, no doubt thinking of the liquid he compared to motor oil. "Tea," he insisted. "And yes, that's an order, in case you were wondering." The look in his eyes was dead serious—disturbed, almost— and it sent Esther into a fit of hysterics once again.

They fell into step together as they strolled aft, walking leisurely, simply enjoying each other's company. Esther wished she could hold his hand, but the reality of their divided ranks made her banish the thought entirely. Winds cold as ice crept over them, clearing the boat deck once again as passengers sought the warmth of *Titanic*'s glittering labyrinth of cabins and corridors. Murdoch's nose had begun to redden in the chill, turning the same shade as a ripened tomato, and Esther teased him about it the entire way, grinning at his half-amused scowl.

She was still taunting him by the time they reached the mess hall tucked away on the other end of the ship. Murdoch reached for the door, but his gloved hand barely grazed its handle before Esther softly spoke.

"Will…wait."

He studied her curiously as she led him away from the mess and toward the nearest row of lifeboats. Esther waited until two chatting crewmen passed before leaning in close to Murdoch with a whisper.

"I've given it some thought," she said, "and I really think you should accept the chief officer position aboard the *Olympic*."

Murdoch stared at her in utter bewilderment, brows arching as high as they could go. "Lass…don't take this the wrong way or anything…but I think you've gone 'round the bend."

She laughed, beaming at him. "I haven't! Look, think about it. I could speak with Smith or even with my uncle to request a transfer along with you. If we convinced them how complementary our work is, they might consider extending my apprenticeship. You never know, right?"

Murdoch studied her for a long moment, head tilted to one side, warmth flooding the depths of his eyes. And when he finally spoke, his scratchy, Scottish burr was soft in her ear.

"It's certainly worth a try," he told her. "But I'll be honest, Esther. You should know I don't give a damn which ship I work, or what rank I have, so long as I'm with you."

His fingertips brushed hers. It was a quiet gesture—subtle in a way that no passing soul would take notice of it, but intimate enough to make her heart beat faster.

No other words were said between the two officers. They stayed together on the boat deck for a long while, their tea forgotten, marveling at the ocean spread before them until the last gleam of daylight faded along the horizon.

TWENTY

THE ICEBERG

April 14, 1912 | 20:15

A S MURDOCH SAT in the smoking room hours later, forced to endure a rather trying game of poker before the start of his nightly watch, he found himself fighting an internal battle to keep from staring at Bailey.

She was sitting on his left, transfixed on the spread of cards in her hand, her green eyes glinting with a challenge. Murdoch was amused; he had never seen this competitive edge to her before. Hell, he hadn't even known she could play poker until tonight.

But despite her obvious determination to win, Bailey was still good-natured, chatting and laughing with her opponents as they traded crude jokes and tongue-in-cheek remarks.

The atmosphere was lively, the table obscured beneath a clutter of cigarette butts, pound notes, shillings, teacups, and platters of crackers and fine cheeses. Smoke coiled from the heady cigar at the corner of Wilde's mouth, lending the room a dim gray haze. Pitman smirked at the hand he'd been dealt, while Lowe sipped from a bottle of ale at his side. And although Murdoch enjoyed the company of his fellow officers, he considered poker to be something of a bore. He was only here for Bailey, and had she not asked him to come along, he would have steered well clear from the smoking room.

As the game stretched on, Murdoch tried to focus on the cards splayed in his hands. But his thoughts were elsewhere, swirling around his head like the swells of choppy seas.

He couldn't stop thinking of the intimacy he and Bailey shared earlier, hidden away in the privacy of his cabin. The way she'd gasped and writhed beneath his hands. How wonderfully tight she had felt against him. How quickly she'd managed to come when he'd shagged her hard and whispered her name. Murdoch was longing for more—was yearning to be with her once again.

But he wanted those softer, quieter moments, too, when he'd twined his legs with hers and kissed her scars and played with her hair. And when they had both let their guards down, laughing and joking around in the bath. It was surreal to think he and Bailey finally reached this point, working past all their animosities and differences to wind up together.

This certainly wasn't going to be easy, of course. Murdoch knew the risks they were taking, sneaking around and sharing themselves behind locked doors. He knew they could be sacked at any moment.

But as he sat beside Bailey in the smoking room, watching her laugh and curse and shoot him sly glances from time to time, he knew she was worth it all. She was worth everything.

He watched her take a hasty swig of tea, a little wrinkle between her brows as she scowled at her cards. Then Murdoch realized he was staring at her again, so he quickly turned his attention back to the game instead. He was beginning to wonder how much longer this would take when Lowe heaved a sigh and slapped his cards down on the table.

"Bloody hell," the fifth officer growled. "That's it. I fold."

"Oh ho," Pitman chuckled. "Color me surprised."

Lowe buried his cigarette butt into an ashtray with a glare. "Sod off, will ya? Not my fault I was dealt a piss-poor hand."

"Sure, blame the cards. You're just piss-poor at poker, if you ask me. Admit it, son. Go on."

"I admit nothing. Only that poker is stupid, and I hope Henry or Esther destroy you to bits."

Wilde flicked his gaze down at his cards, gray eyes glittering with amusement. "My goodness, someone's a bit sore, aren't they?"

Lowe's voice was flat. "Yeah. How'd you guess?"

The chief officer laughed. "See here, lad," he said slyly, "if you're hankering to see Bert get his ass handed to him, I daresay there's a slim chance you might get your wish."

"Be waitin' with bated breath, I will," Lowe grumbled, casting a smug-faced Pitman one last glower.

Murdoch, who was scarcely paying attention, idly placed his cards on the table. Only Pitman, Bailey, and Wilde were left in the game. The chief officer wore a cunning smile, half his face wreathed in clouds of cigar smoke. Pitman shot him a calculating glance before snapping his cards flat on the table, revealing two pair. Bailey smacked her cards down as well, and Murdoch peered closely to see she had a full house.

But then Wilde laid out his hand with a flourish, wrecking the lot of them with a straight flush.

An uproar followed, with Pitman groaning in protest and Lowe snickering at his defeat. Bailey looked just about ready to flip the damn table. Wilde, however, grinned as he scooped his winnings toward him.

"Why, thank you lads. *And* lady," he added with a smirk, sparing an amused glance at Bailey's grouchy face. "I'll be using this for pub money once we make port in New York."

Lowe laughed, looking a great deal more chipper now that Pitman had been bested at poker. "That doesn't sound very officer-like," he said.

"Nonsense." Wilde chuckled around his cigar. "We're free to do as we please once we dock—so long as we're not getting blind drunk or running around with trollops, mind you. That's where the line is drawn, I'm afraid."

"How disappointing," Murdoch said dryly. He'd merely been joking, but Bailey still shot him a look that was half-amused, half-scathing.

Wilde barked with laughter at her expression before turning back to Lowe. "Dropping into a pub once a night to have a drink or two isn't much of an issue," he reasoned. "In fact, there's a charming little spot in Lower Manhattan I've frequented during my stays. Has a decent view of the Hudson. Damn good frankfurters, hamburgers—everything you can imagine. And the barmaids aren't bad-looking either, if I do say so myself…"

Lowe grinned. "Well, now I'm intrigued." But his smile faded when he stole a glance at Bailey, and he changed the subject at once. "What's it like, anyway? New York, I mean."

"You never been?" Pitman looked astounded.

"Nah." Lowe shook his head. "First time across the pond, remember? I've never set foot on American soil in all my life."

"Consider that a blessing, lad," Murdoch remarked, and Bailey looked at him once again, only this time with a glare that amused him. "What?"

Wilde snorted. "Oh, don't bother listening to Will. New York's not too shabby. Tall buildings, busy streets, excellent food. And the Statue of Liberty's a fair sight to see, too." Grinning at Bailey, he added, "But the Americans could stand to learn some manners, I reckon. Rude, loud, quick-talking heathens, the lot of 'em."

"Gee, thanks for the glowing praise, Mr. Wilde," Bailey said flatly.

He smirked, tobacco smoke cascading from the edge of his crooked mouth. "Not a problem, miss."

Pitman yawned. "Well, Americans aside, at least we'll be docked in New York soon enough, eh? Three more days to go."

"True." Wilde nodded, brushing a spot of tobacco off his coat. "What's the first thing you lot'll do when we reach shore?" he asked around the table.

"Wouldn't mind visiting that pub you were going on about," Lowe admitted.

Pitman looked thoughtful as he snapped a lighter against the tip of his cigarette. "I second that. Could do with a nice pint. Or two. Or three."

"I'll likely look around for something new to read with my brother," Bailey said. "He's fond of this little hole-in-the-wall bookshop in Midtown. We try and go there whenever we're in the city."

Wilde finally turned to Murdoch. "And what of you, William, darling? What are your plans once we make berth?"

Murdoch's voice was wry. "Besides drown m'self in Scotch and count the days till we're back on the open sea, you mean?"

"Oh, very funny. Perhaps you'll join us for a drink, then?"

"Possibly," Murdoch replied.

But the first officer already had a plan in mind—one he'd been mulling over for the last hour, in fact. Once in New York, he would rent a room at one of the finest hotels in the city, either the Plaza or the Waldorf Astoria, where he and Bailey could be alone together. There would be nothing to trouble them. No need to worry about being seen or overheard. They could spend the afternoons and late evenings together, tangling themselves in the sheets, dozing peacefully and ordering room service to their door. It would be out of the question to spend the night at the hotel, of course. Officers were expected to keep their quarters aboard the ship whenever in port, and they would only arouse suspicion if the pair of them were missing throughout the night.

But there were still plenty of hours for them to fill during the day. Plenty of time to make love again and again, tucked away in their own quiet haven before heading out to sea once more.

The thought cheered him, and he was glad when the officers finally disbanded from the smoking room, yawning and heading off for a kip. Murdoch remained seated, however, nodding at Bailey to do the same. Wilde looked between them with mild amusement as he tugged on his coat.

"Have a lovely watch tonight," he said with a smirk. "See the pair of you at two o'clock, dark n' early as always."

Casting a subtle wink over one shoulder, Wilde followed his colleagues out the door. Glad to be alone at last, Murdoch reached for Bailey's hand and laced their fingers together.

"Well?" he said cheerfully, regarding her with amusement. "Did you enjoy losing, then?"

The scowl on her face made him chuckle. "Oh, be quiet," she grumbled. "I think you seem to be forgetting that you lost, too."

"Aye, that I did. But the difference is that I was never really trying in the first place."

She snorted. "Yeah, no kidding. I don't think you even looked at your cards."

"I looked at them," Murdoch insisted. "Once, I think." When she laughed, he tightened his fingers around hers before adding, "I was far too busy planning what to do once we make port. And I have some idea, if you'd like to hear it."

"I would." She looked curious. "Though I take it this means you won't be drowning yourself in Scotch, then?"

Murdoch grinned. "Not exactly." He stole a cautious glance at the door before leaning close to her, cupping the side of her face in his heavy palm. "Was thinking of taking you out for brunch, first and foremost. Going for a walk 'round the beach after. Browsing the shops for a proper world atlas for all your future travels. And renting a room in one of the nicest hotels in the city, just for the two of us."

His lips brushed hers, soft and teasing, and he smiled when he heard her breath hitch. "We wouldn't be able to stay there at night, naturally. But we'd have the entire day and early evening together." He trailed one feather-light finger along her collarbone, enjoying the way she shivered beneath his touch. "We'd book the room in a false name. Arrive in our plainclothes so no one would look twice at us. Tell anyone who asks that we've merely gone sightseeing, perhaps. They'll be so busy exploring New York, I doubt they'll wonder about us, anyhow." His eyes danced across her face, wondering and curious. "What d'you think?"

She beamed at him, the delight on her face enough to warm his heart.

"I think it's a crazy idea, Will," she said. "And I want to do it all with you. I want nothing more."

Her green eyes sparkled as she snagged the lapels of his coat and suddenly yanked him forward, kissing him with all her might. Murdoch felt his heartbeat stumble as their lips met, her mouth so soft and warm against his own. He could feel her emotions cascading through her kiss— the affection, devotion, desire that he so irrevocably echoed back.

It felt like an eternity before they finally broke apart. Her freckled cheeks were full of color, and there was a crafty glint in her eyes as she grinned at him.

"Geez," she remarked slyly, "a hotel room all to ourselves, huh? I can't imagine what we might get up to."

"Sleeping, obviously."

She chuckled at his wry humor. "Okay. That's a given. Anything else?"

Brushing back her hair, Murdoch brought his lips to her ear. "I want to hear you moan, Esther. Properly. We've had to keep quiet here in the cabins, but I think we can afford to be a bit louder in a room of our own."

She was almost breathless. "I—I quite agree."

He nipped her earlobe before moving lower, drinking in her scent of soap and lavender, his breath hot against her neck, her hammering pulse.

"And I wouldn't mind shagging you against the wall, if you'll let me."

The heat between their bodies was a firestorm of its own, and Murdoch could feel his skin blaze as she looked longingly at him, her eyes brimming with a desire he wholly reciprocated.

"Why wait until New York?" she asked, chest heaving, looking about ready to fling herself on him. "Why not now?"

He laughed softly, enjoying her enthusiasm. "Because it's noisy?" he offered. "Because I won't be able to control myself once we start? And because our watch starts in fifteen bleedin' minutes?"

Smirking a little, Bailey crossed the length of the smoking room and snapped the lock shut. She walked back to the table, but instead of taking her chair, she clambered onto his lap. Murdoch felt his pulse quicken as she mounted him, skirt draping over his legs, her hands roaming across the thick wool of his coat.

"We could be quiet," Bailey reasoned with a grin. "You could keep your composure. And I think we both know fifteen minutes is more than enough time for us to finish."

She ground her hips against his, her smile wicked, and Murdoch inhaled a sharp breath, eyes rolling back as the blood rushed straight to his groin.

Though his head was spinning, swimming with lust and her smell of lavender, he tried to weigh their situation logically and rationally. The door was locked tight. Any remaining officers who were off-duty had already retired for the night. And the chance of being overheard was next to none, given the low hum of the engines and the distance from the rest of the cabins.

A wiser man might have refused and shown proper restraint, of course. But Murdoch wasn't in the mood for being very wise. Bailey drove him wild, and the thrill of having her right here and right now was all too enticing. He needed to kiss her, to touch her, to be inside her once again.

Murdoch watched her rise to her feet before he stood along with her, catching her face between his palms and pressing his lips roughly against hers. His kiss was hard and deep, full of an insatiable need as he eased her across the room.

Neither of them had regard for their surroundings as they went, stumbling and banging into furniture until Murdoch pressed her up against the nearest bulkhead—right where he wanted her.

There was little time to tease and explore, not with their watch hanging over their heads. Thus they were quick, clumsy and urgent, not even bothering to remove clothing besides hiking up Bailey's skirt and yanking down her hosiery and undergarments. Murdoch simply undid the button of his trousers, and he bit back a groan as she took him in her hands, caressing and stroking him until he was fully hard.

Self-control shattered, he snagged one of her wrists and slammed it against the wall above her head, pinning it in place. His other hand slipped up her skirt and between her thighs, and a rasp of satisfaction escaped his lips when he found the wetness already waiting for him. His fingers worked her, caressing and teasing and swirling in slow, lazy circles.

"Christ, lass," he sighed in between kisses against her throat. "You're so wet…"

Murdoch wanted to keep touching her like this, but the minutes were ticking by. He wasted no time in hoisting her up against the white wall behind them, supporting her thighs with strong hands while she hooked her legs around his hips. Her hand slipped downward, guiding him inside her, and Murdoch was overcome with pleasure as he felt her stretch around him, the feel of her hot and tight, the sound of her gasp soft and breathless against his ear.

It took them a moment to get comfortable as he shifted his grip, and she had to adjust herself to accommodate the thickness of him. But his lips soon found hers, and not once did their kiss break as he thrust into her, his hands bracing her against the smooth wall behind them. Murdoch wasn't rough or hard; there would be other times for that. For now, all he cared about was this—this feeling of closeness and togetherness, of a connection he had never felt with any other woman before.

She was *his*, and he was hers. And no ranking or bloody policy could ever change that.

While her wiry frame was easy for Murdoch to hold up, there was still a dull, expected ache in his muscles after a while, threatening to tire him. But it was a small price to pay as he pounded into her again and again, holding her close in his arms, longing for her to come for him.

She finally broke their kiss to beg him not to stop, the words coming up in short, strangled gasps against his ear. And the more he gave, the more his control began to slip, that former restraint yielding to senseless desire entirely.

His pace quickened, every deep thrust sending the clock and coat hooks rattling against the wall. They were bordering on being too loud between the uncontrollable pitch of her moans, and the sound of his hips meeting hers.

But Murdoch couldn't find any reason to care. Not now, when he was heedless of anything but her. He loved the flush in her freckled cheeks. The sound of her breathing. The way she gripped his tie between her fingers, clenching it like a tether.

Murdoch lifted her higher, his nails digging into her thighs, and a sudden whimper fell from her lips as her orgasm overtook her.

She came harder than he'd ever felt, and he nearly swore aloud. He could feel her tighten around him—could feel her bite down on his shoulder to keep quiet. It was enough to make him come as well, and he held her tighter in his hands, his kisses soft and tender, the release a ridiculously strong wave crashing over him before tapering away into a ripple.

They were breathing heavily as they righted themselves and cleaned up, snagging fresh towels from the pantry. Murdoch rebuttoned his trousers, watching her with a mesmerized look on his face as she pulled on her undergarments and tugged down her skirt.

"Jesus, Will," she panted through a laugh, breathless. There was a wily gleam in her eyes. A glow to her freckled skin. She looked wholly radiant, even standing there with her hair mussed, tie crooked, and face flushed. "See? That wasn't so difficult. It was incredible, in fact. And we still have another five, er—" She stole a glance at the now-lopsided clock hanging on the wall. "—four minutes before we're expected on the bridge."

Murdoch straightened his tie and then hers, shaking his head at her with amusement.

"You're a bad influence. You know that?"

She bellowed with laughter. "As if you're any better. You're supposed to be my mentor, after all. *Sir.*"

He laughed sheepishly as he swept his cap back on his head. "I suppose I'm not doing the best job of it, am I?"

There was a short pause as Bailey quietly stood on tiptoe, closing the distance between them, and Murdoch felt his heart stutter as she cradled his jaw with one tender hand.

"On the contrary, Will," she said, her voice soft, "you're doing wonderfully."

She looked as if she wanted to say something more. But Murdoch swept her into his arms, chin resting on top of her hair, merely holding her close as he realized this was the happiest he'd been in twenty years.

20:55

The cold was nearly unthinkable as Lightoller kept his post in the port bridge wing, looking out into the watery veil of sea spread before him.

It was almost nine o'clock, and there was an hour left of his watch. Just one more measly *hour*, and then he would make his rounds before sinking into the warmth of his bed, electric heater cranked on at full blast.

It was a jolly thought, enough to make the chill somewhat bearable as Lightoller faced the unnaturally calm stretch of sea.

He tried not to think of earlier, when he'd woken from his nap to fetch a drink of water and had heard an unmistakable noise in the cabin next to his. Murdoch's cabin. It had been the sound of a creaking mattress and a sequence of muffled thumps, and it hadn't taken Lightoller more than half a second to put two and two together.

Murdoch must have sorted everything out with Miss Bailey, and it was clear that the pair of them were closer than ever. Lightoller was glad for this; he knew how much his friend cared for the girl, after all. But even he couldn't deny the slight rush of envy, knowing Murdoch was shagging in the cabin right beside his while Sylvia was still an ocean away.

The lucky bastard, he thought to himself. *Lucky, but still daft...*

A door snapped open behind him, and he glanced down the length of the bridge wing to see the captain emerging from the wheelhouse, teacup and saucer in hand. Lightoller was surprised to see him; Smith had been away for most of the night, attending a first-class dinner party in honor of his maritime achievements before retirement. But perhaps he'd wanted to retire early from the celebrations, seeking the muted calm of the bridge instead.

The second officer watched Smith stroll to windows, peering out at the still, black ocean nearly smoother than a millpond. Lightoller had never seen it so flat, in all his years at sea. He flexed his gloved hands, which were chilled and stiff with cold, and made to join his captain.

The bridge was quiet, save for the distant rumble of storming water, and the echo of engines murmuring deep beneath him. Lightoller stole a cursory glance into the wheelhouse as he passed, watching Moody pull open the binnacle lid in a blaze of gold light, Boxhall at his side.

All was calm and quiet, just as it should be.

Lightoller approached Smith in an unhurried manner, hands held smartly behind his back, footsteps soft on the pine decking beneath him.

"Cold, isn't it?" Smith remarked, as Lightoller stepped to his side.

"Yes," Lightoller agreed. "Very cold, sir. Only one degree above freezing, in fact. I've already sent word to the carpenter and the engine room."

"Good." Smith nodded with approval, twirling his spoon in his tea. "Haven't seen weather this clear in quite some time."

A faint, wondering smile tugged at the corner of Lightoller's mouth.

"Nor have I," the second officer said. He tilted his head to one side, blue eyes curiously studying the sheet of dark, motionless water. "Come to think of it, I don't believe I've ever seen such a flat calm."

"A flat calm," Smith echoed thoughtfully.

"Yes, sir. Quite flat."

"Like a sheet of glass, almost." Smith chuckled at the comparison. "Not a breath of wind to speak of."

An unpleasant notion occurred to Lightoller as he weighed his captain's words. Without wind, there would be no waves foaming and rippling along any ice in their path. It would make the icebergs all the more undetectable, when darkness already hindered their visibility.

Pity the breeze hasn't kept up, he thought to himself. Turning to Smith, Lightoller decided to voice his concerns.

"Little wind will make the bergs harder to see," he reminded the captain, "with no breaking waves at the base."

Smith hummed in a contemplative manner, glancing down at his tea and shifting his spoon around with a few *clinks*. Lightoller watched him with equal quiet, expecting his captain to decrease speed as a measure of caution, perhaps. So it came as some surprise when Smith merely asked, "Even without wind, surely we have enough indicators to recognize the ice?"

He had a point, admittedly enough. There was nary a whiff of sea fog or haze in the sky, and they could clearly see the stars rising and setting along the horizon. But the captain did not seem too troubled, so Lightoller let his misgivings slip from his mind.

"I'd say so," he replied. "In any case, there will still be a certain amount of light reflected from the bergs. That will give us ample warning, I imagine, even if the berg shows its blue side."

Smith nodded, looking satisfied. "Very good. Maintain speed and heading, Mr. Lightoller. But should anything become in the slightest degree doubtful, let me know at once. I shall be just inside."

Lightoller could do little more than salute and acknowledge the order. "Yes, sir."

21:05

There was something oddly thrilling about reporting for duty with Bailey, Murdoch thought, after making love only moments ago.

The first officer was in a pleasant mood as he stood within the wheelhouse, listening to Lightoller's briefing about the clear weather, the peculiarly calm sea, and other minutiae regarding the previous watch. *Titanic* was holding steady, it seemed, with little to no vibration. They were expected to maintain speed and heading as per Smith's order, steering a course north of seventy-one degrees west.

As the topic turned to bergs, Murdoch decided to send Bailey along to the wireless room to check for any recent ice reports. She flashed him a pretty smile before stepping down the hall, and Murdoch, who was staring after her retreating back longer than he should have, turned when Lightoller cleared his throat.

"Looks as if the two of you had a pleasant evening, then."

"Haven't the faintest idea what you're talking about," Murdoch said cheerfully.

Lightoller snorted. "Oh? Because your crooked tie and red face certainly say otherwise."

"I was exercising," Murdoch lied, while Lightoller regarded him with amusement. "In a manner of speaking," he added.

Before his colleague could say anything else, Boxhall passed through the wheelhouse door, and Murdoch felt a glacial rush of air chill him through his greatcoat. "It's pretty cold," he remarked, surprised.

Lightoller nodded. "Yes, it's freezing." He peered out at the frozen darkness before them, a curiosity to his eyes. "Seems an ice field is near."

"Oh, good," Murdoch said dryly. "Something to look forward to."

"Indeed," Lightoller laughed. "I can sense your enthusiasm already, Will." Gesturing toward the door behind him, he added, "If the wireless report is correct, we should come upon the ice around eleven o'clock, I suppose. The captain said to wake him if there's any issue."

Murdoch nodded as they strolled out onto the bridge, leaving the warmth of the wheelhouse behind them.

"Did you ever happen to find the binoculars for the lookouts?" he asked idly, gloved hands adjusting the lapels of his greatcoat to shield his neck from the bitter cold.

"I'm afraid I didn't," Lightoller replied. "Seems they've been missing since Southampton."

Murdoch felt a twinge of annoyance as he stepped up on the raised platform running along the bridge wing, frowning out at the sea. How the binoculars vanished during the short course of their journey was a mystery to him—but it was even more absurd to think they had yet to be found. Murdoch didn't like being without them during times of smooth seas. It would make icebergs all the more difficult to spot, when already they were working against the clear weather and the darkness of the cold Atlantic night. There wasn't even a hint of definition between the horizon, the sea, and the sky—just a wall of deep, endless blue-black.

Lightoller, however, did not seem too troubled as he started across the bridge; perhaps fatigue and cold had begun to catch up with him.

"Well, I'm off to take my rounds," his colleague drawled, sweeping one hand through the air in farewell. "Have a good watch with Miss Bailey. Cheerio."

With a nod, Murdoch turned back to face the bow, propping his elbows up on the wood of the bridge wing rail. He wasn't sure how much time passed before the sound of footsteps made him turn, and his heart leaped when he saw Bailey strolling out of the wheelhouse to join him.

"Nothing new to report, sir," she said, her breath misting the air before her lips. "Mr. Phillips said there was a brief ice warning from the SS *Mesaba* around nine-thirty, but I believe Lightoller addressed it."

binoculars and it's black as pitch out there."

She shot him a confident smile, hiking herself up on the bridge
platform to stand beside him. "Very well, sir. I'd be happy to oblige."

The brutal chill became little more than a distant memory as
Murdoch kept watch with Bailey for the next hour and a half, their gazes
fixed upon the sea, their elbows brushing through their coats. He was cold,
of course—so was she, judging by the slight shake of her shoulders. But
despite the miserable weather, there was something about tonight that
made Murdoch happy to be alive. The stars, the sea, the remarkable girl
at his side—all of it brought him a contentment he had never known
before. He couldn't ever remember being so at peace.

At length, something glimmered in the corner of his eye, and
Murdoch turned to see tiny motes of white blustering around the deck.
Thinner than mist, they caught the deck lights with brilliant prisms of
color. Bailey stared at the wisps in utter astonishment, mouth wide open,
watching them shimmer through the air.

"What are they, sir?" she asked excitedly.

"Splinters of ice from nearby floes." Murdoch smiled, liking her

342

curious, bright-eyed enthusiasm. "Or 'whiskers 'round the light,' as the crew calls them. We get them whenever the temperature drops."

"They're beautiful…" she murmured, her voice soft. "And cold!" she added with a yelp, wrinkling her nose as the glittering particles swept against her face. "Jesus shit."

Murdoch swallowed hard, desperately trying to hold back his laughter. But the crew were within earshot, and he forced himself to reprimand her.

"Language, Miss Bailey."

"Right." She looked sheepish. "Sorry, sir."

They spent several moments admiring the iridescent wisps of ice, watching them glisten between the diamond stars and deep, abyssal ocean. Once Moody disappeared to fetch a cup of tea, Bailey finally spoke, her voice barely audible over the wind and sea spray.

"I wish I could stay the night with you, sir."

Murdoch saw the disappointment in her eyes—which likely mirrored his own—and he sighed, "I know, lass. I'd like nothing more than to fall asleep beside you. Trust me. But we both know how risky that would be. Even I wouldn't push that boundary, I'm afraid."

"Neither would I," she said, and Murdoch snorted.

"*Really*, now? Given your boldness in the smoking room, I somehow find that very hard to believe."

Bailey bit her lip, clearly holding back laughter. "Listen, I know I'm rash, but I'm not that rash. I can certainly hold off until New York." When Murdoch arched one disbelieving eyebrow, she insisted, "I can! It gives me something else to look forward to, Will, among the many other marvelous things you have planned for us in the city." She smiled shyly at him, her cheeks suddenly pink. "I simply cannot wait."

Murdoch felt her fingers gently brush the back of his knuckle, and he closed his eyes, longing to feel the warmth of her skin and wishing the leather of their gloves wasn't between them—

A door snapped open, making them start.

Pulling away from Bailey at once, Murdoch glanced down into the forward well deck to see two people sneaking their way out of the third-class passage. He was surprised to see Harold Bride—whom he'd thought had retired to his cabin for the night—walking hand in hand with a female passenger. The young woman looked familiar to Murdoch, though he couldn't quite put his finger on where he might have seen her before. She wore a weightless gown that flowed from her frame in a waterfall of pastel blues and lavenders, and he watched her and Bride slip beneath the shadow of a cargo crane. There, the young wireless operator pulled a thick cigar from his jacket, and they passed it back and forth, with the woman taking surprisingly deep drags that made her and Bride laugh between fits of coughs and clouds of smoke.

Bailey spoke up from Murdoch's side, a wide grin spreading across her face. "What are they doing here?"

"Was just wondering that m'self," Murdoch remarked with mild interest. "You know that woman, I take it?"

"Yes, and so do you! That's Miss Fay Harlow. The woman who nearly fell overboard a few nights ago, remember?"

"Isn't she engaged to—?" Murdoch started to say. But he stopped when he looked down into the well deck and saw the young couple kissing passionately, the cigar long-forgotten between them. "Never mind," he chuckled. "I suppose that answers the question well enough." Amused, Murdoch turned away from the bow to smile at Bailey now, his gaze dancing across her freckled face. "They've the right idea. No better way to stay well warm in this dreadful weather, if you ask me."

"Perhaps I can warm you up later then?" she offered with a clever grin.

Murdoch didn't respond immediately. He gazed at Bailey instead, captivated by her, wondering how a person could have eyes so green. Pale and light, like shallow seawater. They were utterly remarkable.

When he answered her, his voice was soft.

"Perhaps," he murmured, resisting the urge to cup her face with his hands and kiss her right then and there.

Clang. Clang. Clang.

The warning bell from the crow's nest rang out through the night, splitting the stillness of the briny air.

Three tolls, he realized. The mark of danger ahead.

Whirling around, Murdoch stole a sharp glance up at the crow's nest before squinting out into the night. His hands clenched the rail as he searched the sea, scouring for the faintest sign of trouble. But he could see nothing—just a plane of impenetrable darkness and starry sky.

Bailey spoke uneasily at his side. "I can't see a thing," she whispered. "Can you, sir?"

Murdoch was about to reply when the ring of a telephone pealed shrilly in the distance. Bailey started for the wheelhouse, but Moody was already on the move; he strolled to the telephone with an unhurried stride, carrying a cup of tea in one hand and snapping up the telephone earpiece with the other. Murdoch turned back to the horizon, eyes narrowed against the salt and the chill, seeking whatever danger lay ahead.

Then he saw it, and the blood rushed cold in his veins.

An iceberg loomed out of the deep night, rising up from the blackness of the glass-smoothed sea.

It was a monstrous thing—a glistening mountain of sleek, blue-gray ice that suddenly appeared from nowhere.

And they were heading straight for it.

It took Murdoch less than a single logical second to realize what had to be done. What he had no choice but to do.

And in that one gut-wrenching moment, as he quickly weighed the speed of the *Titanic* and her distance to the berg, he knew they would have to maneuver around it.

That was his decision. That was it.

No questions, no doubts, no hesitations in his mind.

He didn't even look twice at Bailey as he barreled across the bridge toward the wheelhouse, swallowing back his shock and clinging to pure instinct instead.

Moody burst from the door as he arrived, eyes wild, teacup hanging haphazardly from one hand.

"Iceberg, right ahead!"

But Murdoch scarcely heard or even noticed him as he braced one hand against the wall and bellowed the order into the wheelhouse.

"*Hard-a-starboard!*"

"Hard-a-starboard!" Moody echoed his shout, and Quartermaster Hichens threw his weight into the wheel, hands scrambling from one wood handle to the next.

Murdoch hurtled to the bridge, slamming into Moody's arm and splattering the contents of his tea in a spray of milky amber. But the first officer paid no notice, blind to anything but the danger ahead of them.

He rushed to the port engine telegraph first, and bells trilled within its frame as he clenched the lever and yanked it to *Stop* and *Full Astern*.

Behind him, Moody called out to Hichens again.

"Turn! Turn! Smartly!"

Blood roared in his ears as Murdoch sprinted to the main engine telegraph and wrenched it with all his might, sending another burst of bells jangling across the bridge. Behind him, Moody hollered from the wheelhouse.

"Helm's hard over, sir!"

Sweating and winded, Murdoch sped back to the bridge with his pulse thundering in his chest. He could see the iceberg draw even nearer, its size enough to make Bailey curse somewhere behind him. But Murdoch couldn't even look at her. He spared another quick, urgent glance at the telegraphs, double-checking that their levers were fixed on *Full Astern*. Panic crackled underneath his composure, and he clenched his jaw, praying the engine crew would receive the orders in time—

Gradually, blessedly, *Titanic* began to slow beneath him. But she was still drifting straight toward the berg, bow pointed straight for its icy mass.

Murdoch could see starlight smoothing the crest of the berg now. He could see every ridge and crevice and cold, sharp edge stretching before him. Far below, a seaman hurried to the bow of the ship to watch for a collision, and Murdoch clenched the rail with a death grip, shoulders heaving as he fought for breath.

"Come on..." he whispered, blue eyes blazing with focused calm, never once looking away. "That's it....that's it, come on...*turn*..."

It felt like an eternity before the bow eased toward port, slowly but surely steering clear of the perilous tower of ice.

Murdoch held his breath, a shred of hope flaring in his chest.

Perhaps they could make it out of this. Perhaps they could avoid this mishap and continue onward without a scratch.

But then the bow dipped beneath the shadow of the iceberg, pooling the forecastle deck in darkness.

Too close. Much too close.

Murdoch could already see the porthole lights shimmering upon its smoothed surface. Down at the bow, the seaman raced away as the wall of ice descended upon them.

And in the few breathless seconds that followed, Murdoch felt it—a shuddering jar as *Titanic* made impact.

There was a muffled, grinding, sickening crunch of metal as her hull tore along the berg, deep beneath the water but still loud enough for all to hear. The sound was chilling, but it was nothing compared to the violent wrench that rumbled down the length of the ship, shaking the floor beneath their feet. Murdoch clenched the rail as it rattled and trembled beneath his hand, and horror flooded every inch of him as he watched the berg drift past, lamplight glistening across its wet, icy surface.

He spared a single glance at Bailey—her face pale-white as she braced herself against the nearest wall—before realizing what he had to do.

Clear the stern. Clear the stern. Clear the stern.

The words were branded in his head, clanging through his thoughts again and again—

Wheeling around, Murdoch swept his arm through the air and hoarsely bellowed the order aloud.

"*Hard-a-port!*"

Trusting Moody to repeat the order and Hichens to fulfill the maneuver, Murdoch spun back around to see a chunk of grayish-blue ice snapping from the slope of the berg. It crumbled and exploded into scattered pieces along the well deck, icy fragments glittering across damp wood.

A deathly silence filled the bridge as the rumbling stopped, and the berg drifted out of sight. But Murdoch knew it wasn't over yet. He headed straight for the wheelhouse, thinking only of the flooding below decks— of the icy seawater likely pouring through buckled sheets of metal and popped rivets, swallowing all in its path.

Rushing past Moody to the wheelhouse, Murdoch slammed his hands against the wall to fling himself inside. He went straight to the Watertight Door Indicator Panel and threw the lever. Alarm bells chimed as each tiny white light popped on, and Murdoch waited until every compartment was sealed and illuminated before slowly, shakily turning around.

His face was pale beneath a sheen of cold sweat, his eyes flickering across the bridge. The silence was deafening. Agonizing, almost. Murdoch couldn't even look at Bailey, who hovered at the wheelhouse door.

"Note the time," he ordered of Moody, fighting to keep his voice steady. "Enter it in the log."

Silently Moody obeyed, stealing an uneasy glance up at the brass clock before crossing to the logbook. *11:40,* the numbers read.

Boxhall emerged from the chart room in a scramble of hasty footsteps, a questioning look in his eyes.

"Will," he started to say. "What—?"

But the words were silenced when a door snapped open, flooding the wheelhouse with light.

Everyone turned to see Smith emerging from his quarters. He was in a state of undress, tie hanging loose and waistcoat unbuttoned. Although his expression was controlled, there was a steely tenseness to his eyes as he swept a passing gaze over the bridge and the wheelhouse.

"What have we struck, Mr. Murdoch?" he demanded.

It took Murdoch a moment to find words—to deliver an answer without hearing the quaver in his voice.

"An iceberg, sir."

The captain looked starboard immediately, a shadow of wordless shock crossing his features, but Murdoch found his bearings as he went on, "I put her hard-a-starboard and ran the engines full astern, but it was too close." He inhaled a sharp breath, suddenly clammy beneath all the sweat. "I tried to port 'round it, but she hit before I—"

But Smith was already striding out to the bridge.

"Are the watertight doors closed?"

Murdoch followed quickly, Bailey and Boxhall trailing at his heels. "The watertight doors are closed, sir."

Smith didn't even look twice at his first officer as he crossed to the starboard bridge wing. Murdoch and Bailey hovered in silence behind him, watching their captain lean over the bulwark to inspect the hull for visible damage. He moved to the rail overlooking the forward well deck next, Murdoch rushing to his side, and together they surveyed the chunks of ice littering the wood below.

"Find the carpenter," Smith told Murdoch, the authority sharp in his voice. "Get him to sound the ship." His eyes lingered on Bailey, and he added, "You'd best find your brother and Mr. Andrews as well."

Both Murdoch and Bailey answered without hesitation.

"*Yes, sir!*"

They fell into step together, the two of them stunned into silence. Murdoch knew Bailey was watching him, but he couldn't bring himself to look at her. His thoughts were broken and scattered, unraveling apart. This was the end of his maritime career as he knew it. Murdoch would never become a captain, and it would be a bloody miracle if White Star Line kept him on after such a blunder.

But a ruined career and a loss of captaincy meant nothing, absolutely nothing, compared to the casualties his foolish actions might have caused.

Christ in Heaven, Murdoch thought, gritting his teeth as the self-loathing tunneled through him.

What had he done?

In those few, crucial seconds when Murdoch had first registered the danger ahead, he had acted on immediate instinct. He'd thought an evasive maneuver was their best possible course of action. There had been so little time to decide otherwise.

But his decision had clearly been a mistake.

Titanic had struck an iceberg. Her starboard hull was no doubt breached, and he was certain the stokers below decks were either drowning or swimming for their lives. Murdoch could only pray that the watertight doors would hold, keeping the seawater from rising any farther so no one else would perish from his folly.

If only I had done something differently, he thought, over and over again.

Murdoch could not stop lamenting what he had done. Bitterness swirled and stormed inside him, wreaking havoc along the edge of his nerves. And although he remained carefully composed on the outside, he could feel something else buried deep inside him, lingering beneath the layers of shock and self-hatred. It was raw and agonizing, sinking into his chest like the blade of a knife, and it didn't take him long to realize what it was.

Guilt.

TWENTY-ONE

PROMISE

April 15, 1912 | 00:10

ESTHER WAS IN a state of shock, but it was nothing compared to the state of the Scotsman at her side.

Murdoch seemed to have settled since the initial collision; he was no longer visibly shaking, for one thing, and the cold sweat at his temples was gone. But there was still a distance about him, made all the more apparent by his stiff expression and impassive eyes. His stride was brisk as they headed aft, locked in a tense silence with the sound of their footsteps echoing between them.

Esther couldn't fathom what he was thinking. All she knew was that it wasn't his fault. None of them had seen the berg until the last minute. And by then, it was too late. Murdoch only had seconds to react, and he had responded to the best of his ability. Not a single sailor or honest captain could have done better.

Esther wanted to tell him this, but Murdoch was hurrying faster now, his greatcoat snapping at his heels. She tried to speak his name, but the words came out cracked, catching in her throat. So she tried again.

"Will…"

His pace quickened; he didn't even look at her. Esther grasped his arm with more insistence this time, tugging him to a halt. "*Will!*"

Their eyes met, and the edge in his voice was unmistakable as he said, "Not now, lass. You heard the captain. Go and find Mr. Andrews."

He started down the boat deck without another word, disappearing down the nearest stairwell.

Esther almost considered running after him. But she knew there would be plenty of time to speak with him later—to quell the flicker of blame in his eyes. So she headed off in the opposite direction, making her way to the cabins tucked away on A Deck and praying she would find Andrews there.

She was just swinging open the door to the aft Grand Staircase when two men came barreling out of it, and Esther suddenly found herself standing before her brother and Thomas Andrews. The pair of them were armed to the teeth with rolled blueprints and charts, their clothes slightly mussed, as if they had hastily bolted their way above decks.

"Esther, what's—?" Booker gasped, but the seventh officer only had eyes for Andrews.

"You have to come quickly," she breathed. "The captain sent me to fetch you, sir. You're needed on the bridge at once."

Andrews nodded at once, brow furrowed and expression troubled. As the three of them hurried afore and the tall shipwright shuffled his grip on the mountain of blueprints in his hands, he asked, "What has happened?"

Esther drew in a deep breath, cheeks stinging with the cold. "We hit an iceberg, sir," she explained, and the color drained immediately from Andrews' face. "Starboard side. Mr. Murdoch was the Officer of the Watch at the time, and he tried to port around it, but..." She swallowed, recalling the groan of metal scraping across ice, the vicious shudder beneath her feet. "But we didn't make it, sir. It seems it was a glancing blow."

Andrews and Booker exchanged glances; Esther could see the uneasiness lingering in their eyes.

"Has Smith called for the carpenter?" Andrews asked urgently.

"He has, sir. They'll be sounding the ship any moment now."

The shipwright began bombarding her with all manner of questions, asking for details about the watertight doors, the maneuver Murdoch had taken, and the size of the berg. Esther answered to the best of her ability, though she knew someone like Murdoch would be far more articulate. She stumbled over her words, trying to keep herself calm. But underneath it all, she couldn't stop the slow crawl of dread seeping into her skin, icier than the Atlantic water rippling beneath *Titanic*'s keel.

By the time they reached the bridge, the ship had slowed to a full and complete stop. It was unsettling, Esther thought, sitting amidst the deep, black ocean without the familiar sounds of hissing seafoam and humming engines. She didn't like it one bit.

Her eyes roved across the deck, seeking Murdoch's face among the tangle of whispering officers and crewmen. But he was nowhere to be seen.

At length, the carpenter appeared to inform them that he had already sounded *Titanic*, and that the mail hold was already taking on water. Wide-eyed and shaky, he left the bridge with Andrews, Smith, and a stone-faced Wilde in tow. Esther stared; she had never seen the chief officer so serious, with his gray eyes narrowed and mouth twisted into a grimace, and she watched him with uncertainty as he passed.

Voices echoed across the forward section of the ship now, as passengers emerged from the belly of *Titanic* to see the damage firsthand. Some chatted and laughed in huddles, others played with the bits of broken ice, kicking and punting the larger pieces across the well deck. A cluster of first-class passengers traded gossip and smoked cigarettes on the promenade below, many of them dripping with jewels and dressed in their eveningwear; one mustached gentleman even held a thick cigar and champagne glass in hand, chortling with his companion as they swapped tales of what had happened.

Esther found it surreal how they could be so at ease while everyone on the bridge was quiet and tense, the apprehension hovering like a thick, icy fog above their heads. But then again, she reasoned, the passengers didn't know the severity of the situation. And neither did the officers, until Smith returned with the damage report. All they could do was roam about and hope for the best until they received further orders.

Booker started for the chart room to deposit his blueprints, asking Esther if she wanted to come along. But she shook her head, preferring to stay on the bridge and wait for Murdoch to reappear. As she loitered near one of the telegraphs, running a palm over its cool brass surface, Moody stepped to her side.

"Good God Almighty," he murmured. "Can you believe this?"

Esther numbly shook her head. "It's like a living nightmare."

Moody nodded, looking ill at ease as he studied the ice sparkling along the well deck, remnants of the danger they failed to miss. "Never seen a berg that big. Come to think of it, I don't believe I've ever seen a *berg*. And I hope to God I never will again."

"Christ, me neither." Distracted, Esther peered into the wheelhouse in search of her superior, and she couldn't help but ask, "You haven't seen Mr. Murdoch anywhere, have you?"

"I believe Smith sent him off to the wireless room to have a word with Mr. Bride and—" But Moody stopped abruptly, adding, "Hang on, miss. Here he comes."

Esther turned, and the tension in her muscles relaxed when Murdoch emerged from the wheelhouse. His expression had been smoothed into one of decisive calm, his blue eyes alert and untroubled. He looked so different compared to the pale, shell-shocked man whose nerves had clearly been rattled following the collision. He had reverted back to the William Murdoch she knew well: cool, steadfast, and professional.

Their gazes met, and Esther started toward him immediately, longing to be near him. But she had barely taken a step forward when Bruce Ismay stormed onto the bridge, smoothing one hand through his thinning hair. He was still wearing his pinstriped pajamas, complete with a pair of maroon carpet slippers and a furred dressing robe. When he spotted Murdoch, he rounded on him at once.

"Why the devil have we stopped?"

"We've struck an iceberg, Mr. Ismay," Murdoch explained calmly.

"An iceberg," Ismay echoed in disbelief. "And you didn't once think to bloody steer around it?"

Murdoch arched a brow. "That is exactly what we did, Mr. Ismay," he said curtly. "Or at least, tried to do."

"I don't understand. How could you not have seen it? You, of all people, Mr. Murdoch." The first officer stiffened, but Ismay paid little notice. His gaze swept across the bridge, dark and accusatory as he appraised the sailors before him.

"I could say the same for the rest of your crew. It's absurd and honest to God embarrassing to think honorable seamen such as yourselves could have allowed something of this magnitude to—"

Esther felt her temper snap, and before she could stop herself—before she could remember her place as an officer of discipline—she was raging at Ismay something fierce.

"It wasn't as if we were aiming for it!" she snapped. "It was an accident, goddammit, and if Mr. Murdoch here hadn't given the order to turn to port, we might have—"

"Miss Bailey." Murdoch spoke quietly; she knew he had no choice but to admonish her. "Enough."

The authority in his voice made Esther fall silent, chest heaving against the folds of her greatcoat. But she was still glaring at Ismay, while he glared right back. She didn't care if her outburst was unseemly. She'd start a fight with anyone who dared to put the blame on Murdoch, White Star Line president be damned.

Her anger faded at the sound of quick, hurried footsteps echoing in the distance, and she wheeled around to see Andrews scrambling up the A Deck Stairwell.

The shipwright's eyes were wild with panic, while his entire forehead shone with a nervous sweat. He hurried to the chart room, Smith and Carpenter Hutchinson at his heels. Murdoch followed, nodding at Esther to join him. They hovered in the doorway, their gloved fingertips brushing as they watched Andrews frantically unfurl one of the larger blueprints and splay it on the desk. While Smith and Hutchinson smoothed it flat with paperweights, Ismay prowled at the back of the room, rambling useless platitudes that no one cared to acknowledge. The atmosphere was tense, and Andrews stole a quick glance at Booker before he shakily spoke.

"Water," he breathed, "fourteen feet above the keel in nearly ten minutes." His hand fell against the sprawling blueprint, indicating the forward starboard hull. "In the forepeak." His fingers skated across the sheet. "In holds one and two. In the mail room. And in boiler room six." He glanced at Hutchinson for confirmation, and when the carpenter nodded mutely, Andrews went on, "She can stay afloat with the first three compartments breached. She can stay afloat with four. But she simply cannot stay afloat with five."

The urgency of his voice was unsettling. Even the captain was deathly still, hanging on the shipwright's every word.

"As she goes down by the head, water will flood over the tops of the bulkheads, overflowing from one compartment to the next." His hand skipped across the deck plans, trailing across the lines of white and bold, solid blue. "Back and back, from E Deck to D Deck and on. The weight of the flooded compartments will drag her down, and down, till she's fully underwater."

"But the pumps will work in our favor, surely," Smith insisted. He was clinging to alternatives, not yet willing to accept the horrifying reality of it all. "If we opened the shell doors—"

But Andrews shook his head. "It's no use, captain. Nothing can be done. The pumps, the watertight doors—they can bide us time, certainly. Minutes, at most. But they will do nothing to stop the inevitable. Come daylight, *Titanic* will be no more. She will founder."

Esther felt the breath catch in her throat. Felt the icy despair pool into every corner and crevice of her being.

She reached out to grasp Murdoch's hand on instinct, no longer caring who saw. His stiff fingers came alive at her touch, and she felt them tighten around hers, clenching hard enough to turn her entire hand numb.

Ismay broke the silence with a snort. "But this ship is unsinkable."

Andrews rounded on him, staring hard at his incredulous expression.

"That is not necessarily so, Mr. Ismay. Surely you're a wise enough man to know that anything of any sort can be deemed unsinkable—unbreakable, unbendable—till the day so comes when it sinks, breaks, and bends. *Titanic* is no different. She's built of iron and steel. Of course she can sink." His grave, pained eyes lingered on Booker as he voiced the truth. "And she will. 'Tis a mathematical certainty."

A heavy silence smothered the room as the chilling realization settled over their heads.

The iceberg had dealt a fatal blow. The gleaming ship beneath their feet would sink to the bottom of the North Atlantic. And God only knew how many people would go down along with it.

Esther exchanged a long, anguished look with her brother before leaning into Murdoch, wishing she could close her eyes and be long gone from this horror. She clenched his hand even tighter when she thought of all those poor *people*—the men, the women, the children who had no idea what was coming—and who might not live to see the light of day. Murdoch must have been thinking the same; he swallowed thickly, standing motionless at her side.

Smith was the first to speak, his murmur filling the stunned quiet. "How much time do we have to evacuate?"

There was a momentary pause as Andrews calculated the figures.

"An hour, perhaps," he answered finally.

Heavy footfalls echoed behind Murdoch as Wilde approached the chart room, surveying their stricken faces with a grimace of his own. But despite being in full view of her chief officer, Esther didn't bother releasing Murdoch's hand. She only gripped it tighter.

"And how many passengers aboard, Mr. Murdoch?" Smith questioned.

Esther spared a glance at the first officer, who quietly replied, "Two thousand, two hundred souls on board, sir."

The emptiness in his voice was enough to break her heart. Murdoch couldn't seem to meet the captain's gaze for more than a second; his eyes were hollow, the gravity of the situation carved deep within them. He clearly understood that not all those souls could be saved. Not with so few lifeboats. Not while they were surrounded by freezing seawater in the dead of night.

Blue eyes piercing, Smith shot Ismay a sharp look before turning to address Murdoch. He was so transfixed with the crisis ahead of them that he didn't even notice his first and seventh officers holding hands. "Call the others in, Mr. Murdoch," he ordered. "Quickly, if you please."

"Aye, sir."

Murdoch left to round up the remaining crew on the bridge, and Esther tried not to feel dismayed when his gloved hand left hers. As she hovered in the doorway in wait of his return, she stole a glance at Booker, who stood with Andrews in the far corner of the chart room. They were speaking in undertones, utterly oblivious to everyone else around them. Booker's hand clenched his mentor's shoulder in reassurance, and Esther was surprised by this familiarity. But before she could think on it any further, Murdoch returned with a handful of deck crew, stepped to her side, and slipped his hand into hers once again.

At length, once they were all packed and huddled inside the chart room, the captain carefully explained the predicament ahead of them: the iceberg, the flooding, the breached compartments—and the one, critical hour they had left to evacuate the sinking ship. Shock spilled across the faces of the crew, but no one dared to speak while Smith continued to voice his crisp orders.

"Our primary task is to ensure the safety of all passengers aboard. They will need to be transferred from the ship and into the lifeboats as quickly as possible."

His eyes lingered on Wilde first, who gazed resolutely back at him, spine straight and chin held high.

"Mr. Wilde, you will gather the deckhands to prepare the davits and uncover the boats," Smith commanded. "Mr. Murdoch, you and Miss Bailey will be responsible for mustering passengers throughout the ship. Have the deck stewards inform those in their charge to assemble on the boat deck immediately. Mr. Boxhall, please wake the rest of our officers. And Mr. Moody, please retrieve the lifeboat assignments from the navigating room. It will have all your respective positions for the boats, whether that be the port or starboard side of the ship. Assemble back here in twenty minutes to review the list and see to your posts at once."

A brief silence fell as the officers internalized their roles and recognized what needed to be done. What they had no choice but to do.

Esther glanced around at them, at the faces of the men she had come to care for—and whom she might never see again. But she tried not to dwell on such a hopelessly grim thought. They were professionals of sheer will and loyalty and conviction. They would make it through this nightmare. And they would save as many lives as they could in the process.

Glancing around the room, Smith addressed his crew once more.

"Another thing, lads—and lady—please ensure that lifebelts are distributed to all. And if any of the crew asks what has happened, you are permitted to answer honestly. But do not give the passengers any reason to panic. We must ensure the evacuation moves as smoothly and as calmly as possible. Is that understood?"

He waited until every person had acknowledged the order with a "Yes, sir" before clearing his throat.

"Very well. Good luck, and may God watch over us all."

And with that, Esther spared Murdoch a single glance before they scattered from the room. Her fear was overwhelming now, but she refused to let it hinder her, knowing deep within her heart that she had to fulfill her duty to her captain, to her crew, and to the first officer at her side.

00:20

Esther could feel her pulse thundering in her chest as she struggled to keep pace with Murdoch, the pair of them threading their way through knots of confused passengers and crew.

The Grand Staircase was bustling with activity, its glistening oak steps hidden beneath a sea of men and women donned in various states of clothing—evening gowns, pajamas, fur coats—even bathrobes. It seemed the collision and its shuddering jar had brought a fair amount of people above decks, curious to see what all the fuss was about.

Esther swallowed as she crossed the magnificent room for the very last time in her life, studying everything from the ornate clock to the glowing glass dome vaulting high above her. She tried not to think of how it would all be crumbled and waterlogged, lost to the depths of the North Atlantic, never to be seen again. It was a sad, terrifying thought.

Crowds milled along the upper and lower balconies, their voices spiraling high to the luminous ceiling, their stares questioning as they watched the two officers pass. But Murdoch was ever the professional, heedless of anything but the deck and first-class stewards as he moved purposefully through the throng.

He was swift, rounding them up and leading them into the quiet seclusion of the nearest crew passage. It was here where he gave the orders to start mustering the passengers, distributing lifebelts to all, and passing along the order to their colleagues. The captain had declared a state of emergency, he explained, and they needed to begin the evacuation as soon as possible. His voice was calm, his blue eyes steady as he met the gaze of every steward and stewardess. But Esther could still sense their uncertainty, and she was not at all surprised when one of the chief stewards spoke.

"We all felt the shudder, Mr. Murdoch. And we've heard rumors of an iceberg." His eyes were intent, beseeching. "How serious is it, sir?"

Murdoch did not answer for a long moment. Esther could see that empty, deadened look in his gaze once more. But it was momentary, and she watched it fade beneath a gleam of ironclad resolve.

"I'll not mince words, Mr. Latimer," Murdoch said, "because you have a right to know the truth. We're going down by the head, and we have less than two hours to evacuate the ship."

His words struck the air like a thunderbolt; the gathered crew looked stricken, some gasping, others covering their mouths in shock. But Murdoch pressed on, "Now is not the time to panic. It's our responsibility to ensure the safety of everyone aboard. That is our job, and that is what we must do."

His eyes swept over the stewards once more, remarkably cool considering the danger at hand. "Once again, make sure lifebelts are given to all. And do not give the passengers any cause for alarm, aye? Assure them that this is merely a precautionary measure and nothing more. Are we clear?"

He waited until every steward and stewardess nodded in understanding before dismissing them. They scattered like moths, and suddenly it was just Murdoch and Esther standing alone together.

The first officer didn't waste any time; he simply turned on his heel and hastened down the corridor. Esther scrambled after him, breathless, struggling to match his stride.

"Where are we headed next, sir?" she asked.

"Officers' quarters," Murdoch said shortly.

She waited for him to elaborate, but he was still tight-lipped and impassive, staring straight on ahead.

Esther could understand his urgency at a time like this. But there was something about his demeanor that didn't sit well with her.

Although Murdoch seemed perfectly levelheaded on the outside, his eyes told a different story. Esther couldn't forget the emptiness she'd seen in their depths. The self-blame. The bitter self-loathing, even.

She knew there was a storm of emotion spiraling inside him. And yet Murdoch was clearly fighting it, trying to keep it shuttered away behind a pretense of order and discipline.

Of course, Esther wasn't any better; she was absolutely terrified. But despite her own instinctive panic, she wanted nothing more than to hold Murdoch tight, to quell that storm within him and make him understand that he wasn't to blame. Not in the slightest. There had been so many variables involved—the unusually clear weather, the lack of binoculars, the order to maintain speed—that no single person was at fault. Not the captain, not the lookouts nor the quartermaster, and certainly not Murdoch. Esther stood by this fact with blazing certainty, and she'd fight anyone who dared to say otherwise—even Murdoch himself.

It wasn't until they reached the quarters that her superior finally spoke.

"I'll fetch us some whistles and pocketknives," he said brusquely. "And if you need anything from your cabin, now's the time to collect it, lass."

Esther pondered this, biting down on her lip. "My medical kit, perhaps. Wouldn't hurt to throw it into one of the lifeboats, just in case."

Murdoch merely gave a curt nod. "See to it, then."

He started down the hall without another word, and Esther watched him go before slipping inside her cabin. She felt dazed, almost, as she surveyed her quarters one last time. The very realization that this entire room would soon be underwater was such an eerie thing to comprehend. Her books, clothes, family photographs—it would all become nothing more than sodden, salt-soaked debris at the bottom of the ocean.

Esther could feel the hold on her composure slipping, just as she could feel that fear slithering its way through her veins once more. But she wrestled it down, tucking it away into some dark corner of her mind where it couldn't touch her. She lowered herself flat on her stomach and scoured beneath the bed for her medical kit, dimly reminded of the stinging ache in her cheek and nose. After everything that happened tonight, her scuffle with Lockerbie and Slate seemed a lifetime ago. But the pain was still apparent, and rather let it hinder her efforts during the evacuation, Esther pulled two pills from her kit's aspirin bottle before rising to her feet.

She was quick, snagging a glass from the washbasin cabinet and filling it with cold water. But it wasn't until she'd swallowed down the pills and placed the half-empty cup on the marble countertop that she froze in horror.

The water in the glass was not level.

Its surface was at an imperceptible tilt—subtle at first glance, but apparent all the same.

Esther staggered backward, her heartbeat slamming in her chest. Her eyes roamed wildly around her quarters, and the more she looked around, the more she realized the entire room was slanted—the clothes hanging in her wardrobe, the furniture, *everything*. Seeing the tilt made their situation more horrifying real.

They were going down.

"Jesus *Christ*," Esther cried aloud. She had never felt so damn frightened. Helpless, even. She clutched her medical kit tightly to her chest, trying to prevent the hyperventilating breaths from billowing up her throat.

She couldn't snap.

She was an officer, for God's sake. She had to keep it together. Not simply for the passengers' sake, but also for her own.

Esther bolted from the room, slamming the door behind her and trying with all her might to calm her frazzled nerves.

When she reached Murdoch's cabin, she found his door was left ajar. Esther pushed it open, expecting to see the first officer rushing around the room for equipment. Whistles, flashlights, pocketknives—anything else that might be of use. So when she stepped inside, she was surprised to find him standing hunched over the washbasin, white knuckles clenching the marble rim, shoulders heaving as he drew in slow, uneven breaths.

Esther was quiet as she came up beside him, the fear in her heart gone, crisped to ashes beneath a blaze of unwavering concern for her superior officer.

"Will," she whispered.

Her palm cupped his cheek, cradling it, and he slowly turned to face her, folding his trembling hand over hers. Now that they were alone, Esther could see the slight unraveling of his resolve. The small chips and cracks that were wearing away at him. His eyes were heavy, glazed with guilt, and his voice fell to a throaty rasp when he spoke.

"Forgive me, Esther."

She clutched the side of his face even tighter. "There's nothing to forgive," she said softly. "It wasn't your fault."

But Murdoch shook his head. "I was the officer on duty." His voice was flat, stripped of all emotion, but he was clearly fighting so hard to keep his control. "It was my responsibility to keep watch over the ship. To see these people across the Atlantic safe and sound. And I've failed them all."

Esther wrenched her hand away from his cheek. She snagged the lapels of his coat in her fists, forcing him to look at her, refusing to tear her searing gaze away from his.

"Listen to me," she said fiercely. "You aren't responsible for this. So many things went wrong tonight that you just can't put the blame on anyone. Not Fleet or Lee. Not Smith. And certainly not you."

He was shaking his head once again, and Esther yanked his coat even harder, desperate to make him understand.

"Damn it, Will! What can I say to make you believe it?!"

His reply was quiet. "You can say nothing, lass. I've accepted my guilt. But that doesn't rightly mean I've given up. If anything, it's pushing me even harder to right what I've wronged." He stood straighter, blue eyes burning with conviction, the cracks in his resolve sealing themselves up again. "I'll help as many passengers off this bleedin' ship as I can. And I swear to you, Esther, that I will do everything in my power to make sure you're safe."

"Don't think for a moment I won't do the same for you," Esther retorted. Her eyes were blazing, his resolve only adding fuel to her own. But Murdoch still looked hesitant.

"Esther..." he murmured. His fingers found her chin, gripping it tight. "Esther, if anything should happen, and I have no choice but to give you a direct order, I need to know that you'll follow it. That you'll trust my judgment without question, no matter the cost." His blue eyes were unyielding as they searched her face. "Can you do that for me?"

Esther did not respond immediately. Not even when he tipped her chin up, his fingers gentle, prompting her to look at him.

She knew what he was thinking; it could not have been plainer on his face. There were only so few lifeboats. So few chances to make it to safety. And Murdoch was willing to use his authority to protect her—even at the cost of splitting them apart.

But that wasn't going to happen.

Esther would be with him every step of the way, so her gaze was steady when she finally offered a reply.

"I'll follow any order, Will," she said, "so long as I'm able to keep by your side."

He opened his mouth to protest, but her voice was firm, the words rich with heart and conviction. "You can say whatever you want, but it won't change a damn thing. I already know what's going to happen, and how this is going to end." Her hands roamed across the expanse of his broad, warm chest, feeling his muscles and deep heartbeat beneath his coat. "We're going to arrive in New York. Both of us."

She leaned into him, breathing in the soothing smell of his aftershave, fingers tangling with his. "We're going to stay at the Plaza, like you promised. We'll go for walks on the beaches around Coney Island. We'll make plans to visit San Francisco, and then I'm going to show you all around the bay, and then I'm gonna make you eat clam chowder, even if you don't like it."

He cracked a thin smile, and her eyes locked with his as she swore, "We'll fight our way through this hell and we'll do it together."

There was a long moment of silence as the two officers faced each other—not simply as lovers, not as superior and subordinate, but as equals.

Then Murdoch grasped Esther by the shoulders and suddenly pulled her closer, his lips crushing against her rigid grimace.

His kiss was hard, a promise, a pact that they would live to see daylight. It was enough to scatter the last of her lingering fear—to cut away the horrible thoughts of the icy seawater swirling in the ship, the blame in his eyes, the tilted floor beneath their feet. She kissed him back, clinging to these last few seconds with him, this one moment of calm before the storm.

There was a wetness on her cheeks, and it took Esther a moment to realize that tears were seeping beneath her lashes. But she ignored them, holding the first officer with all her might and knowing in her heart that they would make it through this or die trying.

When they finally broke apart, Murdoch pressed his forehead against hers, echoing her promise.

"Together, lass."

TWENTY-TWO

BULLETS

April 15, 1912 | 00:35

L IGHTOLLER WAS STUNNED as he dressed himself. His breathing was shallow and his hands fumbled as he pulled a dark turtleneck and a pair of trousers over his pajamas.

He couldn't believe that this was happening. That the unsinkable ship was sinking beneath their very feet.

When Boxhall had first knocked on his door and relayed the issue at hand, Lightoller had almost let out a scoff. But he'd seen the urgency in his colleague's eyes, and so he'd slipped back into his cabin at once, swallowing down his own dread and numbing disbelief.

He knew this would not be easy.

He knew how few lifeboats there were relative to the number of people on board. He knew that many would perish in the frigid water, and that he might die as well.

But even with his own mortality staring him in the face, Lightoller refused to let it worry him. It only made him hurry faster, slinging on his greatcoat and looping a white-threaded whistle around his neck before bolting out the door.

He wasn't sure what to expect when he stepped onto the bridge, but it came as no surprise when he saw the flurry of activity surrounding him. Crewmen roamed in all directions, streaming through the wheelhouse in blurs of navy blue. Some carried heaping towers of blankets, others held flashlights and extra lifeboat supplies.

Lightoller spotted his colleagues gathered in the port bridge wing with the captain and started toward them. Almost everyone was present, save for Lowe, who appeared to be missing. But Wilde was there, towering over everyone, his gray eyes sliding to Lightoller and away again. Murdoch and Bailey stood close to each other, their fingers interlaced tight, no longer trying to remain inconspicuous. Moody held a clipboard with the lifeboat assignments, while Boxhall and Pitman murmured in undertones with Smith. Swallowing thickly, Lightoller stood alongside his fellow officers with his chin raised high, ready and willing to face the duties that awaited him.

"Right," Moody called out, voice barely rising over the thundering roar of venting steam from the funnels, "Mr. Murdoch will take the starboard side, with Miss Bailey and Mr. Pitman assisting. Mr. Wilde, you will man the port side with Mr. Lightoller and Mr. Boxhall. And Mr. Lowe—"

He glanced up from the clipboard, suddenly realizing the fifth officer was nowhere in sight. "Erm, has anyone seen him?"

"I'm here."

They turned to see Lowe emerging from the wheelhouse, tucking what looked like a revolver into the waistband of his trousers. Wilde scoffed, "Did you forget where the bridge was, or what, lad?"

With a hasty apology, Lowe shuffled his way forward to stand with the rest of the group. Brows raised, Moody promptly continued, "You will see to the starboard side for now, Mr. Lowe, until otherwise specified by Mr. Murdoch." He glanced at the captain, who nodded in approval.

"Dismissed. Good luck and God bless, everyone."

Lightoller did not waste any time. He strolled purposefully along the port side of the ship, flanked by Boxhall and Wilde. They began with Lifeboat No. 4 and continued down the line, uncoiling ropes and swinging out each boat out until their gunwales were level with the deck.

"*Keep lowering!*" the second officer shouted again and again, puffing on his whistle and sweeping his arms through the cold air. "*Keep lowering!*"

The roar from the funnels was deafening as expressed steam billowed from their tops in great, endless bursts. It only added to the confusion as seamen and officers alike bellowed at each other, some resorting to hand signals to convey their words. Deckhands swarmed from boat to boat, wrenching away canvas covers and stocking extra supplies of blankets, thermoses, oil lanterns, and biscuit tins. Lightoller barked orders and blew into his whistle again and again, struggling to make himself heard. But even the cacophony of the davits was lost to his ears. The clatter of winding hand winches, slithering ropes, and squeaking pulleys were all blotted out by the din.

By the time each lifeboat was swung out on its falls, the deck was beginning to swell with passengers in various states of dress and undress. Some wore bathing robes or thin kimonos. A few gentlemen had donned their top hats and tailcoats, as if headed off for an evening stroll. Many looked baffled, others bored or irritable. Several passengers sipped hot lemonade as they cradled their personal items—jewelry, velvet boxes, picture frames, and other such keepsakes. But Lightoller was relieved to see that they all wore lifebelts, thank Christ above, keeping them fastened above their clothing or hidden beneath thick-furred coats and sparkling shawls.

He weaved his way through the crowd toward Wilde, who watched the crewmen stock the lifeboats with his sharp gray eyes.

"Hadn't we better load the women and children first?" Lightoller asked, feeling hot beneath his thick turtleneck. Yet his hands were freezing, and he wished he had remembered his gloves.

To his surprise, Wilde shook his head. "No, wait." His voice was a firm command. "I'd rather wait until the steam dies down first. Avoid any shouting and confusion, you understand."

Lightoller regarded him in disbelief, the last flicker of amiability he'd ever had for the man guttering out, doused like water to flame.

"Surely not. We mustn't waste any time, Mr. Wilde. We need to begin boarding *now*."

Wilde's stern expression didn't waver. "I do believe I gave you an order, Mr. Lightoller."

But Lightoller refused to heed such nonsense. "And I really don't agree with it, Mr. Wilde," he said bluntly.

Before his superior could utter another word, the second officer strolled purposefully across the deck, stepped beyond the gated partition, and marched straight toward Smith. Wilde trailed behind him, much to his displeasure, but Lightoller ignored the unwelcome company as he approached his captain.

"The boats are swung out and ready, sir," he announced with a dutiful nod. But the captain kept silent, and Lightoller—thinking that perhaps his own voice had been lost to the ear-splitting steam—cupped one hand to his mouth and leaned into Smith's ear to ask, "Shall I put the women and children into the boats, sir?"

The captain merely gave a vague nod, murmuring words that Lightoller strained to hear. There was something about his clouded expression that made the second officer all the more uneasy. But he couldn't let it trouble him. Not here and not now, while passengers shuddered in the cold, waiting to be rescued from the foundering ship beneath them.

"Sir?" Lightoller pressed on, while the git in the chief officer's uniform continued to hover infuriatingly close over his shoulder.

"Yes," Smith agreed, nodding grimly. "Put the women and children in first and lower away."

Lightoller acknowledged the order at once. "Yes, sir."

He spared one brief, cutting glance at Wilde before making his way back to the boats, still trying to push Smith's faraway look out of his mind. Standing before Lifeboat No. 6, he cleared his throat and called out to the crowd, "Ladies and gentlemen, may I have your attention, please!"

His guttural voice reverberated across the deck, arching high above the expelling steam as he urged the crowd forward with his hands.

"Step this way, please! That's right, very good, come towards me!"

Gradually, the passengers shed their timidity and began inching forward, linking hands and arms with their loved ones. It wasn't until they were all huddled before the lifeboat that the hissing steam finally, mercifully stopped. Now there was only the faint creaking of Lifeboat No. 6 as crewmen readied it with supplies, and the deep, booming shouts of Wilde further aft.

Satisfied, Lightoller surveyed the crowd with his chin raised. "Thank you," he said shortly, and his reassuring smile all but disappeared beneath hard-nosed diligence as he got to business. "For the present, I shall require only women and children. So gentlemen, please stay exactly where you are." Already he could see the surprise and hesitancy linger in their eyes. Nonetheless, he continued, "Ladies, please step toward me."

Not a single woman moved in the crowd. Lightoller swallowed back his frustration as he surveyed their reluctant faces. He gestured toward the passenger closest to him, a young lady with a lifebelt tightened over her sequined dress and fancy shawl.

"Have no fear, miss," he told her, offering her his hand, and she looked up at him with wide, doe-like eyes. "Please come toward me."

Her trembling fingers slipped into his, and he carefully eased her forward. She was shivering like mad from the cold, gooseflesh sweeping up her bare arms. Unthinkingly and without pause, Lightoller stripped off his greatcoat and swept it around her shoulders. It draped around her slight frame, but the fear in her eyes gradually faded as he helped her aboard.

"The boats are perfectly safe," he assured her kindly, before turning back to the remaining passengers with a forced smile. "This is merely a precautionary measure."

A handful of women stepped forward, but they moved slowly, cautious to trade the seemingly-safe steamship beneath their feet for the little lifeboat swinging on its falls. Lightoller could feel his patience begin to wane as he observed their unhurried pace. There were other boats to fill, and they only had so little time to load them as the clock ticked above their heads.

One hour, Boxhall had said. *Possibly two, if we've Lady Luck on our side.*

The more time they wasted, the more lives were in peril of falling victim to the icy sea. And so Lightoller's voice grew sharper as he addressed the crowd.

"Come forward, ladies! This way, please, madam. Nothing to fear!"

They did as they were told, meandering forward while the distant melodies of *Titanic's* string quartet drifted, strange and cheerful, through the freezing midnight air.

00:40

Esther followed Murdoch's every order as she helped him prepare the first starboard lifeboat, breathing heavily against her thick greatcoat.

She worked quickly, ignoring the beads of sweat on her brow while she wound clattering winches, helped the men tug the frapping lines, and clambered into the boat to store away her medical kit.

But by the time Lifeboat No. 7 was swung out on its falls, swaying high above the dark water beneath it, only a few passengers were gathered around the starboard deck.

Murdoch surveyed the small crowd before him with a hint of displeasure, his brow creased into a frown. But he clearly wasn't about to wait for more people to arrive. Not while they had so little time.

Nodding at the nearest crewman, he pointed to the lifeboat and ordered, "Mr. Hogg, you are to man this boat." He turned to two more sailors. "And you two. In. Assist the ladies with boarding and then cut the falls once you reach water. Understood?"

"Aye, sir," the three men echoed before hastily climbing aboard.

Now Murdoch turned to face the gathered concourse of passengers with Esther at his side, Lowe and Pitman at their heels.

"We will begin boarding the women and children first," Murdoch announced, his cool voice ringing out across the barren deck. "Men will be permitted to board so long as there are seats available." Esther spared a glance at him, surprised, but he was busy waving his gloved hand forward. "Ladies, this way."

No one seemed to want to step forward. They eyed the lifeboat uncertainly, many of them young couples not yet willing to part with their loved ones. Esther felt her heart flood with emotion as she watched a taller man drop a gentle kiss on his wife's forehead. Her thoughts turned to Murdoch, and she knew how reluctant *she* would be, too, if she were forced to clamber into a lifeboat without him. And so she leaned close to her colleagues with a whisper. "We ought to put the brides and grooms first, perhaps."

Pitman looked hesitant at her suggestion, but Murdoch and Lowe were in agreement.

"Anything to get them in the bleedin' boat," the first officer muttered, a sliver of impatience leaking through his calm demeanor. Turning back to the passengers, he called out, "Newlyweds and all other married couples, please step this way. You may board together."

Men and women shuffled forward now, stepping carefully into the lifeboat teetering over the pitch-black water. A few older gentlemen refused to board in place of the women, pausing to kiss their wives and murmur quiet words of parting.

I'll catch the next one, some would say. *Don't you worry.*

As they gallantly stepped back into the crowd, Esther gestured to the other women, hovering and shivering on the deck.

"It's all right," she said gently, coaxing them forward. "There's nothing to be afraid of. This is only a precaution. We just want to make sure you're safe, ladies. Trust me."

More women stepped from the crowd, though whether they were emboldened by the presence of a lady in uniform or by her encouraging words, Esther couldn't say. But she was pleased and proud to see them brave their fears and climb into the boat, one woman after another, until it was half full.

Once again, Murdoch didn't seem pleased by the lack of filled seats. But what else could they do? Few passengers were left on the starboard deck, and those still present were unwilling to board. The officers had no choice but to launch for now—even at half capacity.

Stepping to the edge of the bulwark, Murdoch addressed the crewmen lining the davits.

"Prepare to lower, lads! Ready the falls!"

Esther stood by the right davit with Pitman, only dimly aware of the charming waltzes echoing somewhere in the distance. How surreal it was, hearing such a merry tune as barely-contained panic simmered around them. She peered over the railing, gazing down at the water rippling so many decks beneath them, and only then did she understand the passengers' misgivings. It truly was a dizzying drop.

"*And lower away!*" Murdoch bellowed, sweeping both arms through the air. "Left and right together!"

Slowly, carefully, Lifeboat No. 7 began its descent to the icy ocean beneath it, the pulleys squeaking and shuddering as thick, heavy ropes slid through their grooves.

"Both sides together, lads!" the first officer continued to shout. "Steady. *Steady!*"

Everything seemed to run smoothly, with the first officer pacing along the rim of the boat deck, orders flying from his lips.

But then screams suddenly rose up from the descending lifeboat, shattering the calm. Esther leaned over the edge, shocked to see the left side of the boat tipping perilously toward the sea, passengers crying and yelping in fear—

She whirled around, ready to raise the alarm to the crewmen, but

Murdoch was quick.

"Hold the left side!" he commanded. "Right side only, right side only! Hold the left side!"

The lifeboat began to level itself, and Esther breathed out a long sigh of relief when it finally touched water.

As Murdoch ordered the crew to move along to the next boat, a peculiar hissing noise rushed through the chilly air. Esther glanced up to see the first distress rocket blazing high above the ship; it split apart the sky with a *crack*, shimmering across the water and flooding the deck with dazzling white light. She watched the sparks glitter and rain down, suddenly feeling nervous all over again. Just like the tilted water glass in her cabin, the distress rocket seemed to cement *Titanic*'s demise.

It was difficult to keep a cool head around the passengers when she knew the fate of the ship. When there were no lights along the horizon. No word of any other vessels on their way.

Her anxious thoughts turned to her brother as she fumbled with the ropes, and Esther found herself wishing he was by her side. She knew Booker was likely assisting Mr. Andrews, but that didn't stop her from worrying. Not when Smith's orders of "Women and children first" continued to whirl like a tempest through her head.

Lowe kept by her side as they readied Lifeboat No. 5 next. Her hands were shaking—not from the cold, but from the frantic thoughts of her brother—and he took immediate notice.

"Esther," he said slowly, eyes dark with concern. "Are you all right?"

"Yes, fine." Her reply was short, and she pointed at the davit to distract him. "Here, help me with this winch."

They rounded up more women next, guiding them toward the boat and assuring them of their safety. Even Bruce Ismay, of all people, offered to help. But with so few seats filled, Murdoch had no choice but to send Pitman to the port side to rally more passengers. And Esther—desperate to move around, to distract herself from her worries of Booker—asked to join in. Murdoch hesitated as he weighed her request, a flicker of uncertainty crossing his face; clearly, he didn't want her gone from his sight. But he knew they needed more people to fill the boats, so he finally relented.

"Aye," he said. "But make it quick, lass. I need you back here." His blue, unwavering gaze held hers. "I need you with me."

Esther nodded, eyes burning with a promise. "Yes, sir."

And with that, she rushed through the wheelhouse with Pitman hard on her heels, crossing to the port side and finding it teeming with people. All first-class, Esther noticed, with very few steerage passengers in sight. The thought troubled her, but she kept to protocol as she and Pitman weaved through the crowd, blowing their whistles and waving their hands for attention.

"This way, please!" Pitman shouted. "We have more boats on the starboard side of the ship! Women and children, this way!"

Some didn't even glance twice in their direction, while a few regarded them as if they were mad. But a handful of women were willing to go with them, including an older matron holding the hands of two frightened children, a young mother nestling a baby against her bosom, and a tall, frightened woman draped from head to toe in Arabian robes. The officers led their group through the wheelhouse, emerging on the starboard side as another rocket sheared its way through the air. One child gasped in amazement at the tumbling smoke and brilliant sparks, but the other shied away from all the light and noise, tears welling in her eyes.

"It's all right," Esther assured the sniffling girl, using the sleeve of her coat to wipe the tears away. "There we are. Don't be afraid, little miss. It's only fireworks. Just fireworks."

The child stopped crying, but she kept close to Esther as they approached the lifeboats, clinging tightly to her greatcoat.

They found Murdoch pacing back and forth upon their return. Although his face was a mask of orderly calm, the relief in his eyes was unmistakable as he locked eyes with Esther. He quickly ushered every last woman and child aboard before turning to her, brushing his gloved fingers gently against her freckled cheek. It was a brief gesture, quick enough for the bustling crew to take little heed of it—save for one officer who stood frozen at the other end of the davit, staring at the pair of them in utter bewilderment.

Harold, Esther realized in dismay.

She swallowed and stepped away from Murdoch at once, her heart overflowing with a cold shock of guilt. But Lowe was still watching her, and when she looked up, she saw the bewilderment in his gaze darken to something else she couldn't decipher. He said nothing, however, and promptly stepped forward when Murdoch gave the order to help the men aboard.

Gentlemen began filing into the boat, seating themselves among the women and children. There was enough room for them, in any case, and Esther knew Murdoch wasn't about to send off another boat at half capacity—regardless of whether it could be rowed back. So the present men were quickly ushered forward, helped aboard by the officers and crew.

As they prepared to lower, there was a scramble of footsteps, and everyone turned as Ismay suddenly bolted from nowhere. He was beside himself, grasping the manila falls and going absolutely berserk.

"Lower away!" he shouted, wringing the ropes with a white-knuckled grip. *"Lower away! Lower away!"*

Esther uttered a heated curse, Murdoch stormed forward with a look of disgust, but Lowe—who manned the frapping lines and stood inches away from Ismay—whirled around in a burst of anger.

"Hey!" he bellowed, snagging Ismay by the waist and flinging him away from the davit. Esther had never seen his temper, and she watched with a mixture of shock and appreciation as Lowe snapped, "Get out the way, you fool! You want me to lower away quickly? You'll have me drown the lot of them!"

Ismay gaped at him in outrage, his voice strangled. "Do you know who I am?"

If he'd expected his words to intimidate the fifth officer, he was sorely mistaken. Lowe rounded on him with fury, his Welsh accent a coarse snarl.

"You are a passenger and I'm a ship's bloody officer! If you'll get the hell out of the way, I'll be able to do something!"

With one last furious glower, Lowe turned his attention back to the lines. Ismay seemed mildly taken aback. It was the second time an officer had snapped at him tonight, and he finally seemed to get a grip on himself.

"Yes," he stammered, smoothing out his mustache with shaking hands. "Quite right. Sorry, I—"

But Murdoch cut in, blue eyes raking over Ismay with menacing calm.

"Look," he said, "if you want to help the passengers board, then help. But don't run 'round screaming like a lunatic, aye? You'll only cause a panic." He did a quick sweep of the half-full lifeboat, then of the deck, his voice hoarse as he bellowed for more passengers. But when no one else moved forward, he made his way toward Esther.

"Lass..." he began.

His eyes flickered between her and the lifeboat. It didn't take her long to interpret his thoughts. Esther took a step back, squaring her shoulders as she faced him. "Don't even think about it. We made a promise."

"I know, lass. But I need someone to take charge of the boat, and you—"

"Find someone else," she gritted out. "You already know I won't go without a fight. You'll have to drag me on board, Will."

Murdoch sized her up through a narrowed gaze. "That can certainly be arranged."

"Oh, really?" Esther challenged, raising her chin at him with defiance. "Then why don't you come over here and try it?"

The two officers glowered at each other before Murdoch finally gave in with a weary sigh. Turning to Pitman, he jerked his thumb at the lifeboat. "Go on, Bert. Get in."

Pitman looked shocked, hazel eyes flitting between Esther and Murdoch. "But surely Esther—"

"Esther is too busy being insubordinate at the moment, I'm afraid," Murdoch said dryly. "You take charge of this boat and look after the others, Bert." He offered a gloved hand, and although Pitman looked hesitant, he willingly shook.

"You're a good man, Will."

"And you. Goodbye, old friend. Good luck."

Esther stepped forward next to shake hands with Pitman, clasping his fingers tight. She wanted to thank him for so many things—his cheery nature, his jokes, his acceptance of her place as a lady officer. But there was little time to waste, so she murmured a hasty farewell instead. As she stood by the falls in wait of Murdoch's order and watched Pitman clamber into the teetering lifeboat, she found herself thinking only one anxious question, circling in her thoughts again and again like the chaotic swirl of a maelstrom:

Who tells the first officer to board?

Heart racing, Esther gripped the line tighter. Lowe was ordered to join her, and as he picked up the sprawl of rope, he said quietly, "I didn't realize you and Will were…"

The words trailed away, as if he didn't quite know what his two colleagues were to each other. Esther uneasily bit her lip. Her throat suddenly felt horribly dry, and she struggled for words, not even knowing what to say to him. Guilt coiled through her chest as she saw the hurt in his eyes. She'd never meant for it to be like this. She had always seen Lowe as a friend and colleague—nothing more. She had never even shown an inkling of romantic interest in him. But that didn't stop her from feeling regret. Esther was aware of his feelings for her, after all. She should have set things straight with him sooner, dammit, rather than have him find out during their darkest hour.

"I'm sorry, Harry," she mumbled.

Lowe nodded at Murdoch, sparks of anger and bitterness in his eyes. "He told me to forget about you, he did. To move on. Now I see he was saving you for himself."

Esther shook her head. "It wasn't like that, Harry, he never intended for it to be like that. Neither of us did." She glanced to her superior officer, her eyes soft as she watched him rove along the deck, calm and unafraid in his authority, and she added, "It just sort of happened. I don't know when or how, but it did. And I'm happy with him, Harry. I really am."

Lowe opened his mouth to speak, but Murdoch came striding across the deck, ordering the crew to move on to the next boat. Esther and Lowe hurried after him, and no further words were said between them as they prioritized their duty over personal matters.

Lifeboat No. 3 was launched without issue. But like the others, it was at half its capacity. Esther could see the agitation on Murdoch's face at the lack of filled seats. Even she was beginning to feel the slow, simmering crawl of frustration herself. Regardless, her superior officer showed no intention of slowing down. He seemed adamant that the half-full boats could row back to pick up more passengers, if need be.

Murdoch swiftly set out to load Lifeboat No. 1 next, while Lowe hurried aft to round up more people. Esther might have gone along with him, but Murdoch needed the extra help now that Pitman was gone. So they started with women and children first, calming them, encouraging them, while the men were ordered to standby. There was no preferential treatment among the passengers. Dark-skinned or fair, Irish or Syrian, first-class or steerage—it didn't matter to Esther. Not one damn bit. So long as they had a beating heart, she and Murdoch would do everything in their power to get them to safety.

"*Any more women and children?*" Murdoch finally bellowed, Scottish burr splintering hoarsely through the air.

But when no one stepped forward, he turned to the gentlemen clustered around the deck.

"Right, gents. Form a line and step aboard, one at a time."

As they clambered into the boat, a plump gentleman stormed from the queue.

"This is *hardly* necessary," he snapped at Murdoch, looking cross. "You realize that, don't you? What's the point of getting into these puny little boats when there's a perfectly sound ship beneath our feet? It's an inconvenience, that's what it is."

Murdoch arched an eyebrow. "My sincerest apologies, sir," he deadpanned, self-control wavering beneath undisguised sarcasm. "I didn't realize saving lives was so terribly inconvenient."

The man looked as if he wanted to snap back, but Murdoch, it seemed, had had enough.

"Jump in," he said shortly, gesturing toward the boat. "And don't make a fuss about it."

The portly man sauntered forward, irritable but surprisingly obedient now that Murdoch had given him a direct command. He swung one stubby leg over the bulwark railing, then the other.

But the rail was far too high, and the man was much too large. He lost his balance, and everyone on deck watched as he slowly, awkwardly rolled into the boat with a *thunk*.

There was a short pause as Esther and Murdoch looked at one another.

Then, before they knew it, they were both snorting aloud with laughter.

The portly man righted himself in the boat with a sheepish look, red in the face but unscathed. Esther was in stitches, breathless, having to brace herself against Murdoch's forearm to stay upright. Perhaps it was the cold air or the rush of adrenaline that made the situation so strangely hilarious, but whatever the case, she couldn't seem to pull herself together.

Even Murdoch was still laughing heartily at her side.

"That's the funniest thing I've seen all night," he declared.

Esther grinned, her grip tightening on his arm as she fought for breath. "No kidding. Phew. That certainly cheered me up a bit."

"Aye, and God knows we could all use some cheering at a time like this."

They sobered up a little, regaining their professionalism once more. Esther was about to return to her station when Murdoch caught her hand, stopping her in her tracks and pressing a swift, tender kiss against her forehead.

Clearly, he no longer cared who might see. And neither did Esther.

She blushed pink, unable to hold back her smile, and she found herself thinking only of how reassuring it was to share a laugh with him—even amidst the throes of disaster.

01:15

Lightoller could feel his patience chipping away, little by little, as the evacuation went on.

First-class passengers frustrated him, dawdling as if they had all the time in the world. Men were arguing, demanding to be seated with their wives, some even begging or pleading with him to board.

But Lightoller refused to relent. His orders were clear. Women and children *only*. And as a loyal, dutiful man with reverence for the rules, Lightoller would strictly abide by said orders until the last lifeboat was gone from the ship.

He had barely finished launching Lifeboat No. 8 when Smith and Wilde made their way toward him, twining their way through the flood of people. Lightoller was relieved to see that the captain seemed to have collected himself; he no longer appeared dazed, and his eyes were sharp and alert as they swept across the deck. It was as if he'd finally come to terms with the fact that *Titanic* was doomed to sink into the abyssal depths beneath them.

Swiftly the captain voiced his orders, placing Boxhall in charge of the boats and pulling Lightoller away from the throng. As they stood in a huddle before the First Class Gym, Wilde leaned close to Lightoller to ask,

"Where are the firearms kept?"

Firearms?

Lightoller was bewildered. He knew why they were asking him; he had been first officer back in Belfast before the reshuffle, after all. And since the first officer was responsible for the guns and ammunition, he would know exactly where they were stored.

Still, Lightoller was surprised that the captain and chief officer found any need for weaponry. The crowds were thick and swarming, true. But they weren't unruly.

Yet, a small voice in the back of his head reminded him.

He was aware that his superiors were waiting, so Lightoller quickly voiced his answer. "I know where they are. Come along and I'll get them for you."

Smith gave a curt nod. "Very good. We'll fetch Mr. Murdoch and distribute firearms to all senior officers. I daresay they'll be necessary by the end of all this."

Lightoller didn't like the foreboding in the captain's voice; he especially didn't like the notion of wielding a gun before terrified passengers. But he knew he had no choice, so he followed Smith and Wilde to the forward part of the ship.

It was quieter and less crowded here, with few passengers in sight. As they walked, Lightoller was vaguely aware of the slanted deck beneath his feet; even Wilde glanced down, mumbling a curse under his breath.

It seemed as if the tilt was growing steeper as *Titanic* slipped further into the sea, and Lightoller tried not to think of the one, harrowing hour they had left.

They fetched Murdoch from the starboard side in a hurry—with Bailey in tow, as Murdoch refused to go anywhere without her—and it wasn't until their group reached the bridge that Lightoller stared across the forecastle in horror.

Both the bow and the forward well deck shimmered beneath clear, shallow seawater—and more cascaded over the railings by the second, flooding everything in its path.

God help us, Lightoller thought.

His own fear had been a small, flickering flame in his chest. But now it threatened to become an entire inferno.

How much time did they have left until even the sodding boat deck was awash? And how could Smith waste what precious minutes they had left to fetch guns?

Lightoller was annoyed he'd been pulled away from his lifesaving duties for something so inconsequential, so he made it quick, leading them to the first officer's cabin and hauling out each Webley from the arms locker. The revolvers glistened beneath the lamplight, dark silver and still freshly-polished.

Though Murdoch studied them with a stoic expression, Lightoller didn't miss the disgust buried in his hooded eyes. Even Bailey, who stood rigid at his side, made little effort to conceal her disapproval as she glowered at the weapons. But no one spoke or even dared to protest before the captain.

Silently, Lightoller passed around the guns to Wilde and Murdoch before turning for the door, weaponless, all too anxious to return to his post. But Wilde suddenly grasped him by the shoulder, stopped him dead in his tracks, and pressed a revolver and cartridges into his hand.

"Here you are," the chief officer said quietly. "You may need it."

They stared at each other for a moment, slate-gray eyes meeting light blue. Eventually Lightoller nodded, dipping the gun and its ammunition into his pocket and hurrying for the door. There was little time for farewells, so he paused to tip his cap at Bailey and grasp Murdoch's arm tight, hoping the gesture could convey how much he cared for his friend. Then he spun on his heel and hurried out into the wheelhouse once more, returning to the freezing hell that awaited him.

Shortly after overseeing the launch of Lifeboat No. 10, Lightoller felt a sudden, tangible shift in the atmosphere as the seriousness of the situation grew apparent among the passengers. Any placidity left on the decks vanished beneath an onslaught of fear and panic, and only now did he understand why Wilde handed him the gun.

The crowd was swelling now, people pushing and shoving their way through the turmoil. Distress rockets bloomed brilliantly in the air. Passengers stood in a crushing huddle before Lifeboat No. 12, while the crew fought to push the men back and usher the ladies forward. Even Lowe had to be called over from the starboard side to help.

And the more the chaos grew, the less Lightoller could control his temper. He was snarling at everyone and everything in sight. A handful of first-class women brought their trunks into the lifeboat, and that was when he lost it.

"What's this luggage doing here?" he roared above the clamor. "There's no room for luggage in this lifeboat!"

He snagged one trunk and heaved it into the sea without a second thought. "*Get rid of it!*" He hurled another one over the edge. "We need the room! Get rid of that! *Out!*"

Lightoller was furious; didn't these people understand what was happening? They were escaping a sinking ship, for Christ's sake, not going on a sodding holiday.

He turned back to the crowd, livid, grabbing any woman or child within sight. An elderly woman in a bottle-green shawl stood directly before him, sobbing as she clung to the lifebelt of her husband. But the leash of Lightoller's last patience snapped. He grabbed the woman by the arms and started pulling her toward the boat.

"This way please!" he insisted. But she held on to the gentleman, and Lightoller had no choice but to push him back. "Let go, sir!"

Crying and sobbing hysterically, the elderly woman allowed herself to be ushered to the lifeboat. "Keep calm and sit down, woman," Lightoller insisted, before urging the passengers to keep budging up. "Make more room, you lot. There we are. That's right, look sharp."

He was leaning over the bulwark to count the number of passengers seated when he felt a sharp tapping on his shoulder. Lightoller whirled around to see a first-class woman standing behind him, donned in mink furs and glistening diamonds. She looked completely unruffled as she addressed him in a posh, lofty drawl.

"Would you hold the boat for one moment? I've left my pearls in my cabin, and—"

But Lightoller wasn't having any of it. With a snarl of frustration, he hoisted the woman up by her lifebelt and dumped her into the boat.

"Sit *down!*" Lightoller commanded, sweeping his hand before her scandalized face.

The next few moments were a rush to fill as many seats as possible, with Mr. Andrews and his tall apprentice helping the apprehensive women and children aboard. Most ladies were receptive toward Booker, Lightoller noted, as though encouraged by his good looks and politeness. But Booker scarcely noticed the attention as he ushered passengers to safety, his eyes meeting Andrews' on occasion, his hand brushing against his mentor's shoulder once or twice.

As Lightoller ordered the boat lowered to the icy sea, a wave of steerage passengers suddenly came storming out from the belly of the ship, shouting and shoving against each other as they surged for the nearest boat. Lightoller could see the wild-eyed terror in their eyes. The desperation to live. But he had no choice but to push them away.

"Back!" the second officer shouted again and again. "Back, I say! Keep order!"

Yet they continued to push forward, heedless of his words—until one man stumbled from the throng and slammed into a first-class woman lingering by the rail.

Her scream was bloodcurdling as she staggered forward, her heel catching in the deck slats, and Lightoller swallowed back a curse as she went plummeting from the ship.

He raced to the bulwark, his heart pounding, only to see the woman hanging from the lifeboat below, clinging to its edge for dear life.

"Pull her in!" Lightoller ordered over the woman's shrieks. "Pull her in this instant!"

It was only after she was hauled away to the safety of the promenade below that Lightoller finally rounded on the crowd, his temper crackling, close to reaching its boiling point.

"*Get back, I say!*" he roared at the top of his lungs, brandishing the unloaded revolver from his pocket and sweeping it before the passengers with a steady hand. *"Or I'll shoot you, so help me Christ!"*

The reaction was almost instantaneous; a fearful hush fell over the passengers as they gaped at the slick, cold metal glinting before their eyes. No one seemed to want to move, suddenly more afraid of a bullet to the brain than of the sinking ship beneath their feet.

"Keep order!" Lightoller shouted at them, the ferocity in his voice dying down as the crowd began to settle. "Keep order, I *say*."

Swinging around, he turned to face his junior officers. Moody stood with a straight back alongside the bulwark rail, while Lowe kept close to his side, scanning the sea of passengers with tense, watchful eyes.

"We'll need an officer to take charge of this boat," Lightoller informed them crisply, hands snapping open his Webley to load its chamber with bullets, "and keep the crowds at bay as she's lowered to the sea." He studied the pair of them expectantly. "Gents?"

There was a short pause as Moody and Lowe looked at one another; it was clear from the hesitancy in their eyes that neither junior officer wanted to leave *Titanic* behind. Before Lightoller could speak another word, Moody purposefully stepped away from the lifeboat and its davits. Though he was far younger than his colleagues, he fearlessly held his chin high, his eyes glinting with resolution.

"You go ahead and board," he assured Lowe. "I'll get the next one."

Lowe stared at him, incredulous. "Don't be thick. You're getting on this lifeboat and that's the truth of it."

Moody shook his head. "I'm not going anywhere, sorry."

"Fat chance of that!" Lowe rounded on his colleague in a temper. "Listen mate, if you think I'm going to let you pass up a chance at safety, then you're not proper right in the head. And you're forgetting that Esther's still on board. You know how I feel about her. I can't leave this ship, I can't leave her—"

But Lightoller was done listening to their indecision.

"That's quite enough!" he snarled. "We don't have time for this! Or did you forget that this bloody ship is sinking? Christ's sake." His gaze settled on the fifth officer, and he made no attempt to conceal the ire in his voice as he commanded, "Mr. Lowe, man this boat."

"Lights—" Lowe tried to protest.

But Lightoller was curt. "That is an order, Mr. Lowe."

Although his eyes darkened, Lowe said nothing, merely pulling out his own revolver from his pocket and clambering into the lifeboat.

Lightoller listened distantly as his colleague calmed and reassured the passengers, but his thoughts were elsewhere. He stood with his back to the crowd, slipping one bullet after another into his Webley and thinking of a time when he could be long gone from this tragic mess—when he could cradle his wife in his arms, and never have to listen to the pleas of terrified, panicked human beings again.

TWENTY-THREE

THE SINKING

April 15, 1912 | 01:20

A S CHILLING, JADE-green water continued to creep further across *Titanic*, slowly but surely easing the magnificent ship into the sea, Murdoch fought to load Lifeboat No. 13 with as many women and children as possible.

It was sheer pandemonium, the aft boat deck teeming with a flood of terrified people, the slant beneath them growing steeper by the minute.

Women sobbed as they were wrenched away from their husbands. Children cried out, scared and confused in the din. Some men quietly and courageously accepted their fate, while others shoved and hurled themselves against one another, scrambling for the closest lifeboat in their desperation for life.

But where Murdoch might once have allowed those men to board, he now had no choice but to turn them away. There were so few seats left as more and more people rushed up from the depths of the ship, fleeing the ice-cold water slithering its way through every cabin, every corridor, every cargo hold. So he, Bailey, and his shipmates did everything in their power to push the men back, quickly lowering away Lifeboat No. 13 before moving on to the next one.

Another distress rocket cracked through the air, illuminating the swell of chaos beneath it. Bailey was shouting, the fire wild in her eyes. Short and slight though she was, she fought with all her might to drive back the buffeting wall of panicked men, slamming her palms and elbows into anyone who dared to breach the line. Murdoch did the same, dimly aware of the cold weight of the Webley in his coat pocket. The first officer had yet to load it with bullets, and he damn well wasn't in any hurry to do so. He knew he'd have to draw it on the mob at some point—if only to drive them back, to keep them from rushing the boats meant solely for women and children. But he would wait until it was an absolute necessity. Until he was left with no other choice.

He simply resorted to physical force for now, Webley still tucked away, voice scratchy and hoarse as he bellowed, "Stay back! Stay back, you lot! Women and children only!"

As they continued to load the boats, the separation between families was swift and sobering. A young girl screamed for her father as she was eased toward the boat by her grim-faced mother. Couples embraced and exchanged words of farewell, a few speaking in foreign languages Murdoch couldn't understand. Some women outright refused to board, preferring to brave the icy sea alongside their husbands. An older first-class couple settled on a pair of deck chairs, holding hands, refusing to part with the other. One first-class gentleman, however, was reduced to a different tactic. He tried to force his wife to the boat, but she was clinging to him, weeping, fighting him the entire way.

"I won't go, damn you!" she sobbed, beating her fists against his chest.

"For God's sake, Helen, be brave and go!" the man cried. His desperate eyes found Murdoch, and he begged, "Sir, please—"

Murdoch did not need to be told twice. He stepped forward, trying not to feel disgusted with himself as he grasped the woman by the arm and pulled her away from her husband. She started grappling with Murdoch now, hurling insults at him as she cried her husband's name.

"Madam," Murdoch said gently, trying to calm her. "It'll be all right, madam—"

But the woman ignored him, still fighting tooth and nail to return to her husband. She stooped to slide off one of her heels, trying to strike Murdoch in the face until he knocked it from her grasp. It clattered on the deck, blue and glittering, and the woman cried even harder. His gaze lingered on Bailey, who was watching him with a conflicted expression, and Murdoch knew all too well that she would offer the same resistance— only hundredfold. Shame swelled in his chest, but he did not slacken his grip as he tugged the hysterical woman to the boat. Her husband looked on, quiet in his courage, clearly fighting back tears before disappearing into the crowd.

Only after another handful of women climbed aboard did Murdoch order Lifeboat No. 15 lowered away. As he stood between the davits with Moody at his side, signaling and bellowing orders to the crew, he couldn't stop thinking of the husband with his tear-filled eyes, and the wife with her pleading screams. His gaze dropped to the lifeboat teetering below, searching for her, and his chest tightened when he found her sobbing into her hands.

Suddenly, the terrible sounds of weeping women and panicked men were overwhelming, a grisly reminder of the hell he had put them through.

It didn't matter what Bailey had tried to convince him. This was his fault. All his bloody fault. He had splintered these families apart, dividing husbands from wives, fathers from children, mothers from adult sons. The guilt was gut-wrenching, sharp enough to hurt. Murdoch could feel it slicing its way through his resolve, threatening to cut away those last slivers of hope and salvation. For even if he and Bailey were to make it through this, how in God's name could he live with himself, knowing that his blunder sentenced thousands of innocent people to *death*—

"*Will.*"

A voice shouted his name, wrenching him from the darkness of his hollow thoughts. Murdoch turned to see Bailey scrambling toward him, battling her way through the thick concourse of passengers.

"Will!" she cried. "*Stop*! Stop lowering! Boat 13 is underneath 15!"

Murdoch didn't even bother peering over the bulwark to confirm for himself; he trusted Bailey's word with his life. He reacted swiftly, noting the screams rising from below.

"Hold both sides, lads!"

His crew followed the order in a heartbeat, halting their pull on the falls. The shrieks faded, and Murdoch rushed to the railing to investigate.

Far below, he glimpsed the rudder of Lifeboat No. 13 poking out from beneath the bulky frame of No. 15. An enormous jet of discharged water torrented from *Titanic*, churning and foaming the inky sea, and Murdoch immediately knew that the boat was caught in its current. The occupants of No. 13 scrambled to cut their falls, and it wasn't until they rowed away to safety that he ordered the lowering of No. 15 to continue.

Murdoch kept calm throughout it all, his sense of duty giving him sheer focus, driving him onward to help the poor souls he had wronged. He was not afraid. There was so much happening around him that he didn't have time to feel fear.

But he could feel one thing. And that was the guilt still clinging to the back of his mind, trapping his thoughts as if they were frozen in ice.

Even as he shouted orders for the left and right lines, it was in that split moment of clarity that he finally came to terms with the cold truth.

There would be no New York. No walks around Coney Island. No quiet hotel room spilling with morning sunlight, the bed sheets soft and white, tangling together as he and Bailey made slow, passionate love between them.

The reason was pure and simple, Murdoch thought.

He did not deserve it.

He did not deserve such happiness and contentment after making so many innocent people suffer. He did, however, have an ironclad obligation and responsibility to help these passengers until his dying breath. That was exactly what he would do, even if there was no hope for him. And if he were to fall victim to the icy sea…well, so be it, then. It was a fate befitting for the man who failed to steer clear of the berg that imperiled them all.

But while he was willing to stay on the ship until the very end, to set aside his own want for survival to give these people a chance at life, Murdoch could not allow Bailey to do the same. He knew they'd made a promise to fight through this hell together. He'd seen the blazing sincerity in her eyes when she held him, swearing to never leave his side. But now, as the chaos and despair only grew, Murdoch had no choice but to break their promise. It would be bloody selfish of him to let her risk her own life for the sake of his. Not when he cared for her so dearly. Not when she was so young, so clever and bold. She was only in her twenties, for Christ's sake, and she still had so much ahead of her—traveling, sailing the seas, setting an example for working women around the world. He needed her to make it through this. To live a good, long life—even if he wasn't part of it. Murdoch knew he had no choice but to get her into one of the remaining lifeboats, with or without her consent.

He turned to her as soon as Lifeboat No. 15 touched water, his forehead and neck glazed with sweat, his breath heavy from the exertion of keeping the crowds back. The mere sight of her looking up at him with those light, lovely green eyes was enough to crack his heart in two. He almost couldn't believe that only a few hours ago, they'd chatted and flirted and made love in the smoking room. How quickly things had changed.

"Collapsibles next," he said gruffly. "Follow me, lass." He reached for her hand on instinct, lacing his fingers with hers, and together they weaved their way through the crowd. But they had barely taken a handful of steps when someone called his name.

"Mr. Murdoch!"

Murdoch turned but did not slow his step, and his expression shifted to cold indifference when he found himself face-to-face with Callum Lockerbie. Hatred tore through him, seeping through the edges of his composure, and he glanced at Bailey, gripping her hand tight. Although she glared straight ahead, she squeezed Murdoch's hand back, a silent reassurance that she was all right.

"I'd like a quick word, Mr. Murdoch," Lockerbie said smoothly. "Without the freckled burden in uniform, if you'd be so kind," he added, shooting Bailey a pointed glance.

Murdoch might have struck him. Bailey looked ready to smack him square in the face, too. But the first officer kept his focus, thinking only of his duty and little else as he shouldered his way through the crowd.

"Perhaps you haven't noticed, Mr. Lockerbie," he said dully, "but I'm a bit busy at the moment." His gaze shifted to three sailors at the nearest bulwark. "You three. With me, now!"

He quickened his stride, still ignoring Lockerbie as he joined Wilde and Ismay at Collapsible C. They made quick work of fitting the collapsible into its davits while Lockerbie and his foul manservant skulked near the wheelhouse, watching. Murdoch didn't know or even care what they wanted; he was more focused on doing his job. Once, he caught Bailey looking across the bow, which was fully submerged beneath the cold, crystalline water. He didn't miss the lingering fear in her eyes, and he knew in that moment she was getting on Collapsible C whether she liked it or not.

But first, they needed to fill the damn thing.

The collapsible wasn't even close to half capacity; there were still seats available, and no passengers in sight. Agitated, Murdoch paced to the A Deck stairwell to check for rising water. It was empty now, but who knew how long they had before the sea came swirling up its steps? He turned his gaze to the deck, which was barren save for a few straggling passengers here and there. His breathing grew heavier—not out of fear, but of frustration—and he turned to the seaman working the falls behind him.

"Where is everyone?" he demanded, his voice harsher than he'd intended.

The man pointed a gloved finger in the distance. "Seems they're mostly aft, sir."

Murdoch clenched his jaw, biting back the curse he longed to say aloud. He started aft without a second thought, motioning Bailey to follow. But he'd barely taken a step before Lockerbie flung an arm out, stopping him in his tracks.

Their eyes met for a moment, hazel against hard, flinty blue. Murdoch was livid that anyone would dare waste his time in a moment of crisis—especially the sick bastard standing before him—but his anger turned to outrage as Lockerbie pulled a thick wad of dollar bills from his pocket and passed them forward, murmuring, "Perhaps we can come to an agreement that will be of your benefit as well as mine, Mr. Murdoch."

Disgusted, Murdoch caught Lockerbie by the wrist, stopping his hand from going any further. Though he was a head shorter than the man before him, he was far stronger, shaped by a great many years at sea. He effortlessly held Lockerbie's wrist in place, his grip crushing, his expression one of pure disdain.

"You're a fool," Murdoch said shortly. He didn't have time for this. "Now get out of my way."

Lockerbie looked affronted, but Murdoch didn't care. He was seething, insulted by such a disrespectful bribe and furious that any man would try and pay themselves out of this tragedy. Callum Lockerbie wouldn't be getting on a boat, and that was that. Murdoch would damn well make sure of it.

He released Lockerbie's wrist with one last look of contempt before returning to Bailey. She stood by the stairwell, waiting for him, a questioning look on her face. "What did the asshole want?"

Murdoch did not answer immediately. He continued aft, and it wasn't until Bailey fell into step with him that he muttered, "He's a right dafty. Tried to offer me cash for a spot on a boat—"

"He what?" Bailey snarled. Murdoch had never seen her so angry, not since the day he'd tried to break off their relationship in the chart room. "Cowardly *sonofabitch*!"

She spun on her heel in a fury, looking ready to storm back down the deck to give Lockerbie a piece of her mind. But Murdoch was swift, catching a handful of her greatcoat and tugging her back toward him.

"Steady." His voice was mild, but it carried a note of curt authority that made her stop in her tracks. "He's not worth it, lass, and we have more important matters to attend to."

She scowled. "Can't I just go over and kick him, please?"

"No, Esther." Even amidst the peril all around them, Murdoch felt a faint smile pulling at the corner of his lips. "You can't kick him."

"Pity," she muttered under her breath, casting a murderous glare at Lockerbie over her shoulder. But she said nothing more as they rounded up a few more women scattered along the officers' promenade, guiding them to the safety of Collapsible C.

By now, Lockerbie and his manservant had disappeared, no doubt slinking away to find some other crewman to bribe. Murdoch helped the last of the passengers aboard before shouting into the cold, "Any more women and children? Any children?"

Ismay spoke up from the side of the boat. "They're all aboard, Mr. Murdoch!"

"*Anyone else, then?*" Murdoch bellowed, turning to the cluster of gentlemen standing on deck, patiently waiting for their turn. There was room for them now that the last women and children in the vicinity had taken their seats, so Murdoch ushered the men toward the boat's gunwale next, bracing his gloved hands against their lifebelts to help them up.

Only after they were safely aboard did he round on Bailey, his heart heavier than stone as he braced himself for the hardest decision of his life.

01:45

Esther was kneeling to pick up the coil of heavy rope sprawled at her feet when Murdoch stepped toward her. She stood at once, surprised by the flinty gaze looking back at her, and straightened up in bewilderment.

"Will?" she asked uncertainly.

Murdoch pointed one gloved finger at the collapsible. "Get in."

"Sorry?"

"You heard me." His voice was curt. "Get in the collapsible. Now."

She dropped the line, letting it fall to her feet with a muffled thud. "Didn't we just have this conversation an hour ago?" she demanded.

"Aye. That we did. But I'm not asking you now. I'm telling you."

"And I already told you *no*," Esther retorted. "I'm staying with you and that's that."

Murdoch spared an impatient glance toward the Engelhardt collapsible before bearing over Esther, a muscle twitching in his cheek.

"You'll do no such thing," he said harshly. His tone was rough and insistent, unlike anything she had ever heard before, and she took a step back. "You will board and take charge of this collapsible. That is an *order*, Miss Bailey."

Esther felt her chest swell with a myriad of emotions, the sharpest of which were hurt and anger. It had been a while since Murdoch had addressed her by her surname. But she would not let his cold formality wound her. She had a duty to the first officer standing before her—a searing loyalty and affection that bound her to him, overriding every last instinct of survival. The thought of drifting passively in a lifeboat and leaving him to fend for himself was almost sickening. Even worse was the wretched thought of arriving in New York without him, knowing he went down with the ship, drowned and alone in the middle of the North Atlantic. She simply couldn't do it. She wouldn't even try.

Esther lifted her chin. "Then I am sorry, Mr. Murdoch, but I must refuse."

"Miss Bailey—" he started to protest, but she spoke over him.

"I made a promise. I can't leave you, dammit. Or my brother. Or any of those passengers that need our help!"

"If you stay," Murdoch said through gritted teeth, "then you are *willfully* disobeying the order of your commanding officer, Miss Bailey."

He was trying to intimidate her, to do anything to get her in the boat. But Esther held her ground. "I am perfectly aware of that, thank you."

"Are you, now? Then I assume you're also aware that you will, in all likelihood, be dishonorably discharged for insubordination?"

"I am." She gathered her wits, willing herself to stay strong as she faced him, blinking the angry tears away. "And I will accept the repercussions of my actions, sir, when I arrive in New York *with* you. The two of us. Together."

Murdoch stared at her in silence, his stern expression faltering, his eyes filling with an anguish he was so clearly trying to hide. Esther watched his composure crumble away, bit by bit—until he seized her by both arms and shook her.

"*Damn* you, Esther!"

Esther struggled against him, but he was far stronger, and she could do nothing but stand there, rigid in his grasp. They were making a scene; passengers and crew alike stared, shocked to see the two officers quarrel, their private matters laid bare for all to see.

But Murdoch didn't seem to care about their audience. Or even notice them, for that matter. He only had eyes for Esther as he held her tight, his gloved hands trembling.

"Please get into the boat. Please, lass."

The crack in his voice cut through her heart. But not her resolve.

She remembered the day that sailor had shoved her down, and how she'd climbed right back on her feet. She remembered when her father had told her she would amount to nothing as a seafarer, but she'd left home and proved him wrong anyway. She thought of the scars marring her skin, the hardships she'd managed to overcome, the people who'd tried to tell her what she could and could not do. Esther was here because she wanted to be. Because she had fought for it. She was a ship's officer, and like Murdoch, she would fulfill her duty until the end.

This work suits you, he'd once told her. *Don't squander it.*

I won't.

Esther faced her superior officer with conviction, trying to separate her personal affections for him from her responsibility. Recollections of the intimate moments they shared together flickered through her thoughts— warm laughter and soft-spoken words, locked eyes and fierce lovemaking. But Esther wrestled them down, standing tall before Murdoch and knowing where she truly belonged.

"I won't go," she told him, unwilling to let the pain in his eyes sway her. "I said we'd do this together and I meant it, Will."

Another distress rocket hissed and crackled through the air, flooding their faces with ghostly light. Murdoch's grip on her arms tightened like a vice until it almost *hurt*, and for one tense moment, she wondered if he was going to drag her over to the boat. She thought of the woman he had no choice but to force aboard earlier, and in that moment, she knew she might have to fight him. She clenched her hands into fists, her eyes unwavering, full of heart as they burned into his.

Perhaps Murdoch was frustrated enough to give in. Perhaps he knew that manhandling her into the boat would not only be unjust and difficult, it would also waste what little time they had left. Or perhaps he respected her resiliency and stubborn determination after all. But whatever the reason, he released her arms and stepped back with a look of resignation. The agony vanished from his eyes, sealed behind a wall of indifference as he accepted defeat a second time. He didn't even look at her as he strode to the collapsible.

"Prepare to lower!" he ordered, cool and professional once more.

Esther wordlessly reached for the line, fighting to stay her trembling hands and trying to convince herself that what she was doing was right.

But she couldn't forget the soft, staggering pain in Murdoch's voice when he'd begged her to get in the collapsible. Pleaded with her. That was the first time throughout this entire disaster that she'd seen his calm facade slip. Now he was stone-faced, refusing to even look at her.

Esther reached for his compass in her coat pocket, letting its cool metal soothe her and hoping he wouldn't stay angry for long. Not *now*, for God's sake. Not at a time like this.

As she stood by the falls in wait of his orders, she noticed a sudden movement out of the corner of her eye.

The breath caught in her throat, and she felt the anger sizzle a hole right through her chest as she stared at the sight before her.

Bruce Ismay had clambered swiftly over the gunwale and into Collapsible C, his back ramrod straight as he took his seat, his panicked eyes staring straight on ahead. Esther couldn't even muster a glare. She could only gape at him as shock and disgust cascaded through her. Of all the people who ought to help these poor passengers until the bitter end,

Ismay should have been one of them. It didn't matter if he wasn't directly responsible for the sinking. As chairman of White Star Line, he had a moral obligation to his paying customers and dedicated crew.

But now, as he settled himself into the little collapsible, fully prepared to leave them all behind, it was clear there wasn't a decent or honorable bone in his damn body.

"*Ready on the left!*"

As Murdoch belted out the order, his gaze fell upon Ismay.

The first officer went motionless, hands dropping rigidly at his sides. Esther saw his jaw tighten. Saw his eyes darken, narrowing with contempt. He didn't look away from Ismay once, his Scottish burr carrying a cutting, knifelike edge as he commanded, "Take them down."

Esther loosened her grip on the line with her crewmates, the pulleys squeaking loudly in her ears.

"Steady," Murdoch ordered, and she was surprised by the sudden weariness of his voice. "Keep it steady. Both sides together, lads, steady."

The collapsible dipped toward the waiting sea, little by little, until Ismay was gone from sight. Murdoch brushed pointedly past Esther, crossing the deck to join Moody and Wilde.

"'Fraid it's Collapsible A next," he told them brusquely, nodding toward the officers' quarters. "And we'll have to get her down from the roof, of all places."

"We'll manage, eh?" Wilde swore. "We can brace the ruddy thing with oars, perhaps."

Murdoch nodded. "S'pose we don't rightly have a choice." Twisting on his heel, he called over one shoulder, "I'll ready her on the roof."

He started for the officers' quarters in silence, still ignoring his subordinate. Esther dissolved into flat-out fury as she stormed after him, climbing the ladder to the roof and trying not to trip over her stupid skirt. It wasn't until she scrambled up the last steps that she caught his sleeve, stopping him in his tracks.

"Don't be like this, Will. You *know* I couldn't get in that damn boat."

"You could have." His voice was bitter; she could see the faint traces of a cold anger in his eyes. "You simply chose not to."

Murdoch shrugged her off, shouting for the crew to start uncovering the collapsible. Esther stepped forward to assist, scowling at him.

"Well, what did you expect? How could you possibly think I could leave you? We made a promise—"

"To hell with the promise!" Murdoch snapped. "It means *nothing*, lass. Not while you're in danger. Not at the expense of your life!"

Esther snarled out a retort, and suddenly she and Murdoch were bickering back and forth as they prepped and worked around the collapsible. It might have been comical, had their situation not been so serious. The deckhands exchanged glances, shocked to see the officers going at it. But neither Esther nor Murdoch paid them any mind.

Murdoch's eyes blazed as his gloved hands worked deftly, snapping off the collapsible's turnbuckles and rolling back the canvas cover.

"I don't understand you!" he shouted. "You know what might happen tonight. You know I only want to keep you safe. And yet, you disregard all that and blatantly go against my wishes—my orders, even—"

"Because I don't have a choice!" she said fiercely, as she helped him wrench the tarpaulin away. "I'm scared shitless that I'm going to die tonight, but I have to help. I *have* to stay. My duty is not only to you, but to all these people on board. I could never forgive myself if I left them. Even less so if I left you!"

"And do you think this is any easier for me, lass?" Murdoch demanded. "Watching you forfeit your last chance at safety—at life, even—and knowing that I was the one who put you in this peril in the first place? I'd never forgive myself if anything were to happen to *you*, either!" He turned away from her to address the crew, his voice raw and hoarse from shouting. "Get some ropes on her, lads! Then we'll rock her to the edge, nice and easy."

The sailors followed the order at once, scurrying around for some lines while oars were propped up below. Murdoch wiped the glisten of sweat from his brow, angry as he faced Esther once more.

"God forbid I try to protect the woman I love," he said, his voice heavy with bitter sarcasm. "I respect your bravery, Esther, I really do. But you should be out *there*, in a boat." He flung one gloved finger toward the sea. "Not here on this ship, damn it, risking your bleedin' neck!"

Esther reared up on her tiptoes, meeting his stubbornness with her own. "And you should be—" she started to argue. But she stopped, thinking she hadn't heard him correctly. Her voice dropped to a whisper.

"What did you say?"

Murdoch stared at her, as if he had never seen someone so daft. "I said you ought to be on a lifeboat, you numpty—"

"No." Her throat felt cracked and dry. "What you said before that."

The words were still running through her thoughts, slipping through her mind like a slow trickle of water.

God forbid I try to protect the woman I...

Murdoch swallowed thickly, a shade of scarlet flaming his cheeks; perhaps he hadn't meant to speak those words aloud. But now he was stepping closer to her, the anger in his eyes softening, turning to something else she couldn't define. And as he closed the distance between them, Esther was dimly aware that the chaos around her was torn away, fading into silence: the groan of stressed metal, the water slithering across the deck, the crew shouting for oars. It was all gone, save for the fitful stuttering of her pulse, and the quiet words Murdoch spoke in her ear.

"I love you, Esther Bailey. With all my heart."

Esther suddenly couldn't think straight. She stared at Murdoch in astonishment, wordlessly lost in his deep blue eyes. Their gazes met for what felt like a lifetime, the heated argument all but forgotten between them, and Esther felt an inexplicable warmth cascade from her chest to her fingertips. It flooded her veins like liquid light, bright enough to scatter away this nightmare of torment and despair, to brand her soul with its blazing sincerity.

She reached out for his hand, twining her fingers with his, more than ready to say those words back—but Murdoch had no choice but to turn away when a deckhand announced that they were ready to lower. He knelt before the collapsible at once, the flush still coloring his cheeks as he braced his palms against the gunwale. Esther joined him without a second thought, his confession of love glowing, soft and warm and wonderful, in the chamber of her heart.

Murdoch's steady orders rang out across the roof. "Keep rocking! Keep her rocking!"

But the collapsible refused to budge. More crewmen were called over for additional muscle, and even a handful of passengers clambered up the roof to help.

Eventually, after a great deal of pushing and swaying, they managed to ease the collapsible to the edge of the roof. Esther was wincing, breathing heavily from the exertion as she clenched the gunwale tight.

"Hold it," Murdoch commanded sharply, as the collapsible began to sway lower, teetering precariously over the deck below. "Hold it—"

And then he bellowed himself hoarse.

"*Hold iiittt!*"

The collapsible tumbled to the boat deck, snapping the oars beneath it. As crewmen swarmed around its frame to attach the falls, Wilde fought to beat frenzied passengers back.

"*Women and children only, damn you!*" he roared, again and again.

Esther turned to Murdoch, but he had already dropped down to the boat deck, not even bothering with the ladder. She did the same, caught up in her haste to follow him. But the fall was higher than she'd thought, and unlike Murdoch—who'd landed nimbly on his feet—she staggered, tripped over her skirt, and almost went toppling down on the deck.

"Shit," the seventh officer grunted in pain, struggling to regain her balance. She rushed to join Murdoch, who stood hunched over the stairwell to A Deck, hands clenching either side of the banister. Shock and horror swelled in his eyes, and when she moved closer to peer over her shoulder, she realized why.

Seawater, foaming and pale green, billowed its way through the stairwell, churning up the steps and flooding the decks far below.

Murdoch spun around, nearly slamming into Esther as he rushed to the collapsible. "Get these davits cranked in!" he bellowed. "And get the falls hooked up!"

"Will!" Esther grappled for his hand, not wanting to lose him in the bustle of crewmen.

But the mere sight of the water-drowned stairwell seemed to have launched him into a state of deadly focus, and he was heedless of anything but preparing that collapsible.

They were running out of time, and Murdoch knew it.

Esther hurried to help him, trying to ignore the dread and fear crawling down her spine as the sea crept closer. Christ, how were they ever going to make it through this?

She was about to pick up the falls when a hand gripped her shoulder, and she found herself looking up at Wilde. His cap was slightly askew, his temples shining with sweat and saltwater.

"Miss Bailey," he said, his voice urgent, "I've a favor to ask of you."

She straightened up at once. "Sir?"

"We'll need lifebelts very, *very* soon. Is there any chance you'd be willing to retrieve them?"

Esther did not answer immediately. She spared an uneasy glance at Murdoch, and Wilde followed her gaze, adding, "Don't you fret, miss. I'll keep an eye on our dashing Scotsman for you. That, I promise."

Esther nodded numbly, trying to swallow down the apprehension billowing up her throat like bile. "Right. Where are the lifebelts stored?"

"My cabin, second bureau. Bring as many as you can carry, please."

Esther let her gaze linger on Murdoch one last time, watching him bellow orders and scramble with the davits. Though she wanted nothing more than to keep by his side, she knew there was little time to waste. They needed those lifebelts. The sooner, the better.

And so she nodded at Wilde once more, kindling her resolve from a spark to a flame.

"Yes, sir."

02:10

Sometime during the mad scramble to ready Collapsible A, Murdoch realized that Bailey had disappeared.

He stood rooted in place, his eyes sweeping over the deck as he scoured for her freckles and dark hair. But where his subordinate had once been glued to his side, now she was nowhere in sight.

Panic seized him, and although all instincts urged Murdoch to start shouting her name, to search for her amid the tumult, he forced himself to maintain his composure. He hastened over to Moody first, who was fumbling to secure the collapsible to its falls.

"Jim!" he called, almost breathless as he spoke. "Have you seen Esther?"

Moody shook his head. "Sorry, sir, I—" he started to say, but Wilde strolled over to answer for him.

"Sent her off to fetch us some lifebelts."

Murdoch rounded on him in a sudden temper. "You couldn't have sent someone else?" he demanded fiercely.

Wilde raised his brows. "Steady on, Will, she'll be all right. And we need those lifebelts, remember? Now more than ever."

As if to prove his point, *Titanic* released a deep, shuddering groan beneath their feet, while the gush of seawater grew even louder.

"Bloody hell," he muttered under his breath, a flicker of uneasiness in his eyes. Wilde turned his back on the passengers to face the flooded bridge wing, and Murdoch watched him load his Webley with bullets.

"There's not much time left," he murmured under his breath. "And the crowds will only get worse, I'm afraid. We'll have to protect the collapsible so the last women and children may board." He slid back the chamber, gray eyes meaningful and steady. "I'll need your help, Will."

Murdoch knew perfectly well what Wilde was implying, and although he wanted nothing more than to avoid drawing a firearm, he knew there was no choice. Already the crowd had grown tenfold beyond the partitioned gate, men pushing and shoving one another in blind, frantic desperation to reach the boat. Neither crew nor officers would be able to hold them back for much longer. Not as the water continued to rise. Not as the chaos continued to worsen. So Murdoch drew his Webley after a reluctant pause, filling its chamber with bullet after bullet and trying to ignore the dread twisting in his stomach.

Wilde waited until Murdoch loaded his gun before voicing stern orders. "You man the left, I'll take the right. We'll pull the women and children through and control the crowd while Mr. Moody oversees the collapsible."

Moody stood tall and determined, nodding his acknowledgement, and Wilde continued, "If anyone tries to break through, well..." His expression was hard, unyielding. "We'll have no choice but to shoot."

Nodding mechanically, Murdoch faced the crowd with his Webley clutched in one gloved hand. But unlike Wilde, he chose not to point it at the passengers—not yet, at least. He kept it at his side instead, ushering the women and children forward and leaving the crewmen to grapple with the mob. But the passengers could not be controlled, and it wasn't long before the deck dissolved into utter chaos. Men shouted and barreled into each other, some plummeting from the ship and tumbling into the deep green water below. Concerned for the women and children in the boat behind him, Murdoch was forced to brandish his Webley, drawing it from his coat and pointing it at the crowd with a practiced hand.

"I will shoot down any man who tries to get past me, get back!"

He refused to lower his gun, knowing he had no choice but to threaten, to do anything in his power to defend those sitting in the collapsible behind him. Though his voice had grown hoarse from all the shouting, his warnings still ripped through the chilled night air.

A first-class passenger stumbled his way to the front of the crowd, haggard and disheveled in his fancy white tie, and it took a moment for Murdoch to recognize the face of Callum Lockerbie. Fury seized him, and he lifted his gun with a brutal snarl.

"Get *back,* I say!"

He trained the barrel of his gun on Lockerbie, thinking of Bailey and wanting nothing more than to silence the man who had abused her.

His finger twitched, so perilously close to drawing back the trigger. It would be quick and effortless. Already Murdoch could picture the bullet driving straight through Lockerbie's skull—the blood bubbling at his lips, the sound of his worthless corpse toppling to the deck in a heap—and he clenched his Webley even tighter.

Shoot him, a voice at the back of his mind urged. *It's all he deserves.*

He wanted to do it. Christ, he wanted nothing more.

But as the cold reality of the screams and despair swelled around him, Murdoch felt his blinding rage settle, smoothed away by duty and discipline. With a tremendous and almost painful amount of self-control, he collected himself and reeled back his vindictive thoughts, knowing nothing good would come of them.

The sea'll claim him, anyhow, Murdoch reasoned. *If we're lucky enough.*

No reason to waste bullets. No reason to strip away his pride and become a murderer, when the frigid cold of the North Atlantic could do the job for him.

Murdoch started to lower his gun, but raised it again as Lockerbie stormed closer. He was no longer the smug, arrogant oil heir he'd once been—just another scared man unwilling to accept death at sea. Defiance and panic burned in his eyes as he fumbled in his pocket, withdrawing a stack of bills once more.

"Take it, damn you, and let me through!"

But Murdoch had enough. He slammed Lockerbie's hand away, sending the dollars exploding into the air and fluttering down at their feet.

"Seems I was wrong about you, laddie," Murdoch sneered. Disgust scalded his voice as he stared into the eyes of the man before him, his words calm but cutting. "You're not only a fool. You're a coward."

Lockerbie spat at his feet. "And you are a pathetic scrap of a man—"

"—who'll die plenty happy knowing your corpse will rest at the bottom of the sea," Murdoch finished coldly. He slammed his palm against Lockerbie's shoulder, driving him back into the crowd. "*Get back!*"

The crowd swelled as Murdoch guarded the last collapsible with his life, pointing his Webley at the sea of terrified faces before him and longing for the woman he loved to return to his side.

02:15

Esther flung herself into the officers' quarters at lightning speed, desperate to find and collect the lifebelts as quickly as possible.

The corridor was still brightly lit, its floor slanted so steeply that she was almost running uphill. Cold, knee-deep water swelled at the end of the hall, lapping at the tilted floor and shedding unearthly, rippling refractions of light along the walls. It frightened her, but Esther ignored her fear as she sloshed through the piercing water and scrambled inside Wilde's cabin.

She found the room in disarray, its floor littered with fallen books, picture frames, and an overturned lamp. Thuds and shouts echoed overhead as deckhands worked to lower the collapsible on the port side roof; even Lightoller's booming voice was discernible.

Esther didn't have any time to waste. She dashed to the bureau first, ripping out the contents of each drawer and sorting through finely-pressed shirts and stashes of cigars and whiskey until she finally, *blessedly* found the lifebelts. Only four in total, but it was enough.

As she gathered them in her hands and turned to leave, she spotted someone familiar through the window. There was no mistaking his ink-black hair and lanky height.

"*Booker!*"

Her brother turned at her shout, frowning through the windowpane.

And when he saw his sister standing in the middle of the untidy room, he scrambled forward at once.

"Stay there!" Esther shouted through the glass. "I'll be right out!"

She dashed down the hallway, stumbling headlong into passengers as she barreled out to the boat deck. The crowds here were just as thick as the starboard side, and Esther stood on her tiptoes, peering above the crushing tide of people.

"Booker!" she yelled again. "I'm here!"

Her brother followed her cries, shoving his way through the throng to reach her, his face pale and strained as he pulled her into an embrace.

"Christ Almighty, why are you still here, Esther? Why aren't you on a goddamn boat?"

"I could ask you the same question!" Esther gasped. "And where the hell is your lifebelt?" She shoved one at him. Three left now, but it was enough for Murdoch, Wilde, and Moody. And that was all that mattered. "Take it and come with me," she told her brother. "Murdoch will let you on a boat so long as you can pull an oar, I know he will—"

But Booker shook his head. "I can't do that, Esther."

Esther stared at him, almost sightless in her rage. "Are you insane?" She shuffled her grip on the lifebelts, freeing her left hand and snagging his wrist tight. "You're coming with me whether you like it or not—"

"Esther, *no*." Booker yanked free from her grasp, his voice suddenly firm. "I won't take the place of a woman or child. And I..." His eyes flickered across her face, his chest heaving with slow, deep breaths. "I can't leave Thomas. I'm sorry, Esther, but I can't."

"I—what?" Esther was bewildered. "Why? Where is he?"

"He's inside the ship as we speak. I tried to get him abovedecks, but he won't..." Booker looked absolutely wretched. "He won't go."

Esther bit her lip hard, fighting against the gut-wrenching ache in her chest. It was heartbreaking to think such a brilliant man would trade his own life to rest with *Titanic* at the bottom of the sea. But that didn't mean Booker had to die along with him.

Livid and terrified, Esther spluttered, "Surely you're not thinking of going down with him? You can't sacrifice your life for the sake of his, Booker!"

Before her brother could respond, a booming voice made them turn.

"…Do your best for the women and children, and look out for yourselves."

Esther glanced to the port bridge wing to see Captain Smith addressing the nearest crewmen with a megaphone, swirls of seawater lapping at his feet. Their eyes met, and to her surprise, he tipped his cap in a gesture of farewell. She did the same, somewhat perplexed but refusing to question the matter. But her confusion turned to immediate understanding as Smith lowered the megaphone, stepped inside the wheelhouse, and closed the door behind him.

Esther choked on a gasp of horror as she realized what was happening. She took an instinctive step toward the wheelhouse, but Booker gripped her shoulder, holding her back.

"Let him go. A captain is meant to go down with his ship."

Esther snapped her blazing eyes up at her brother. "A noble captain, yes. An honorable shipwright, certainly. But not you." She snagged a bundle of his coat with her free hand, desperately trying to drag him back to the starboard side along with her. "You're an idiot if you think you're staying behind with Mr. Andrews."

But Booker refused to move. "I can't leave him, Es. You should understand this more than anyone. I'm not stupid; I know how you feel about Officer Murdoch. Would you be any more willing to leave him, if you were given the chance?"

Shock swept over Esther as she stared into his pained eyes, suddenly wondering if Andrews meant more to her brother than she'd realized. She struggled for a reply, but her mind went still as the unmistakable crack of a gunshot split the air.

Esther whirled around, seeking Lightoller and assuming her colleague fired a warning shot. But the second officer hadn't even drawn his revolver; he was too busy barking orders in his haste to bring down Collapsible B.

Another gunshot sounded off, rising above the turmoil like thunder. And only then did she realize where the sound was coming from.

The starboard side of the ship.

Esther felt the breath catch in her throat. Felt the icy fear consume her, snaking through her veins like liquid poison and clouding all reasonable, rational thought.

Will, she thought frantically.

The blood roared in her ears as she rounded on her brother, pleading with him, begging him to come with her.

"For the love of God!" she cried, "I have to find Will, I have to go to him! But I need to know you won't do something stupid! I need you to come with me!" Her voice rose in pitch, cracking with the weight of mindless fear. "Please, Booker. I can't lose another brother!"

Booker swallowed, and Esther knew he was thinking of Brighton. She watched, breathless, as something shifted in her brother's eyes. Wordlessly he nodded his assent, and Esther wasted no time in racing toward the bridge, stumbling her way through passengers and crew alike. She raced through the gated partition with Booker at her heels, breathless and sweating, fighting to get a decent grip on the lifebelts tucked into her arms. But when they arrived at the bridge, they found it completely awash, the wheel and lit telegraphs surrounded by cold, clear, waist-deep seawater.

"*Shit!*" Esther swore, while *Titanic* released another deep, rattling groan.

A white ladder clung to the side of the officers' quarters, but Esther's arms were laden with lifebelts; she'd never make the climb with them. So they doubled back, crossing through the eerie, listing quiet of the officers' quarters before spilling out to the starboard side. They found themselves standing at the back of the crowd, which had become uncontrollable. Esther couldn't even see Murdoch beyond the tangle of lifebelts and limbs. But she could hear him, thank Christ, his raspy, Scottish burr bellowing for calm, rising above the roar of voices and distant ragtime waltzes. She kept elbowing and shoving her way through the wall of bodies, refusing to stop—not even as another gunshot cleaved the air.

"Make way!" Esther shouted, fighting to wade through the crushing swell of people. "Come on, *move!* Officer coming through!"

After a great deal of jostling, she and Booker reached the edge of the mob at long last. Esther could see Murdoch now, and Wilde along with him, the pair of them wielding their firearms before the unruly passengers.

"*Will!*" Esther shouted. She tried to call his name again, but the words became a snarling curse as someone slammed into her from behind, sending her staggering from the throng.

She stumbled forward with a hiss of indignation, the lifebelts spilling from her hands.

And in those few, fleeting seconds, Esther barely had time to register the Webley pointed at the disturbance in the crowd—the disturbance her stumble had created—when the gun went off with another *crack*.

A squeak of surprise escaped her lips as searing, white-hot pain plunged through her, burrowing through layers of flesh, blood and bone.

The breath was whisked from her lungs, and Esther tried to regain it, gasping as the agony laced through her veins like fire. Gun smoke stung her nose, bitter and metallic, sharp enough to make her gag.

Shakily she fumbled for the wound, hands searching, scrambling against her coat. And when she withdrew her fingers, she found them wet, dripping with blood.

Esther was almost numb with shock, her breathing shallow, her eyes wide and uncomprehending.

She had known many types of pain. A broken brandy bottle to the skin. A heavy pistol to the face. A clenched hand to her windpipe. But this…this was something far different.

This was absolutely excruciating.

Her knees buckled beneath her, and a desperate voice bellowed her name as she crumpled.

"*Esther!*"

But she scarcely heard the shout as she went toppling to the deck, dark hair spilling out from underneath her cap, shivering hands stained with blood.

Warmth suddenly enveloped her, smelling of soap and sandalwood aftershave. Esther felt an arm hook under her knees, while another slid around her shoulders, and before she knew it, she was being lifted off her feet. Someone swept her up into their arms like a bride, holding her with careful tenderness. But Esther was too disoriented to recognize who it was; she didn't even know who fired the shot. Thoughts muzzy and eyes unfocused, she merely leaned her head against their chest and let herself be carried away.

Gentle hands sat her down, lowering her beside the collapsible. The listing deck was cold and damp beneath her hands, slick with sea spray, and she was dimly aware of someone saying her name, over and over. She blinked away her dizziness, slowly recognizing his voice and letting it soothe her, pulling her away from the pain and back to her senses.

"Stay with me, lass."

Esther sighed, knowing she was in safe hands with Murdoch at her side. Familiar blue eyes searched her face, dark and frantic, before dropping down to her greatcoat. His coarse hands unfastened the buttons, quickly but carefully pulling the folds apart. He tore apart the sleeve of her blouse next, the white fabric soaked to crimson, and the two officers were silent as they stared at the dark, dime-sized hole cut into her upper left arm. Hot blood cascaded from the bullet wound, speckling the deck with dots of red, and Murdoch uttered a soft Scottish oath under his breath.

Esther clenched her teeth. "Could've been worse." She cracked a smile, trying to stomach the pain. "'Least it's not sprained wrist—"

A furious voice sliced the air before her superior could reply.

"That's my *sister!*" she heard Booker roar. "Let me through, jackass!"

Wilde must have allowed him to pass, because her brother stumbled forward, clutching a spare lifebelt to his chest. He knelt on the deck beside his sister, his wide, watery gaze studying the puncture in her arm.

Murdoch only had eyes for Esther as he applied pressure to the wound, bracing her arm with the heel of his hand.

"What else can I do?" he asked pleadingly.

"Bandage," she managed to grit out. "Please. And make it tight. It'll stop the bleed—"

She had barely finished the sentence before Murdoch grasped the fabric of her torn sleeve and tied it around her arm, wrenching it tight enough to stem the flow of blood. As he fastened the knot, she was suddenly aware of the water swirling closer to her feet, soaking into the hem of her greatcoat. It was a chilling reminder of the cruel, dark sea they would soon have to contend with.

Her breath quickened as the harsh reality of it all set in once more— the frightful screaming, the icy water, the bullet buried in her arm.

And she lost it.

Tears burned in her eyes as her fears finally spilled over, breaking through her resolve. She'd fought with all her might to remain professional, to keep it together for the sake of the passengers. For Murdoch, even.

But now Esther couldn't take it anymore.

She leaned into Murdoch and let the tears silently fall, sinking into his chest and wishing they could be long gone from this hell.

"I won't be able to swim for a boat when we go down," she wept, burying her face deeper into the fabric of his coat. "Not with this arm. I won't—"

But Murdoch pulled her away from his chest to look straight into her eyes. His gaze was steady, his voice firm as he promised, "You *will*. I'll help you. I'll be with you. I promise." His fingers swept beneath her lashes, wiping her tears away. "And we can still get you in the collapsible, if need be. Then I'll swim to you."

He cradled her face between his palms and gently kissed her forehead, the mere brush of his lips building up her strength again. "Here. Let's get a lifebelt on you."

Esther glanced around for the rest of the lifebelts she dropped. But they were gone, likely claimed by panicked passengers. Her eyes widened.

"But Will," she gasped. "You—"

"I'm a dead good swimmer," Murdoch said calmly, as he redid the buttons of her greatcoat and slid the lifebelt over her head. "Don't you worry about me, lass." He braced his hands underneath her good arm, helping her rise to her feet. "Up you get now." His voice was soft and murmuring against her ear. "Come on, lass. I'm here. I'm—"

But his words were drowned out by a terrifying, rushing roar.

Horrified, Esther turned to see the bridge wing plunging beneath the surface, swallowed beneath the foaming whitewash of the roiling sea. *Titanic* groaned as she sank, the sound low and ominous, rumbling from deep within her hull. Seawater spilled onto the deck in tides of vivid, frothy green. Colder than ice, it crept at Esther's ankles, then her knees—and finally came swirling all the way up to her waist. She cried out, shocked and freezing and nearly breathless. Murdoch grasped her hand tight and tugged her toward the collapsible, Booker and Moody wading frantically alongside them. But the water was swelling now, surging over the deck and pouring into the windows of the officers' quarters, its fast-flowing rush scattering terrified passengers and crew.

"*Cut those bloody falls!*" Wilde bellowed to the crew swarming around the collapsible. "*Cut 'em, for God's sake, cut 'em if you have to!*"

Esther did not have time to think. Only act.

Adrenaline lanced through her veins as she scrambled up on the gunwale and drew a penknife from her pocket, the searing pain of her wound suddenly driven from her mind. Murdoch joined her without hesitation, pulling his own knife from the folds of his greatcoat and climbing up beside her.

Together they balanced on the teetering collapsible, struggling to hold the first line taut as they sawed through the heavy manila threading.

They managed to slice through one rope, then another.

But they had barely moved on to a third when an enormous wave came crashing onto the deck in a sheet of ice-cold saltwater and foam, swallowing everything in its path.

Esther lost her footing as the collapsible swayed and rocked beneath her. She wobbled, Oxfords slipping on the water-soaked wood, hands scrabbling to cling to something, anything—

But her fingers clasped only air, and the last thing she heard was Murdoch shouting her name as she tumbled backward into the sea.

Water closed over her head, swallowing her whole, and for a few terrifying moments, Esther saw nothing but bubbling, foaming darkness.

Salt stung her eyes, her mouth, her wound. Her greatcoat grew heavy and waterlogged, dragging her down, rendering her lifebelt useless. Debris slammed against her head as the wave washed over her, whirling with a maelstrom of ropes, luggage, and deck chairs. The cold was agonizing, as if needles were drilling deep into her lungs, scraping against her skin like shards of broken glass. Yet she fought to ignore it, clawing her way to the surface, struggling to find the smallest shred of air before she blacked out entirely—

A hand reached out for her, barely discernible through the whirling haze of foamy water.

Esther recognized the dark leather of Murdoch's glove, and she clasped his fingers tight, gripping them with what little strength she had left. Her head broke above the water as he pulled her to the surface, and she gasped, coughing and spluttering, drawing in deep lungfuls of air. Murdoch waded close beside her, his cap swept from his head, his fingers still holding fast to hers.

The water crashed and roared around them, chilling her down to the bone, threatening to pull them apart. But Esther refused to let go of his hand, clinging to him with all her might as they were swept away into the icy sea.

TWENTY-FOUR

SEAWATER

April 15, 1912 | 02:15

THE WRENCH OF violent seawater dragging Charles Herbert Lightoller beneath the surface was just as sudden as it was terrifying—and it was in that moment that he finally allowed himself to panic.

His fingers scrambled madly, desperate to reach air, but something kept him pinned beneath the tides of foam and freezing water.

A grate, he realized. *Of all the sodding things.*

In his haste to swim away from the foundering vessel, Lightoller had somehow ended up trapped against a ventilation shaft above the officers' quarters. It sucked greedily at the back of his turtleneck, holding him beneath the surface, seeking to bring him down with the ship.

Saltwater stung his eyes and flooded his mouth. His vision sputtered and crackled with bright spots as his lungs burned, begging for the smallest sliver of oxygen.

As his strength began to fail him, and his struggling limbs turned to lead in the icy water, Lightoller thought of his wife one last time, hoping the memories of her love and laughter would be enough to make drowning painless—

A rush of pressurized heat suddenly burst at his back, slamming him away from the vent and propelling him through the water.

Roaring and screaming for air, Lightoller clawed his way up through the sea. Cold, blessed oxygen filled his lungs as his head broke the surface, and he gasped, drawing in the deepest breaths he'd ever taken in his life.

He didn't have a moment to wonder what happened, let alone how he'd escaped the suction. He was focused on only one thing—and that was swimming as far away from *Titanic* as possible.

His long arms worked quickly, slicing their way through the painfully cold sea. But Lightoller could feel an odd weight impeding him, dragging him down in the water, and he realized he still had the Webley in his pocket. He discarded the pistol into the abyssal depths before swimming on, fighting for his life like so many others around him.

In the turmoil of terrified people, Lightoller eventually found himself facing the overturned keel of Collapsible B. He clambered up its side, hands slipping and sliding on the water-slick wood.

It took him several tries, weak as he was, but soon Lightoller managed to scramble aboard. He crouched there for a moment, shaking with cold, gaping at the sight before him.

Titanic was slipping away into the North Atlantic, her forward end swollen with frothy turquoise water, her aft end arching high into the air. She was at a horrifying list, porthole lights sparkling across the glassy sea, some of them dimming red before they were extinguished, one by one, beneath the sheet of cold water. Her funnels and tall mast stood silhouetted against the blue night sky, contrasting with the bright promenades still blazing with light.

Lightoller could see passengers scrambling up the steepened slope of the boat deck, desperate to prolong their entry into the frigid ocean awaiting them. Some were already abandoning ship, leaping from brightly lit decks and promenades, willing to brave the freezing water beneath them.

But worst of all was the screaming, the collective cries and keens of the poor souls who were scared. Who didn't want to die.

It was a terrible sound, worse than anything Lightoller had ever heard, and he knew that if he lived through all this, he would never forget it.

The longer he watched *Titanic* sink, the less Lightoller could believe this was the same ship he'd first set eyes upon in Belfast. The same stunning vessel that had sat proudly in her berth all those weeks ago, her paintwork fresh, her plated hull glistening. Lightoller had boarded her with dignity, the title of first officer on his shoulders and his old friend William Murdoch at his side.

But now that day was only a distant memory as this tragic nightmare played out before him, and *Titanic* cried out, wounded and dying, her metal groaning, rumbling, and clanking as she bowed to the icy sea.

Lightoller uttered a curse as the tilt of *Titanic* grew even steeper, unable to tear his eyes away from the horror in front of him—until a sudden splashing caught his attention.

Glancing down, he saw a young man struggling to climb up the capsized boat, his face ghostly-white beneath a mop of soaked dark hair.

Lightoller was quick, shimmying to the edge of the hull and offering his hand.

"I've got you!" he promised, as their ice-cold fingers locked tight. "Up you get, son!"

The young man was hauled aboard, coughing and choking out seawater, and Lightoller was momentarily stunned when he recognized the familiar face before him.

"Mr. Bailey?"

Before either of them could speak, a tremendous noise like the crack of a whip struck the air.

Lightoller wheeled around, searching for the source of the commotion, and it took him mere seconds to realize what was happening.

Steel cables were snapping from the forward funnel, lashing hard against the water with a series of hissing splashes. One of them struck a man clinging to a deck chair, killing him instantly. Another whipped across a cluster of people struggling to swim, cracking their spines in half and turning their bodies limp in the sea.

The funnel swayed, no longer supported by its cabling, and Lightoller could only watch in helpless terror as it toppled in an explosion of seawater and soot, crushing the poor souls beneath it.

An enormous wave surged out upon impact, pitching against the collapsible and slamming against his back. Water doused every inch of him, pouring off him in streams.

But Lightoller held tight, adjusting his grip on the keel and ignoring the wet chill soaking him straight to the bone.

He had to hang on. He had to keep fighting.

He had to see Sylvia again.

02:17

Thomas Andrews pressed one last lifebelt into a frightened woman's hands when he saw the clear, cold water flooding up the steps of the Grand Staircase.

He swallowed, bracing himself against the nearest balustrade with one hand and caressing his wedding band with the other.

Screams of the drowning pierced the air, rising from the decks far below. Glass windows buckled in their frames, dragging passengers and torrents of water inside.

Some people fought to swim, flailing their limbs with all their might. Others clung to support beams and statues, desperate to stay afloat. Freezing water and seafoam tunneled in faster and faster, swallowing the oaken steps and their scrollwork until even the panel of *Honour and Glory* was submerged, its opulent clock face finally claimed by the sea.

And as Andrews watched the destruction of his ship unfold around him, he knew there was nothing more he could do. He had hurried around the decks for hours, ushering passengers to safety, flinging deck chairs overboard, and distributing lifebelts to anyone in sight.

But now, as the ocean hissed and barreled its way onto the Grand Staircase, and *Titanic's* tilt steepened beneath his feet, Andrews knew his time was running out. It was only a matter of minutes before fate caught up with him, and he became little more than a nameless pair of shoes on the seafloor.

Looking down at his shaking hands, Andrews struggled to come to terms with the inevitable.

But as he prepared to meet his demise, he found himself thinking not only of his wife…but of Booker Bailey.

Andrews thought of the way his apprentice had kept by his side, rushing to help as many passengers as possible. He recalled the fight in the young man's eyes. The refusal to let his mentor go down with the ship.

Booker had tried to stay with him, even until the bitter end. And although Andrews had sent him away, he would never forget that.

Booker had been a good soul. An earnest young man with a thirst for knowledge and a keen eye for shipbuilding. They would have worked well together. They would have gone on to draft blueprints and design steamships unlike anything the world had ever seen. If only they had had

more time—

There was a deafening crash as the glass dome buckled and shattered. A series of bloodcurdling screams. A lurid flash as waterlogged lights shorted and crackled out. And it took less than a second for Thomas Andrews to realize that this was the end.

His death was painful.

Not because of the endless cascades of whitewater roaring over top of him, pummeling his bones and starving him of breath.

It was because in his last few moments of awareness, he felt as if he'd failed not only himself, but thousands of innocent people.

02:20

As he struggled to stay afloat in the chilling water, James Moody could do nothing but watch as *Titanic* sank from sight.

He couldn't believe his eyes.

As her deck steepened, passengers could no longer stand on their feet. They were sliding down into the water below, hands scrambling for purchase on the smooth wood beneath them. Eerie noises echoed in the depths of the ship—the crash of shattered chinaware, the clatter of deck chairs tangling together, and a series of thuds and gruesome cracks that suggested worse damage deep within her hull.

The deeper the bow ducked beneath the surface, the higher the stern lifted into the air, parting with the sea until her propellers and keel—parts of a ship meant to stay underwater—were visible. Water washed the decks, slopping its way through the promenades and corridors Moody had once roamed on his daily rounds. Lights flickered and dimmed, fading from bright yellow to dull, dying red. Chilling screams pierced the air.

And as *Titanic* arched higher, seawater trickling in sheets down her plated hull, it seemed her metal could take the stress of the tilt no longer.

She broke amidships, snapping almost cleanly in two with an explosion of split steel and sparks.

Pillars and promenades collapsed like matchsticks, flattening to pieces. Sheet metal tore and rivets speckled the air as the magnificent ship was ripped apart.

Her aft end plummeted down to the water below, throwing up a tremendous wave of whitewater as she settled on an even keel. Even in the starlit darkness, Moody could see her tunnels toppling over, collapsing and clanging their way into the sea.

Broken and mangled, *Titanic*'s forward end quickly flooded with water; it didn't last long, disappearing beneath the surface in a matter of seconds. But the stern arched back up with a rumbling metallic groan unlike anything Moody had ever heard, raising higher, and higher, until it was vertical—just a mere silhouette pointed straight up at the starry sky.

Moody could hear the panicked screams. He could see people clinging to the ship for dear life. Some of them managed to hold on, but many lost their grip and fell, slamming into vents and rails with sickening crunches before tumbling into the sea. Moody gritted his teeth; he clasped his hands over his ears and closed his eyes. He wished this was all a dream—a nightmare—and that he would wake warm in his bunk, ready to step on the bridge for his next watch.

But this terror was too real, too brutal to be a dream. Moody almost couldn't stand it—the freezing water that made his teeth chatter, the screams of those still clinging to the upright stern—and now, the slithering, rushing roar as the once-magnificent ship descended into the depths of the North Atlantic.

She slid smoothly beneath the surface, deeper and deeper until only the white rails edging her stern were visible. Moody caught one last glimpse of the words *LIVERPOOL… TITANIC* in the darkness.

Then her flagstaff slipped under the foam of the roiling sea, and she disappeared completely.

Suddenly, the screaming and splashing around Moody only intensified. Held afloat by his lifebelt, he kicked his legs through the water, struggling to propel himself away from the chaos. But he could only go so far before the cold overpowered him—a deep, brackish chill so agonizing, he felt as if his skin was aflame.

He clung to a nearby deck chair, blowing his whistle as over a thousand of people floated around him, crying, wailing, and praying into the black, hopeless night.

"*Come back! For God's sake!*"

"*Please, help us!*"

"*Help me, God!*"

Their screams tore at his heart. Moody longed to answer their pleas—to spare them from their suffering in any way possible.

But there was nothing he could do. He was no longer an officer, but a mere speck in a scattered ocean of drowning souls. He could do nothing else except blow into his whistle, clinging to his deck chair and hoping a boat might pass by.

Somewhere in the distance, Moody heard another whistle ringing out across the sea. Then another. He wondered which of his fellow officers it might be. He had lost Bailey, Murdoch, and Wilde when the first wave overran the decks. But he prayed they were still out there. Still alive. Still fighting, like him, for survival.

A sharp cry made him lower his whistle, and he turned to see a young woman floundering in the water. Her hair was slick against her skull, her eyes wide and terrified. Although a lifebelt was fastened around her middle, she couldn't seem to swim properly, and Moody wondered if she was injured. He called to her, his voice rasping from the cold.

"Miss! Miss, here!"

She couldn't hear him. Or perhaps she couldn't understand him. But Moody used the last of his strength to glide toward the flailing woman, gripping her by the lifebelt and tugging her over to his deck chair. They held on, shivering, breaths misting the air to white.

"*Det är så kallt*," she kept saying, over and over. "*Det är så kallt. Jag fryser.*"

Although Moody couldn't understand her, he still heard the trembling fear in her voice.

"It's all right," he said, trying to console her. "We'll be all right."

She started to cry, and Moody held her frozen hand, not letting go.

He wasn't sure how much time passed before the wailing began to quiet. People gradually fell silent, one by one, their skin paling to blue, their bodies turning slack in their lifeboats. Moody could already feel frost crusting his hair and eyebrows. And when he turned to the young girl whose hand he was holding, he saw her eyes staring blankly at him, glazed over in death.

He tried to fumble for his whistle again. But his hands were far too heavy, white as bone and caked with ice. He couldn't even feel them now. He couldn't feel any part of his body.

His thoughts stumbled and slowed, growing hazy until he felt sleepy, almost. But at least he wasn't cold. At least he wasn't hurting anymore.

James Moody slowly closed his eyes, thinking only of his mother and wishing he could have seen her one last time.

02:25

Henry Tingle Wilde was not ready to die.

He had a family waiting for him back home in Liverpool. He had two young sons and two beautiful daughters to care for. He damn well wasn't going to leave them parentless, let alone freeze to death in the middle of the North Atlantic. So he blew his whistle as hard as he could, pausing only to roar his orders into the frigid night.

"*Return the boats!*"

His cap was gone, hair soaked and spilling across his forehead. Though he was a larger man with a good bit of muscle, the chill was unbearable, plunging into the submerged half of his body like needles.

But Wilde refused to let the cold thwart him.

It merely drove him onward, coaxing him to breathe into his whistle with every last scrap of strength he could muster. Hope was a flame that flickered brightly in his chest, and he let it burn—let it blaze through him, reassuring him he would see his children again.

He couldn't help but think of Esther Bailey—the spunky girl who in every way reminded him of his daughters—and a sudden, shuddering guilt crept through him as he recalled the shot he'd fired. Her wide, shocked green eyes as the bullet pierced her. The blood dripping from her trembling fingertips. The way she'd collapsed to her knees.

Wilde had never meant to shoot her. He had only tried to stop the last boat from being overridden amid the crushing panic on deck—and she'd gotten caught in the crossfire.

But Bailey was strong. She was a fighter. Even with a bullet to the arm, Wilde knew she would make it through this. Same as Murdoch.

He licked his lips, tasting saltwater, and blew his whistle again.

And again. And again.

But as the screaming and thrashing around him began to settle, and the waters became glassy and still, Wilde felt his own resolve crumble.

It dripped away, bit by bit, like water leaking from the cracks of a shoddy roof. And only then did he realize what would become of him.

He felt the anger first—anger that he had been transferred to *Titanic* in the first place. Anger that he was dying, when he still had so much to live for. Then came the grief as he imagined his children growing up without him. And finally, he was seized by the raw, harrowing fear of death. Of the unknown that awaited him.

This was the end, and he ruddy well knew it. Wilde could feel the ice building on his eyebrows and lashes. He could feel the whistle start to cling to his mouth. His limbs deadened, until he couldn't feel them at all.

And the pain—the heaving and burning of his overtaxed lungs, the excruciating cold unlike anything he had ever known before—it all tapered away into nothingness.

Henry Wilde was not ready to die.

But in those last few moments before the icy seawater claimed his life, he found peace in the notion that he and his wife would be together again.

02:30

Esther Anna Bailey could not swim any farther.

She had tried her damnedest to swim beside Murdoch in the deep, frozen water. But now she found herself struggling, slowing him down.

The sea was chilling. Brutal. So cold that she wanted to scream.

Salt scalded her gunshot wound, only adding to the pain, and it wasn't long before her injured arm seized up entirely. It became useless—a dead weight hanging listlessly at her side as she floundered after Murdoch, fighting to keep up with him.

He hadn't lied about being a decent swimmer; even in the freezing water, with no lifebelt and a heavy greatcoat weighing him down, his strokes were swift. And although the lifeboats were indiscernible beyond the darkness and desperate splashing, Esther was sure Murdoch would be able to reach them. He could keep going, even if she couldn't. He could make it out of this. And that was all that mattered to her.

Breathless, weak and wounded, Esther finally came to a stop. "Will," she struggled to say, as she shuddered with pain and cold. "I can't."

Murdoch turned to face her in the dark, bottomless water.

"You can," he urged. "Swim, lass. Swim."

Esther tried again, emboldened by the sound of his voice, willing to fight for him. She clawed her way one-handedly through the sea. She kicked her legs with all the strength she had left.

But the exhaustion and agony overtook her once more, and she suddenly found herself unable to move, drifting weakly in the water.

She tried telling him to go on without her—to get to a lifeboat and save himself. Although her words were raspy and jumbled together, he got the gist of what she was saying, and it didn't take him long to staunchly refuse. His gloved hand latched on to her lifebelt, and he kept swimming through the icy water, trying to tug her along, ignoring her feeble protests.

But the exertion of hauling another person was enough to diminish his own strength. His strokes grew slower, his breathing uneven, ragged. They had gone so far, and yet there were still no lifeboats in sight. Only a churning sea full of thrashing, floating people.

A chunk of debris drifted nearby, glistening wetly beneath the dim light. It wasn't large, but it was buoyant. It was enough. Murdoch led her over, swimming very weakly now, and together they clung, half-submerged, to the woodwork.

"We'll just have to get them to come to us, then," he told her.

His voice was calm but terribly quiet, shaking from the cold. Already she could see his lips turning blue. He reached for his whistle and blew into it, hard. Its shrill cry echoed across the water, rising above the terrifying chorus of screams.

Esther blew into her own whistle as well, and they kept at it for some time, trying to alert the boats floating somewhere in the distance.

But none came. Not a single one.

Time became nonexistent as they drifted, cold and silent, beneath the stars. Murdoch had stopped blowing his whistle. Not because he had given up, she knew, but because like her, he had no strength left. He leaned against the debris, quiet, simply holding her hand.

Esther clutched his fingers tight. She could feel the ice clinging to her hair. The frost smoothing its way over her skin. She could hear the cries grow quieter, and quieter, until only the frail, feeble moans of the dying echoed around them.

There was a point when the cold stopped being painful. When it was just there, and Esther was too numb to even feel it. She was scared. She thought of her brothers. Of her parents. Of the many wonderful places that she had yet to explore with Murdoch at her side. Her heart swelled with a fear that stretched deeper than the ocean chasms miles and miles beneath her, and she shifted closer to him in the water, whispering, "I'm sorry, Will. I tried. I tried to swim."

His grip tightened on her hand. "I know, lass," he said softly. "You don't have to apologize. I'm the one who ought to be sorry." The words faded as he fought for breath. "I'm the one who put you through this bleedin' hell."

Although she was afraid, Esther felt something fiery blaze through her, some dying flame that flooded a sliver of life back into her veins.

"Don't," she pleaded. "Please don't say that. It wasn't your—"

"It was." The pain in his voice broke her heart. "It was, lass."

But she refused to listen. "No, Will. You did everything you could. And you risked your life to help so many people tonight."

"It wasn't enough."

"It was more than enough," she insisted. "You fought for those people just as you fought for me." She swallowed painfully, her lungs straining, her limbs shaking uncontrollably in the freezing water. But she held his gaze, her eyes unwavering as she spoke the truth aloud.

"And I love you, too, Will. I'll always love you."

The words were soft with their sincerity, rising up from the bottom of her heart. Murdoch couldn't seem to look away from her now. His grip tightened on her hand, a weak smile twitching at the corner of his mouth, and he didn't hesitate to lean into her cold ear, whispering words of love back. The guilt in his expression was gone, swept away by a tenderness reserved only for her.

For a while they gazed into each other's eyes, their mutual bond of respect and love and loyalty burning strong, brilliant and bright in the cruel, icy darkness. It was enough to protect her, to strengthen her, to chase away the cold and crippling fear of death.

Her glove was beginning to freeze in place, but Esther fought to scrape it off. She just wanted to touch him, to feel him one last time. Murdoch did the same, gently brushing his frozen lips against her knuckles before lacing their bare fingers tight.

And as they drifted, together and unafraid, Esther let her eyes wander to the heavens glimmering above their heads. A single star stood out to her, hanging like a fixed point amidst the swirling constellations, and she squeezed Murdoch's hand.

"Look," she said. "Polaris. We m-must be facing north."

His grip on her fingers tightened, and she heard the smile in his scratchy voice as he murmured, "You've b-been practicing, then."

"A little. You w-were right. Guess they weren't so s-stupid after all."

"Aye...Not too late to say 'I told you s-so,' is it?"

When she managed a weak laugh at his teasing, he rasped, "Tell me what else y-you see."

It was surprising how easily she could list them off, now that they were surrounded by nothing but deep ocean water.

Ursa Minor...Ursa Major...Vega...Capella...all the stars and constellations burned so beautifully, she wondered how she'd never cared to notice them before.

Murdoch had fallen silent again, listening to her name the stars. But as silence settled over them, and Esther lost feeling in the submerged lower half of her body, the first officer quietly spoke.

"You were brilliant tonight. Pure b-brilliant. A proper officer. Wearin' the proper uniform she so rightly deserves."

He swallowed, his breathing growing slower, weaker. Her heart swelled with emotion at his words, but she did not cry. She only kissed each of his shuddering fingertips and let herself mumble her thoughts and memories aloud, wanting nothing more than to share it all with him.

"And t-to think, you once hated my guts," she taunted. "I still get a k-kick outta all the shit we used to give each other. R-remember that day you helped with the t-tailor? You were such an *ass.* Said s-something about how you thought you were my superior officer, n-not my nanny."

He coughed out a laugh then, but it was hoarse and brittle.

Esther managed a smile, lips cracking with frost. "You were so d-damn cheeky. But you were there for m-me. It meant more than y-you'll ever know, Will. And I'll never forget that."

Murdoch closed his eyes, sighing softly, contentedly, leaning his head against the soaked debris.

She was aware that his breathing had gone silent. That his frosted hand had grown still. And yet she kept talking, her voice frail, cracking with exhaustion and grief.

"And then there was that d-day you stood up for me in front of that horrible passenger…and when you lied to the captain just so I c-could keep my job…and you were there for me that night I got hurt, helping me and h-holding me when I cried…"

Esther could not stop the words from tumbling out, even though his eyes refused to open, and his breathing faded away into silence.

William Murdoch was dead.

"Please," she whispered. She didn't know who she was pleading with. God, perhaps. Anyone who might hear her. "Please. Please, no. I have to go to New York w-with him. We have to go. We have to…"

Esther tried to grapple for her whistle, but she couldn't feel her hands. Or any part of her body, for that matter. She couldn't even turn her head. Her limbs had gone numb, her skin frozen and blue. Her pulse was slowing. Her breaths were short and shallow.

And only then did she realize what was happening.

She was dying beside him, on this spit of mangled furniture in the middle of the North Atlantic, clinging to his frosted hand and feeling nothing but love in her heart.

But her last thought was not of the lifeless bodies littered around them, nor was it the sight of Murdoch lying motionless, his hand frozen to hers. It was of a hope that was not yet lost in her mind—a glowing, gossamer dream that stretched across distant shores of time, beckoning her, pulling her from the throes of grief and fear and sadness.

She could see it and she could feel it, even as she drifted in the cold darkness of the sea: *Titanic* arriving in New York City amid a hail of cries and cheers; the waves of Coney Island stretching before her as she roamed its beaches, laughing and exchanging witty quips with the first officer at her side; Murdoch lying beside her in their quiet hotel room deep within Manhattan, exhausted but content after hours of lovemaking, finally able to hold her in his arms until they both fell asleep.

That was her last thought. A lovely thought.

And she clung to it, cherishing the warmth it brought her until she drew her final breath.

TWENTY-FIVE

AFTERMATH

April 15, 1912 | 02:30

FROM THE MOMENT the screaming started, Harold Godfrey Lowe
knew that they needed to go back.

The sound was like a roar, an endless cry that trembled and shook
the heavens above. There had to be over a thousand people stranded in
those frigid waters, frothing the sea in their struggle to swim. Lowe could
hear them crying, pleading, begging for mercy. And somewhere, in the
distance, the shrill shrieks of whistles split the air—a reminder that his
fellow officers were still out there, fighting for their lives.

He had to go back. There was no doubt in his mind.

Clenching his electric torch tightly in one fist, Lowe shone its light
across the passengers adrift in the nearby lifeboats, illuminating their pale
skin and fearful eyes. He moved quickly, rounding up the boats in a
floating huddle, his boiling blood cutting right through the Atlantic chill.

"*Right!*" he bellowed to the crew. "Bring in your oars, men. Tie these
boats together, please, and make sure they're knotted tight!"

It was only after the boats were properly tied that he turned back to
the commotion roiling the sea, his heart slamming against his chest. A
nervous energy crackled inside him—a fierce anticipation he couldn't
swallow down.

Lowe needed to do something. He longed to help, to answer their
pleas across the ocean. He couldn't sit around and wait any longer.

Not when innocent people were dying.

Not when Esther Bailey might be among them.

His commanding Welsh lilt broke the stillness as he roared, "*Lads, we have to go back!*"

Some crewmen exchanged looks of shock, but others nodded with agreement, already rising to their feet.

Lowe wasted no time in clearing out Lifeboat No. 14, barking his orders in his haste. "I want all women and children transferred from this boat into that boat as quick as you can!" He motioned with his hands to the second of the two lifeboats. "Make space, the lot of you! There we are, move smartly now!"

The seamen helped the women and children from boat to boat, their voices firm but encouraging in the chilly darkness. One woman moved forward clumsily, her head bowed, her face hidden beneath a heavy shawl. But her lumbering gait only raised Lowe's suspicions; he snagged the shawl back, yanking it away to reveal the wide, fearful eyes of a young male passenger who looked no older than twenty.

Lowe was almost speechless. Blinded by his rage, he bore over the young man with a menacing snarl.

"Filthy coward! How *dare* you!"

Though he wanted nothing more than to chuck the spineless little blighter overboard—right over the gunwale and into the cold, cruel water so many others were fighting to conquer—he merely shoved the boy into the adjacent boat, watching with vindictive satisfaction as he went toppling down in a heap.

After a great deal of shifting and shuffling, Lifeboat No. 14 was readied to collect survivors, belly filled to the brim with thermoses, blankets, and heavy coats. Lowe was edgy, longing to charge off to the wreckage right then and there. But as he settled himself near the tiller, the fifth officer had to force himself to weigh reason. Should he return now, his lifeboat would only end up overrun by God knows how many desperate people. It would mean the flooding of another precious boat—and the risk of sentencing his men to a watery death themselves. Lowe couldn't allow this to happen. They had to wait, he knew. Give it time for the screams to subside—as much as it pained and disgusted him.

It was a hard choice…but a necessary one.

And so he waited and waited and *waited* until the roar of cries and keening began to fall, becoming little more than a frail murmur. It was only then that he ordered his men to set off, gliding their way through an ocean still as glass, not entirely sure what they would find.

The quiet was unsettling, broken only by the faint creaking of Lifeboat No. 14, and the soft splash of oars cutting through water.

They came upon a few deck chairs first. Some bits of furniture and other drifting debris.

But as they drew nearer, they suddenly found themselves looking upon a graveyard of frozen bodies stretching as far as they eye could see.

The corpses were utterly motionless, bobbing listlessly in their lifebelts or slumped over floating wreckage. Some looked as though they had fallen asleep. Others stared out with frozen, whitish eyes. All were coated in layers of frost and ice.

"Are there any moving?" Lowe demanded, roaming his electric torch across the eerie, glistening water. "Any at all?"

One man answered him, his voice hushed. "No, sir."

"Check them!" Lowe insisted, the sharpness of his voice merely hiding his own desperation.

The men began using the oars to gently shift and prod the bodies, but to no avail. One seaman, Burley, lifted a woman up from the chilling water. The light fell upon her, illuminating her chalk-white skin and gray, glazed eyes.

"They're dead, sir," Burley murmured with a strained swallow, lowering the corpse back into the water and watching it drift away. "All of them, sir."

As the field of bodies thickened, Lowe tried to keep his voice from trembling as he gave his orders to continue onward.

"Mind your oars," he reminded softly, as he watched his crew shift bodies before the prow. "Careful not to hit them."

His grip on the electric torch became vice-like as he swept the beam across the dead. He could see women, children—babies, for Christ's sake. One mother held an infant to her chest, the pair of them frozen stiff. Lowe took one look at them and clenched his teeth tight, the anguish and guilt overwhelming him as he realized the truth.

They had waited too long.

But Lowe would not yield to his grief. Even amidst all this icy death and hopelessness, there had to be survivors out there.

He was certain of it.

"Keep checking!" he ordered of his men, and the prow glided forward once more. His face was set, eyes dark with resolve, blood blazing through his veins. Clenching the tiller with one white-knuckled hand and his electric torch in the other, Lowe bellowed out into the darkness.

"*Is there anyone alive out there?*"

But his calls were met with only silence.

Lowe felt the dread and frustration return. *Just one*, he thought desperately. *Please, just let us find one bloody person—*

A sudden, strangled cry had him turning his head, beaming his torch toward the sound.

Lowe spotted a man crouched in the distance, balancing precariously upon what looked like a floating door. His dark, ponytailed hair was caked in ice, his clothes soaked—but he was *alive*, by Jove, shouting in a foreign language as he waved his hand toward the light. One of the crew muttered something about him being Oriental, and Lowe almost considered turning the boat away.

But then he swallowed down his prejudice and changed his mind, swinging the tiller towards the ponytailed man without a second thought, simply desperate to save a life. *Any* life.

"Haul water, men! Put your backs into it!"

As their boat came upon the survivor, Lowe found himself snarling out his orders in his urgency. Burley reached for the man and heaved him aboard; he tumbled down into the boat, frozen and weak and dripping with seawater.

"Cover him in blankets!" Lowe commanded. "Keep him warm, lads!"

He waited until the man was bundled beneath a mountain of warm wool and fleece before continuing the search, sifting through the dead, scouring for signs of life.

And then he heard it.

A shrill whistling pierced the air somewhere behind them. Lowe turned, hope flaring in his chest.

An officer, he thought.

It damn near had to be. Almost every one of his colleagues had wielded a whistle—Bailey included. Christ, how he wanted it to be her. It didn't matter if she had feelings for Murdoch. Lowe still cared for the girl, and he would give anything to see her again.

"Come *about*!" Lowe roared at the crew, yanking the tiller with all his might.

The boat gradually swung, drifting in the direction of the whistling.

And as they drew closer, cutting through the somber expanse of frosted bodies and broken wood, Lowe could discern a young woman with long hair. She clung to a deck chair alongside a lifeless body, breathing furiously into the whistle at her lips.

Esther, Lowe thought wildly.

But then he realized this woman had blonde hair, not brown that was almost black, and her skin was smooth as porcelain, no freckles in sight.

Grief flooded through him, pouring through the cracks of his heart. But Lowe shut his mind against it, remembering where he was, who he was, and what needed to be done.

He would mourn Bailey later. He promised he would.

But for now, this woman needed his help.

Nearly there, Lowe thought restlessly. Now that they were closer, he could see who was clinging to the opposite end of the deck chair.

And who the whistle belonged to.

Lowe felt the grief return as he recognized the slumped frame of Henry Wilde. He was motionless, his head tilted at an angle, his eyes closed as if he were sleeping. Ice dusted every inch of him—everything from his skin, to his chief officer's uniform. He was missing his cap, locks of his dark hair splayed over his forehead, and his hands seemed to be frozen to the woodwork beneath him. It was a heartbreaking sight.

Lowe swallowed thickly, fighting to hold the electric torch steady in his hand. He almost couldn't believe this was the same bloke who joined him in the smoking room hours ago, cracking jokes and smoking cigars and sweeping everyone at poker. But here he was, this great, distinguished officer now frozen in the middle of the North Atlantic.

An overwhelming sense of loss slammed through Lowe, hurtful and cold as it scraped through his chest, but his voice still ripped through the air like thunder as he howled orders at his men.

"Haul her in! Haul her in! Cover her with blankets! *Quickly*!"

The woman was lifted into the boat by her lifebelt, shaking and shuddering with cold. Her hair was wreathed in icicles, her eyes sightless, unseeing.

Lowe took one look at her ashen face and was seized by a desire to protect her. Perhaps the grief of Wilde and Bailey sent him into a frenzy, but he didn't care.

Brushing Burley aside, Lowe bundled the woman with blankets and kept her close. He saluted Wilde's corpse in one last gesture of farewell. And then they continued onward, scouring for the smallest signs of life amidst the floating bodies of over a thousand perished souls.

03:40

For many hours afterward, there was only darkness, unbearable cold, and an ocean of seawater and stars.

Lowe rested his back against Lifeboat No. 13's gunwale, spine stiffened against the chill as he studied the swath of constellations he'd once taught Bailey how to name. He had refused a spare blanket on principle, more concerned with keeping the passengers warm than himself. Now he sat hunched over, heedless of the cold, swallowing back the survivor's guilt threatening to tear at him.

He hated this; he hated the waiting, the wondering, the questioning of when or even *if* a ship might appear on the horizon. It was harrowing, almost, sitting around as their boat rocked with the slow pitch of the water, and a few women erupted into hysterical sobs and screams. Lowe couldn't take much more of this. His thoughts felt clumsy, like broken machinery struggling to work right. He rubbed his eyes, trying to keep lucid.

Or sane. One of the two.

His gaze lingered on the body of the girl they'd plucked from the sea, sprawled at the bottom of the boat with his greatcoat still tucked around her. She had died sometime during the dark morning, shaking and shuddering against him. He'd held her hand the entire time, desperately trying to bundle her in blankets and reassuring her that help was on the way.

But she had been too cold. Far too cold.

Lowe couldn't forget the way the light faded from her eyes before she went limp, slumped against his knee. He hadn't even known her name. And when he'd closed her eyelids shut with one tender hand, he wondered if he ever would.

Sighing, Lowe rummaged around the boat for a second oil lamp when light bloomed suddenly in the distance.

It was a signaling rocket exploding in mid-air—and beneath its sparks, he glimpsed the speck of a ship in the distance, steaming straight for the lifeboats littered across the open water.

The *Carpathia*? Lowe wondered, catapulting to his feet.

He leaped into action at once, scrambling and shouting orders until his voice grew hoarse. He had all nearby lifeboats lift their masts and sails. He ordered the crewmen to retrieve their flares before igniting one of his own. And then he had each lifeboat strike out for the steamship, where their salvation awaited them.

Daybreak broke over the horizon as they rowed their way to the steamer in the distance, battling the choppy waves and enduring their exhaustion in silence. Watery sunlight glistened almost menacingly upon the broken ice floes and bergs still adrift around them, but even so, the sight of its glow kindled a newfound hope in Lowe's chest. It was a reminder that they were still breathing, despite having stared disaster in the face. That they lived to see another day.

But then he remembered the poor souls who didn't make it...the colleagues he had lost...the people he couldn't save...and the crushing weight of their deaths extinguished his hopefulness at once.

When they reached the *Carpathia* at long last, the sun had fully risen in the gray, frozen sky. Sailors awaited them, standing at the open shell door and throwing down rope ladders. Lowe was the last to climb; he waited until every passenger, corpse, and crewmen were safely aboard before stowing away the sailing gear and clambering up himself.

His limbs felt like lead when he reached the top of the ladder, and he was dimly aware of how sorely he'd missed standing on a solid, stable deck. How strange it felt in comparison to *Titanic's* steepened list.

Exhaustion threatened to catch up with him, rippling on the edge of his awareness. But before he could rest his wearied bones, a voice spoke behind him.

"Excuse me, sir, but are you one of *Titanic's* officers?"

Lowe turned to face a slim man donned in the garb of a captain. Although his eyes were grave and face grim, he carried himself with an air of crisp authority.

"I *was*," Lowe answered, too tired to hold back the flippant remark. "Harold Lowe. Formerly fifth officer."

The man scrutinized him for a moment before holding out his hand. They shook, Lowe's freezing fingers slipping into his sturdy gloved ones.

"Captain Rostron," he said. "Welcome aboard, Mr. Lowe. We have a few of your colleagues already situated in our officers' lounge. Given space might pose an issue as more survivors come aboard, it will have to be your sleeping quarters until we reach New York…"

But Lowe had stopped listening. He was thinking only of his fellow officers, wondering which of them might still be alive. Although he kept a level head, he could feel the instability shocking through him as a sailor led him to the officers' lounge on the boat deck. He stepped through the door with a deep breath—but relief flooded through him when he recognized Pitman and Boxhall. The pair of them were seated before an electric heater, mugs of hot tea in hand. While Boxhall stared unseeingly into the pit of flames, Pitman shot from his seat. He didn't bother with formalities as he yanked Lowe into a tight embrace, his voice heavy with exhaustion.

"Thank Christ," he murmured. "Thought we'd never see you again, lad."

"Was thinking that myself, honest," Lowe admitted. "But it's good to see you alive and well, Bert. Joseph."

He dropped into an easy chair with a groan and burrowed himself into the pile of flannel blankets, never wanting to rise to his feet again. Pitman fetched him a cup of hot tea at once, buzzing as if he were in dire need of something to do, while Boxhall ran a weary hand over his face. Lowe pressed the mug against his lips but didn't drink.

"This all of us?" he asked.

Pitman nodded. "So far at least."

"Bloody hell," Lowe gritted out, closing his eyes. He and his colleagues were silent for a long while after, simply lost in their shock, their guilt, their troubling thoughts. His mind was a dark pool he couldn't quite clamber out of, overflowing with the memories of the screaming. The frozen corpses. The groan of buckling iron and steel.

He sank deeper into his chair and tugged the blanket tightly around him, wishing he could have done something more. That he could have pulled one more person out of the wreckage. And that he could have seen Esther Bailey's bright green eyes one last time.

Lowe tried not to think of what her final moments had been like. He wondered if she'd been with Murdoch. And if she had, then he was glad for that. At least she hadn't died scared and alone in the middle of the North Atlantic.

His thoughts turned to his chief officer, and Lowe could not forget the sight of Wilde's lifeless body frozen to the deck chair beneath him. He'd looked as if he'd fallen asleep. Lowe wondered if he'd died fighting, blowing into his whistle before succumbing to the cold. He thought of Moody, whom he had only known for a short while but had come to like over the course of their journey. He had only been twenty-four. Far too young to die at sea.

He thought of Murdoch, and Lightoller, and Smith, and the young woman who froze to death at his side—and he suddenly found himself consumed with anger, wondering why it had been *them*.

Why had they been claimed by the sea, and not him?

Lowe gritted his teeth and clenched his fists, breathing heavily through his nose to suppress a roar of rage and grief. Were his colleagues not present, he might have stormed around the room, knocking over chairs and overturning tables and breaking everything within goddamn sight—

A door creaked open, and they all turned in shock to see Lightoller stepping inside.

He looked haggard, his face pale as bone and eyes vacant. But when he saw his men on their feet, waiting to greet him, a glimmer of life returned to his deadened gaze. He clasped hands with each of them before collapsing into the chair closest to the electric heater. And only then did he tell them the hard truth.

He had been in the last lifeboat, and he was the highest-ranking officer to step aboard.

"The others are gone," he said quietly.

A mournful silence followed his words as the harsh reality of their loss set in. The officers took their seats, grim as they sipped tea and warmed their frostbitten hands. Lowe stared hard into the glow of the heater, once again lost in his thoughts.

But this time, he did not dwell on death or grief.

In that dark pool of his mind, he was able to rise above it, and reflect on the best of times rather than the worst.

He thought of the day he'd met Bailey during their tour of *Titanic*, and the clever way she'd put Murdoch in his place. It was the first time Lowe had heard her witty sense of humor, and his heart flooded with weightless warmth as he recalled the banter they'd exchanged back and forth at sea. He thought of Moody with his friendly charm and penchant for writing. He thought of Murdoch, the cool and professional senior officer who'd rarely let his composure crack. Who had seemed so comfortable at sea, and had clearly cared for Bailey until the end. He thought of Wilde with his strength and good sense of humor, never hesitating to share a story about his daughters. And Smith, always so distinguished with his white beard and war medals.

He recalled his excitement the day *Titanic* set sail from Southampton. The laughter and wisecracks he'd shared with his colleagues. And the immeasurable pride and duty in knowing he would be working alongside so many fine seafaring men and women.

It was an ocean of his happiest memories since becoming fifth officer, and Harold Lowe was content to let himself drift, reveling in every last one of them.

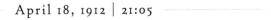

April 18, 1912 | 21:05

A drizzling rain fell as the *Carpathia* arrived in New York at last.

Lightoller stood upon a bridge that was foreign and unfamiliar to him, watching the Statue of Liberty and its glowing torch rear up from the rainy darkness.

He had anticipated this sight ever since his departure from Belfast.

But now it felt empty, colorless and wrong.

It should have been Smith manning the helm in the wheelhouse, not Rostron. And Lightoller should have been standing on the glistening bridge of *Titanic*, not the *Carpathia*.

But the magnificent steamship once deemed "unsinkable" now rested at the bottom of the Atlantic Ocean, broken and buckled and flooded with saltwater. And she had taken so many innocent lives—including the lives of his friends and colleagues—along with her.

Though several days had passed since the sinking, Lightoller couldn't process the notion that he was still living, while the others were long gone. It was a hard thing to swallow, and he wasn't even sure that he'd ever be able to come to terms with it. Not until the day he died. The hardest part of surviving would be accepting his grief and moving onward. It wouldn't be easy. But Lightoller would have to try, for the sake of Murdoch, and Bailey, and Moody, and Smith…and Wilde.

Admittedly, Lightoller knew his relationship with the chief officer had been problematic. They fought and bickered and bantered like children rather than grown men. But now that Wilde was gone, Lightoller could admit how much he would miss him.

He combed his thoughts as he watched the downpour, trying to think of the last time he had seen Wilde alive. In the chaos and the confusion, he remembered the chief officer ordering him to man a lifeboat.

Not damn likely, Lightoller had said, dismissing the command before continuing with his duties. Nothing more had been said between them, and Wilde was eventually called away to the starboard side to help, vanishing beyond the frightened swell of people with a grave determination in his eyes.

That was the last time Lightoller had seen Henry Wilde alive.

He knew he would never forget it—just as he'd never forget the sight of Murdoch strolling out of the first officer's cabin shortly after they'd retrieved their guns, looking calm and more than ready to fulfill his duty. Lightoller only glimpsed him a handful of times throughout that wretched night, as they'd been working on opposite sides of the ship.

But in the few moments they'd crossed paths, he had always seen Murdoch keeping close to Bailey, his hands linked with hers. They were together, side by side, until the end.

Lightoller sighed, keeping his eyes on the rain as they sailed onward through the Hudson. When they docked and disembarked at long last, he wasn't surprised to see the enormous crowd of people edging the drenched slipway, kept back by police officers and stevedores.

Reporters barked questions into megaphones, demanding to know what had happened, how many had died, and what had become of them. Families wept and sobbed, holding up picture frames and crying out the names of their loved ones. Others cheered and hailed the officers as heroes, which Lightoller thought couldn't be further from the truth. Photographers snapped pictures again and again, the flashes of their cameras speckling the rainy gloom.

But Lightoller was oblivious to it all.

He walked in a daze as he followed his colleagues down the gangway, the cries and commotion muffled, nonexistent, as if sealed behind a pane of glass. And somehow, hours later, he found himself sitting numbly in a shared suite in the Waldorf Astoria, surrounded by a huddle of colleagues, lawyers, and White Star Line executives. The officers would be called to an inquiry for the sinking first thing tomorrow, Bruce Ismay informed them, and they were advised to get plenty of rest that night.

Lightoller couldn't see how such a thing was possible, but he damn well had to try. He went to clean himself up in the washroom and ended up retching over the sink for a good ten minutes. And when he tried to run a bath, the sight of clear water swelling in the tub was enough to make him scramble halfway across the room, stumbling against the wall and drawing in deep, panicked breaths.

Lightoller was an utter mess now that he was alone, hidden away from the public eye—and from his fellow officers. It was clear the horrific events of *Titanic* could not be forgotten so easily. Even the sea, which had once called to him, sang to him, drawn him away from land and to the wilds of seafaring instead—now felt like a treacherous enemy, a cruel mistress that he wished he'd never braved in the first place.

His dreams were nightmares that evening, dragging Lightoller back to the terrors he would never escape: the drowning, the darkness, and the cold, chilling water that had felt like a thousand knives piercing right through him, inside and out. Unsurprisingly, he managed only two hours of sleep before he awakened with a jolt, shooting upward and gasping like a drowned man resurfacing from deep water.

His colleagues were fast asleep around him, snoozing on the spare bed, the sofa, or else sprawled across the floor. Reaching for his watch on the bedside table, he squinted at the time.

4 o'clock, it read.

Still hours before the inquiry. But Lightoller knew he wouldn't be able to fall back asleep. He rose to his feet and dressed, pulling on trousers, a sleeved shirt, and a long overcoat for the morning chill.

As he topped a bowler hat over his hair and started for the door, a voice filled the hushed room.

"Where you off to, Lights?"

Lightoller turned toward the sofa with a start, realizing that Lowe was wide awake. The young Welshman stared unblinkingly up at the ceiling, and Lightoller wondered if he'd even slept at all. Perhaps he, too, had been kept awake by horrific memories. Come to think of it, Lightoller realized he had heard someone sniffling in the room late last night, in the moments before he'd traded his trauma and torment for a few restless scraps of sleep. He wasn't entirely sure if it had been Lowe or Boxhall or Pitman—but given that only Lowe had returned to the sinking site to sift through the bodies, Lightoller wouldn't be surprised if it had been him.

Clearing his throat, he explained, "Heading off for a bit of fresh air and a smoke. I'll be back shortly."

"Right you are."

As Lightoller turned for the door, Lowe spoke quietly once again.

"Fifteen-hundred dead, Lights. That's what the papers are sayin'. Fifteen-hundred."

The second officer closed his eyes, his grip tightening on the cold doorknob beneath his fingers. "Yes. Yes, I know."

"There were still seats on the boats we sent away."

"Yes."

"D'you...d'you ever wonder how many we could've saved if...?"

Lowe didn't have to finish the question; Lightoller knew exactly what he meant. He felt his shoulders slacken and his chest turn cold as he recalled those lifeboats fanning out across the sheet of icy, dark ocean—most of them not even close to being filled—and his words were pained in the darkness of their hotel room.

"I do. Every day."

Lowe sat upright, shaking his head, one hand coursing through his mussed dark hair. He stole a glance at the newspapers sprawled upon the end table, the boldest headline almost screaming at them:

*TITANIC SINKS, WORST MARITIME DISASTER IN HISTORY, GREAT
LOSS OF LIFE.*

"You know," he murmured, "there's a tidy little pub Mr. Wilde and I
planned to visit here in the city. Was thinking that perhaps, well…we
could grab a pint there before the week is out. Have a proper toast to him.
And to Murdoch…Bailey, Moody, Smith…all those good people, the
whole lot of 'em."

Lightoller nodded, recalling those they lost and wondering if
someday—after the bodies were recovered—he would be able to visit each
of their graves. He wouldn't simply pay his respects and move on. He
would take his time, and apologize to those he might have wronged: to
Esther, for being cold and dismissive to her the first day she'd set foot on
the ship; to Jim, for not ordering him to step aboard the lifeboat to safety
that night, essentially sealing his fate; and to Henry, for always quarreling
with the man, when he'd held an unusual soft spot for him all along.

A tear swelled at the corner of Lightoller's eye, and he quickly brushed
it away before Lowe could see.

"I'd like that, Harry. Truly, I would."

And with that, he bade a goodbye before departing the hotel.

The downpour had long since passed, but the streets were still
shimmering, slick with rain. Lightoller started northward, not caring
where his feet might take him. He just needed to walk, to move, to feel
the wind against his skin and the cool air in the depths of his lungs—all
the little nudges and reminders and reassurances of living.

He wasn't sure how far he walked, let alone how much time passed,
before daybreak crept up on him. Lightoller paused on an unfamiliar street
corner, withdrawing a cigarette from his pocket and lighting its tip.

It was then when he noticed a familiar man crossing the avenue, tall
and lean with his dark hair slicked back. Lightoller almost didn't recognize
him in the fine suit he was wearing.

"Mr. Bailey!" he called.

Booker Bailey stopped short, surprised. But when he recognized
Lightoller, he started forward at once. He carried a bulky object under his
arm, and as he drew closer, Lightoller was struck by the curious color of
his eyes. They were pale green, and so identical to his sister's that it stung

Lightoller's heart. Even their freckles were awfully similar.

I miss her, he couldn't help but think. *I really do.*

"Mr. Lightoller." Booker greeted. His eyes were weary, his voice hollow. "Good to see you again."

"And you as well," Lightoller said, dipping his head.

"You're up rather early. I thought the inquiry didn't start until nine o'clock."

"Couldn't sleep a wink, I'm afraid."

"That certainly makes two of us." Booker looked down at his feet with a heavy gaze, scuffing one shoe against the curb. "Everything that happened that night…It was something darker and worse than hell. I can't get it out of my head. I don't reckon I ever will."

Lightoller wasn't sure what to say, so he passed him a cigarette, thinking of the cold struggle they and thirty others endured aboard the overturned collapsible. He thought of the ice that clustered their frostbitten hands. The crisp wind that stiffened their sodden clothes. The way they had to shuffle their weight, obeying his steady orders to adjust with the shifting tide.

He could still hear the waves lapping against the wood of the collapsible, hollow and unending. And worst of all, he could hear the sobering splash as another man or woman succumbed to the clutches of death, curling over the tiny boat and disappearing into the sea.

Grimacing slightly, Lightoller exhaled another cloud of smoke and pointed at the bulky object underneath Booker's arm, all too willing to change the subject.

"Might I ask what you're holding?"

Booker held it out for him to see, and Lightoller realized what it was.

A medical kit.

"They found it when they were salvaging the lifeboats last night," Booker explained. "It belonged to my sister, you see. Had her name scribbled in it and everything. So they made sure it was sent to me. She must've thrown it into one of the boats before she…"

His voice cracked beneath a sob, eyes glistening with the beginnings of tears. Lightoller didn't care if it was unseemly for a grown man to cry in public; he clasped a hand on Booker's shoulder and spoke his words meaningful and true.

"She was a brilliant woman and a fine officer. Clever, hardworking—and so extraordinarily brave, from what I saw and heard from that night. I won't lie, we all had our misgivings about her at first. Myself included. Her temper took some time getting used to, I'll admit…to say nothing of her sailor's mouth."

His lips curved into a wistful smile as he remembered all the filthy curses she used to drop here and there—and how often he had to reprimand her—before pressing on.

"But she proved herself to be more than worthy of our ranks. She died with honor, Mr. Bailey, doing her duty and helping as many people as she could. And she will always be remembered for that."

Nodding, Booker wiped his tearful eyes with his sleeve. "Quite so. This was what she always wanted, sir. To set a good standard for women in the maritime business. To make a difference. I'm proud of her for what she's done, Mr. Lightoller. I really am. But I…" His words grew strangled, thick with sorrow. "I miss her something awful. I didn't even have a chance to say goodbye. Not to her. Not even to Thomas."

He pressed a hand to his temple, looking as if his entire world had splintered apart. "It all happened so fast. She fell into the water when the wave hit, and Officer Murdoch dived in after her. But that was the last I saw of her before I went under myself."

A light drizzle began to fall, so thin that it was little more than mist. They ignored it, still standing on the street corner, smoking their cigarettes. After a while, Booker spoke.

"Mr. Lightoller, I understand you were close friends with Mr. Murdoch, and I know you spent a great deal of time around my sister. It seems as if there was something going on between the pair of them and…Well, I have a hunch, but I was wondering if perhaps you knew the truth, and whether or not you could share it with me."

Lightoller sighed, his heart aching as he thought of his colleagues, both claimed by the sea. Murdoch was gone, and Lightoller would never hear his hearty laugh and biting Scottish wit again. Nor would he see Bailey's lively smile and shining eyes.

Grief and guilt swept through him, but he chased them away, gathering his bearings once more.

"I'm not sure whether they were in love," Lightoller admitted, "because Will never had the chance to confide it to me before he died. But I do know that they cared for one another very much."

An unexpected laugh rumbled in his chest as he added, "I remember they used to bicker like mad. Quite the entertaining sight, really. I don't think Will had ever met anyone as stubborn-headed as him, and it showed. But even though they quarreled, they were always soft on each other. She was happy with him. And I know that Will would have fought to keep her alive until his dying breath."

Swallowing against the lump in his throat, he turned a curious gaze to the sky. "Perhaps they're together now. I like to think that."

Booker nodded, a small, sad smile crossing his face. "As do I."

He kindly thanked the second officer for his help and shook his hand. Then the two men parted ways, and Lightoller traced his steps back to the hotel, hands tucked deep into his pockets.

As he walked, he found himself thinking not of the inquiry that awaited him, but of his wife. Already he could see himself hurrying up the front steps of their little home, and sweeping her off of her feet and into his waiting arms. It was enough to lighten the heaviness in his heart and bring him a shred of peace, warming him from the chill as he made his way through the early morning quiet of Manhattan.

The rain began to lighten, and beyond the sleek, towering buildings that soared high above him, Lightoller could catch a glimmer of daylight along the horizon.

Everything will be all right, he told himself, inhaling a deep breath as he watched that glow light up the sky.

In time, everything would be just fine.

EPILOGUE

She awoke in darkness.

There was nothing here. Only a vast, unbroken emptiness surrounding her from all sides, dimming her thoughts and awareness.

But somewhere in the black void, she could see a pinprick of light—blurred and distant, as if shining through deep water. It gradually became brighter and brighter, until the darkness around her fell away completely, and in its place rose a stretch of brilliant, blinding white.

Glowing warmth slipped across her skin like bathwater, awakening her senses along with it. She could smell the tang of salty sea air. She could feel her limbs again, no longer frosted or frozen. She could hear the lull of rippling waves along with the quiet, murmuring heartbeat within her chest.

Gradually, shapes began to manifest and take form in the strange void of white. She could see a long wall broken by arched glass windows, a maze of pipes and water valves above her head, and finally, an expanse of polished wood stretching seamlessly beneath her feet. She started walking along it, her footsteps soundless, her eyes curious and wondering as she looked around.

Another wall appeared to the left of her, looming out through a fog of white. But this one was lined with familiar square openings pouring with soft sunshine. She stepped closer, peering out of them, and that was when she saw it—the bright, beautiful blue of the ocean, stretching as far as the eye could see. Her eyes closed as she savored the sunlight on her skin, the salty breeze running through her hair.

And it was then that she realized exactly where she was.

She kept walking, but her steps were no longer aimless. She was searching now, glancing around the bright corridor she recognized as A Deck Promenade. The doors to the forward Grand Staircase were to her right; she could see could see a cluster of people gathered at its steps, as if they were waiting for something. Or someone, perhaps. Maybe they were waiting for their own loved ones. She wished them well.

Something tugged her onward, and she kept walking, making her way to the forward part of the ship. The stairwell leading up to the boat deck stretched before her, and she climbed the steps without hesitation, heart fluttering excitedly against her chest. Now that she was topside, she was greeted with so many wonderful sights she had sorely missed: the towering grace of the funnels soaring high above her; the expanse of a glittering ocean, swirling beneath the sky; the lifeboats pristine and secure in their davits, canvas covers flitting in the saltwater breeze.

She smiled, letting all the colors and smells and sounds wash over her. Then she made her way toward the bridge, where the swell of a crowd was waiting for her.

They lined the bridge and the wheelhouse, standing in two rows to admit her through. It was a sea of familiar faces, many of them belonging to those who had poured their hearts and souls into the ship beneath their feet. She could see the stokers, the electricians, the engineers. She could see the stewardesses, the waiters, the bakers. The band was there, still holding their instruments as they dipped their heads in greeting. The captain stood beyond the windows of the wheelhouse, his hands braced on the helm in a relaxed manner, his eyes sparkling at her with welcome. She spotted Mr. Phillips with his wireless headset hanging from his neck, Miss Fay looking stunning in a dress of sheer white, and Mr. Andrews, who smiled kindly at her as she passed.

She continued onward, making her way through the bridge so perfect and pristine, its brass machinery glistening beneath the sunlight. Moody stood before the helm, sweeping his cap respectfully from his head. Wilde was there as well, tall and dignified, gray eyes crinkling as he smiled.

It was everyone she had come to care for since the day she'd first boarded the ship.

But a few were missing, she noted.

Her brother, for one. Lowe and Lightoller. Boxhall and Pitman.

They must have made it. She was happy for this…and a little sad. She would miss them with all her heart. Perhaps they would meet again, in time. Though for now, she was glad to stand before the faces of those she thought she lost. The people she never thought she'd seen again.

But there was still one more face she needed to see, and it didn't take her very long to find him.

He was standing in the starboard bridge wing where they had first met, smiling, waiting for her. He was dressed handsomely in his first officer's uniform, his arms held behind his back, his eyes just as deep and blue as she remembered. He offered her his gloveless hand, and she took it without pause, letting him pull her closer until he could press his forehead against her own.

They stood together for a long while, finally reunited again, quietly savoring their closeness as the waves rushed all around them. She felt his fingers lace hers tight, so warm and wonderfully familiar. And in that moment, she knew all would be well.

AFTERWORD

William McMaster Murdoch perished in the sinking. He was 39. His body was never recovered. Memorials for Mr. Murdoch were erected in his hometown of Dalbeattie, Dumfries and Galloway, Scotland to honor his heroism. He was remembered as an honorable seaman who fulfilled his duties ably and admirably, despite the controversy surrounding his death.

Esther Anna Bailey perished in the sinking. She was 26. Her body was never recovered. She was honored by her hometown of San Francisco, California for her fearless actions during the night of the sinking. Her brother later established a foundation in her name, seeking to educate and train women in the maritime industry, and later in the United States Marine Corps following the Great War.

Charles Herbert Lightoller testified at the American Inquiry alongside his fellow officers after the sinking. He would return to sea as first officer of *Oceanic* before serving in the Great War as Lieutenant Lightoller. Years later, he would pilot his own yacht, Sundowner, across the English Channel to collect stranded soldiers at Dunkirk. He also wrote a memoir detailing his experiences aboard *Titanic*, which he dedicated to "My persistent wife, who made me do it." Mr. Lightoller passed away at the age of 72 on December 8, 1952.

Harold Godfrey Lowe married Ellen Whitehouse and later had two children, Esther Josephine and Harold William. He continued to work at sea, taking on the role of commander in the Royal Naval Service during the Great War, and later retiring in North Wales with his wife. He passed away at the age of 61 on May 12, 1944.

Booker Hamilton Bailey returned to his hometown of San Francisco, California following the sinking. He arranged a small memorial service for his sister overlooking the Pacific Ocean. He resigned from Harland and Wolff a year later to establish a maritime foundation for women at the Presidio. Mr. Bailey lived with his long-time partner, Matthew Harper, before passing away at the age of 98 on April 18, 1975.

Henry Tingle Wilde perished in the sinking. He was 39. His body was never recovered. He was survived by his four children: Jane, Harry, Arnold and Nancy. A memorial for Mr. Wilde was built in Kirkdale Cemetery in his hometown of Liverpool, England to remember his bravery and sacrifice.

James Paul Moody perished in the sinking. He was 24, the youngest officer to die in the sinking. His body was never recovered. He was commemorated with a monument in Woodland Cemetery, Scarborough, England. Mr. Moody was remembered as a selfless young man who fought to help passengers and fellow crew until the end.

Herbert John Pitman continued to work at sea with White Star Line, joining *Oceanic* and later *Olympic*. He married Mimi Kalman in 1922. Due to deteriorating eyesight, he would work as a purser for over 20 years. He passed away at the age of 84 on December 7, 1961.

Joseph Groves Boxhall would later work aboard the *Adriatic* as fourth officer, until he served as lieutenant in Royal Naval Service in 1915. He married Marjory Bedells in 1919, serving Cunard-White Star Line until 1940. The longest surviving officer, Mr. Boxhall passed away at the age of 83 on April 25, 1967.

Edward John Smith perished in the sinking. He was 62. His body was never recovered. He was last seen near the bridge with a megaphone in hand, giving the orders to abandon ship. A statue of Mr. Smith was erected in his memory in Beacon Park, Staffordshire, England.

Thomas Andrews Jr. perished in the sinking. He was 39. His body was never recovered. He was remembered as a hero who gave his life to help his passengers to safety. A memorial was made to honor his gallantry in his hometown of Comber, County Down, Ireland. Today, the SS *Nomadic* is the sole surviving ship he designed.

Callum Niles Lockerbie would marry Margaret Carnegie Miller, daughter of prominent industrialist Andrew Carnegie. His net worth stretched into the millions until he was convicted of racketeering in 1919. He was unable to recover from financial ruin and was mysteriously shot after his release from prison that same year. He was 47.

HISTORICAL NOTE

It has been a long journey into the tragic history of the RMS *Titanic* this past year. What began as another re-watch of the 1997 film during my last semester of college turned into something much bigger. While I wish I could include every fascinating detail of the ship and her crew, I had to be selective for the sake of storytelling. There were some aspects I tried to keep as accurate as possible, such as the timeline of events, the architecture of the ship, and the sinking itself. But in other cases, I made a conscious choice to deviate from the historical record.

One major example is the creative liberty I took with the officers themselves, specifically their character personalities and appearances. For example, the real William McMaster Murdoch was married during the events of *Titanic* but has been written single for the purpose of this narrative. Henry Wilde was more serious and authoritative than I have depicted him here, while Charles Lightoller was less posh and straight-nosed. Wilde and Lightoller's disdain for one another is also purely subjective, though there is some evidence to suggest Lightoller didn't particularly favor Wilde's authority, given that he went above his orders twice during the sinking. As for their appearances, they are not reflective of the real *Titanic* officers and were loosely inspired by actors such as Ewan Stewart and Jonny Phillips instead.

Another deviation from history is the invention of Esther, Booker, Callum, Fay, Florence, and Slate. They are fictional characters created for the story alone, with Esther serving as a vessel for the reader by introducing the duties of a White Star Line officer from an outsider's perspective. It is worth noting here that while there were no female officers in active service in 1912, a few underwent officer and maritime educations during this time period. If you are interested in women in the naval forces, the WRNS (founded in 1917) are a fascinating place to start.

As for other changes, I also wanted to rectify the misconceptions created by rumors, speculations, and the 1997 film—specifically Murdoch's "suicide." Although eyewitness accounts state an officer did indeed shoot himself and fire on passengers, there is no conclusive evidence to confirm this officer was Murdoch. Research merely suggests Murdoch or Wilde would be the most likely candidates, largely due to variables such as where they were stationed (Collapsible A), the weapons they were issued, and even specific psychological factors, such as Wilde's grief for his late wife and Murdoch's potential guilt over the collision. But with so many conflicting eyewitness accounts and so much mystery surrounding the sinking, the identity of the suicidal officer—if there truly was one—has never been confirmed. Given the ambiguity surrounding Murdoch's death, I decided to shy away from the suicide and write a different outcome for him altogether.

But even with these narrative changes, I still made a conscious effort to keep as close to history as possible. There are too many examples to list, but some instances in this story that are based on fact include Murdoch's refusal to allow a French commander aboard *Titanic* in Cherbourg, Lowe's outburst at Bruce Ismay during the evacuations, Moody willingly turning down a spot aboard a boat to remain on the ship, and Murdoch laughing aloud and remarking "That's the funniest thing I've seen all night," after witnessing a larger man tumble into a lifeboat—all fascinating tidbits I wanted to include within this story to maintain a respectful balance of fact and fiction.

The sinking of the RMS *Titanic* was an unimaginable and deeply poignant moment in human history. But despite the horrific events that occurred that night—and the compounding mistakes and hubris that only added to the devastating loss of life—it serves as a reminder of those brave individuals who died or otherwise risked their lives for the sake of others. *Titanic*'s officers are one such example, and we can only hope their stories and sacrifices will continue to live on through history.

GLOSSARY

Afore	Forward part of the ship, before the mast.
Aft	Rear part of the ship, toward the stern.
Amidships	Middle of the ship.
Astern	Distance behind a ship; opposite of ahead.
Berth	Space where a ship is docked or anchored; officer slang for their individual quarters.
Binnacle	Housing of the ship's compass.
Bow	Forward end of a ship.
Bulkhead	Walls that divide the hull into separate compartments.
Bulwark	Railing along the sides of a ship.
Collapsible	Lifeboats with folding canvas sides for storing.
Davit	The overarching crane that suspends or lowers a lifeboat.
Docking bridge	Platform at the stern used for docking operations.
Falls	Lines that lift or lower the lifeboat.
Forward	Toward the bow of the ship.
Full astern	Maneuvering backward (reversing the engines).
Greatcoat	Large wool overcoat worn to protect from cold and rain.
Growler	Small iceberg or ice floe.
Gunwale	Upper edge of a ship's railing.
Hard-a-starboard	Turning the ship to the left (port side).
Hard-a-port	Turning the ship to the right (starboard side).
Helm	Steers the ship; another word for the wheel.

RMS	Short for Royal Mail Ship.
Keel	Bottommost structure of the ship.
Knot	Unit of speed equivalent to one nautical mile per hour.
Officer of the Watch	Responsible for watch-keeping and navigation on the bridge.
Marconigram	Messages sent by the Marconi wireless system.
Master-at-arms	Responsible for law enforcement and discipline.
Mal-de-mer	Another term for seasickness.
Port	Left side of the ship.
Quartermaster	Responsible for steering and navigating the ship.
Starboard	Right side of the ship.
Stevedore	Unloads and loads ships; also known as a dockworker.
Stern	Rear of the ship.
Stoker	Tends to the furnace and boilers on steamships.
Telegraph	Relays orders from the bridge to the engine room.
Telemotor	Transfers wheel movements to the steering gear.
Topside	On or toward the upper decks of a ship.

OFFICER WATCHES

SENIOR OFFICERS

Wilde   2:00am–6:00am
                     2:00pm–6:00pm

Lightoller   6:00am–10:00am
                     6:00pm–10:00pm

Murdoch | Bailey   10:00am–2:00pm
                     10:00pm–2:00am

JUNIOR OFFICERS

Lowe | Pitman   Middle, morning,
                     forenoon, afternoon,
Boxhall | Moody   & dog watches.

TIMELINE

April 6, 1912
Esther Bailey arrives in Southampton Port.

April 10, 1912
Passengers board in Southampton; crew are mustered, and lifeboat inspections carried out; *Titanic* sets sail on her maiden voyage, sailing south to Cherbourg.

April 11, 1912
Titanic arrives in Queenstown before setting out for sea.

April 12, 1912– April 13, 1912
Titanic sails through calm waters and clear weather.

April 14, 1912
Heavy ice warnings received; that night, iceberg spotted dead ahead at 11:40 p.m. Despite the hard-a-starboard maneuver ordered by Officer Murdoch, *Titanic* brushes the iceberg on her starboard side. Water floods above the keel; Andrews determines the ship will sink; *Titanic* begins a slow and gradual list.

April 15, 1912
Officers load the lifeboats, with Lightoller manning the port side, Murdoch manning starboard; only 20 lifeboats launched in total, with many at half capacity; last radio message sent at 2:17 a.m.; *Titanic* snaps amidships and takes her final plunge at 2:20 a.m. Officer Lowe returns to the sinking site to look for survivors; *Carpathia* collects those stranded in the water shortly after sunrise.

April 18, 1912
Carpathia arrives in New York with survivors.

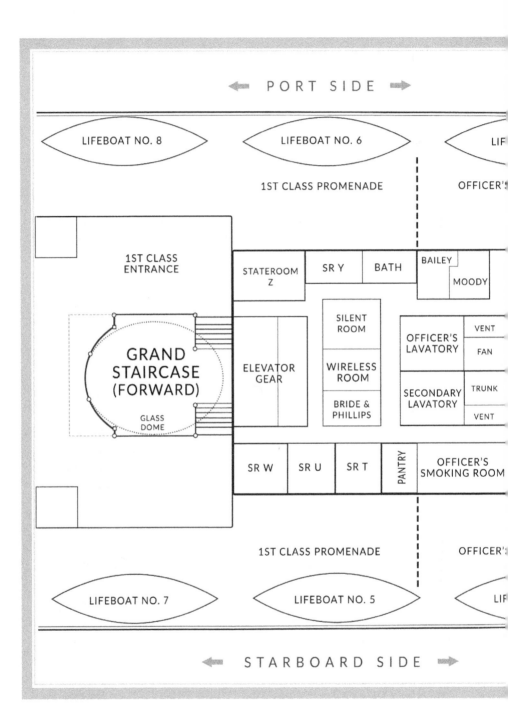

PORT SIDE

LIFEBOAT NO. 8

LIFEBOAT NO. 6

LIF

1ST CLASS PROMENADE

OFFICER'S

1ST CLASS ENTRANCE

STATEROOM Z

SR Y

BATH

BAILEY

MOODY

GRAND STAIRCASE (FORWARD)

GLASS DOME

ELEVATOR GEAR

SILENT ROOM

WIRELESS ROOM

BRIDE & PHILLIPS

OFFICER'S LAVATORY

VENT

FAN

SECONDARY LAVATORY

TRUNK

VENT

SR W

SR U

SR T

PANTRY

OFFICER'S SMOKING ROOM

1ST CLASS PROMENADE

OFFICER'S

LIFEBOAT NO. 7

LIFEBOAT NO. 5

LIF

STARBOARD SIDE

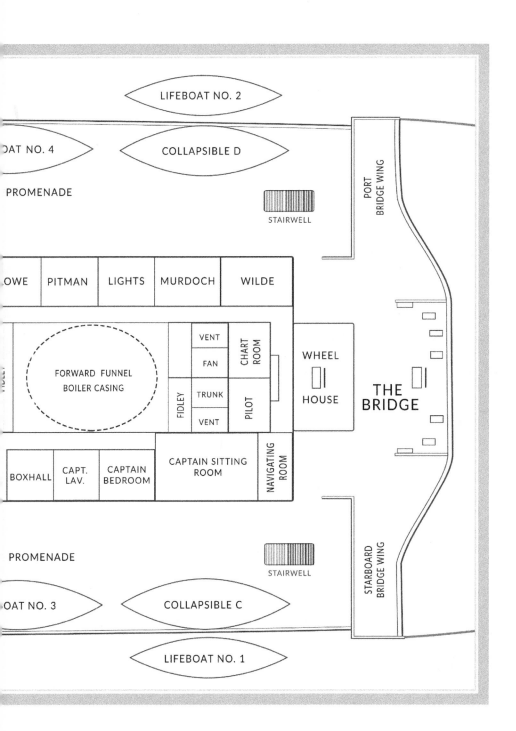

LIFEBOAT NO. 2

BOAT NO. 4

COLLAPSIBLE D

PROMENADE

STAIRWELL

PORT BRIDGE WING

OWE | PITMAN | LIGHTS | MURDOCH | WILDE

FORWARD FUNNEL
BOILER CASING

VENT

FAN

CHART ROOM

FIDLEY

TRUNK

VENT

PILOT

WHEEL

HOUSE

THE BRIDGE

BOXHALL | CAPT. LAV. | CAPTAIN BEDROOM | CAPTAIN SITTING ROOM | NAVIGATING ROOM

PROMENADE

STAIRWELL

STARBOARD BRIDGE WING

BOAT NO. 3

COLLAPSIBLE C

LIFEBOAT NO. 1

ARTWORK

Officers Murdoch
& Bailey
April 1912

ACKNOWLEDGEMENTS

I'd first like to thank everyone who followed this story from its inception. You kept me writing. You kept me going. You followed the path of our characters along with me as I scribbled out chapter after chapter, update after update, not even knowing how the story would end. I'm not bullshitting when I say that you all played an incredibly huge part in the publishing of this story. Honestly, without your encouragement, this book wouldn't be here today. I also owe thanks to my editors, Holly and Katherine, for helping me polish this massive tale, which was no easy feat. Thank you to the wonderful Melissas (Melissa P. and Melissa W.), who have always, and will always, be there for me. And huge thanks to Melissa P. for convincing me to publish this story, even when I had my own doubts and misgivings. And finally, thank you to Sean for tolerating my sudden obsession with Titanic, for sitting through the 2017 Dolby re-release of the film with me, when I was so excited to see it in theaters for the first time, and for always telling me I could, when I always thought I couldn't.

Thank you.